The
Curse
Breakers

✝HE CURSE BREAKERS

BOOK TWO OF THE CURSE KEEPERS

DENISE GROVER SWANK

47N⬤RTH

Published by 47North, Seattle
www.apub.com

ISBN-13: 9781477820216
ISBN-10: 1477820213

Cover illustrated by Larry Rostant

Library of Congress Control Number: 2013955183

Printed in the United States of America

*To my daughter Jenna, who loves to create stories
almost as much as I do*

THE
CURSE
BREAKERS

∿ CHAPTER ONE ∿

The rain came down in thick sheets, drenching through my cotton tank top and denim shorts. I welcomed it. I welcomed anything that made me feel something.

I stood inside of the Elizabethan Gardens, next to the goddamned tree that had ruined my life more than four hundred years before I was even born. The gate to Popogusso.

The gate to hell.

And my daddy was on the other side.

I leaned back my head and shouted into the night, taunting the god who had sent him there. "Ahone! Come out and face me, you fucking asshole!"

The only answer was the rain that pelted my face and filled my open mouth.

I spat on the ground and slapped my palm on the rough bark of the ancient oak tree. The mark that had appeared on my hand almost three weeks ago had power, after all, but that power was so much stronger when my mark was pressed to the identical one on the other Curse Keeper's right palm.

His betrayal sliced through me again. It was still impossible to believe that Collin had purposefully opened the gate.

I'd forced him to close it again. But at what cost? The Native American gods and spirits had still escaped and now they were in hiding, killing hundreds of animals as they regained the strength they'd lost over their centuries of exile. And my father had died as a sacrifice. The gate might be closed again, but it would take two Keepers to send the gods and spirits back. Which meant the assholes weren't going anywhere since Collin believed they should be free.

Even if they were after me.

"Okeus! Where are you? You said you wanted me, well here I am!" I stepped back from the tree, throwing my arms wide. "Come and get me!" Taunting him was pointless, but I felt the need to rage at someone. A temporarily incapacitated god probably wasn't the best choice, but it was safe enough for the moment. He had to regain strength before he could face anyone . . . even me.

Lightning flashed in the sky and thunder boomed.

"Ellie."

I spun around, my long wet hair whipping against my arm. Tom Helmsworth, an old high school classmate of mine, stood behind me, hands on his hips. I suspected he was here in his official capacity—as a police officer of Manteo. "How'd you know I was here?"

"Every time a thunderstorm appears out of nowhere directly over the botanical gardens, it's a safe bet that you'll be here too."

Fucking wind gods. They loved to torment me every chance they got.

"You can't bring him back, Ellie."

I knew Tom meant that I couldn't bring Daddy back from the dead, but Daddy hadn't died under ordinary circumstances. For all I knew, I *could* bring him back.

Tom took a few cautious steps toward me, and I understood why. The first few times he'd found me here, I was crying and kneeling on the spot where Daddy died. Two nights ago, he had found me pounding on the tree. Tonight I was shouting at the gods. Sadness had slipped into anger.

How much had he actually heard?

He stopped in front of me. "You can't keep doing this. I haven't arrested you because I know how hard it was for you to lose your dad. Everyone knows how close you two were." He put his hand on my arm and gripped lightly.

His touch sent a bolt of pain through the zigzag scar on my bicep, and I tried not to wince.

Tom bent his knees and lowered his face to mine, his expression gentle. "Ellie, this is illegal. You're trespassing."

I looked back at the oak tree. Someone needed to tell that to the gods.

"You need to go home."

Tom slid his arm around my back and gently guided me toward the gate. "Let me drive you."

I shook away from his touch. "I can drive myself."

His eyebrows rose. "Can you?"

I stopped in my tracks. "You think I've been drinking."

"Ellie." His voice softened and he looked down at me, water dripping from his bangs. "You're hurting. There's no shame in drinking a little to numb your grief, but I can't let you drive and hurt yourself or someone else."

"I'm not drunk, Tom."

"Nevertheless, I'm going to drive you home." His mouth lifted into a smart-ass grin. "Unless you'd rather I drive you to the police station."

Some choice. "Fine."

As soon as we reached the parking lot, the torrential downpour immediately stopped. If Tom noticed, he didn't comment.

Instead, he guided me toward his police cruiser, which was parked next to my beat-up car. Tom opened the passenger door for me. I offered him a tight smile and climbed in. At least he was letting me ride up front.

He made his way around the back of the car and popped the trunk. After he climbed behind the wheel, he tossed me a beach towel. "Here."

I grabbed it. "I didn't know towels were standard issue in a police car."

He chuckled, using another towel to dry his face. "They're not. But I was a Boy Scout."

He must have stopped to grab the towels before driving out here. "Why are you being so nice to me, Tom?"

He stopped rubbing his hair with the towel and slowly lowered his hand to his lap. "Maybe we weren't in the same grade, but we were friends through Claire's sister." He paused and tilted his head. "And I know that you're all alone now that your dad's gone. You don't have any grandparents around. No aunts and uncles. No siblings."

"I have Myra. And Claire."

"True," he acknowledged. "But Claire is getting ready for her wedding. And your stepmother is in mourning herself, not to mention all the overtime she's putting in at the Fort Raleigh visitor center and the bed and breakfast."

My eyes widened. He must have really been paying attention to my life to know all of that. I wasn't sure I liked it.

"You need someone to keep an eye on you."

My back stiffened. A few weeks ago someone else had insisted on keeping an eye on me whether I liked it or not. Look how that had turned out. "I can take care of myself."

"No one's disputing that. I just feel better watching out for you."

It was pointless to argue with him so I stared out the windshield as we drove down Highway 64 back to Manteo.

A voice over his police radio broke the silence. "Helmsworth, we got a call about another mutilated dog off of Highway 64."

Tom's shoulders stiffened and he cast a sideways glance at me before answering. "Roger. I picked up a stranded driver, and I'm dropping her off in town before I head out there."

"Roger." The dispatcher gave Tom the address.

"Mutilated dog?" I asked, my stomach churning with dread. Had the spirits' campaign of terrorism escalated?

Tom groaned. "As if animals dropping dead all over the island wasn't bad enough, now something is attacking dogs and ripping their guts out without eating them."

"What do you think it is?"

Tom's eyebrows lifted. "Why don't you tell me."

My stomach dropped to the floorboard. "How would I know?"

Sighing, he ran his hand through his hair. "Sorry, it's been a rough few weeks."

He didn't know the half of it.

"So, Ellie." Tom shifted in his seat. "What do you know about the Native American gods?"

What *had* he heard? I shrugged. "Not much. Why do you ask?"

"Well . . ." His hand twisted on the steering wheel. "It just seems a little odd for a woman who can practically trace her ancestry back to the *Mayflower* to be shouting at Algonquian gods."

I could go back further than that. I was a direct descendant of Ananias Dare of the Lost Colony of Roanoke, but I wasn't about to tell him that. Especially when all the history books said there were no survivors. "I don't know what you're talking about."

"I notice you're still marking your door with those symbols."

I twisted in my seat. "Are you investigating me?"

Tom parked at a stoplight and turned to look at me. "Ellie, two weeks ago there was a local death every day for four days and each person had ties to you. Of course I'm investigating you."

My mouth dropped open, my anger rising to the surface again. "You really think I'd kill my own father?"

His face lost all expression. "I thought your father had a heart attack."

Shit.

"Ellie, I've known you since you started kindergarten. There's no way in hell you killed anyone, least of all your father."

I turned away, trying to get it together. Tom was trained to get information from people. I needed to start thinking before I spoke, not a natural impulse for me.

The light turned green and Tom drove through the intersection. "So are you going to tell me the real reason why you have those marks on your front door?"

I didn't answer.

"When I asked you after Marlena's death, you said it was for protection. Protection from what?"

I closed my eyes and resisted the urge to shake my head. "I told you—it was insurance."

"Where did you learn how to do that?"

I decided to turn the question around on him. "Where did *you* learn about Algonquian gods and markings?"

"My mother is part Lumbee. I asked my great uncle after I first saw them on your door." He stopped at another stoplight.

This had to be the longest drive ever.

"And what's with the marking on your back?"

Goddamn it. How on earth had he seen that?

As if reading my mind, he reached over and shifted the strap of my tank top to the side. "Your shirt isn't exactly covering it. What's it for?"

"It was a dare from Claire. She knows how much Myra hates tattoos. So before Daddy died, I got a henna tattoo and pretended it was real." It was all true except for the dare part. "It's fading." Which also meant I was almost out of time. Okeus's symbol on my back was a temporary protection from the gods and spirits. Once it was gone, my Manitou—or life force—would be fair game. And they'd all made it quite clear that they considered my Manitou a gourmet feast.

"More Native American symbols, Ellie."

He was starting to piss me off. "When did it become a crime to be fascinated with another culture? People get Asian symbols tattooed on them all the time."

The light turned green, and I held back a sigh of relief. We were only five blocks from my apartment.

"You have to admit that the timing is a bit coincidental."

"How do you know I haven't been interested in Native American things for a while?"

"Call it a hunch. You just admitted you got the henna tattoo right before your father died, and that's around the time you started marking your door. Something fishy is going on here."

I needed to learn to keep my mouth shut. I sucked at this covert crap.

We rode the rest of the way to my apartment in silence, although Tom kept sneaking glances at me. When he pulled into my parking lot, I reached for the door handle like it was my lifeline. He grabbed my arm. "Ellie, wait."

I paused, refusing to look at him.

"Like I said, I know you're not a murderer. I'm not accusing you of anything. In fact, I think you're in trouble, only I've done a piss-poor job of telling you that." He tugged on my arm. "Ellie, look at me."

I slowly turned to face him.

"You're scared of someone or something, and I want to help you. But I can't do that unless you tell me what's wrong."

As I stared into Tom's earnest face, I realized I felt like telling him everything. That I was one of two Curse Keepers, the descendant of the Ananias Dare line. As the eldest child of the previous Keeper, my father, my job had been to watch and wait for the breaking of the curse that made the Lost Colony of Roanoke disappear over four hundred years ago. The other Keeper was Collin Dailey, a commercial fisherman from Buxton, North Carolina, and part-time petty thief, who took his role more seriously than I did mine. He was the descendant of the line begun by the Croatan chief Manteo. Only Collin had purposely broken the curse . . . and instead of closing the gate to hell before the morning of the seventh day, he had tricked me into opening it wide.

Everyone was scrambling for a reasonable explanation for why the Lost Colony had suddenly reappeared a few weeks ago, preserved down to the food in the colonists' bowls. I wanted to tell Tom the truth: Collin had shown up in the New Moon restaurant while I was working and pressed his right palm to mine, breaking the curse.

I would have loved to tell Tom about the horrifying things that had escaped and how they now lay in wait, regaining their strength before seeking their revenge against humanity for locking them away. That the mutilated dog he was about to investigate had undoubtedly been butchered by one of them.

But if I told him any of it, he would think I was crazy. If I told him all of it, he'd have me committed. The curse was my cross to bear.

I offered him a tired smile. "Thanks, Tom. If I find myself in a situation where I think you can help me, I'll be sure to call you."

Before he could ask more questions, I hopped out of the police car and headed up the two flights of outside stairs to my apartment. When I reached the landing, I realized that I'd left my keys and purse in my unlocked car, but I wasn't about to let Tom know that. I bent over and pulled my spare key from underneath the mat and slipped it into the door. As I swung it open, I froze. There were fresh markings on the door.

Collin had been here.

I swallowed the lump in my throat and summoned my anger. Collin Fucking Dailey didn't deserve my tears. I had given him my heart—not to mention the fact that my soul was now literally bound to his for all eternity—and he'd thrown it away. He'd thrown *me* away for whatever reward Okeus had promised him in exchange for opening the gate.

So why was he still helping me?

After the curse was broken three weeks ago and the first spirits were released, Collin had started to mark my door with symbols that represented the day and the night, forces of nature, and, in the center of each side, his symbol for the land, asking all the forces to lend me their protection.

Collin was the son of the earth, and I was the daughter of the sea. Our power was stronger combined than it was individually. So right before the end—before he betrayed me—we intersected our symbols for added protection.

Now, every few nights, he would sneak up and either scratch on fresh markings or place his symbol over mine.

He was protecting me even now.

I wanted to hate him—I *did* hate him—but this very act had softened my heart to him before. And look where that had gotten me . . . I needed to grow up. Collin wasn't doing this out of love.

Collin Dailey loved one person—Collin Dailey.

He was helping me out of guilt. It would only be a matter of time before he decided he'd paid his dues. Either that, or he thought he still needed me for something. Perhaps it was a combination of the two.

Any way I sliced it, I was in deep shit. The henna tattoo had faded so much it was almost gone, and Collin would soon stop lending me his marks.

I needed to learn how to protect myself or I was as good as dead.

~: CHAPTER TWO :~

When the curse first broke, animals began parading through my dreams, calling out to me for help. And I also began to have nightmares about the past, dredging up memories that had been buried long ago. But after the gate opened all the way, and my henna tattoo began to fade, other creepy crawlies started to invade my dreams . . .

The creatures varied from night to night, but tonight the creature resembled a badger, although it was many times larger than it should have been. It crouched in front of me, its eyes glowing red. Its teeth were huge, sharp, and dripping with blood.

"Curse Keeper," it said. "Daughter of the sea and witness to creation. Okeus is waiting for you to be ready, but I have other plans."

Panic washed through me and I took a step backward, holding up the mark on my palm. I had the power to send him away—not permanently, but I could get him to leave me alone for now.

The animal laughed. "Your mark won't always work."

It wasn't exactly news. His children had screamed and hissed about these great plans as they spilled out of the gates of hell. Their first order of business was to regain their strength. Torturing me for four centuries as punishment for my ancestor's role in locking

11

them away was a close second. Despite the way I'd taunted Okeus in the botanical gardens, I knew the last thing I wanted to do was confront him. "Tell Okeus I'll take a rain check."

"Tell him yourself," the creature snarled. "He'll visit you soon. Unless I get to you first."

A dog appeared behind the badger, hunched down and whimpering, restrained by unseen forces. The badger turned around and attacked with a loud growl, throwing the dog to the ground and ripping open the flesh of its abdomen. Screaming and howling, the dog tried to get away, but the badger continued its attack, ripping intestines from the still-living creature and flinging them to the ground.

I fought to wake from the nightmare, but the badger looked over its shoulder, intestines hanging from its teeth, and mumbled, "This is only the beginning."

I awoke screaming, my nose still filled with the scent of blood. I jumped out of bed and ran to the toilet, throwing up what was left of my dinner from hours earlier. I tried to purge the image from my head along with the contents of my stomach. The image wasn't as easy to lose.

After I rinsed out my mouth, I made sure all the window ledges were protected with salt, which helped keep out the nasties. I went into my living room and grabbed my laptop, hoping to uncover some information about the creature from my dream. I wasn't even sure what to look for. My biggest problem was that four hundred years ago the colonists had been more intent on converting the Native Americans to Christianity than they were on recording their belief system. Multiple tribes had been wiped from existence without making more than a blip on the historical record, which meant that finding specific information about the gods and spirits was next to impossible. I'd already checked the local library and bookstore and performed every conceivable Internet search. I needed to know what I was fighting—or at the very least defending myself against—but there was so little to find.

I curled up on the oversized sofa with an afghan and glanced at the clock, surprised I hadn't yet had a visitor. Maybe they'd skip tonight since I'd been out by the tree.

But that was wishful thinking. The banging on my front door started at 4:00 a.m., close to dawn—when the spirits were usually at their strongest.

The mark on my palm itched and burned, making me cringe. I wasn't in the mood to deal with a messenger, but it wasn't like I had a choice. If I didn't answer, the thing would keep pounding and moaning and might awaken my neighbors. And if anyone came to investigate, there was a good chance the spirit would take their Manitou, the essence of life in all living things. So I either answered the door or risked killing my neighbors and condemning them to hell. Too bad I liked my neighbors.

"Curse Keeper! I summon you."

Setting my laptop on the sofa, I threw off the afghan and padded to the front door.

"Who's there?"

"Who are you to speak to me this way!"

I groaned. It had to be Kanim, the messenger spirit of Okeus. As if the badger thing hadn't been enough for one night. Taking a deep breath, I cracked open the door and spread my legs apart to brace myself against the wind with which the spirit would most likely blast me.

The cold gust hit me in the face, and instead of the usual dark blob hovering over the wooden floor of my deck, a large bird with a human head and flowing white hair was perched on the rail of my front porch.

It was Wapi, the northern wind god.

Oh, crap. He was just a shadowy spirit the first time I met him. I'd seen his true form when the gates of hell burst open, but most of the messengers who'd visited me after that night still showed up as shadows. Wapi had been free the longest of all the gods, so there'd been more time for him to regain his strength. What did it mean about the others if Wapi was already strong enough to come to me in his corporeal state?

Part of me was terrified. If he'd regained his true form, what was he capable of doing? The marks on my door would only keep him from coming in to get me. They wouldn't protect me once I left the apartment.

I gripped the edge of the door. "What do you want, Wapi?" There was no love lost between us. He'd tried to suck out my Manitou a couple of days after the curse was first broken.

"Okeus has placed his mark on your arm."

My hand self-consciously rubbed the zigzag scar made by Okeus's claw. "Ahone has claimed me."

"Ahone," the bird spit. "Ahone is a weak coward. He hides in the heavens. Where is your Ahone now? Where will he be when Okeus comes to claim that which is his?"

I couldn't help thinking that "that which is his" meant me.

I rested my temple on the edge of the door frame. "I'm tired, so cut to the chase. What do you want?"

"You are running out of time. You must choose a side. Okeus or Ahone."

"And if I don't?"

His leer sent chills down my spine before I slammed the door closed. I expected him to howl and scream in protest, but it remained blessedly silent outside. After a moment, I turned and rested the back of my head against the door.

14

The bottom line was that Wapi was right. I would have to choose . . . and it wasn't much of a choice. Okeus promised me an eternal life in hell. Ahone promised little other than his protection, but at least my soul wouldn't be damned. Not that I knew of, anyway.

Not like Collin's.

Perhaps I could put Ahone's mark on my back if I knew what it was. One thing was for sure: I really was running out of time.

I stumbled back to the sofa in exhaustion and dozed there for a few hours, my dreams remarkably quiet, until Claire let herself into the apartment.

"You look like shit," she said as she kicked the door closed behind her and handed me a cup of coffee from the shop across the alley.

"Gee, I love you too." I took a sip of the coffee, burning my tongue and nearly dropping the cup.

She plopped down in the overstuffed chair across from me, dug a muffin out of a paper bag, and handed it to me. "I heard you were in the botanical gardens last night."

I peeled the lining paper off the muffin, giving it my full attention. "And where did you hear that?"

"Tom Helmsworth stopped by my house this morning to have a chat."

My gaze jerked up to meet hers.

Claire watched me for several seconds and when I didn't answer, she continued. "He said it wasn't the first time."

I took a bite. "He's watching me."

"Why?"

"He knows that all those deaths are connected to me."

Her eyebrows rose. "He thinks you killed those people?"

"No, but he heard me shouting to Okeus and Ahone, and he's

studied the symbols on my door. I'm pretty sure he knows something's up."

"How does he know about the symbols?"

"He says he's part Lumbee. He asked his great uncle."

Claire shook her head. "It doesn't mean he *really* knows anything. How could he?"

I ran my hand through my dirty hair and looked up at her. "My dreams are getting worse."

"What did you see?"

"When Tom brought me home, I heard a call come over the radio. The dispatcher said a mutilated dog had been found. I don't think it was the first one." I groaned. "I mean, I know hundreds of animals have already died—in fact, it's a wonder there are any left—but this time, they've been tortured."

"What does it have to do with your dreams?"

"Last night, the creature in my dreams ripped a dog apart in front of me."

The color drained from her face; then she sat back in the chair and tucked her feet underneath her. "Maybe it was the power of suggestion, Ellie. It could have just been a dream."

I shook my head. "No, this was real. And the thing talked to me. It told me that I had to make a decision soon, that Okeus was coming for me."

"You're okay as long as you have the symbols on the door, right?"

"For now, sure. But the spirits are growing stronger. Soon they'll be strong enough to show themselves in the daylight. I'm no closer to finding Ahone's symbol for my back. What am I supposed to do?"

Her eyes widened in fear. "I don't know."

I crossed my legs and leaned forward. "I'm not going to sit here and wait for them to come and get me, Claire. I need to learn how to protect myself. And I have to figure out how to protect everyone else too. Sure, it's dogs now, but it won't be long before the spirits move on to people."

"How are you going to do that? We've looked at every resource we can find, both at the library and online. Are you going to visit the Lumbees or something?"

Pressing my lips together, I considered my options. I needed an expert who knew more about Native American spirits than anyone else. Someone who'd studied these religions in depth. Then an idea struck—one so perfect I couldn't believe I hadn't thought of it before. I grabbed my laptop and searched for universities that offered Native American studies. "If you want an expert, who else knows more than a professor teaching the subject, right?"

Claire considered it. "You might be on to something there. What are you going to do?"

It looked like the closest university with a strong program was the University of North Carolina at Chapel Hill. Digging into the faculty page, I pointed to the screen. "Here, Dr. David Preston. He's the head of the American Studies Department and it says he's an expert on North Carolinian Indians. That means he might have the information I need, right?"

She looked doubtful. "I guess . . ."

I stood and stretched. "It's worth a chance. I'll leave as soon as I finish up at the bed and breakfast this morning." I only hoped the anxiety I always felt when I left the island—a wretched side effect of the curse—wouldn't be too debilitating. But I'd suffer through just about anything to improve my chances of long-term survival.

"You're going to go *today*?"

"I need this information as soon as possible, Claire."

"How do you know if he'll even be there? It's summer."

"I'll call and see if he's available. Maybe he teaches summer classes." I sat down and turned my back to her, pulling aside the top strap of my tank top. "The henna tattoo is almost gone. It's my only protection. I have a few days left at most."

"So just replace it with what Collin put on you."

"But he used Okeus's mark on my back. The spirits keep telling me I have to choose. If I put Okeus's mark on my back permanently, it will mean I've chosen him. I have to wait until I find Ahone's symbol."

She sighed, nodding reluctantly. "Yeah, that makes sense."

I got up and headed for the bathroom. "I'm going to take a shower. I'll call you later."

"Ellie, wait."

I paused next to my bathroom door.

"Let me go with you."

"But you have to work."

"I'll work for a few hours and then tell them I'm sick." She gave me a wry smile. "I'm worried about you. Chapel Hill is a good four hours away, and I don't want you going by yourself. What if . . ."

"What if what? I get attacked by the badger thing that showed up in my dream?"

She looked down into her coffee.

"All the more reason for you to stay home."

Her face shot up, a determined look in her eyes.

I sagged against the door frame. I couldn't bear the thought of something happening to her. But I also couldn't stand the thought of being alone all day. "Thanks, Claire. You're right. I'm scared to death, and I need you."

Claire got up and walked over, pulling me into a hug. "I'm here for you. As long as you don't try to back out of wearing the maid of honor dress I picked out for you." I tried to pull back and swat her arm, but she tightened her hold as she giggled into my ear. "I know you hate that dress, but you're going to have to wear it. It was a concession to my sister for picking you as my maid of honor. So get over it."

"I know, but orange taffeta ruffles? Really? I'm going to look like a pumpkin."

"Nah, you're not round enough. Maybe a squash."

I laughed, breaking free. "Lucky for you, I'd wear a burlap bag if you asked."

She patted my cheek with a sneaky grin. "I'm counting on it." Her smile slid off her face and she stared into my eyes. "I'll help you any way I can, Ellie."

"I know, Claire. And I love you for it." But when things started getting really bad, I'd turn away from her rather than put her in harm's way. I wasn't sure how I'd manage that, but I was determined.

"I know how hard all of this has been for you; losing your dad—"

I waited for the usual tears to fill my eyes, but they stayed dry. Maybe I was cried out. For now. "The best thing I can do for Daddy is carry on his legacy. And that's exactly what I intend to do."

"He'd be so proud of how brave you are."

Daddy would have been prouder if I'd taken the curse more seriously from the beginning, but it had sounded like a fairy tale passed down from generation to generation for over four hundred years. I'd stopped believing in the curse when I was eight years old. Right after my mother was murdered. Every piece of information he'd told me completely disappeared, something I'd attributed to the trauma of witnessing her death. Daddy had done his best to reteach me, but I'd turned my back on it. My mother hadn't believed, and I felt I owed it to her to give the curse up as well. For the last two weeks I'd beaten myself up about it, wondering if Collin would still have been able to trick me if I'd remembered all the details. I'd like to think he still would have snowed me, but there was no way of knowing.

Claire left for work with the plan that she'd develop a convenient case of food poisoning as soon as I called her with confirmation that the professor would be at the university. I grabbed a quick shower, trying to keep my left shoulder blade out of the water. Anything to make the henna tattoo on my back last longer. I would have skipped showering for another day or so if I weren't going to see Dr. Preston.

I left for Myra's bed and breakfast to help out with the morning chores. It was odd to think of it as Myra's now and not Daddy and Myra's. It may have been handed down several generations in my father's family, but the truth was, it had been Myra's place for some time. Daddy's Alzheimer's had stolen him from us years before his physical death.

Myra was sitting at her desk in the small office when I walked in through the back door, the heavenly smell of cinnamon rolls and bacon hitting me as soon as I entered.

"Good morning, Ellie." Myra looked up and smiled, but dark circles underlined her almond-shaped eyes. My stepmother was second-generation Chinese, which drew quite a bit of curiosity when I introduced her as my mother. "How are you?"

I leaned over and kissed her cheek. "I'm fine," I lied. "How are *you*? You look tired." I'd lost my daddy, but Myra had lost her husband. Sometimes I forgot I wasn't the only one affected by his death.

"I am." She closed her eyes and rested her cheek in her hand. "I'm working overtime at the park site, and we're sold out here at the B&B for several weeks, which is good since we're in financial trouble. But with the funeral . . . and everything . . . I'm having trouble keeping up with it all."

I squatted next to her. "I'm sorry I haven't helped more with the inn—"

She looked down into my face and cupped my cheek. "Ellie, you just lost your daddy, and not under normal circumstances. I don't expect you to help. I expect you to grieve. You don't even need to be here now."

"What am I going to do, Myra? Sit around and wait . . ." I stopped myself from saying "for the end of the world." I had told Myra about Daddy sacrificing himself to close the gate, but I hadn't told her that the supernatural beings had escaped before that happened. She had enough to worry about without adding fear for my safety to the mix.

"Wait for what?"

"Nothing. I'm being a bitch and feeling sorry for myself."

She frowned. "Don't say that."

I rested my head on her lap, and she stroked my hair like she used to do when I was having nightmares as a girl.

"I love you, Ellie. I may not have had children of my own, but you know I consider you my daughter. I wish you didn't have to go through this."

I looked up into her face. "Myra, I barely remember my mother. Just bits and pieces. I love her, especially what she did for me." I paused as the usual pang of guilt struck me. "But you've been there for me for all the big stuff. Makeup. Boys. Daddy." My voice broke. "I know I call you Myra, but I think of you as my mom too."

"Oh, Ellie."

I rose to my knees and threw my arms around her neck.

She squeezed me tight. "We Lancaster women need to stick together."

"We always have." I hugged her again and stood up. "I'll be able to help out more at the inn until the restaurant reopens."

"You don't have to."

"I know, but I want to. The inn's part mine too."

The reminder looked like it pained her. Not because she didn't want to share the ownership, but because it made her think about all the money I'd scraped together over the last couple of years to keep the bed and breakfast afloat.

"How have you been doing without working these past couple of weeks?" She looked worried. "Any word on when the New Moon is going to reopen?"

I sucked in a deep breath and let it out slowly. The restaurant I worked at had been closed for two weeks because the manager had been found dead. "No. But Tom Helmsworth thinks all these mysterious deaths have something to do with me."

Her eyes widened in alarm. "Are you in trouble?"

I gave a quick shake of my head. "No. If anything, he's worried about me."

Fear flickered in her eyes. "Is everything okay?"

My mouth lifted into a tight smile. "Of course."

Myra had never believed in the curse. It had been pretty much the one and only long-standing argument between her and Daddy, especially when he tried to goad me into relearning everything I'd forgotten after my mother's death. But on the night of Daddy's death, Myra had seen Okeus's messenger spirit—the one who had come to try to take Daddy's soul. She had seen enough to make her a believer.

"They're going to have to replace Marlena with a new manager." My voice broke and I forced the hurt back down. Marlena was dead because of me. Just like Dwight, a guy I'd dated a few times, and Lila, one of the waitresses who'd worked with me. When I let the truth of their deaths sink deep down, I nearly collapsed with the guilt. But I reminded myself that I was just as much a victim as they were. I had never asked for this. Collin had just thrust it upon me. Their deaths weren't on my head. They were on his. "I don't know when they'll reopen. But I can pick up hours on the lunch shift at Darrell's Restaurant if I need money. They get all that courthouse business, and they're busier than ever with the reappearance of the Lost Colony. They told me I had a job there if I want it."

"You can always move back home, Ellie."

"I know." But I'd probably live on the street before I did that.

"I should be home in time to relieve the caregiver . . ." Her voice became tight and then trailed off.

I squeezed her shoulder. I knew what she'd been about to say: she should be home in time to relieve Daddy's caregiver. It had been her routine for two years. It was hard to forget something so deeply ingrained.

Myra's gaze turned to the picture window along the back wall of her office, following the neighbor's dog, a big golden retriever that was chasing a squirrel in the yard. At least one dog was still running around on the island. "I tell myself that he's happier now. He hated losing his mind piece by piece. He was one of the most intelligent men I've ever met." She smiled as tears slid down her cheeks. "On my first day as a part-time park ranger, I was so nervous to meet him. He was the head ranger and renowned for his knowledge of the colony. I thought he'd be intimidating. But he was so nice, and there was something about him . . ." She laughed softly. "You probably don't want to hear this."

"I do." I forced down the lump in my throat. "I like to remember what he was like before his memories began to fade."

"Your mother had been gone a couple of years, but I could still see the pain in his eyes. It was like he'd lost part of himself." She paused for several seconds. "I never once thought I could replace your mother . . . I was just grateful to be part of his life." She looked up at me with a shaky smile. "And yours. I don't want to lose you too, Ellie."

I hugged her again, my tears breaking through the dam. "I love you, Myra. Like I said, I'm not going anywhere."

Myra's friend Becky appeared in the doorway. "I'm sorry to bother you, Myra, but there's a police officer here who wants to talk to you."

Her eyes widened in concern as she pulled away from me. "Do you think this is about you?"

I squeezed her arms. "It's probably Tom. I promise he doesn't think I killed anyone. This is his way of looking out for me. We went to school together, remember? Claire's sister dated him when Claire and I were freshman. I think it makes him feel kind of responsible for me since Daddy's gone."

She nodded, wiping her tears. "What should I tell him?"

"Tell him the truth, except for the part about the curse, of course. You didn't believe the curse until a couple of weeks ago anyway. Just tell him what happened and how you saw things before you learned the truth."

"What about Collin?"

My back stiffened. "Tell Tom the truth about that too."

"But it might look bad for him."

I shrugged, pretending not to care. "Then he brought it on himself."

I walked into the small kitchen, passing Becky, and poured a cup of coffee and then took it out into the great room. As I'd suspected, Tom was sitting there waiting. Dressed in jeans and a T-shirt, he was perched on the arm of a leather sofa, staring at an old family portrait on the wall. It was of Daddy, Myra, and me and was taken when I was in the eighth grade.

"Long time no see, Tom."

He turned toward me. "You look tired, Ellie."

Lifting my shoulders in a half shrug, I gave him a wry smile. "Busy night." I held the cup out to him. "When did you become a plainclothes policeman?"

Laughing, he stood and took the coffee. "I'm here unofficially. Your keys were in the ignition of your car, so I drove it to the parking lot of your apartment. When you didn't answer the door, I decided to bring the keys here. I figured I might as well ask Myra a few questions while I was at it."

"You might have mentioned that to Becky. You just about gave Myra a coronary."

Cringing, he took a sip of the coffee. "Sorry about that." Tom walked toward the photo. "I used to envy you, you know."

"Me? Why?"

"Your dad was awesome. Mine was never around, but the summer when I dated Melanie, your dad always made a point of talking to me. Like he was really interested in me as a person."

I reached out and stroked Daddy's smiling face with the tip of my index finger. "I'm sure he was. That's who he was . . . at least until he got sick."

"I bet you didn't know I got in trouble that summer. I was caught vandalizing the school."

I whipped my head around in surprise. "You?"

He hung his head, a sheepish grin on his face. "Yeah. I went through a rebellious patch. Got in with those Morris boys; they were nothing but trouble. I was about to get kicked off the football team, but your dad was on the school board and he spoke up on my behalf. I got that football scholarship to UNC because of him. Without him I never would have gotten my criminal justice degree."

I turned back to look at Daddy's smiling face again. "I didn't know."

"He never made a big deal out of it. That's just the kind of guy he was." He shifted his weight. "So now I feel like I owe it to him to make sure you're okay."

"I'm fine, Tom. You won't find me in the gardens again."

"It's not just that, Ellie. I can tell that you're in some kind of danger."

"I'm not. I assure you." I hated lying, but I saw no other way around it. "Questioning Myra is only going to upset her more."

Tom didn't look convinced.

"Fine," I lowered my voice. "Talk to her, but promise that you'll be gentle. She looks like she's handling all of this well, but I suspect she's hiding most of her pain from me."

"I wouldn't dream of hurting her."

"I know." I dropped my hold on him. "I've got work to do. Thanks for sharing that story about Daddy with me."

"You're welcome. I suspect there's a lot more stories about your dad that you've never heard before."

I suspected he was right. If only some of them could help me now.

⌁ CHAPTER THREE ↜

After Myra left, I went outside and called the phone number listed on the university's web page and confirmed with a departmental assistant that Dr. Preston would have office hours from one until three. Which meant that if Claire and I left between nine thirty and ten, we'd have at least an hour to spare. I called her and arranged to pick her up at ten.

After changing the linens and starting the laundry, I told Becky that I needed to leave for the day. She was used to my sporadic schedule and didn't say a word, but I had to wonder if she was getting tired of all my slacking lately.

Claire and I were on the road by ten, crossing the Virginia Dare Bridge to the mainland.

"This marsh gives me the creeps," Claire mumbled, hunched down in the passenger seat.

"What are you talking about? We have marshes all over Manteo." I was just grateful I wasn't feeling the usual anxiety that troubled me when I left the island.

"I know, but something about this stuff doesn't feel right."

The reeds growing along the side of the highway looked exactly like the marshland on our island, but I had to admit that Claire was right. Something about it set my nerves on edge. I couldn't help wondering if some of the spirits had hidden here, lying in wait as they preyed on squirrels and salamanders, growing stronger.

I shuddered. This is what my life had become—a constant battle with enemies, real and imagined.

We stopped a couple hours later and grabbed some deli sandwiches to eat on the way. The closer we got to the university, the more nervous I became.

"Do you know what you're going to say?" Claire asked.

"I don't know. I can't tell him the truth, obviously."

"I agree. You can't be in my wedding in a couple of weeks if you're locked up in the psychiatric ward at the Outer Banks Hospital. Then I'd have to move Melanie up as maid of honor, and all that fighting will have been for nothing."

"I still feel bad that you and Melanie fought over me being your maid of honor."

"Hey, it's *my* wedding. That's something I get to choose. You and I are much closer than she and I will ever be."

"Hmm . . ." I twisted my lips together as I thought about it. "Do you remember when Melanie dated Tom Helmsworth?"

She rolled her eyes. "I think he's spent the past nine years trying to forget it. She treated him like crap."

"He came by the B&B to talk to Myra today."

Claire sat up and grabbed the dashboard. "About you? He's really making the rounds, huh?"

"Yeah. He drove my car back to my apartment from the Elizabethan Gardens, and he was bringing her the keys since I wasn't home. He was actually off duty . . . He told me he felt a responsibility to watch over me."

Her eyebrows shot up. "You think Tom has a thing for you?"

I shook my head. "No, it's not like that. He said Daddy helped him when he was in high school. He got into trouble and was almost kicked off the football team, but Daddy spoke up for him. He said he wouldn't have gone to college and gotten his criminal justice degree without his football scholarship. He feels like he owes it to Daddy to make sure I'm okay."

"Wow. I had no idea."

"Me neither." I sighed. "But that means he feels a personal connection to this whole thing, so he might not back down. I'm going to have to convince him I'm okay . . . I don't want him to get hurt."

"You have to admit that you could use some help since Collin's hiding from you."

"Tom wouldn't be of much help, Claire. It takes two Keepers to send a spirit or god to Popogusso."

"But you said Collin thought you could probably send the minor ones back on your own."

"But I don't even know how to do *that*. I don't know anything."

"We can look through your dad's things again. See if we can find the notes he says he wrote down. Maybe there's something in there about what to do in the case of an absentee Keeper."

"Yeah . . ." Daddy had recognized Okeus's mark. Maybe he had Ahone's mark written down somewhere. Still, we'd been through his office and his old bedroom three times without turning up anything. If there were notes somewhere, they had been hidden well. My current hopes were pinned on the professor at UNC. He couldn't know about the curse, but I hoped he'd know Ahone's symbol. And maybe he had enough knowledge about the gods and spirits to at least help me understand the nightmare I was facing.

It was after two when we arrived at the UNC campus and found a place on the street to park.

"Are you sure he's here?" Claire asked as we walked through the campus bookstore toward Greenlaw Hall. "This place looks like a ghost town."

"I called this morning and his secretary told me he had office hours from one to three. He's in office 232."

"Did you get an appointment?"

"No, she said it was first come, first serve." My stomach knotted.

"Do you have a plan?"

"I was just going to wing it."

"Excuse me, Dr. Preston," Claire mimicked. "My name is Ellie Lancaster and I need you to help me send Okeus back to hell before he tortures me for four hundred years."

"Not helping." But she was right. I should have come up with something better than that. "He's the head of his department. He's bound to be an old guy. I'm sure he's dealt with all kinds of crazy questions."

"Yeah, which is bound to make him cranky."

Crap. I hadn't considered that. We were already inside the small lobby of Greenlaw. I stopped and took a deep breath.

Claire stopped too and looked me up and down. "Well, you've got a damsel-in-distress look about you. When all else fails, go for the pretty, helpless girl act. How can he resist? You'll have the old fart eating out of your hand."

"Shut up, Claire." I tugged up the neckline of my T-shirt to show less cleavage, then tugged down my above-the-knee cotton skirt. "I want this to be a professional conversation."

"Then you should have tried to look frumpier, not that I've ever seen you look frumpy."

"You think I look slutty?"

"God, no. I've never seen you look slutty either. You're a pretty girl, Ellie. Guys notice, even if you ignore them most of the time."

"I'm not here to get a date. I'm here to hopefully save my life . . . and the rest of humanity." That made me think of Collin, and a wave of pain flowed through my body, anger fast on its heels. I had thought we were saving humanity then, when in fact we'd been condemning it. I didn't have time to think about Collin right now. Fucking asshole.

We climbed the stairs to the second floor, still without seeing anyone. I wiped my sweaty palms on my skirt and sucked in a deep breath.

"Two thirty-two." Claire pointed toward a door several feet away. It stood ajar and voices were coming from inside the office. "Do you want me to come inside with you?"

"No. I need to do this myself." I tried to slow my racing heart. Why had I not come up with a better plan—or any plan at all?

"Okay, I'm going to look up ideas for the centerpieces for my reception on Pinterest while I'm waiting down there pretending I don't know you." She pointed toward the end of the hall, raising her phone. "Hallelujah for smartphones."

"I'll find you when I'm done."

She walked past the door and peeked inside before glancing over her shoulder at me with an amused grin.

What did *that* mean?

Just as I was about to knock on the door, a girl shot out of the room, tears streaming down her face. My heart kick-started as I watched her rush toward the stairs.

"Are you going to just bloody stand there or are you coming in?" a gruff voice asked from inside the office. The door was now gaping open.

My head whipped around to face the speaker, and I tried to hide my surprise. Dr. David Preston didn't even begin to resemble the fusty old professor I'd imagined. The man standing at his desk had to be in his thirties, with dark brown hair and a handsome face. He was tall and even though he had on a long-sleeve dress shirt, it was obvious he didn't have a beer belly. And his accent suggested he was British.

"Well . . . ?" he asked, looking exasperated as he stuffed several overflowing folders into a messenger bag.

Why couldn't he be a freaking old fart?

"I need to ask you a few questions."

He kept his eyes on his bag as he closed the flap. "Sorry, but my Introduction to Native American Cultures classes for the fall are full, and I'm not approving any additional students. You'll just have to get on the waiting list like all the others, although last I heard, the list is quite lengthy."

The English accent was throwing me. Talk about a contradiction. An Englishman who specialized in Native American history.

He was staring at me, waiting for an answer. "That's not why I'm here." But I understood why there was a waiting list. Dr. David Preston was like a real-life Indiana Jones. Only hotter. And British.

His eyebrows rose. "You don't look familiar. Are you a history major?"

"No, actually, I'm not a student here at all."

His shoulders relaxed. "Oh, then my apologies. Over the last two weeks, I've been barraged with requests from female undergrads begging to get into my classes. I've heard every excuse under the sun, so forgive me for assuming you were in the same position." He slung his bag over his shoulder and moved around the side of his desk.

"That's okay. Are you leaving? Your secretary said you had office hours until three."

"Usually I do, but I'm going on a research trip tomorrow, and I'm leaving early today to take care of some personal business."

Panic ate at my resolve. "I just drove four hours to see you, Dr. Preston. I really need to ask you a few questions about the Croatan Indians."

He looked surprised. "I'm honored that you drove all that way, but I don't have much time to spare at the moment. Perhaps you could make an appointment for when I return to the school in August." Walking to the door, he waited for me to follow him into the hall so that he could lock his office.

"That will be too late."

He chuckled as he put his keys into his pants pocket. "The Croatan tribe has been thought to be extinct for over two hundred years. I assure you that five weeks won't be too late."

"Please, this is important."

He looked skeptical, but he tilted his head toward the stairs. "You can accompany me to the exit and ask any questions you can fit into the thirty-second walk."

Thirty seconds? I had no idea where to start. I hurried to keep up with him as he headed for the staircase, his long legs making the trek even shorter. "Do you know anything about the Croatan gods and spirits?"

"Yes." I waited for him to expand upon that, but he just gave me a slightly irritated look. "While I admit that my knowledge of their spiritual beliefs is scanty, it would certainly take more than thirty seconds to discuss it."

When we reached the staircase doorway, I cast a quick glance at Claire. She looked up from her phone with raised eyebrows. I just shrugged and hurried down the stairs after the professor.

I decided to ask him about my most pressing concern first. "Do you know about a spirit that looks like a huge badger and attacks animals, ripping out their internal organs but not eating their meat?"

He stopped at the bottom of the stairs, narrowing his eyes. "Excuse me?"

"Do you know what it is?"

He abruptly started walking again, hurrying for the exit. "I don't know what you're up to, but I've heard enough."

I grabbed his arm. "Dr. Preston, *please*."

He stopped and looked from my hand to my face, his expression all wariness.

"I promise you that this is important. Have you heard of a spirit that does that?"

"No. Look, Miss . . ."

"Ellie. Ellie Lancaster." He tried to pull out of my grasp, but my fingers dug in deeper. "I know this sounds crazy, but you have no idea how important it is for you to tell me what you know."

"*Ellie*, I suggest that you do an Internet search and perhaps read the book *Indians and English* by Karen Ordahl Kupperman."

"I already have."

"Then I'm afraid I won't be of much help to you." He pried my fingers off his sleeve.

"Wait! Please!" I begged, digging my cell phone out of my purse. "Can you just look at this photo for me?"

Indecision flickered across his face before he closed his eyes with a sigh and then reopened them, shaking his head. "I'm going to warn you right now that if you're showing me a naked photo of yourself, I *will* call security and have you arrested."

I looked up from scanning my photos for the one Claire had taken of my back a week ago. "What? No! God, no." I handed him the phone. "Here. I know the mark's faded, but if you zoom in, you can see it better."

He reluctantly took the phone, pulled a pair of glasses from his shirt pocket, and put them on his nose. "Is this a tattoo?"

"Yes, but it's henna."

He rolled his eyes and started to lower the glasses. "Miss Lancaster."

"Dr. Preston, *please.*"

The desperation in my voice must have swayed him, but he didn't look happy as he examined the picture. "The symbols look Native American . . ."

"Can you make out what they mean?"

"Well, yes. They stand for forces of nature." He pointed to the screen. "The sun, the moon. I believe these symbols in the corners stand for rain and storms."

"What about the one in the center?"

He tilted his head to the side as he examined the image. "Some obscure texts show that symbol in relation to an Algonquian deity."

"Okeus."

His gaze lifted toward me, now tinged with curiosity. "Yes, but very few laypeople know that. Where did you learn of it?"

I ignored his question. "What about all the symbols put together? Are they like our alphabet? When you put a bunch of symbols all together, do they mean something different? Does this tattoo have a deeper meaning?"

He studied me with an expressionless gaze. "Yes."

For the first time in weeks, I felt like I was getting somewhere. "Really? What?"

He slowly handed the phone back to me. "It means some drunk college kid went out and got a bad henna tattoo during spring break. Now if you'll excuse me, you've wasted enough of my time."

I followed him toward the exit, tears springing to my eyes as I kept pace with him. "Dr. Preston, this isn't a joke. I need your help. Do you know the symbol for Ahone? My life depends on it. Please."

He looked back at me with disgust and pity. "Miss Lancaster, if this isn't a joke, the only help I can give you is to suggest you check yourself into a hospital for psychiatric screening." He pushed the door open. "Now if you'll excuse me."

I watched him walk across the courtyard, my last bit of hope leaving with him.

"That was painful to watch." Claire had followed us downstairs, and she stood next to me, looking out the glass doors.

"If he won't help me, I'm as good as dead, Claire. He was my last chance at answers."

"No, Ellie. You and I both know who you need to go see."

I hated her for suggesting it, but I supposed there was no way around it.

It was beginning to look like I would have to pay a visit to Collin Dailey.

∴ Chapter Four ∾

I was already having a shitty day, and then my car broke down in the Alligator River National Wildlife Refuge when we were almost home. I sat on the side of the road and allowed myself ten minutes of tears while Claire called her fiancé, Drew, to come and get us.

"It could be worse," she said as we sat on the trunk, watching the cars speed past us as we waited for our rescue. "We could be two hours from Manteo instead of forty minutes."

"I know." She was right, but I barely had enough money to pay my rent, let alone the bill for a tow and car repair.

Claire wrapped her arm around my back and pulled my head to her shoulder. "You deserve a good cry. You've had a hell of a few weeks."

"I don't know what to do," I said, wiping my face. "Dr. Preston was my Hail Mary plan."

She turned to face me. "Ellie, you know you need to ask for Collin's help."

I shook my head and leaned my arms on my thighs. "He was the one who wanted the gate open in the first place. What makes you think he'd help? He doesn't give a shit."

"Yeah, that man doesn't give two fucks about you. Which is why he sneaks to your front door in the middle of the night to put his protective marks over yours."

"But I told him I never wanted to see him again. It would be humiliating."

"How could it be humiliating?" She leaned back and stared into my face with disbelief. "He's the shithead who made you a buffet for a bunch of vengeful gods. He owes you more than a few marks on your door."

"Yeah." Claire was right, and my head knew it, but I wasn't sure if my heart could handle seeing him. The wound was still too raw. As much as I hated him for what he'd done, I didn't feel whole without him, which seemed ridiculous given that we'd only known each other for a few weeks, and we'd only been together for less than a week of that time. But I also knew my feeling had more to do with the fact that our souls were bound together than it did with our attachment to each other.

Claire shivered. "This marsh still gives me the creeps."

"Me too."

The sun was setting, and a shiver ran down my spine as I watched it bow beneath the clouds. Over the past several nights, I'd noticed a new heaviness in the air for about thirty minutes during the merging of day and night—all shadow, substance, and danger. As the mark on my back faded, I could feel myself becoming more and more vulnerable. The things in the night were getting stronger while I was becoming weaker. It was only a matter of time before they overpowered me.

I had hoped Dr. Preston would know the symbol for Ahone. I had already accepted that I had to permanently etch a protective mark onto my skin. I just needed that final piece of the puzzle. Sure, I could ask Collin, but I couldn't trust his answer. After all, he was the one who had originally put Okeus's mark in the center of my henna tattoo.

"Curse Keeper," a voice hissed.

I jerked upright, a slight tingle in my palm. "Did you hear that?"

Claire looked around, her forehead wrinkling with worry. "Hear what?"

"*Shh.*"

We sat in silence for a moment, the only sound the cars whizzing past.

I turned my ear toward the marsh. "Shouldn't there be some kind of sound? Birds? Bugs?"

Claire's eyes widened. "Yeah."

I slid to the ground, my heart racing. How could I be so stupid? This was a wildlife refuge, and the spirits had been targeting animals. "Get in the car."

I walked to the edge of the marsh as she scrambled off the trunk and ran to the passenger door.

"Ellie, what are you doing?"

Ignoring her, I looked into the canal that ran alongside the road. "What's out there?"

"*Curse Keeper.*" A low hiss filled the air. "You've come out to play."

"Holy shit," Claire murmured, swinging her door open. "Ellie, *get in the car.*"

I steeled my back and tried to stop my hands from shaking. "Spirit, show yourself."

"*Ellie!*"

The water splashed and the marsh grass rustled. The movement headed my way.

"Ellie," Claire begged. "You don't have to do this. Just get in the car."

I wanted to run to safety, but this was my chance to get some answers. I needed to know what I was fighting. "Who are you?" I asked, willing myself to be brave.

The rustling stopped in front of me, but the canal was covered in shadows, and I couldn't make out what was hidden in the vegetation.

"I am your nightmares come to life." A giant snake's head rose from a patch of reeds six feet in front of me. Its scales were green, its eyes were red, and it had horns. Shiny green scales covered the snake's lithesome body, and its head was probably over three feet long.

When it said it was from my nightmares, the creature was right. I'd dreamed of it several nights ago.

The snake's head bobbed, and the image shimmered and became hazy. The spirit still hadn't regained enough strength to have a solid form. That would hopefully work in my favor.

I flexed my hand, ready to lift the mark on my palm toward it and send the beast away. It would only be banished temporarily, but at least I'd be protected for the moment. I wasn't about to let it know I was scared. "Who are you?"

"I am Mishiginebig." Its forked tongue slipped out of its mouth and quivered. "Have you heard of me?"

I lifted my chin. "No."

"Before long, you will know me well. I slither through the water, hunting my favorite prey. *Humans*." His eyes lit up with excitement. "The *nuppin* feared me, and soon, so shall the *tosh-shonte*."

What the heck were the *nuppin* and the *tosh-shonte*? I tried to hide the fear that turned my knees shaky. The snake would feed off of my weakness. "Why are you here?"

"To see the witness to creation for myself."

I didn't like the sound of that. "Why?"

The snake slid from side to side, its red eyes tracking me. "You're not so special."

"That's right. I'm not. Now go tell all your spirit friends."

Mishiginebig lifted his head high and slid back several feet, looking haughty and regal. "Okeus has special plans for you."

"Yeah, your badger buddy told me the same thing last night."

"Okeus wants to have an audience with you."

"Since when does he ask for permission?"

The giant snake's red eyes blinked, then narrowed to slits as it leaned closer. "You're alive because Okeus wishes it. Many of us would rather it was otherwise. Do not doubt that for a minute."

I didn't, but there were several ways they could do me in. One, I was pretty sure they could outright kill me, but Collin was certain they wouldn't. Because my Manitou had never been recycled, my life essence had been pure since the creation of the universe. That had earned me the title of witness to creation, but it also meant my Manitou was much stronger than other creatures'. For beings that gained strength from consuming the life essence of other creatures—including most of the beings that had escaped from the gate to Popogusso—I would be the ultimate catch. Collin had assured me that the mark on my back would protect my Manitou. But I wasn't sure if his information was trustworthy, and even if it were, the mark would soon be gone.

A car approached from the other direction, its headlights illuminating the snake in gruesome detail.

"Drew!" Claire shouted, waving her arms in desperation.

"You're almost ready," Mishiginebig hissed. "Okeus will visit you soon."

"Almost ready for what?"

Drew made an illegal U-turn and pulled up behind my car. Mishiginebig faded into thin air.

Getting out of his car, Drew looked from one of us to the other, his expression alarmed. "What happened?"

Claire ran to him and threw her arms around his neck. "Let's get the hell out of here!"

I was still standing at the side of the road, my eyes glued to the spot where the snake had appeared and then disappeared.

"Ellie, let's go!"

I felt nauseated. Okeus was waiting for something before he was ready to come for me. He had to be waiting for the mark to disappear. How long could I make it last?

Claire grabbed my arm and dragged me away from the side of the road. "Ellie!"

I turned to her, surprisingly calm. "The snake won't hurt me." Not yet. But that didn't mean he wouldn't hurt Claire and Drew if he managed to regain his physical form. I grabbed my purse from my car, locked it up, and got into the back of Drew's sedan.

As soon as he pulled away, Claire let loose. "What were you thinking?" she hissed, turning in her seat to glare at me.

"I told you he wouldn't hurt me, Claire. He said Okeus has plans for me."

"And you believe that . . . that thing?"

"Yes. Without a doubt. At least I got some information."

"You have to go see Collin. Immediately."

I leaned my head back on the seat and groaned. "No."

"*Ellie!*"

She was right, but I still didn't want to see him. I still had a few days. Maybe I could come up with something else. Anything else. My pride was on the line. "I don't even know where he is."

"I do."

My mouth dropped. "You *what*?"

"I know where he is. His boat is in Wanchese. He seems to live on it. Sometimes his truck disappears for a few days, but his boat stays docked. You find one or the other, and he'll return to it soon enough."

"What the hell, Claire? You staked him out?"

"I knew you'd need him."

I wasn't sure why I was surprised. Claire always had my best interests in mind. "Well, it doesn't change anything. I'm still not going."

"You'd rather let those things kill you than go talk to him?"

"Yes!" I leaned forward. "Yes! I don't trust him, Claire. He *betrayed* me." My voice broke. "If he could put my life in danger after everything we shared, why would he help me now?"

She clenched her jaw. "I'll go find him myself."

"No you won't!"

"Yes I will, and you damn well know it. I'm giving you twenty-four hours. Tomorrow night. And if you don't go, I will."

Drew had been silent for our entire conversation, but he cleared his throat and spoke. "Claire's right. You need to see him, Ellie."

"*Et tu*, Drew?" I asked, my tone a little more hateful than intended. "You only found out about all of this last week." Up until a few weeks ago, I'd kept the curse secret, telling only Claire about it. But between my involvement with Collin and the marks on my body and door, Drew had grown suspicious. Now that hell had literally broken loose, I'd spilled all the details.

"You're running out of time. If you don't do it, I'll help Claire find him and drag him to you."

Gritting my teeth, I looked out the side window, intent on ignoring them for the rest of the car ride. I knew for a fact that they meant it . . . and I also knew I couldn't let that happen. But what could I possibly find out in the next twenty-four hours?

I tossed and turned that night, worrying about how to pay for my car repair bills—but also worrying about my mark. Even if I found Ahone's symbol, I was smart enough to know that getting the tattoo wouldn't just mean putting a mark of protection on my skin. I would be committing my soul for eternity. I needed more reassurance. One way or the other.

When I went to bed, my dreams were filled with animals begging for my help, but the spirits left me alone. They didn't even show up at my front door. Seeing Mishiginebig must have been message enough.

The next morning, Myra pushed open the back door of the bed and breakfast as I walked up. "Good morning, Ellie," she said with a worried smile.

"Were you waiting for me?"

She shrugged. "I just wanted to say good morning." Myra had always been a terrible liar.

"What's wrong?"

"Is it a crime to want to see you?"

"Something's up, Myra. What is it?"

"There's been . . . an incident."

My breath caught as I spanned the rest of the distance between us. "What kind of incident?"

She put a gentle hand on my arm. "Don't worry. Everyone is fine, but Tom is here . . ."

"Tom Helmsworth? Why?"

She looked worried again. "Tom thinks some kind of wild animal is on the loose."

I looked around her to see if he was in the great room. "Tell me what happened, Myra."

"Something attacked the neighbor's dog."

"*Chip?*" My chest tightened, and I knew what had happened before she said anything else. It stood to reason the spirits would taunt me this way. I pushed past her and through the dining room, ignoring the startled looks of the guests who were eating breakfast. "Where is he?"

Myra followed me. "Outside, on the west side of the house." She grabbed my arm as I reached the front door. "You don't want to go out there, Ellie."

"Yes, I do."

When I reached the side yard, Tom had his back to me. He was standing next to his partner, and their bodies were blocking my view of the dog. Hearing my approach, Tom swiveled around at the waist. "Ellie, this is a mess. Go back inside."

Ignoring him, I made myself stand next to him. The gods and spirits wanted me to see this. That's why the badger creature had chosen this dog and left him next to my house.

I took one glance and had my worst fear confirmed. His abdomen had been ripped open.

Spinning around to face the street, I sucked in huge gulps of air.

"Ellie, why don't you go sit on the porch," Tom said. "I'll join you in a second."

This time I didn't argue. I sat in one of the rocking chairs, staring at the giant oak tree in the front yard. When I was younger, I had spent one whole summer climbing that tree whenever I could. My mother would yell at me to be careful, but Daddy would tell her to let me be a kid and have fun. But they hadn't been fighting, not really. They never fought . . . not unless they were discussing the curse, anyway.

That goddamned curse had ruined everything in my life.

Several minutes later, Tom sat down in the rocking chair next to me. "Tell me what I'm not seeing, Ellie."

I turned my gaze to his police car parked by the curb. "I have no idea what you're talking about."

"Yes, you do."

I stopped rocking. "What is it you want me to say, Tom?"

"Tell me what you know about the mutilated dogs."

I glared at him. "Do you know how ridiculous and paranoid you sound right now?" I stood and moved toward the front door.

"Whatever's attacking these dogs isn't normal. The claw marks tell me it has to be some sort of animal, but whatever it is rips them apart and only eats one thing."

My curiosity got the better of me. "What?"

Tom shot me a meaningful look. "Their hearts. What animal in nature does that?"

I rubbed my forehead. "I don't know, Tom. Isn't there some department you can call about that? Like Animal Control?"

"We've already called the Department of Fish and Wildlife."

"Well, there you go. Why do you need my opinion? I'm just a waitress."

"I'm not letting this go, Ellie."

Of course he wasn't. "Fine. You do whatever you want." I opened the door to the house. "Now if you'll excuse me, some of us have *real* work to do."

To my surprise, he didn't follow me. I looked for Myra and found her in her office.

She frowned when she looked up at me. "I hope you didn't see him too closely. It was quite upsetting."

"I'm sorry, Myra."

She shook her head and turned to look out the back window. It was odd to think we'd never see Chip running around the yard again. He'd been part of my life for ten years.

I sighed. The world was in danger, but I had mundane things to worry about at the moment. "I hate to ask, but my car broke down as I was driving through the Alligator River Wildlife Refuge. Can I use your car today? I can take you to work and pick you up."

"Do I want to know why you were driving through the wildlife refuge?"

"No."

A ghost of a smile twitched at her lips. "Of course you can use my car. And I'm sure I can find a ride home. You don't have to worry about that."

"Thanks, Myra. I'm going to do some work upstairs. Let me know when you're ready to leave."

After I put the linens in the industrial washing machine in the main house, I went into Daddy's office and stood in the doorway. It looked exactly as it did two years ago, before his mind started getting worse.

I went inside and trailed my fingertips across the old wooden desk, my eyes scanning the floor-to-ceiling bookcases on both sides of the room. I thought about searching the room again for the notes Daddy had told me about—the ones about the curse—but I knew it was a lost cause. Especially when my time would be better spent figuring out which antique I could pawn next.

Myra knew I'd pawned a set of candlesticks from the dining room a few weeks ago, and she'd told me I didn't need to hide it the next time I had to take something, but it still felt slimy and underhanded. Maybe I could find something in the attic that wouldn't be missed. As I walked past the door to my old bedroom, the familiar ball of anxiety that had been born after we opened Popogusso tightened in my stomach.

The attic was musty and full of cobwebs and a multitude of discarded items. I scanned the room, my eyes stopping on an engraved wooden box on top of an antique chest of drawers. I clambered over the cardboard and plastic containers in front of the dresser and picked up the box. I held my breath as I opened it. There it was, just as I'd expected—my grandfather's pocket watch collection. Three antique watches nestled in a rich velvet lining.

When I was a little girl, Daddy used to take turns wearing two of them. Each day I'd try to guess which one he had on his chain. A wave of melancholy washed over me as I picked up my favorite of the two, a dull gold, well-worn watch, and placed it in my palm. The face was hidden behind a hinged cover that was engraved with a large four-pointed star surrounded by smaller stars. The other watch he used to wear had a crystal face and a shiny silver back decorated with my great, great grandfather's initials and elaborate scrollwork.

The third was particularly old and ornate. The oval timepiece had a silver cover with a bas-relief of a Greek bathing scene, and the inside face was etched with cherubs. I figured it had to be worth a lot of money, but I also knew it had been in the family for centuries. Hopefully, the newer silver watch—a relative term when I considered the fact that the piece was well over a hundred and fifty years old—would bring enough money to cover my car expenses.

I decided to bring all the watches to see what they were worth. I found an old duffel bag in the corner and wiped off as much dust as I could before stuffing the wooden box inside.

I decided to just set the bag in the backseat of the car without telling Myra what was in it.

As suspected, she didn't say anything, at least not until we arrived at the Fort Raleigh National Historic Site Visitor Center.

"Ellie, I know money's tight right now, and I don't judge you for anything you do."

I couldn't answer.

"Just be careful what you choose. Some of those heirlooms have been part of the Dare line since the beginning. I know the money's attractive, but certain things can't be replaced."

Her words were sobering. "Thanks."

"Be careful with whatever you're doing today."

I paused. "I will."

After Myra got out of the car, I headed straight to the pawnshop in Kill Devil Hills. Oscar, the owner, was helping another customer. The first time I'd come here over a year ago, his hard rock band T-shirt and his scruffy beard and hair had almost sent me running back out the door. Thankfully, I'd given him a chance.

He gave me a quick nod when he saw me wander into the store. When his customer left, I waited until he was entirely out the door before I started toward the counter.

"What's going on, Ellie?" Oscar sounded irritated with me. The last time I saw him was when I tried to buy back the four-hundred-year-old pewter cup I'd pawned multiple times. Oscar had already sold it. After doing some snooping in the back, Collin figured out who the buyer was, and we managed to buy it back from her. Had she told Oscar about the whole thing?

"What did I do?"

"Why were there thugs coming in here looking for you?"

I froze. "What are you talking about?"

He leaned on the counter. "What kind of trouble have you gotten into?"

"I . . . I don't know what you're talking about."

He stood up. "Cut the bull crap, Ellie."

If he wasn't so upset with me, I would have teased him about saying "bull crap." His language was usually more colorful.

"Let me guess: that guy who was here with you last time has gotten you into a mess." Oscar shook his head in disgust. "I told you that he was trouble."

I shifted my weight, slinging my bag onto my other shoulder.

His eyes narrowed. "He took you to Buxton, didn't he?"

My gaze lowered to the counter.

"Please tell me you didn't pawn something to that snake Marino."

I looked up with a grimace. "Would you rather I lie?"

"Ellie." He sounded more disappointed than angry, driving a knife of guilt into my gut.

"It wasn't my fault, Oscar. I wanted to come to you, but Collin took me there before I realized what was happening." Why were they looking for me at Oscar's place? It didn't make sense. Collin had told Marino's guys I was from Greenville, which was over a hundred miles away. "Are you sure they were looking for *me*?"

"They said they were looking for, and I quote, 'a redheaded spitfire who goes by the name Ellie.' What do *you* think?"

Shit. "But why would they come *here*?"

"You told Marino you usually sell to Mikey in Kill Devil Hills. Is that true? Do you sell to that weasel?"

Shit. I scrunched up my nose and waved my hand. "No. That was a misunderstanding."

"A misunderstanding? With Marino?"

I rolled my eyes. "Look, Oscar, it all happened so fast. I wanted more money than he was offering so I told him my guy in Kill Devil Hills would give me more. He asked if it was Mikey and I didn't correct him."

"I still don't get why he wants you."

This part was embarrassing. "Collin was sort of . . . protective of me, and apparently that's not normal behavior for him. Collin does regular work for Marino, so he thought if I was important to Collin, there was a financial reason. He thinks I know something about some job."

"Do you realize what serious shit you're in?"

"Yeah."

He grabbed my arm, fear in his eyes. "No, Ellie, I'm not playing around. Do you realize what serious shit you're in?"

I swallowed. Marino seemed so tame next to the monsters waiting for me in the darkness, but the fact was that he would kill me in an instant if he didn't like what I had to say. And he wouldn't. I didn't know anything about any job or any other business that would interest him. At least Okeus wanted me alive . . . for now. "Collin said it would blow over in a few weeks."

Oscar groaned. "No, Ellie. That's not the way it works with guys like him. The longer it takes him to find you, the more pissed he becomes. This won't end well."

I looked up at him, defeated. There were too many odds against me in both the physical and spiritual worlds. I glanced at the symbol on my palm, the square and the circle intersecting. Daddy said it represented the connection between the physical and spiritual worlds. I guess it stood to reason that if they were intersected, both would go to shit at the same time. "I don't know what to do."

"Leave town?" He shook his head. "I don't suppose that will work. You can't leave your stepmother now, can you?"

My eyes widened.

"I heard about your dad, girl. I'm sorry."

My eyes burned, and I blinked to keep from crying. "Oh."

"Ellie, I'm here for you if there's anything I can do to help. I'm serious."

I flashed him a cocky grin. "All part of the full pawnbroker service."

His mouth drooped into a frown. "You know you're not just one of my regular clients."

He was right. Given the number of times I'd pawned the pewter cup, he'd heard my entire tale of woe about my father's illness. I was certain he gave me more and more money each time because he felt sorry for me. But then I reminded myself that he'd sold the cup—after holding onto it a month longer than he had to—for a whole lot more than he'd given me.

He lowered his voice. "Go to the police. They're your best bet right now."

"Are you serious?"

"Yes. I'm dead serious."

"That's going to get . . . messy."

"Suck it up. It got messy the minute you walked through Marino's door."

He was probably right, but I didn't have time to deal with the whole situation. I set the bag on the counter. "I have something to pawn."

Oscar unzipped the bag and pulled out the wooden box, setting it on the glass counter. When he opened the lid, he released a soft whistle. "Where did you get . . . ?" His face softened. "Ellie, these belonged to your dad, didn't they?"

I swallowed the lump in my throat. "Well, Daddy doesn't need them anymore, does he? And my stupid piece of shit car is dead on Highway 64 in the Alligator River Wildlife Refuge." I shoved the box at him. "I don't think I want to lose them all, but I wanted to see what they're worth before deciding which ones to sell."

He picked up the silver watch and turned it over to examine the back. "I wish you could catch a break, girl."

"Yeah, so you say every freaking time I walk in that door, yet here I am again." I squared my shoulders, refusing to let self-pity creep in. "What are they worth?"

Oscar studied each watch and after he did some research, he released another low whistle. "I'm not sure I'm the one you want to sell these to. I can give you eight hundred for the silver one and twelve hundred for the gold. But you'd be better off going to a bigger city to sell the other oval one. It's centuries old. You're looking at *thousands* for that piece."

"Thousands?"

"As in it should have its own insurance policy."

"Wow."

"What do you want to do? Sell one or both?"

I picked up the gold starry-sky watch. If I was going to sell one of them, it was the logical choice. Chances were my car repair and tow bill would be more than eight hundred dollars. But I just couldn't part with it. I might have to sell it at some point, but I wanted to hold onto it a little longer. "The silver."

As I stuffed the money into my wallet a few minutes later, I glanced at the tattoo on his arm. "Do you have a tattoo artist you can recommend?"

"Where'd you get the one on your palm? That had to hurt like a son of a bitch."

I stretched out my hand. Of course he'd seen it. I couldn't go through life with my right hand in a fist.

The mark had appeared the day Collin showed up in the restaurant and touched me, setting this whole disaster in motion. "He's no longer an option."

"Considering the trouble you're in with Marino, getting a tattoo seems like it should be low on your priority list."

I put a hand on my hip. "So you're not going to recommend one?"

He scowled. "Rusty, up toward Duck at Purgatory Ink."

Purgatory Ink seemed like an appropriate place to commit my soul for all of eternity. "Thanks." I put the box back in the bag and headed for the exit.

"Ellie."

My palm rested on the door, ready to push it open as I spun at the waist to look at him.

"Be careful."

"I'm always careful." Or at least the old me had been. Three weeks ago I was a full-time waitress and part-time bed and breakfast employee who dated boring guys. My idea of excitement was driving up to Norfolk, Virginia, to shop at the mall.

How quickly my life had changed.

◦ CHAPTER FIVE ◦

I drove back to Manteo and stopped at the car repair shop Daddy had always used. Unfortunately, they were used to seeing me walk in their door.

When I parked and got out of Myra's car, Bruce, the owner, caught sight of me from inside the garage. He picked up a rag and wiped his hands before approaching me. "Hey, Ellie. You here for your car or Myra's?"

I leaned against the side of the sedan. "Mine. It's waiting for you on Highway 64 in the Alligator River Wildlife Refuge."

"So you need it towed?"

I nodded.

"What happened?"

"I don't know. I drove to Chapel Hill and back. It just lost power and died. I've got eight hundred dollars, so see what kind of magic you can work with that."

He stuffed his hands in his back pockets. "You should just put your money into a new car. Nickel and diming repairs on that clunker is costing you more in the long run."

I lifted my eyebrows with a smirk. "Somebody's got to keep you in business. And I wouldn't call five hundred dollars here and seven hundred dollars there 'nickel and diming.' You and I both know it would cost me thousands of dollars to get a decent car that's not going to be in your shop every few weeks. And we also both know that I don't have it."

He looked back at the garage. "I'll do the best I can to help." He paused, wiping his stained hands again. "I was sorry to hear about your dad."

I resisted the urge to sigh. "Thanks."

"He was a great man and one of the pillars of this town before he got sick. He helped me with a zoning permit when I first opened this garage. Did you know that?"

"No." It turned out there were all kinds of things about Daddy I'd never known about.

"I'll call you when I find something."

"Thanks."

When I got back in the car, I glanced at the clock. It was almost noon, and I had about eight hours before Claire started to hunt down Collin. I'd rather find him myself than have her go after him.

Which was probably exactly what she'd planned.

Before I consciously realized what I was doing, I was crossing the bridge back into Nags Head. It wasn't the first time I'd done this since we'd opened the gate to Popogusso. This call to the sea was a part of me now.

I pulled the car into the public beach parking lot and kicked off my sandals when I reached the sand. It was hot beneath my feet, but I barely noticed—some primal part of me was craving the sea too much to be derailed by anything.

The first wave of water that washed over my feet nearly brought me to my knees as power surged through my body. I walked deeper into the ocean until the waves hit my waist. I was sure I had to be drawing curious stares from tourists. While they wore swimming suits, I was dressed in capris and a T-shirt. But I was too overwhelmed by the energy of the sea filling every cell of my body to care.

I was one with the sea. I was one with the fish that swam around me. The clams that buried themselves in the sand, only to be washed up with the next wave. I was one with the seaweed and the algae. I was one with the amoeba and the plankton.

I felt the life force of millions of creatures in the sea and I stood with my hands spread from my sides in awe.

Experiencing the Manitou was the only good part of the curse. I'd discovered I could feel the Manitou of all the life forms in the ocean on my own, but when Collin and I touched palms I could feel *everything*—all life both in the sea and on the land. Other than when the animals came to me in my sleep, it was the only way I could feel the full impact of what I was being charged with protecting.

Other than the rare moments of total connection I'd experienced with Collin, standing in the ocean was when I felt the most complete.

When I turned around to walk out of the water, I realized I'd drawn a crowd. About twenty people stood on the rise of the sand, watching me and murmuring amongst themselves.

A woman with a baby on her hip approached me as I reached the edge of the water. "Are you all right?"

"I'm fine. Why?"

"You've been standing out there for over a half an hour. Every time someone tried to get close to you, a wave pushed them away. It was unreal."

That was new. It had felt like less than five minutes. "I like the ocean so much I guess I lost track of time." It was a lame excuse, but it was the best I could come up with on the fly.

The crowd watched as I walked back to the parking lot. I struggled with the knowledge that they all thought I was some sort of freak. I knew I couldn't let it bother me. I'd never see any of them again, but it was one more reminder that my life had turned to shit.

As I scooped my flip-flops off the sand by the parking lot, I realized I didn't know where the keys to the car were. I found them in the ignition, my purse on the passenger seat. After parking, I'd given no thought to anything other than my need to get to the water. I was lucky no one had stolen my purse or Myra's car. Or what if someone had taken the remaining watches? I might not be so lucky next time.

I was still soaking wet, but thankfully Myra had a blanket in the trunk for me to sit on. I rolled the windows down as I drove back to Manteo, and the wind was so loud I almost missed Myra's call on my cell phone.

"I'm not sure Bruce will get my car done tonight," I said when I answered.

"Don't worry, Ellie. I have a ride home, and I suspect that in the morning I'll be able to get a ride with one of the researchers who will be staying at the inn. In fact, that's why I'm calling. Are you busy this afternoon? Can you help me out at the inn?"

"Sure. I'm free." I'd been planning to go back to the inn anyway. I wanted to do a last sweep for any clues Daddy might have left for me. I knew I was putting off the inevitable, that I would have to go see Collin eventually, but so be it.

"A team of researchers came to Roanoke Island today to study the Lost Colony. There was a mistake with some of their reservations at one of the local motels. They can't find anywhere else to stay, so I offered to open the main house for them to stay in. I figured we could use the extra money."

"That's a great idea, Myra."

"But the rooms aren't ready. No one's stayed in them for years."

"Don't worry. I'll take care of it. What time are they arriving?"

"I think they're planning on staying on site until sunset."

"That gives me plenty of time."

Once I got home, I hid the box with the pocket watches in the back of my closet. Myra would never miss them, and while I hated to think about selling the remaining two watches, I knew it might come to that.

I headed to the inn, happy to have a productive task to fill my afternoon. The Dare Inn consisted of two separate houses taking up half a block. The main building featured five bedrooms with their own private baths, a living room, a dining room, an office, and a small kitchen. The main residential house was where I grew up. Myra usually cooked the breakfast we served to the guests in the house's big kitchen, and it also had a dining room, a large office, a half bath, and a large living room on the first floor. There were five bedrooms and two hall bathrooms on the second floor. After Daddy married Myra, he added a huge laundry room to the back of the residential house and a large guest room with two beds above it. The bedrooms in the main house wouldn't be ideal since the guests would have to share a bathroom, but it was better than having to drive back and forth to the Outer Banks.

Myra and Daddy's room was at the end of the hallway, so I started with the room next to it, making my way down the hall but skipping my old room. After I started the sheets in the washing machine, I headed back upstairs with cleaning supplies. Not only had no one stayed in these rooms for years, it had been months since anyone had cleaned them. I opened all the windows to air them out, dusted and swept the hardwood floors, and vacuumed the wool rugs.

My phone rang when I was on my way to the laundry room to switch the sheets to the dryer. When I saw that it was Bruce calling, I forced myself to stay calm. "How bad is the damage?"

"You lucked out this time. The good news is that it was just the alternator. I found you a used one, so with the tow, it should set you back by about five hundred."

"Okay, that sounds good." That meant I would have a few hundred left to put toward my rent.

"The bad news is that I can't get the part today. Your car won't be done until tomorrow afternoon."

I shoved the wet sheets into the dryer, trying not to sound out of breath. "That's fine. Myra said I can keep using her car for now."

"Okay then. I'll call you when it's done."

"Thanks." I hung up and was about to set my phone on the table behind me when it started ringing again. This time it was Claire.

"So? Which one of us has a date with Collin tonight?" she asked.

"I'm going to see him after I finish helping Myra at the inn. She's renting out the bedrooms in the main house."

"Oh, that's a good idea."

"But they haven't been touched for years so I'm cleaning them out."

"I'll come help."

"You don't have to."

"I know. I want to."

"Thanks. Just let yourself in the back door and come on up."

I'd finished with two of the rooms and had started in on the third when Claire showed up. "What's left?" she asked.

"This bedroom, both bathrooms. The end bathroom is the one Myra uses, but I'm sure she'll share it." I paused and looked down the hall. "And my room."

Claire put her hand on my arm. "I'll take care of yours."

My anxiety settled. "Thanks."

She held up a handful of flowers. "I stopped by the florist and got some fresh flowers to set in the rooms. I figured it might make up for them having to share the bathrooms. If they're women, anyway."

"Good idea." I was so lucky to have her for a friend. "But I'm still not taking your cousin as my date to your wedding. I'm wearing the pumpkin dress. Don't push it."

She smacked my arm as she backed up. "Why not? He's always had a thing for you. He doesn't wear braces anymore and he outgrew his acne."

I snorted. "I should hope so. We're twenty-three, so he has to be at least twenty-six by now."

She walked down the hall, heading backward, toward my room. "Don't ever accuse me of not trying to help you find a boyfriend."

"As if." I forced a laugh. "You're trying to set me up with a guy every other week."

Stopping in my bedroom doorway, she held onto the doorjamb and turned serious. "I just want you to have what Drew and I have."

"I know." I wanted that too, or to be more exact, I wanted what Daddy and Momma had shared—fireworks and magic. I'd gotten that with Collin . . . for a while. Would it be possible for me to love someone else when my soul was tied to his? I faced the very real possibility of spending the rest of my life alone, never experiencing great love.

But then again, I might not live long enough for it to matter much.

When I finished with the bedroom I was working on, I stood in the doorway to my room, watching Claire put on fresh sheets. "I found these in the linen closet."

"Yeah, that's fine."

She tucked the fitted sheet around the top corner of the mattress. "When did you stop coming in here? You grew up in this room. What happened?"

"I started dreaming about Momma's death. Terrible things I didn't remember before." Without saying anything else, I turned and stepped into one of the bathrooms. It was in good shape and didn't need much work beyond dusting and cleaning the toilet. When I finished, Claire was in Myra's bathroom, so I slipped into my room and made myself look around.

I'd never harbored any fear of my old room until recently. As though my nightmares of animals begging for help and the spirits that tormented me while I was asleep weren't enough, I'd had several dreams of Momma's death over the last couple of weeks. In the most vivid one, I was hiding in my closet while her attacker stood in my room, my mother's blood dripping onto the floor from his knife. I wasn't sure if it was just a nightmare or a suppressed memory because I couldn't remember anything about her murderer . . . I definitely didn't remember being that close to him. He had broken in and stabbed my mother while I was upstairs.

I stared at the place the attacker had stood in my dream. The spot was now covered with a large wool rug. In fact, the rug was much larger than any of the ones in the other rooms. How had I never noticed? Taking a deep breath, I grabbed it by the corner and pulled it back.

A six-inch dark spot discolored the floor.

"What are you doing?" Claire asked from behind me. I jumped. "What are you looking at?"

"That." I pointed at the spot.

"What is it?"

"A bloodstain." I knew beyond a shadow of a doubt that it was true.

"From what?"

"The night of my mother's murder."

Claire walked around the lifted rug and squatted next to it. "I thought he didn't come up here. I thought he . . . attacked your mother and left."

"I don't know, but I've been having this dream where I'm hiding in the closet and he's standing in front of me, blood dripping from his knife onto the floor in that exact spot."

"Oh my God, Ellie. Did it really happen that way?"

"It has to be, I guess. What else would have caused that stain?" I felt like I was going to throw up, but I didn't dare mess up the now pristine bathrooms.

"Maybe that's not what it is. It could be anything."

I dropped the rug and went out into the hallway, where I lifted the edge of the runner. A large stain took up several feet of floor space. "That's where she died. Right there. Daddy paid people to sand the floor, but it never went away." I pointed to the discolored wood. "You tell me that's not a bloodstain in my room."

Claire lifted her hand to her mouth, shaking her head. "It doesn't make sense, Ellie. Your dad had to cover the stain with the rug, which meant *he* knew the guy was in your room. Why didn't he say anything to the police?"

"I don't know."

"Are you going to tell Tom?"

"What would I tell him? How would this help? And even if it did, her murder was fifteen years ago."

She waved her hand in frustration. "Police solve old cases all the time."

I dropped the rug. "For God's sake, Claire, this is *not* a television show." I started for the stairs and stopped, keeping my back to her. "I'm sorry. That was uncalled for."

"It's okay . . ."

I pivoted to face her. "No. It's not. My life is a fucking mess right now. It feels like it would be pointless to dredge up the past and Momma's murder." I brushed stray hairs from my forehead. "We're almost done. Why don't you go home, and I'll finish making the other beds."

"Are you sure?" She cringed with guilt. "Drew and I are supposed to taste-test wedding cakes in an hour."

My eyes bugged. "Well, why didn't you say so? Get out of here. And pick a good one. I hate eating dried-out cake."

"Drew wants a red velvet groom's cake shaped like an armadillo."

"What on earth for?"

She rolled her eyes in disgust. "Lord only knows. I've definitely got my work cut out for me."

I pulled her into a hug. "I love you, Claire. Thank you for helping me keep my life seminormal right now."

She pulled back, tears in her eyes. "I'm scared for you, Ellie."

"I know."

"Promise me that you'll go see Collin tonight."

I pressed my lips together in resignation. "I told you I will. I'm just trying to psyche myself up for it."

"Be firm. Be strong. Don't let him fuck you."

"*Claire!*"

"You have a weakness for that man and you know it."

"I hate him. I loathe him. I never want to see the shithead again. You're the one who's making me go."

Her eyebrows rose as she studied my face. "They say love and hate ride a fine line. Now don't you go riding that fine line with him."

Ignoring her, I started back down the stairs to get the linens. "I want chocolate cake," I yelled back over my shoulder.

"Hey! Whose wedding is this?"

"You're making me go see Collin Fucking Dailey. You owe me."

I could hear Claire grumbling to herself behind me as I headed into the laundry room. After I finished getting the beds made, I straightened the vases of flowers. I was stalling and I knew it. My one bright spot was that I might not even see him. This might be one of those times he disappeared for days.

I hopped in Myra's car and hesitated before turning over the ignition. I knew I had to do this. My life depended on it.

❧ CHAPTER SIX ❧

Wanchese was quiet when I drove through town. While Manteo was the flashy, touristy end of the island, Wanchese was the practical, no-nonsense side. Many of the houses here were older and run-down. Recently imposed federal regulations had hit commercial fishermen hard over the last decade, and plenty of them had lost everything thanks to overexuberant fines. Many had given up, deciding the hassle wasn't worth it. As a result, the town had suffered.

My heart raced as I reached the docks. I had no idea what Collin's boat looked like, but I remembered it was named the *Lucky Star*, and I was well acquainted with his truck. A few memories in particular made me flush.

Claire was right. I couldn't let him touch me . . . not even a handshake.

I found his old red pickup parked in a gravel parking lot across the street from several docked boats, and I felt like I was going to throw up from nerves. What would he say when he saw me? I definitely had the upper hand. The last time we saw each other, he'd begged for my understanding. I'd told him to go to hell.

They were wasted words. He was going there anyway.

I made myself take a deep breath and count to three. I could do this. I could be strong.

The area around the docks was deserted, without another person in sight. I parked Myra's car several spots away from his truck and gathered my courage to check out the boats at the dock. If his truck was there, he was probably out on his boat. But when I scanned the names of the boats, none were the *Lucky Star*. I wasn't sure whether to be upset or relieved.

The windows of his truck were wide open, not that I was surprised. He'd told me that he wasn't worried about anyone stealing it or anything inside of it. His theory was that the truck was so old and run-down, no one would think it was worth their while.

His smug assurance made me feel a bit self-righteous when I opened the driver's door and slid into the seat. I might as well snoop while I was here. I pulled down the visor and a bunch of receipts fell onto my lap. I thumbed through them—gas, food, a CVS pharmacy receipt for sunscreen. Part of me was relieved he hadn't bought condoms. At least he wasn't screwing anyone else. Unless he hadn't run out of his current stash.

I made myself examine my reaction. "Elinor Dare Lancaster, you do not care who Collin Dailey screws." But a strangling pain wrapped around my heart at the thought of him with anyone else.

I tucked the receipts back where I'd found them and tried to open the glove compartment, which—to my surprise—was locked. "So you're not worried about someone stealing anything out of your truck, huh?" I jerked on the latch again. "You're a big fat fucking liar!" I smacked my left palm onto the dashboard. "Fucking. Liar!" I shouted again, hitting the dash with each word, amazed at how empowering it felt.

Grabbing the steering wheel, I shook it as hard as I could. "I hate you, you asshole! You ruined everything! You ruined my life!"

I beat the car until my hand ached and shouted until my voice was hoarse, thankful no one was around to witness my meltdown.

I laid my head back against the seat, surprised at how worn out I suddenly felt.

The trunk pointed west and the sun was dipping low in the horizon. Another hour and it would be dark. Another hour before the creatures began crawling from their holes.

I sat up.

The map was what I needed.

Collin possessed a map showing where the Croatan Indians had thought their gods lived. If it was accurate, and the gods and spirits really dwelled there, maybe I could perform some sort of pre-emptive strike. Collin might not want to give the map to me, but I needed it more than he did. In any case, the map had helped land me on Marino's most wanted list. Might as well have Marino after me for a reason.

For the first time since the gate had been opened, I felt like I had some sort of plan. I hadn't figured out how to defeat the spirits yet, but it was something. I closed my eyes and felt some of the tension slip away. I was so exhausted from lack of sleep that I decided to let myself rest for a moment.

When I awoke, something warm and comforting was pressed against my cheek. The overwhelming feeling that I was safe seeped through my skin, rolling through my entire body. I turned my head to the side, drawn to whatever was next to me, and then opened my eyes.

This had to be a dream.

Collin stood outside the open truck door, his face only a few feet from mine, awe and wonder in his eyes as they traveled across my face. His hand cradled my cheek, and I sensed the desperation and the need in his touch.

I felt the same way.

"Ellie." His mouth lowered to mine as his hand slid behind my head, lifting me toward him.

It felt so right, like a missing piece of myself had been replaced . . . and yet it wasn't enough.

His tongue parted my lips and explored my mouth, coaxing my tongue to join it.

My arms wrapped around his neck. My heart exploded with urgency, and hot desire rushed through my body. I needed more.

His other hand grazed up my leg and under my skirt, skimming my ass. He turned me sideways so that my legs hung over the side of the seat. He moved between them, pressing me against his crotch. I wrapped my legs around his waist as his mouth and tongue drove me crazy with want. Lifting the bottom of my T-shirt, he pulled it up and over my head, his mouth breaking contact for only a second before claiming mine again. The lack of contact was agony to every nerve ending in my body that was crying out for more.

My body craved his with an unnatural, unstoppable need.

One of his hands tangled in my hair as the other lifted my skirt to my waist, exposing my panties.

I wanted him like I'd never wanted anything in my life.

His hand cupped my breast before his fingers dipped inside my bra to caress my nipple. I moaned as a jolt shot straight to my core. I reached for the button of his jeans, frantic for more . . . frantic for him to fill the missing part of me and make me whole.

He pushed me back on the seat, pulling my panties off and throwing them to the floor of the truck. I watched him strip off his shirt and his jeans, the sight of his strong shoulders and rippling abs rushing heat through my veins, making my skin feverish. His underwear were next, and then he was standing there in the open door of his truck, stark naked and ready to claim me on the side of the deserted road. Both of us were so frenzied we didn't care.

This is wrong.

But the insane part of me pushed the thought aside. I needed this man. I was empty without him.

He leaned over me, moving between my legs, lifting my thigh to his waist as he paused.

I stared into his agonized face. Nothing had ever felt so right, had made me feel so complete as when we were joined, body and soul.

His right hand reached for mine, ready to press our marks together as he prepared to enter me . . .

Something in the back of my head screamed: *stop!*

My body resisted the warning, desperate to see this through.

No!

My conscience clawed to the surface, pushing past the raw physical and supernatural urgency, begging for my attention.

This was the man who betrayed me.

My body stiffened. What the hell was I doing?

Claire's words echoed in my head. *Don't let him fuck you.* That's exactly what I was about to do.

Confusion flickered in his eyes as he saw the change in me, but he still lowered himself over me, our palms inches from touching. I jerked my hand away, surprised that it was so hard. Our hands were being physically pulled toward each other by a force that wasn't from either of us, like a strong magnet clinging to its polar opposite.

I pushed on his body, my tattooed right palm landing square on the tattoo on his chest. A raw energy filled my hand, shooting through his body. We both gasped.

I fought my overwhelming desire and pushed him hard. "Collin, stop."

"Ellie." His mouth found mine and I was lost in a sea of longing, but I regained my senses as he began to enter me.

"No!" I scooted back and took several quick breaths to regain control. My body and soul screamed in protest, desperate to have what I knew only he could give me.

Hurt replaced confusion on his face for a mere second before his trademark cocky look returned—the one I'd first seen when we met at the New Moon.

The day he'd come in to purposely break the curse.

I scooted back more. "You owe me answers, Collin."

"*Now?*" He lifted up, panting.

I realized the absurdity of it. We were both naked in the front seat of his truck, millimeters away from giving in to what we not only wanted but apparently supernaturally needed. The implication of that thought scared me, but I couldn't focus on it right now. "Yes, now. You owe me answers."

Collin still hovered over me, his face close to my waist, and my treacherous body reminded me how close his mouth was to my crotch. My eyes rolled back in my head as I suppressed the desire to lift myself up to him. But I knew myself enough to realize that if I went through with this, I'd regret it for the rest of my life.

Collin lowered his body onto mine, driving me crazy with the skin-to-skin contact. "I tried to give you answers, Ellie." His voice was husky as his mouth traveled up my neck to my ear, pulling my earlobe into his lips. "You didn't want to hear them then." His hand slid between my legs and my head shot back as I arched my spine, my body begging me to give in.

Still, that persistent part of me screamed for attention. *Listen to what he's saying, Ellie.*

I focused on his words, a tiny flame of anger sparking to life.

He's using you now, just like he used you to open the gate.

My anger exploded into fury, replacing my desire and bringing me to my senses. "Are you fucking serious?" I pushed on his

71

chest to get him off of me, but he resisted, his lower half still pressing me down on the seat, the evidence of how much he wanted me hard against my thigh. "I had just watched my father die, after you betrayed me and released hundreds of creatures that vowed to torture me for hundreds of years. How *could* I listen to you then?"

He watched me for a second, and I could almost see the wheels turning in his head as he tried to figure out how to play me.

How had I never noticed that before?

Contrition filled his eyes, and one of his hands cupped my cheek. "You're right."

I waited for him to continue speaking, but he merely watched my face while his thumb stroked my cheek in slow circles.

"I'm not one of your whores, Collin. You can't use me and then toss me away when you're done."

His eyes widened. "Is that what you think I did? You think I tossed you aside? You were never like any other woman in my life, Ellie."

"I'm sure of that. No other woman could help you break a four-hundred-year-old curse."

He sighed, his shoulders slumping.

"You walked into that restaurant and thought, 'Stupid Ellie doesn't remember anything about the curse. I can play her like a fiddle.'"

His head lifted. "It wasn't like that."

"*It wasn't like that?*" I pushed hard, and he finally got off me. I scrambled back until my spine was pressed up against the passenger door as he took a seat behind the steering wheel.

"You knew damn good and well who I was the moment you walked through the door. How long had you known?"

He closed his door and leaned his forearms on the steering wheel, looking out the windshield. The moonlight swathed his naked body like a blanket, and I wanted to cry at the irony. The most gorgeous man I'd ever hoped to be with had probably only slept with me to get what he wanted. Just like the way he'd dealt with every other woman in his life.

"How long, Collin?"

"A couple of weeks."

A couple of weeks. Why did it shock me? "And you came in planning to break the curse?"

His jaw worked and his shoulders stiffened. "Yes."

He'd already told me that, of course, but I still didn't get it. "Why? You were the one who took it seriously. You were so pissed that I didn't remember anything. You said I didn't deserve to be a Keeper. You were all about the commitment and responsibility . . . I mean, you have a goddamned mark tattooed on your chest. Why did you do it?"

His features hardened, but he still didn't look at me. "The fucking curse destroyed my family. I just wanted it to end."

"You really think it's over? You've opened up one huge can of worms. And you destroyed *my* family in the process. Was that what you wanted? To get even?"

"No." He closed his eyes and ran a hand through his hair. "I'll admit that I didn't give a lot of thought to how it would affect you before we met."

"That's obvious."

He turned to me. "But when I took you to Marino and you started crying in the truck, I realized I actually cared about what happened to you. And that night . . . when I put the henna tattoo on you, I realized I was in trouble."

"*You* were in trouble? Are you fucking kidding me?"

He grabbed my left hand. I tried to pull back, but he held firm. "We may have bound our souls together outside of Morehead City, but I lost my heart to you that night."

I jerked my hand out of his. "You fucking liar."

Hurt flashed through his eyes. "I've never been this honest with anyone, Ellie. Ever."

I shook my head in disgust. "You wouldn't know honesty if it bit you in the ass. You used me, tricked me, screwed me, and then screwed me over. Tell me what I'm missing here."

His eyes narrowed. "You know we can't hide our feelings from each other when our marks touch." His left hand grabbed my right wrist. "We can touch them together now, and you'll know I'm not lying."

I tried to jerk my hand from his grasp, but his fingers tightened around mine. "No! You know what happens when we touch." Which was exactly why I was sure he was pushing the matter. Pressing our marks together is what got me here in the first place.

"Ellie," he whispered, his right hand reaching for mine now. "We're meant to be together. *You know it*. Let me show you how much you mean to me."

"No!" I jerked my wrist hard, panicked. "If you do this, I will hate you forever."

He glanced into my face and his mouth dropped open in shock. "You really are afraid of me."

"Do you have any idea what you've done?" I finally pulled my hand from his grasp. "You killed my father! People I cared about died because of you. No, you didn't personally do it, but you purposely freed the things that did. And now they're after *me*, Collin. They're appearing in the flesh and coming to my door each night. The dead birds they left on my front porch before? That's *nothing* compared to the mutilated animals they're leaving for me now. They killed my neighbor's dog."

"Why would you think they killed your neighbor's dog?"

"Because as Police Officer Tom Helmsworth pointed out, normal animals don't rip open a dog's guts and eat its heart."

His confidence fell away. "If you just wait it out, the spiritual world will stabilize and we'll all be able to live together as one. This is the way it's meant to be."

"You truly believe that?" I asked, incredulous.

His face hardened. "I have to."

"Well, bull fucking shit. I don't have to believe that. In fact, I don't. Those motherfuckers won't stop until they've tortured me for eons."

He shook his head. "No."

"They come to me in my dreams."

That got his attention. "What are you talking about?"

"The animals come every night begging me to help them, and each night one of the escaped spirits visits me in my dreams and tells me that Okeus is waiting for me to be ready."

"Be ready for what?"

"To kill me? To suck my Manitou? How the hell would I know!"

"Is your henna tattoo still on your back?"

"It's fading."

He looked panicked. "You need a new one."

I didn't answer. That much was obvious.

"I know you're reluctant to get a permanent mark. Let me give you another henna one."

I snorted. "Are you kidding me? I trusted you before, and you painted Okeus's mark on my back."

"Ellie," he grabbed my hand again. "If you willingly choose Okeus, you'll save yourself."

"And I'll condemn my soul to hell. No thank you."

"He'll provide you riches greater than you ever imagined."

"So where the hell are your riches, Collin?"

He paused. "You heard Okeus. I lost my reward because I helped you." He reached for my face. "Doesn't that prove how much I care?"

"Are you serious? You found out *after* you helped me. You didn't give that up for me." I smacked his hand away and sagged against the passenger door. "Besides, I don't think that would work anyway. The curse is based on duality. The sea and the land. Ahone and Okeus. Good and evil. You can't have one without the other. You've chosen Okeus and Ahone has chosen me."

"So why haven't you put his mark on your skin?"

"Because I don't know what it is. Do you?"

He closed his eyes for a long moment. When he opened them again, he looked me in the eyes. "I don't know either."

Anger surged through my veins. "You liar."

He reached for me, but I backed away. "I swear to you, Ellie. I don't know."

"How could you possibly know Okeus's but not Ahone's?"

He scrubbed both hands over his short, dark hair. "I don't know. It wasn't passed down. We pledged ourselves to Okeus so that we'd be protected from his wrath when he was freed." He grabbed my left hand before I could snatch it back. "I put Okeus's mark on your back for the same reason." He pulled me closer, but I resisted. "Please don't be so stubborn. If you pledge yourself to him now, you'll be safe."

"You know I can't, even if I wanted to."

Agony covered his face. "Then you're as good as dead."

"And whose fault is that?"

He dropped his hold on me and looked out the windshield.

"I want the map."

He shook his head as if trying to clear it. "What are you talking about?"

"The map we stole from Marino. You remember our field trip to Buxton? Marino's men were at the Kill Devil Hills Pawnshop asking Oscar if he knows who I am and where they can find me."

"You're shitting me."

"You have no idea how much I wish I was."

He shook his head. "No. There's no way. I told them you were from Greenville."

"But I told him I had a guy in Kill Devil Hills when I was negotiating."

He groaned.

"I'm surprised all the women you've screwed since you left me haven't thrown him off."

His face contorted with rage and he leaned toward me, his body shaking with anger. "Say what you like, Ellie, but the minute I joined my soul with yours, I *became yours*. Completely. You're the one who ran away. You're the one who doesn't want anything to do with me."

"Can you blame me? You're just a man whore who uses people to get what you want. You told me so yourself."

"Goddamn it, Ellie. I tried to resist you. I tried not to sleep with you. You're the one who taunted and tempted me. I've never put so much effort into not sleeping with a woman in my life."

"Finally!" I shouted. "Your first truthful answer since I showed up here tonight." His desire for me had been so evident when we joined our marks, yet guilt had kept him from following through until I drove him crazy enough to cross the line. "But you're right. I coerced you into sleeping with me. I just didn't realize what the consequences would be." I laughed, but it was a bitter sound. "Everyone who fucks up says that, huh?" I turned to him. "Isn't that what you keep telling me? You didn't mean to screw up my life?"

Hope filled his eyes. "Exactly!"

"And yet I'm stuck in this hell, and you get to live your life like nothing ever happened."

His eyes glittered with rage. "That's bullshit and you know it. You know what you mean to me. You've felt it, Ellie . . . and I've felt it with you. If you want to sit there and pretend it doesn't exist, then go ahead and do it. But who's the liar now?"

"What we have between us isn't real, Collin!" I shouted, balling my fists. "What we have is hormones and magic. Nothing more and nothing less."

"Not real? *Are you kidding me?*" I'd never seen him so angry. "This is the most real thing either us will *ever* experience, but if you want to throw it away out of pride and immaturity, go ahead. I'm done begging." He opened his door and jumped out of the truck, grabbing his underwear off the ground and stepping into them. He glared at me as he pulled them over his hips. "You must love this. You think I'm a man whore, and I'm standing here groveling. I bet you're eating this shit up."

"Screw you, Collin!" I shouted. "Don't you go and act like I'm the one who hurt you!"

"You think you're the only one with feelings?"

"I don't think you've ever felt a goddamned feeling in your life." As soon as I said the words, I regretted them. They hung in the air, and I watched the last bits of hope and softness slide out of Collin's body.

"Yeah, you're right, Ellie." He pulled up his jeans and fastened them, flashing me an ugly sneer. "You were just another fuck. I'll admit that you were a good one, which is why I hated for things to end. I wasn't bored with you yet, but if you want to move on first, I can live with it."

I knew it wasn't true, but his words ripped my heart to shreds.

He picked up my panties and lifted them to his face to smell them before tossing them at me with a leer. "I'm going to miss fucking you, but I might miss going down on you even more."

My breath caught at his crassness. Never once in the time we'd been together had he ever talked to me this way. Not even in the beginning, when he'd been full of resentment. "Don't be ugly, Collin."

"Why not? Look at the way you've been acting." He grabbed his shirt and pulled it over his head. "Get out of my truck."

Anger rushed through me. "Not until you give me the map."

"I'm not giving you anything. Now get out of my truck."

"No!"

He lunged across the seat and opened the passenger door, pushing me toward the opening.

I tried to grab hold of the dashboard, but my hands slipped. "You owe me that map, Collin. What the hell do you need it for? Why won't you give it to me?"

An ugly look spread across his face. "I thought you would have figured me out by now, Ellie. I don't need a reason to keep it. The fact that you want it is reason enough." He gave me one last shove out the door.

The gravel poked my bare feet and I stumbled to remain upright as Collin slammed the door.

I gaped at him through the open window. "You'd let those monsters kill me?"

He tossed my T-shirt and panties out the window at me. "You know what you need to do to save yourself." He started his truck and backed out, shooting gravel in every direction as I jumped out of the way.

I really was as good as dead.

~ CHAPTER SEVEN ~

I watched his truck lights disappear, still dazed. Although I wasn't sure what I expected, this definitely wasn't it. I stood there in shock, wondering what I should do next. I had two choices: I could go home and cry into my pillow, or I could fight.

It wasn't a question, really. I was going to fight. Too bad I still didn't know how to do that.

Headlights appeared, rounding the curve behind me, and I realized I was standing on the side of the road in my skirt and bra, my T-shirt and panties in my hands and no shoes on my feet. Somehow I'd lost my flip-flops in Collin's truck. The sun had set and I needed to get home. Standing out here like this, I was vulnerable in both the spiritual and the earthly worlds.

I jerked my T-shirt over my head as I gingerly walked across the gravel to Myra's car. I'd left my purse and keys inside again since I hadn't planned on falling asleep in his truck. And I sure hadn't planned on anything else that had happened.

My skin flamed at the thought and horror quickly followed. How could I so quickly and easily lose all control with that man?

The approaching car slowed down, and a man leaned out the open passenger window. "Hey, baby. It's still early. Want to hang out? We'll make it worth your while." He waved several twenty dollar bills in his hand.

They had seen me standing half naked on the side of the road as Collin drove away. They thought I was a prostitute. *Thank you, Collin Fucking Dailey.* I squared my shoulders and shot the guy my meanest glare. "Fuck off."

I continued heading toward my car, but the beat-up Cadillac shifted into reverse, keeping up with me.

"Oh, come on, baby. Don't be like that."

Fear squirmed in my gut. *I might be in serious trouble here.* Just one more reason to hate Collin.

I reached for the door to the car as the guy opened his door and hopped out. I had my door open when he reached me, pushing me into the inside of the door panel.

"My money's just as good as that other guy's."

I balled my fists to hide my shaking. "See, that's where you're wrong. You can't afford me, asshole." I knew it was wrong to provoke him, but anger was still rushing through my veins. If I couldn't take out my frustration on Collin, the stupid part of me wanted to take it out on this potential rapist.

Brilliant.

The guy leaned closer, an ugly leer spreading across his face.

"Bobby," a guy called from the idling car. "Let it go, man."

Bobby's beer breath blew into my face and I nearly gagged, clenching my jaw to keep from adding a smart-ass comment. Bobby was drunk and teetering on the edge of violence. My next words might topple him over.

He blocked my escape with one arm. "I don't think so." Snagging the panties out of my hand, he threw them to the ground.

Oh, shit.

If I could get into the car and lock the door, I'd have a chance to escape. "Listen to your friend, Bobby," I said with just a bit too much attitude.

He grabbed my arm and pulled me toward him, and I tried to dig into the ground, stumbling when the gravel stabbed the bottom of my feet.

"Bobby, what the fuck are you doing?" his friend wailed.

"This bitch thinks she's too good for me."

"Not thinks," I snarled, my feet in agony as I tried to get away. "I *know* I am."

His free hand grabbed a handful of my skirt and started to lift it up.

Oh, God.

Slapping his hand away, I fought harder to shake his hold on my arm, which only made him laugh. "Too good for me now?"

"*Bobby!*" his friend shouted.

Bobby laughed and dropped my skirt, tugging me across the road toward the docks.

There was no way I was letting him get me onto one of the fishing boats. I kicked his shin, ignoring the pain that shot through my toes and up my leg. My blow barely fazed him.

The water began to ripple in the small cove beside us.

Bobby chose the second boat and stepped over the edge, pulling me with him. His hand slid up my leg and under my skirt, cupping my ass as he hoisted me over the edge.

"Get your hands off me." I jerked backward, but he laughed and tightened his grip.

He pulled me toward the cabin door, and I frantically searched for something to use as a weapon. I spotted a wrench lying next to an open hatch in the center of the deck, but I was going to have to break free to reach it.

When we were next to the hatch, I forced myself to go limp. His hold slipped and I dropped to the deck. He was only momentarily surprised, but it was long enough for me to grab the tool with my left hand and smash it into the side of his head.

His eyes widened and he stumbled backward.

As I ran across the deck, trying not to get tangled in the loose fishing net, the wrench still clenched in my fist, I glanced over my shoulder and saw a shadow rising behind him accompanied by a loud hiss.

Oh, shit.

Bobby wobbled, then fell to his knees, blood streaming down the side of his face.

Frantic to escape two different threats, I climbed over the edge of the boat onto the dock. But the hissing grew louder, and I turned around to face the creature from my nightmares.

The shadow shimmered, then took the nearly opaque form of a giant snake.

Mishiginebig appeared, his red glowing eyes narrowing on Bobby. "Who dares to touch what belongs to Okeus?"

Bobby fell, landing on a pail. The blow to his head still had him befuddled. He looked up and his eyes widened. "Holy shit."

"Let's get out of here, dude!" Bobby's friend shouted, climbing out of his car.

Bobby tried to stand but got caught in a pile of net and fell to his knees. He leaned over to untangle himself, his eyes on the snake.

"This witness to creation does not belong to you," Mishiginebig said in a menacing tone as he rose even higher, towering at least fifteen feet over us.

After making another effort to stand, Bobby lost his balance again, his legs becoming even more twisted in the net. "I'm sorry!" He shook his head. *"What the fuck! I'm talking to a giant snake!"*

I backed up, terror rushing through my blood as I dropped the wrench and flexed my right hand.

Mishiginebig leaned over the boat until he was about six feet over Bobby, his forked tongue darting in and out of his partially open mouth. His fangs gleamed in the moonlight. "You must make atonement."

Giving up on the net, Bobby tried to scoot away from the creature. "Whatever you say! I'm sorry!"

The snake grinned and rose higher, his mouth opening wide.

I backed into a pole, my heart beating hard against my rib cage.

Bobby began shouting and tugging at the net in frantic fits and starts.

So quickly I almost missed it, Mishiginebig dove, engulfing my attacker's body up to the waist in his gullet. Bobby's legs kicked frantically, and his muffled screams filled the silent night. The snake reared up and tossed back his head, swallowing the man to his knees.

Bobby's friend, who had been standing next to his car in silent awe and terror, made some incoherent shout. I stayed plastered against the pole, watching in horror as the snake tilted back its head one final time and swallowed the rest of the man, tangled fishing net and all.

The car in the street sped off, tires squealing.

I had to be dreaming.

The lump in Mishiginebig's throat moved lower as the snake's muscles contracted. The serpent sank into the water until its head was level with mine. His red eyes watched me as his tongue darted out of his mouth.

My body screamed for flight, but my head told me to stand strong. There was no way I could outrun this thing. "Am I next?"

"As much as I covet your Manitou, I dare not defy Okeus."

So why was it here? To save me? I knew I should take comfort in the fact that the creepy crawly things in the night planned to protect me instead of eat me, but I couldn't help thinking something even nastier was waiting for me in the end.

"But Ahone has claimed me."

The snake grinned. "That's what makes it even better." Then he lowered into the water, waves gently rippling across the cove.

I watched the spot where he'd disappeared, still frozen against the light pole.

Move, Ellie!

I barely felt the gravel beneath my feet as I ran to Myra's car, locking myself inside. My fingers shook as I turned over the ignition. Barely looking behind me, I jerked the car in reverse, then slammed it into gear and sped through Wanchese on the way back to Manteo.

Several minutes after I took off, my phone started to ring.

"I've been calling you for an hour, Ellie!" Claire shouted. "Why haven't you answered?"

"I . . ." I didn't even know where to begin.

"You chickened out, didn't you?"

"What?" I looked down at the speedometer. I was driving twenty miles over the speed limit. "No. I saw him."

It felt like it had happened days ago instead of less than ten minutes.

"And?"

"He's a prick, that's what happened. He claims he doesn't know Ahone's mark and says I need to use Okeus's. And he refused to give me the map. When I asked him why he wouldn't give it to me since he didn't need it, he told me it was because I *did*."

"Are you serious?" she asked in disbelief.

Sure, I had left a whole lot out of the conversation, but I wasn't ready to get into the near sex miss. Not after what just happened.

"He would really leave you defenseless like that?"

I swallowed the lump in my throat. I'd cried enough tears over that man to earn my title of daughter of the sea. But I still couldn't believe how cold he'd been in those last few minutes. "He told me that I know what I need to do to save myself."

Claire was silent for several seconds. "What are you going to do?" She sounded like she was about to cry, something I'd only seen her do a handful of times.

I ran my fingers through my hair, my panic rising with her concern. "I don't know. Someone has to know about these things. Dr. Preston isn't the only professor specializing in North Carolina Native American tribes."

"But he's the best."

"Not helping, Claire!" My terror mounted the closer I got to town. "He wouldn't help me, so I'll just have to find someone who will. I'll do more research when I get home. Surely someone knows *something*." My voice broke.

"Ellie, come over here tonight. I'm worried about you."

"No." I sucked in a breath and steeled my back. "No. It's safer for you if I stay away." I couldn't help wondering if any and all contact with her was dangerous. The spirits had targeted people who were close to me before. What was to stop them from doing it again? If I were truly selfless, I would disown them all and hide somewhere until I sorted this out, but I couldn't bring myself to do it.

"Are the marks still on your door?" Claire asked. "Are they still dark enough?"

"Yes, they're fine."

I'd redone the marks at the inn and the house after I'd finished cleaning out the upstairs.

Claire's voice lowered. "Do you want me to go with you?"

"Won't you get in trouble if you take off work again?" I turned down my street, eager to get behind my closed and marked door.

"Well . . ."

"I won't be able to go anywhere until the day after tomorrow anyway," I lied. "Bruce is still working on my car."

"Okay."

Red flashing lights appeared in my rearview mirror and I groaned, looking down at the speedometer. I was going ten miles over the limit. "I have to go, Claire. I'll call you tomorrow."

I was close enough to home that I pulled into my parking lot and got out of my car, slinging my purse over my shoulder.

Tom pulled in beside me and got out of his cruiser, wearing his uniform. Did that man ever take a day off? "In a hurry to get home, Ellie?"

I shrugged. "It's been a hell of a day."

He walked around the hood of his car and stood four feet in front of me. "You look a little pale."

I glanced up at the streetlight. "I'm not sure how you can tell under this light, but you're right. The curse of the English."

"Where've you been, Ellie?"

I narrowed my gaze. "Is there a town curfew I'm unaware of?"

Tom crossed his arms. "I'm serious."

"So am I."

"Were you in Wanchese?"

Oh, shit. I held my ground. "I'm sorry. Does Wanchese have a restraining order against me?"

"This is serious, Ellie." He moved closer, hooking his thumb on his belt. "Were you in Wanchese?"

"I don't think I have an answer to that question."

His eyes narrowed. "Well, let me make it really clear for you.

The Dare County Sheriff's Office got a call from a freaked-out guy who said his buddy got swallowed by a giant snake at the docks at Wanchese. Know anything about that?"

"Sounds like your meth lab busts haven't hit hard enough."

"This man claimed his friend was with a redheaded woman wearing a white skirt and blue shirt."

I resisted the urge to look down at my clothes. "So what's this got to do with me?"

"Where are your shoes?"

"Is it a crime to go barefoot now, *Officer*?"

He bristled, and I felt like an ass. But the deeper Tom tried to dig into this mess, the more his life was at risk.

"I'll have to ask you again. Know anything about a giant snake eating a man down by the docks?"

I tried to laugh. "Do you know how ridiculous you sound?" I lifted my hands in surrender. "You got me. My pet snake Big Nasty got loose and ate a guy. Oops." But the memory of Mishiginebig chowing down on Bobby shot through me, making me nauseous.

"There's a dead man floating in the cove with giant holes in his body, Ellie."

Good, God. How fast was the response of the Dare County Sheriff's Office in Wanchese? Perhaps I should consider relocating.

"Are you accusing me of a crime, Tom?" Weariness washed over me.

He noted the defeat in my voice and leaned in closer. "No, Ellie. Like I said, I think you've got yourself mixed up in something bad."

"And what do you think this something is?"

He shook his head, looking frustrated. "I don't know."

It occurred to me if I told Tom everything about Marino, it might solve two of my problems. I had the potential to get both men off my back. But I was too tired to deal with it now. I'd save that idea for when I needed to use it.

I offered him a tired smile. "Tom, I appreciate all that you're doing for me, but you're wasting your time and Manteo's taxpayer dollars. I promise if something comes up that requires police assistance, you'll be the first man I call."

He frowned. "Is that supposed to make me feel better?"

"It's the best I've got right now."

Sighing, he pulled a card out of his pocket. "I had a feeling you'd say that." He handed it to me with a stern expression. "My cell phone is written on the back. If it's an emergency, call 911. But if it's not, and you want to talk to me, call my cell. I'll get back to you as soon as I can."

I took the card, hating myself for actually considering using it. "Okay."

"I'm going to let the speeding issue go with a warning, and I'm going to watch you head inside your apartment to make sure you're safe."

Little did he know that I was safer than he was.

For now.

∿ Chapter Eight ∿

I spent over an hour searching the Internet for professors of North Carolina Native American studies. I found Dr. Debra Higgins at UNC in Pembroke, almost a five-hour drive away. I planned to call in the morning and see if I could make an appointment with her. Perhaps a woman would be better, since I seemed to have zero luck with men.

Next I searched for information on Mishiginebig, and after a little reshuffling of my search terms, I found a reference to him at the bottom of a Wikipedia page. Only he wasn't just part of the Algonquian/Croatan belief system, he was part of the folklore of many native religions.

This changed everything.

Collin had led me to believe we were dealing with just Croatan gods. Maybe this meant I could expand my search.

Sleep was elusive again. I got my usual visit from the animals begging for my help, and the badger was back too. My neighbor's dog, Chip, lay on a patch of grass, his guts exposed. The badger was rooting around in his open body cavity, but he lifted his bloody face when he saw me. "Do you know why I eat their hearts, witness to creation?"

"No," I whispered.

"That's where their Manitou is purest."

The full implication of what he was saying sunk in and I fell to my knees.

I was awoken by a banging on my door and I sat upright, clutching my sheet to my chest, my palm itching.

Okeus had come to eat my heart.

No, Okeus had plans for me, although those plans might very well include my heart. But I didn't think he'd just show up to bang on my front door. Okeus seemed like a god who went for pomp and circumstance and special effects. When he was ready to pull off whatever he had planned, it would be a production.

Convincing myself it wasn't Okeus, I padded to the door, nearly hyperventilating with fear. "Who is it?"

Please let it be a human. Three weeks ago, it would never have occurred to me that there'd be an alternative.

"Curse Keeper," the spirit hissed.

Closing my eyes, I rested my head against the door. Couldn't I catch a break? Just one?

"What do you want?"

"Ahone wishes me to relay a message."

Ahone?

From what little I'd learned, Ahone was a standoffish kind of god and my experience with him had borne that out. Sure, he'd sent his messenger to me after the curse was broken, warning me not to align myself with Okeus, and then right before the ceremony at the inn to tell me that Daddy was my sacrifice. And Ahone had possessed enough balls to show up and take Daddy's Manitou, but I hadn't heard from him since. He told me I could bear his mark, and then the bastard had taken off without bothering to tell me what that was. Okeus and his merry band of baddies were much more faithful.

I opened the door a crack. "What is it?" A white owl sat on my porch railing. It would have resembled a real bird if I couldn't see through it.

"Your time is running out."

"Tell me something I don't know. Maybe if I knew Ahone's mark, I could do something to protect myself. Collin says he doesn't know it."

"Your father knew."

My chest tightened. "But my father's dead."

"He left his legacy to you."

What was he talking about? Then I realized. "His notes? I can't find them! If Ahone wants me so badly, why won't he show me what it is?"

"All warriors must be tested. You are on a journey."

"Is this what this is? *A test?* Shutting the damn gate and sacrificing my father wasn't enough proof of my loyalty?"

The owl remained silent. I didn't need an answer. I already knew.

"Let's say I discover this magical mark and I get it tattooed on my back. What does it mean? I'm not stupid enough to believe there's no price."

"You forfeit your soul to Ahone."

My chest heaved as I tried to control the tidal wave of emotion washing over me. Sell my soul to one god or let the other torture me. Not that it mattered.

"How long do I have?"

"Two days. Maybe three." The owl faded.

I still had at least two days to find the mark. Maybe the professor at Pembroke could help. All the more reason to go see her after work.

I couldn't go back to sleep, so I washed my body off with a washrag. I would have given anything to take a shower, but I was desperate to keep my mark for as long as possible. I did a little housekeeping before walking to the inn at around six fifteen.

Myra was surprised to see me when I walked into the kitchen, but she seemed happy to have me there. When she looked up from stirring her breakfast casserole and got a better look at me, though, the smile fell off her face. "You need more sleep, Ellie. You can't keep going on this way."

I suppressed a yawn. "I know."

"I have some sleeping pills my doctor prescribed me after your father died. You can take one of those tonight."

I was tempted. I hadn't slept more than three consecutive hours in weeks. "Thanks, Myra. I'll think about it."

"What are you doing here this early?"

"I've been up awhile, and I figured you could use the help. Did the new guests get settled in all right?"

She poured the egg and sausage mixture into two baking dishes. "Yes, and thank you for cleaning up the rooms. The flowers were a lovely touch."

"That was Claire's idea." But thinking about the rooms reminded me of the stain I'd found in my old room. "Myra, did Daddy ever talk about Momma's murder?"

She froze for a second, her eyes wide, but then recovered enough to put the casseroles in the oven. "That caught me off guard."

"I'm sorry."

Shaking her head, she put the bowl in the sink and turned on the water. "No, there's nothing to be sorry about. It's just that no one has mentioned her death in ages."

I sat on a bar stool at the counter. "So did he ever talk about it?"

Myra poured a cup of coffee and added creamer before handing it to me, then poured one for herself. "Not much. He didn't like to think about it." She sat on the stool next to mine and leaned her elbow on the counter with a sigh. "I think he felt responsible."

"Why? The man was after me."

"Maybe he thought he should have been here." She took a sip of her coffee. "He said he wished he'd never left the house that night."

"I don't remember much about the attack and nothing at all about the investigation after. I only know what Daddy told me. He said they thought the man who did it was someone who didn't like him."

"Yes, he told me there had been some kind of zoning meeting and his was the deciding vote against the man who had made the zoning request. I don't even remember what it was about." She frowned and reached over to tuck a loose tendril of hair behind my ear. "It seems wrong of me not to know."

"It's okay, Myra."

She shook her head. "No, it's not. It's normal for you to ask questions. Especially after what happened to your dad. Honestly, I'm surprised you haven't asked sooner."

I never thought to ask because I carried so much blame myself. But the new dreams and the stain on the floor made me wonder if what I remembered was true. Why it mattered now, of all times, was more of a mystery.

"The man made threatening calls to your father and mother. Then he started mentioning you, threatening to harm you. That's when your dad called the police. The police questioned him, your dad filed a restraining order, and that seemed to be that. In fact, the man moved off the island, so everyone thought you were safe."

"But I wasn't."

She frowned. "No, you weren't."

"If they knew who did it, why didn't they arrest him?"

She sighed and crossed her legs. "Well, for one thing, they never had concrete proof it was him. They only suspected. And for another, they couldn't find him. He left the island about a month before your mother's death. And when the police tried to find him to question him, it was like he fell off the face of the earth. They had no idea where he was."

I leaned my elbows on the counter. "So he got away with murder."

"If he did it, yeah, I guess so."

I expected to feel bitter at the realization. Instead, I only felt profound sadness. "I remember being upstairs getting ready for bed. A storm was blowing in, and I was scared, especially since a tree branch kept banging against my window. Momma told me to pick a book for her to read to me, but first she went downstairs to make sure the doors were locked. Then I heard breaking glass."

Myra took my hand in hers.

"There was shouting, and I went to sit at the top of the stairs, too scared to go down even though I heard the man yelling for me." I still lived with the guilt of my cowardice. I looked into Myra's face. "I didn't know that man had threatened me before that night until you just told me."

"I'm not surprised. You were only eight. They probably didn't want you to be scared."

"I should have gone downstairs, Myra. If I'd gone downstairs, Momma might still be alive."

Tears in her eyes, Myra squeezed my hand and shook her head. "No, Ellie. You would have been killed."

"But I could have saved her."

"Do you really think your mother could have lived with the knowledge that you were murdered in front her and she couldn't stop it? I assure you that she very willingly sacrificed herself for you. And she'd make the exact same choice again. Just like I would."

My voice broke. "It's not fair. Daddy sacrificed himself for me too. I didn't ask either of them to do that."

She smiled through her tears. "Oh, Ellie. You carry so many burdens, sometimes I forget how young you really are." Tears streamed down her cheeks. "Of course you didn't have to ask them to do it. That's what it means to be a parent."

I threw my arms around her neck and clung to her, needing to feel close to her. I knew that soon I'd have to sacrifice my own needs to keep her safe, just as my parents had done for me. I was dangerous to Myra. I had to figure a way to send her away. Even if it meant losing her.

"You have no idea how much it hurts me to see you with all this responsibility heaped on your shoulders."

I sat up. "You know I don't mind helping with the inn."

"That's not what I'm talking about."

My mouth parted, but no words came.

She grabbed my right hand and spread my fingers open, exposing the mark on my palm. "I know what this is. Your father drew it from time to time when he wasn't himself. Sometimes he'd try to draw it on his own palm." She paused. "It's the mark of the Keeper."

"The gate's closed, Myra. Thanks to Daddy." I choked on my tears.

"It may be closed, but you and I both know that the spirits and gods were set loose all the same."

My eyes widened and I took a deep breath. Myra had enough to worry about without adding me to the list. "My job was to close the gate."

"So you say. But I noticed the fresh marks on the doors last night."

"It's insurance."

Her chin quivered as her fingertip traced my palm. "We both know your job isn't done," she said with calm resignation.

I didn't know how to respond.

"I've told you time and again that you're my daughter. You may not have been born to me, but you're firmly implanted in my heart. If I could sacrifice myself for you—"

I gasped and closed my hand around hers. "Myra! Don't say that!"

"I would do it, Ellie. If it would give you peace, I would do it willingly." She swallowed. "It kills me wondering what terror you've faced . . . what terror still awaits you. I know those things are trying to bait you. Chip . . ." She looked at her coffee cup, then stared into my eyes again. "I don't want you to be alone in your apartment. I want you to move back home so I'm not worried about you every minute of the day. At least when you're here, I'll know you're safe."

"Myra . . ." I understood, but I didn't know if I could do it. Although my financial circumstances might make the decision for me.

"Just promise me you'll think about it, okay?"

I nodded. "Okay."

Myra slid off her stool. "I have to leave an hour early today. The research team will be leaving at about seven forty-five."

"I can take you, and my car should be done sometime this afternoon."

"Don't worry about it." She waved her hand at me. "We're just as behind out there as we are at the inn. I'll have plenty to do." She looked over her shoulder at the sink full of dishes. "I have some paperwork I need to take care of. Would you mind cleaning up this mess and serving breakfast?"

"Of course not."

"Since the guests upstairs are all leaving together, I thought it might be easier to serve them in the dining room. There aren't enough tables and chairs for everyone in the other house."

"That makes sense."

"I told them breakfast would be on the sideboard at seven."

"Okay."

I hopped off the stool and pulled her into another hug. Myra and Claire were the only two people I had left, and Myra could have easily walked away from all this craziness. Yet she was staying for me. The significance was not lost on me. "I love you."

Her arms squeezed around me. "Child of my heart, I love you too." Dropping her arms, she grinned at me, her eyes glassy. "We're turning into a Hallmark movie." She swatted my arm. "If I don't see you before I leave this morning, be careful today."

"You too."

I filled up the dishwasher and washed the remaining dishes in the sink, staring out the window at the side yard. It seemed empty without Chip running around. Myra was right. The spirits had killed Chip to bait me, just like they'd killed people I knew to coerce me to open the gate the rest of the way. Was it time to walk away from the rest of the people I cared about?

Myra had already prepared a tray of biscuits, so I put them into the second oven and then moved into the dining room, carrying the coffeepot. I set up a coffee station and arranged the table with plates and silverware. I heard the timer go off for the biscuits, so I turned back toward the kitchen. As I was heading down the short hall to the kitchen through the butler's pantry, I saw a man entering the dining room from the entrance on the other side.

"Coffee's ready if you want some. I'll have breakfast out in a minute."

"Thanks," he mumbled.

I glanced at the clock in the kitchen, making sure I was still on time. 6:50. He was early.

After I had everything out of the oven and the biscuits arranged in a cloth napkin–lined basket, I carried the casserole in and set it on the sideboard.

The man was standing at the window, looking out toward the downtown area. "Cute little town you have here." He had an English accent, which caught my attention.

"Most people who live here like it," I said, giving him a second look before heading back into the kitchen. It wasn't uncommon to get foreigners on Roanoke Island, but something about him seemed familiar.

I grabbed the biscuits and the tray of butter, jellies, and jams and carried them into the dining room. The man was where I'd left him.

"You say most people. Are you not one of them?" he asked.

He was perceptive. Although these were researchers and not tourists, I still needed to be careful not to damage the image of our town. "No, of course not. I was born here and will die here." Of that, I was certain. And it would probably happen sooner rather than later.

"Again, a strange way to put it."

I cringed. Damn my need for honesty. Rearranging things on the sideboard, I kept my back to him. "I love Manteo, but things have been a bit crazy here lately."

"Since the appearance of the colony?"

"Yes."

"And what about the marks on the doors? The Native American symbols?"

I froze for a few seconds. Several guests had asked about them over the last couple of weeks, and I'd told them it was all part of the experience. This man's question seemed more pointed.

I turned to look at him and was surprised to find myself face-to-face with Dr. Preston.

"You." His eyes widened. "We met outside my office a couple of days ago."

I froze, speechless and stunned.

"Why are those symbols on your doors?"

While hope surged inside me—*He's here! Maybe he can still help!*—I had no idea how to go about getting the information I needed without scaring him away. "Are you part of the research team?"

He set his coffee cup on the table, his eyes narrowing in on me. "Not officially. I'm a guest of one of the researchers. He told me that Manteo's hut was on site, and he asked me if I wanted to check it out."

"Manteo had a hut in the village?" Myra had never told me. I knew the village had reappeared completely intact, as if it had been picked up in 1587 and dropped back into place over four hundred years later, with edible food and water still in washbowls. Everything had returned in usable condition. Except for the inhabitants, of course. They had returned as fully clothed skeletons. But those were the only details that had been released to the public. It had never occurred to me that Manteo would have lived with the colonists and kept a home there. Along with Ananias Dare, my multiple-great grandfather.

I needed to get into those huts.

His head tilted slightly as he observed me. "You didn't know?"

"No."

"What is your interest in Manteo and the Croatan?"

"How long are you here for?"

My question surprised him. "A couple of weeks. What does that have to do with anything?"

I could go about this one of two ways. While I'd love nothing more than to charge forward and tell him everything, I was sane enough to realize that it would scare him off. Slow and steady seemed the best way to go about this. I had two weeks to get information out of him. Even if I wasn't sure the gods would wait that long.

He was watching me warily and I could tell he was becoming suspicious. The longer I took to answer, the stranger I looked. "I grew up on stories about the Lost Colony. We all know about Manteo, especially with the Lost Colony reenactment play. Shoot, I was the Dare baby."

"What's the Dare baby?"

"Every August they pick a baby to be baby Virginia Dare in the play. It's quite an honor. You have no idea how badly people want their baby to be picked."

He looked confused.

"I'm just saying that I've grown up living and breathing the legend of the colony. The Croatan are a part of it."

"That still doesn't explain why there are symbols on your door."

I shifted my weight, trying to come up with a reasonable-sounding explanation. My standard answer wasn't going to work on this guy.

He decided to take a different tactic. "Why did you come see me?"

"I already told you that." I heard voices coming down the stairs. The other researchers were on their way to breakfast, and I really didn't want to get into this with other people around.

Becky, the woman who helped with the inn, came in through the butler's pantry, humming to herself. "Ellie, your mom wants to see you before she goes."

"Okay." But my eyes were still locked with Dr. Preston's.

Becky put her hands on her hips. "Did you hear about that guy in Wanchese getting eaten by a giant snake?"

"A little." I couldn't hide my cringe. Why was I surprised word had spread already? And if word had spread, Becky was sure to play a part in its broadcast.

"The rumor around town is that the guy was about to rape some poor girl and this giant snake with horns on its head rose up out of the water and ate the guy. They found his body floating in the water with big ole holes in it from the fang marks."

Dr. Preston's gaze shifted to Becky.

I shook my head. "You don't believe that, do you? If the snake ate him, why was he floating in the water? Wouldn't he still be in the snake's belly?"

Becky shrugged. "Beats me, but after that colony just appeared out of nowhere, a giant man-eating snake doesn't sound too odd. Not to mention that wild animal on the loose that's going around eating dogs' hearts right out of their chests. I heard it got a cow last night."

I turned to her, wide-eyed with exasperation. "Becky, you know better than to be talking like that in front of a guest. We don't want to scare off the tourists."

"But he's not a tourist. He's a researcher. I'd think he'd want to know about it."

Dr. Preston opened his mouth to say something, but two men and a woman walked in before he could.

"Good morning, David," an elderly man with gray hair said as he patted Dr. Preston on the shoulder. "I see you're eager to get a start on the day."

"I was having a chat with . . ." He looked at me with new interest.

"Ellie." I wiped my hands on the apron covering my shorts and extended my hand to the newcomer. "Ellie Lancaster. I'm Myra's daughter."

"Ellie Lancaster!" A warm smile spread across his face. "I met you when you were a little girl. I bet you don't remember me."

I shook my head as I tried to place him. "I'm sorry. I don't."

"Steven Godfrey. I knew your parents professionally." He shook his head with a laugh. "I should have put it together when Myra said she owned the inn with her daughter, but her last name isn't Lancaster and she's . . ."

"Chinese." I smiled. "And I am the furthest you can get from that. I'm her stepdaughter. And she goes by her maiden name. Myra Long."

"I knew about your mother. In fact, my wife and I came to her funeral. But I didn't find out about your father's death until right before we came to the island. Anyway, when Myra told us she owned the Dare Inn, I thought perhaps your father had sold it to her when he got sick. I should have known better. Your father took great pride in the inn."

I nodded, unsure of what to say. His words only added to my huge pile of guilt. The inn was such a financial mess that we would likely have to sell it in spite of the new boom of guests who had been lured in by the once lost, now found colony.

"I heard about your father's remarriage, but I didn't know any of the details. We fell out of touch years ago."

"Myra came to Roanoke Island a couple of years after Momma died to take a job as a park ranger. She wanted Jamestown, but there wasn't an opening, so Fort Raleigh was supposed to be temporary. Her master's degree is in early American history."

The man chuckled. "We early American history buffs are a dying breed."

"Daddy met Myra and fell in love, and the rest is history, as they say. She never made it to Jamestown." I suddenly wondered if she regretted it. I'd never considered the possibility before.

"And she runs a bed and breakfast on the side, just like your parents did? I have to say she got us out of a real pickle by offering to let us stay here."

"I'm happy we could help."

Steven smiled. "I can't help thinking how much your father would have loved to see the colony. Such a shame."

"Yeah, Daddy would have loved it." My voice broke, much to my embarrassment. "If you'll excuse me, I need to check on something. I'll be around in the mornings and some afternoons and evenings. If you need anything, please don't hesitate to ask."

I turned around and headed for the kitchen. Out of the corner of my eye I saw Dr. Preston start to follow me, but Steven stopped him with a question. I realized that Steven had to be the researcher who had invited Dr. Preston to the site.

Dr. David Preston was interested, which meant I had a real shot at getting some answers. That was a good thing . . . so why did I have a feeling that I was dragging yet another person down a dangerous path?

✌ Chapter Nine ↜

My phone rang midmorning while I was making the beds. I answered, hoping for some news about my car.

"Hey, Ellie. It's Carly from Darrell's Restaurant. Remember when I mentioned that I could offer you some work while the New Moon's closed?"

"Yeah."

"One of my waitresses called in sick this morning and another one's pregnant and has to cut her hours. Is there any way you could come in and work the lunch shift? You'd be doing me a huge favor."

"Sure." Since Dr. Preston was literally at my doorstep, I didn't have to drive to Pembroke anymore. And I definitely needed the money. "That would be great, Carly. Thanks. What time should I come in?"

"It's nine thirty now. How about ten thirty so Howie can go over the menu with you? And you can just wear khakis and a white shirt for your uniform."

"Thanks. I'll see you then."

I finished giving a quick scrub to all the bathrooms before I told Becky I had to leave. "I can finish freshening up the rooms in the main house after my shift. Myra told me the team would be out until after dinner."

"Are you sure?"

I knew what she was asking. I was about as reliable as a fox in a henhouse lately. "I'm positive. I'll be working the lunch shift until three, and then I'll hopefully pick up my car and be back by four at the latest."

I had to scrounge through my clothes to find a khaki skirt and a clean white shirt, but I was on time—I even had one minute to spare. It didn't take me long to get up to speed with the menu, and by the time I'd figured out my station and everything else, the lunch crowd was flowing in. I'd known that Darrell's was a favorite for employees at the courthouse about a mile down the highway, but the number of law enforcement officers surprised me.

"Ellie." I heard a voice call out from behind me as I was heading for the kitchen. Tom was sitting at a table with a sheriff deputy.

Shit.

"Hey, Tom."

"Can I talk to you for a moment?"

I would have loved nothing more than to blow him off, but after last night I had a feeling he'd haul me to the police station if I wasn't cooperative. "Sure, let me just take this order to the kitchen." I pointed my thumb toward the back.

He nodded and I gave the order to the cooks before heading back to the officers' table.

"You're not in my station, Tom, so I'm afraid I can't take your order."

He rested his elbows on the table and looked up at me with a smile. "Then it's a good thing I already gave my drink order to one of the other waitresses."

I jutted my hip to the side. "Then what can I do for you? As you can see, we're pretty busy."

"You're new here, aren't you?" the sheriff deputy asked. He looked to be in his late thirties or early forties, but he didn't appear to be hard and jaded like so many police officers his age. He seemed friendly, so I let down my guard a notch.

"I'm just filling in. I usually work at the New Moon, but we're temporarily closed."

"A couple of the waitresses who worked there were killed, right?" the deputy asked.

My smile froze on my face. He was fishing for information. "Seeing how that's public knowledge, and you look to have half your wits about you, I'm surprised you don't know that for certain. Have you been on vacation?"

The deputy's face reddened, and Tom choked back a laugh.

Tom took a moment to gather himself. "Ellie, this is Deputy Moran, and he's with the Dare County Sheriff's Office."

I raised my eyebrows as I stared at him.

"He's investigating the death last night."

I put a hand on my hip. "Is that supposed to mean something to me?"

Tom rolled his eyes. "Ellie, you know damn good and well what I'm talking about."

I heaved out a loud exhale. "Tom, I'm really busy. This is my first day, and I'd really like to keep this job seeing as how I don't have another one at the moment. Do you have a question or not?"

The deputy cleared his throat, no longer looking as friendly as he had a few moments ago. "Were you in Wanchese last night?"

"Is this an interrogation? Really?" I looked around the restaurant. "Now?"

"Ellie," Tom growled. "Just answer the goddamned question."

I could lie, but what if they had proof? "Yes."

Relief flooded Tom's face.

"What were you doing in Wanchese?" the deputy asked.

I glared at him. "What I do or don't do is my business. If I wanted the world to know, I would have tweeted about it."

The deputy leaned forward, his eyes hardening. "We can do this at the sheriff's office if you'd prefer."

Anger singed my chest. "Are you accusing me of a crime?" My voice rose louder than I'd intended and several people looked in my direction.

Tom's eyes pleaded with me. "Ellie, we're not accusing you of anything."

The deputy's face was expressionless. "I'm reserving judgment."

I rolled my eyes and then put my hands on the table and leaned closer to them. "I like to go to Wanchese and skinny-dip. Okay? I'm not exactly proud of it, but there you go." I stood up. "Anything else?"

The deputy didn't look happy at all and neither did Tom.

"Did you see a giant snake by the docks last night?" Deputy Moran asked.

I gave him a saucy look. "I know that's what lots of guys like to call it, but no. I didn't see any *giant snakes* in Wanchese last night." I used air quotes around giant snakes. "Not that I'm maligning Wanchese," I added. "I'm sure there's a few there. I just haven't seen them."

Tom tried to keep from laughing, earning a disapproving look from the deputy.

"Is there anything else? Because my customers at the table over there need a refill and every second I'm here with you is costing me in tips."

The deputy shook his head. "No. But I'm going to want to talk to you later."

I gave him a smile. "Tom knows where to find me." I quickly left and got refills for the table that was waiting, offering the customers my apologies.

The fact that the deputy wanted to question me set me on edge. At least I knew where I stood with Tom. This other guy was a wild card. I knew he couldn't accuse me of anything—after all, I clearly hadn't put those holes in that guy—but I didn't want to be tied to anything supernatural.

When I brought plates to one of my tables, I noticed that I had a new customer in the back, his head bent, his face looking down at the menu.

My heart stopped, leaving me light-headed.

Collin looked up, and the blood rushed from his face.

I was stuck. This was my first day, so there was no way I was going to ask the hostess to move him. I had to suck it up and be a big girl.

I walked toward him, my back stiffening. "Can I get you something to drink?"

Collin's mouth moved like he was about to say something, but then a wry smile lifted his lips. "We have to stop meeting this way, Ellie."

I tilted my head with a fake smile. "You already broke the curse, so what dastardly deed could you have in mind this time?"

He leaned back. "This time is a coincidence. In fact, I've been here almost every day for over a week. I could accuse you of staking *me* out."

I curled my upper lip. "You wish."

"You did it last night." But the smile fled from his face.

I refused to acknowledge anything about last night, especially since Tom and the deputy were still on the other side of the room. "Can I get your drink order?"

"Water."

I checked on my other tables before I got Collin's water, but I noticed that my interaction with him had drawn Tom's attention. Thankfully, the deputy hadn't noticed.

When I returned to Collin's table, he had a serious look on his face. "What happened after I left you?"

My eyes narrowed and I lowered my voice, leaning closer to him. "You lost all right to ask me what happened the moment you drove off."

He had the nerve to look pissed. "Like it or not, we need to keep track of each other."

My mouth dropped. "Are you shitting me?"

The couple at the next table turned their heads toward us.

Great. Between Collin, Tom, and Deputy Moran, I was going to lose this job on the first day. "I need your order, Collin."

He shook his head in disgust and slid the menu toward me, looking out the window. "A hamburger, medium rare."

I leaned over to pick up his menu with my right hand and his right hand snatched my wrist, pulling me close. Our faces were less than a foot apart. The call of his mark sent a shiver down my spine, and I struggled to catch my breath.

"Say what you like, Ellie," he whispered, his eyes burning with desire. "But we still need each other."

My temper flared, and I lowered my voice. "I need you to help me send those awful things back, but you refuse to do it. I need you to show me Ahone's mark, but you say you don't know it. I'm not sure what you could possibly need *me* for. Other than the obvious."

"Did a giant horned snake really save you from some . . ."

He couldn't bring himself to say it, so I did. "*Rapist?*" I whispered. "Yeah. Big Nasty saved me, because apparently I'm some big prize for Okeus, and all the creatures of the night are making sure to save me for him." My eyebrows lifted. "Forgive me if I don't feel protected."

"Ellie . . ."

I glanced toward Tom, who had dropped any pretense of not watching me.

Leaning close to Collin's ear, I whispered. "Those two officers behind me are already watching my every move, and now Tom is *very* interested in this interaction. I suspect this little show will cost me a trip down to the police station, all thanks to you *again*. So if you will kindly take your *fucking* hand off my wrist."

His grip loosened, and I slowly stood.

"I'll have your order out shortly."

Tom watched me as I headed into the back, and I found a corner to hide in to regain my cool. On the plus side, I'd been in close proximity to Collin and other than the twitch in my palm when my mark was almost pressed against his, I hadn't felt an overwhelming urge to jump him. But now Tom had even more material to fuel his quest to solve the mystery of Ellie Lancaster. What the hell was I going to do about that?

One problem at a time.

By the time I left the kitchen, Tom and Deputy Moran had already left. I ignored Collin while I waited on the other tables in my section. When I finally set his plate on the table, his face was expressionless.

"What do they know?"

"It's none of your business."

"Ellie."

"Why have you been here every day over the last week?"

A hesitant smile spread across his face, making my heart ache. It was another painful reminder of why I'd fallen for him.

He looked up at me. "The cops love to eat here, and they chat about what's going on when they think no one's listening."

"Why . . . ?" Then it made sense. Collin hadn't completely divorced himself from the situation. He was keeping tabs on what the police knew about the spirit world.

"I want to see you when you get off work."

I shook my head. "No way."

"Grow up, Ellie."

I gasped, astounded at his nerve. Instead of responding, I turned around and printed out his ticket, then tossed it onto his table. "You can pay me when you're ready."

He pulled a twenty-dollar bill from his wallet and left it on the table. "You can keep the change," he said as he stood to leave, his food barely eaten.

I considered throwing it back at him but decided he owed me the ten-dollar tip. That and so much more.

When my shift was over at three, Carly asked me if I could work the lunch shift the next day. After my confrontations with the police officers and Collin, I was baffled that she wasn't going to fire me. But then again, she was desperate, just like I was.

"Sure." I had a feeling both Tom and Collin would be back, but that was a cross I could bear for financial survival.

Bruce had had left a message saying my car was ready, so I called Claire to see if she could help me pick it up. "Yes, but you have to come inside when you come and get me. I have something to show you."

"If it's another weird sexual position, tell me right now. I'll ask the homeless guy who hangs out at the Food Lion in Nags Head to help me instead."

"One time! I showed you something *one time*, and you're going to hold it over me forever."

"I was scarred for life."

"Well, it's not. And Drew and I have amazing sex, so you should be so lucky."

I groaned. "Spare me the details."

"It's about my wedding."

"Oh. Why didn't you say so? Did you bring me a piece of chocolate cake from your taste testing?"

"No. It's better."

"You brought me red velvet cake."

"It's not cake! It's better than cake."

"There's nothing better than cake, so I'll have to be the judge of that when I get there."

When I got to Claire's, I knocked on the door. "I'm in the bedroom!" she shouted, loud enough for me to hear her from outside.

When I reached her room, I pushed the partially open door wide and gasped. Claire was standing in the middle of her room wearing her wedding dress.

She lifted the sides of her skirt and dropped it with a fluff. "Well, what do you think?"

"That you're the most beautiful bride I've ever seen." And she was. Her satin dress was a halter style with a short train and scattered appliqués around the waist and bodice. It was simple but elegant. So her.

"Who would have thought I'd get married first? You were always the one who wanted a husband and kids."

My mouth twisted into a sideways grimace. "I know. Go figure." Then I realized how awful that sounded. "But I'm so happy for you. I hope you don't think I'm not."

Claire grabbed my hands in hers. "Don't worry, Ellie. You'll find the right guy. I know it. I have a feeling he's right around the corner."

I nodded, but given the ins and outs of my current situation, I knew it was unlikely. "Well, this will be your big day, and you'll be so gorgeous that it won't matter if I wear a gunnysack standing next to you. So I retract my protests about the dress."

Her face broke into a wide grin. "That's the surprise." She grabbed a dress swathed in a plastic bag from the closet and handed it to me. "Surprise!"

I took the garment bag. "Is this my dress?"

"Open it."

I laid the bag on the bed and unzipped it, gasping when I saw the green satin fabric. "It's not orange."

"Nope, it's emerald green. You look so pretty in that color. And the halter top will make your tits look amazing."

I ignored that comment. "But you ordered orange dresses. And your sister . . ."

"It's my wedding, and I can do what I want." She smirked. "You've had a shitty few weeks, and if this dress makes you even the tiniest bit happy, then . . ." Her voice trailed off as she shrugged.

"I don't know what to say. Thank you."

"Try it on."

I went into the bathroom and put on the silky dress, which clung to my curves and flared at my calves. It was a similar style to Claire's, only a different color and not appliquéd. And Claire was right about the V neckline showing off my cleavage. When I walked into the bedroom, she was sitting on her bed, still wearing her wedding dress.

"You're beautiful." She pulled back the hair from my face. "I think you should wear your hair down in the back but pulled up in the front. The auburn looks great against the green."

114

"Thanks, Claire." My eyes burned and I blinked. I knew the fit her sister would throw.

"I got a deal on it, so think nothing of it." She hopped up off the bed. "You can take it to the bridal shop in Nags Head and see if you need alterations." Turning around, she lifted her hair. "Unzip me. I need to take this off before Drew gets home. We need all the luck we can get with the craziness going on around here."

I grabbed the zipper and pulled it down. "Are you still going to help me get my car?"

"What? Was the homeless guy busy?"

"Very funny."

After we changed, we headed for the garage and I realized I hadn't talked to Claire all day. "You won't believe what happened this morning."

"You got laid?"

"*Claire.*" But I knew she was just trying to make me feel better. I still hadn't told her how close I'd come to following through with Collin the night before, and I didn't plan to. "No. Get your mind out of the gutter. One of Myra's researcher guests is Dr. Preston from UNC."

She sat up and turned to me. "The one we went to see? You've got to be kidding!"

I shook my head. "He asked about the symbols on the doors."

Claire's face lit up with excitement. "This is good! Did you tell him?"

"No. He said he'll be here for two weeks, and I don't want to do anything to scare him off. But Becky came in talking about the giant horned snake and the animal that's been eating dogs' hearts, and it got his attention. I'm hoping he might be ready to talk to me tonight."

"Tonight?"

"I told Myra I'd help in the main house in the afternoons and evenings. I did a shift at Darrell's today so I didn't get a chance to finish fixing up their rooms."

"Is the big snake in Wanchese the one we saw in the wildlife refuge?"

I didn't answer.

"Was that really you in the story I've been hearing?"

I grimaced and twisted my neck to look at her. "What did you hear?"

"That some guy was raping a woman he found by the docks, and the snake ate him."

"It was me, but that's not what happened. The rape part, anyway."

She sank back into her seat. "I should hope not. You would tell me about something like that, right?"

What kind of world had I descended into that nearly getting raped had fallen to the bottom of my list of concerns? "If I got raped, you'd be the first person to know." It wasn't entirely a lie, but it wasn't entirely the truth either. I had to accept that and push the guilt aside. Things were only going to get worse.

↤ CHAPTER TEN ↦

Claire drove my car to my apartment. I changed before I dumped my laundry in the backseat and drove her home before heading back to the inn. My apartment didn't have a washer and dryer, so I used the commercial units at the inn. One benefit of working without pay.

We kept the small kitchen in the guest house stocked with drinks and a few snacks for the guests, so I set up some snacks and drinks at the main house too. I'd changed all the linens and freshened the bathrooms earlier, so after straightening a few things up, I had nothing left to do but wait.

I found myself standing in the doorway to Daddy's office. I wondered for the umpteenth time where he could have hidden his notes about the curse. I didn't even know what I was looking for. A notebook? A journal? Folded papers? Claire and I had looked through all the drawers and obvious places, but what about the less obvious ones? Daddy had never been an overly suspicious person before he started losing his memories. But as his sickness spread its roots, he had become paranoid. He could have hidden his notes during one of his delusional states.

The office still seemed the most obvious place to look. Maybe the actual hiding spot was really obscure. I lifted a large framed map of Roanoke Island off the wall and examined the back for any signs of tampering, then moved on to the next picture. I removed five pictures from the wall, stacking them in a pile, and then turned to the bookcases. What if he'd hidden something *behind* the books?

I removed a big stack from the middle shelf on the end case and set them on the desk. Once I had the shelf cleared off, I felt around the back of it for any indentations or bulges.

"Looking for something?"

Startled, I bumped my head on the shelf above as I whirled around.

Dr. David Preston stood in the doorway.

He was gorgeous, only he didn't seem to flaunt it. I suddenly felt warm all over. He was over six feet tall, with dark wavy hair and broad shoulders. He came across as a man who was confident enough in his intelligence that his looks were a side bonus. Plus he had that sexy accent. It was an intoxicating blend. I could see why he had to fight off the undergrads at UNC.

I rubbed my forehead. "Oh, hi, Dr. Preston. I didn't realize you were back."

He smiled. "Call me David. Please. I insist on doctor or professor at the university to keep some of the students in line, but it feels so pretentious off campus. And I'm back because the section of the colony I'm most interested in was temporarily closed. The others are still working." He paused. "I was hoping you'd be here."

"Me?" Why did that make me nervous? That was a good thing.

He took several steps into the room, rubbing the back of his neck. "I was quite rude to you when you came to Chapel Hill. I'd like to apologize."

"Oh." I leaned my hip against the desk. "I'm sure I caught you off guard."

"Yeah. You asked some unexpected questions." He glanced over his shoulder, as if making sure we were alone. "You didn't answer me this morning, you know. I recognize several of the symbols on the doors. Why are they there?"

I stared at him for several seconds before I sighed. He didn't waste any time. But he recognized some of the symbols, giving me hope that he could actually help. "The less you know, the better. But I'd really like it if you could talk to me about the Croatan."

He gave me a lopsided grin. "Do you really expect a researcher to be presented with something so intriguing without wanting to know everything?"

I *couldn't* tell him everything. In spite of the mounting evidence that supernatural forces were rocking the island, I was sure he'd think I was crazy. Besides, the fewer people who knew, the better.

"Do you need help?" he asked, staring at the pile of books. "I take it you're looking for something."

I fumbled for an answer.

"Your stepmother told me that your father had an extensive library about all things Roanoke. I can look at the titles while I help you search for whatever it is you're seeking. And I'll answer your questions. At least all the ones I can answer."

My eyes narrowed. "Why?"

"If I help you, maybe you'll appease my curiosity."

I ran my fingers though my hair in frustration as I surveyed the room. He already knew I was looking for answers. That's why I had come to his office. "The day my father died, he told me that he wrote down some information that I need and hid it somewhere. Only he neglected to tell me where exactly he hid it. I've searched this room several times without finding anything, so I decided to try ripping it apart. I'm running out of time."

"What happens when you run out of time?"

I turned my back to him and repressed a groan.

"Okay, so you don't feel comfortable telling me what happens when you run out of time. How about this: Are you looking for information about the symbols?"

I hesitated. "I hope. Among other things."

"Can I look at your photo again?"

"The one on my phone?" I asked. "Aren't you worried about me flashing you a naked picture of myself?"

He laughed. "You'd be surprised by how many I've seen."

"It must be a real burden," I teased, grabbing my phone off the desk and pulling up my photo app.

"It's a pain in the arse."

He was serious. I couldn't help thinking that Collin would eat it up if women showed him naked photos of themselves. At least until I showed up. Would he change his ways now that our souls were joined? Probably not. They had all been meaningless before me, so why would it be any different now? Collin was right about one thing: his feelings had been laid bare when our marks touched. I had meant something to him—I still did. It just wasn't enough.

"Ellie?"

I looked up, mentally shaking myself. I still hadn't handed him the phone. "Sorry. I've been a little scattered lately."

"Since the colony reappeared?"

"You have no idea." I regretted the words the moment they fell out of my mouth—they were bound to pique his interest even more.

"Can I ask when you first started putting marks on the doors?"

The more cooperative I was with him, the more cooperative he might be with me. I just had to be careful. I always let things slip when I was tired, and I was beyond my usual state of exhaustion.

"Around the time the colony appeared," I replied. Collin had first marked my door the night he broke the curse, but I wasn't about to say that to this guy.

"Why?"

I lifted my eyebrows and handed him my phone. "I answered your question, now you can answer mine. What does it mean?"

He moved beside me and rested his backside against the desk as he lifted the phone for a closer look. "You said this tattoo is henna?"

"Yes."

He grimaced. "I wish I had my reading glasses. Thirty-one years old and I need reading glasses. I feel like an old man."

David was about the furthest thing from an old man I'd ever seen, but it didn't seem wise to mention that.

"I have some." I moved around to the back of the desk and grabbed a pair from the top drawer. "Here. They were Daddy's."

He perched them on his nose and studied the photo, moving the image a little closer so he could see it better. "Like I told you, they're symbols for forces of nature. I've never seen them put together in this type of an arrangement, but that doesn't mean anything." He looked up from the screen and over the frames. "You asked if the symbols were like our alphabet, and the answer that I so rudely withheld is no, they aren't."

"But Okeus's mark in the middle. Would it mark the person bearing the symbol as belonging to Okeus?"

He pulled the glasses off, lowering his hand to his side while he still cradled my phone in the other. "Belonging? I've never heard of the Algonquians marking themselves to belong to Okeus, but it's not outside the realm of possibility. They often made sacrifices to him."

"But not Ahone?"

"No. From what little we know, the Algonquians believed that Ahone didn't interact much with the human world."

"So if someone put Okeus's symbol on their body, would it protect them *from* Okeus or claim them *for* Okeus?"

He was silent for several seconds, and I could tell he was searching for the answer. "I don't know. I'm guessing claim them. But again, I've never heard of that being done."

"What about Ahone? What is his symbol?" Butterflies threatened to explode from my stomach.

His eyes narrowed as he studied me. "I'm not sure."

"Please, Dr. Preston. This is important."

"Why?"

I closed my eyes and took a deep breath.

His voice softened. "You're running out of time. Okay." He studied the phone for several seconds. "The symbols on this tattoo are very similar to the ones on the doors. Can you tell me why they're there?"

It seemed like a small favor to grant. "Protection."

"Against what?"

I didn't answer.

He sighed and handed me the phone, then placed Daddy's glasses on the desk. "Off hand, I don't know the mark for Ahone. Frankly, I'm surprised I remember Okeus's. But he is much more prominent in the few stories we've gathered. The Native Americans said he was the god who walked among them."

I snorted. "That doesn't surprise me." That had proven true from my experiences as well.

He grabbed my right hand, and I resisted the urge to pull back. He spread my fingers open, revealing the mark on my palm. "What's this?"

"What's it look like?"

His eyebrows rose as he stared up at me. "Are you always this defensive?"

I forced my shoulders to relax. "I didn't used to be."

"But things have been crazy over the last few weeks?"

I gave him a soft smile. He'd thrown my words back at me. "Yeah."

"This town must have been chaos when the village first appeared. I bet it's like when Kennedy was assassinated and 9/11. People here will always remember what they were doing when it happened."

He still held my hand, examining my mark. I didn't answer, wondering why his touch made me feel equally tense and relaxed.

"What were *you* doing when you heard, Ellie?"

"Um . . ." Why did he want to know? Idle curiosity? I doubted it, but I also saw no harm in answering. "I'm a waitress at the New Moon restaurant a couple of blocks away. I was working the lunch shift when the manager of Kitty Hawk Kites came in and told us."

"Roanoke is such an important part of your life here in Manteo that it had to be traffic-stopping news. What was the first thing that came to mind when you heard the Lost Colony was no longer lost?"

"I don't know." I shrugged in frustration.

"Yes you do. What was it?"

"Why do you want to know?"

A devilish grin crossed his face. "Indulge me."

"I thought we'd get more tourists and would have to increase our shifts."

"What else?"

I shot him an irritated look. I couldn't tell him that I'd almost passed out when I heard the news, that it had confirmed the curse.

"Do you know what I thought?"

"What?"

"That this was a once-in-a-lifetime opportunity to get a look at a remarkably well-preserved archaeological site." He lifted my hand again. "These are the symbols for the spiritual and earthly planes. They intersect. Why?"

"I don't know. I didn't design it."

"Who did?"

My eyebrows rose, and I gave him a stubborn look.

"When did you get it? This one isn't henna, is it?"

"No."

"It had to hurt like bollocks. I can honestly say I've never met someone with a tattoo on their palm."

"I'm one of a kind."

He studied me again, with a different kind of interest this time. "I suspect that you are, Ellie Lancaster."

A warm tingle spread throughout my abdomen. *Focus, Ellie.*

His hand still cradled mine. "What caused the scar? It's a perfect diagonal across the symbol, and it looks fresh."

"I thought you had a PhD in history, not an MD."

He laughed. "It doesn't mean I don't recognize a knife slash when I see one." He looked up, his playfulness fading. "Was it a self-defense wound?"

I jerked my hand from his. He was too smart for his own good. "No. It wasn't from self-defense."

"But it was a knife, right?"

"Yes. I slipped with a knife while I was cutting onions."

"When I was in the village today, one thought kept running through my head: *This isn't normal.* Four-hundred-year-old villages do not just appear out of nowhere. The people's skeletons are immaculate. There's food in the pots. Fires that look like they've only just been extinguished. Have you been out there? Have you seen it?"

"No." While it was on my radar, it hadn't occurred to me that it could be a helpful source of information. Until his mention of Manteo's hut earlier.

"Everyone is scratching their heads trying to find a logical explanation for *why* it just appeared this way, but there just isn't one. This sort of thing just doesn't happen. There has to be some other reason for it."

"Supernatural?"

He lifted his eyebrows in question.

I had to turn this conversation around fast. "Dr. Preston, the supernatural isn't real. I would think that you of all people would know that."

He tilted his head with a smug look. "And yet you mark your doors with three-hundred-year-old symbols for protection."

Four hundred, but pointing it out seemed unwise.

His eyes narrowed. "Do *you* know why the village appeared?"

"How would I know?"

He didn't answer.

"Do you have any idea how ridiculous that sounds?"

"Any more ridiculous than a woman who seems completely sane telling me her life depends on finding out Ahone's symbol?"

I pushed away from the desk and moved to the bookcase. I had more shelves to clear off. "We all have our little eccentricities. Especially those of us who live in small towns."

"I told you I don't know the symbol, but what if I told you that I might have a text that does?"

I twisted at the waist a little too eagerly.

"Is your life really in danger, Ellie?"

"Over the mark of a Croatan god?" I asked incredulously, turning back to the bookcase. "You yourself told me that the Croatan have been extinct for centuries."

"So you don't need the symbol?"

My hand froze midreach. Damn him. "I do."

He shifted his weight, still perched on the edge of the desk. "Can it wait two weeks?"

I closed my eyes, resting my arm on the shelf. "No."

"Can it wait two days?"

Could it? Ahone's messenger had told me I had two or three days. At the moment, this seemed like my best hope.

"I own several texts that could possibly help, but I've loaned them to a friend in New York. I can get him to overnight them to me, but I still won't get them for two days. I can even ask him to see if he can find the symbol and scan it."

I turned to look at him. "You would do that? Why?"

"You said it was important. What kind of knight would I be if I let something happen to a damsel in distress?"

I'd been bullshitted before and look where that got me. "You had no qualms about letting me flounder in Chapel Hill. What changed?"

He straightened his posture and moved toward me. David Preston was not only intelligent and good-looking, he was also built. He towered over me and I could see muscles straining against his shirt. "You want the truth?"

I looked up into his hazel eyes. "Always."

"Then how about we make a deal to only tell each other the truth."

I hesitated.

"And if either one of us doesn't feel comfortable sharing the truth, we can plead the fifth."

I shook my head. "Why are you doing this? What's in it for you?"

His mouth turned down in a frown. "Some wanker's done a number on you, huh?"

"Wanker?" He had no idea. "Let's just say I've been burned one time too many."

"So at the risk of scaring you off, here's the truth: I'm intrigued. First this attractive young woman shows up in my office looking for help and I turn her away. Then I go to see the biggest archaeological find in recorded history and not only is she there, but she's at the center of this fascinating riddle that begs to be solved, holding pieces of information no one else knows. Have you heard the story of the Great Horned Serpent?"

This man's conversation shifted from topic to topic enough to give me whiplash. Had I heard of Mishiginebig? He wanted the truth. "Not until a few days ago."

"It has many names and crosses multiple tribes—the Algonquian, the Cherokee, the Cree. I heard three different people mention it today. Only not by name. They said someone saw a giant horned snake."

"So?"

"The last time I heard someone mention a giant snake was on the Discovery Channel."

I was having trouble keeping my breathing even.

"What's with all the animals dropping dead on the island and the surrounding area?" he went on. "It all started around the time when the colony reappeared."

"Why ask me?"

"What about the wild animal that's been attacking dogs and eating their hearts?"

I swallowed the bile in my throat.

"Back on campus, you asked me if I'd ever heard of such a creature. Why did you connect it with an Algonquian legend? No one else did. And you're the only one who has called it a badger."

I stared into his intense eyes, wondering what kind of Pandora's box I had just opened. My heart was thudding so hard, he had to hear it. He believed me, or at least he didn't think I was a stark-raving lunatic. "You think that I'm part of all this, that I'm some riddle to be solved?"

"More like an enigma."

I looked down, unable to hold his gaze.

"I think you know something most people don't, but you only know pieces and you need someone to fill in the blanks. Which is why you came to see me."

I turned to the window.

"I bet you're dying to know what's in Manteo's hut."

He had no idea. "I suspect I couldn't make heads or tails of it, but *you* could. Did you see it?"

"Yes." He crossed his arms over his chest. "I'd like to help you if you'll let me. But I want to know the rest of what you know."

Did he even know what he was asking? I stepped backward to lean against the desk, feeling light-headed. Was it too much to hope that I'd found someone who not only had answers but was eager and willing to help me?

"Does that upset you?"

"Not in the way you think."

"Will you let me help you?"

"How do you know I'm not some crazy woman? Or this isn't some big practical joke? How do you know you can trust me?"

"I just do."

I sat down on the edge of the desk again. This was so completely different from my experience with Collin. Maybe I *could* trust him. "You might have answers to so many of my questions . . . But I have to warn you, I'm not sure it's a good idea to get mixed up with me. It's dangerous."

He grinned. "You *do* know that the best way to get a guy to help you is by challenging him by saying, 'You can't handle it.'"

"That's not what I meant."

"You're just making me more intrigued."

How could I turn down his offer? I needed him. "Okay. But we'll start out slow. I'm still not sure it's a good idea to let you in on what's happening."

His eyes lit up like I'd given him a Christmas present. "I can live with that." He held out his right hand to shake.

I extended my hand and his engulfed mine. I waited for the familiar call of the Manitou that I always felt with Collin, but I felt peace and acceptance instead. How could I feel so comfortable with someone I'd just met?

But as we shook, the significance of the event sobered me. By accepting his help, I was dragging him into danger. Could I let him help and live with the consequences? Could I afford not to?

CHAPTER ELEVEN

Still holding my hand, David turned it over. "So what's with the mark?"

I shook my head and blinked. "You really don't waste any time."

"From what you said, time isn't on our side."

Our side? My side. There was no *our* anymore. Not after Collin. David might be helping me, but I was still on my own when it came to fighting the gods and spirits. I walked across the room, running my hand through my hair. "I'm the one setting the rules for now, and I need a crash course on the Algonquian gods and spirits."

He didn't look too happy, but he didn't argue either. "All of them?"

"As many as you know about."

"I haven't had dinner yet. Are you hungry?"

Again with the lightning-fast change in topic. "Uh . . ." I'd worked through dinner, and the thought of food made my stomach growl. I looked around at the mess I'd made. I could stay here and keep looking for notes that might not even exist, or I could eat with a man who had answers. The decision was obvious. "I'd make something, but Myra only seems to be stocked with breakfast food and snacks. I help her out, but I don't actually live here. How about we walk a couple of blocks down to Poor Richard's Pub and get takeout? Then we can go back to my apartment. I'd rather talk about this in private, anyway."

"What about the mess here?"

I considered leaving it and closing the door, but Myra would ask all kinds of questions I didn't want to answer. "It'll just take a couple of minutes for me to clean up. Do you need to go upstairs to get anything?"

"No, I'll help you and we can get going."

David reshelved the books while I hung the pictures on the wall.

"Do you need to leave a message for anyone?" I asked, heading for the door.

"No one will be interested in seeing my face until tomorrow morning. What about you? Is Myra expecting you to stay?"

"No, I'll just send her a text."

We walked out into the sultry July evening and started the short walk downtown.

"What made you want to study Native American history?" I asked.

"You mean because I'm British?" he asked. "I was born in England, but my mother is American. We used to come visit every few years. We stayed with some relatives in the southern part of North Carolina one summer after I graduated primary school. My uncle took me to a museum about the Cherokee because I had a strong interest in Native Americans, and I was equally enthralled and horrified. I spent the rest of my summer learning everything I could about them." He glanced in my direction. "It's a combination of my love for history and my taste for good mysteries. You can't find much more of a mystery than the disappearance of the early tribes. It's a challenge trying to piece things together."

That explained his interest in helping me. Good to know.

"What about you?" he asked. "Why are you interested in the Algonquian gods and spirits?"

"Honestly?"

"That's our agreement."

"Three weeks ago, I didn't give a rat's ass about them. On the other hand, my father did, and my lack of interest was a great disappointment to him." I snuck a glance at David. "And that's all I'll say about that for now."

"Fair enough. I can wait."

Was I really going to tell him everything? Why did part of me crave the opportunity? Maybe because I was terrified to do this alone, and he was the one person other than Collin who might actually be able to help me.

He cleared his throat. "At the risk of you changing your mind, I think it's only fair that I tell you that my real focus has been on the Cherokee. I may be known as an expert on the Croatan, but considering the lack of available information, that's not saying much."

"But now you've seen Manteo's hut, and you have firsthand knowledge."

"I hardly know what's inside it. I only saw it briefly yesterday and today. They're concentrating on the outside and I'm just a guest."

"How soon until you'll see more?"

"A couple of days? The entire site is being cataloged. It's slow work. What little I saw of the inside resembles a sixteenth-century English home more than an Algonquian dwelling, which isn't that surprising given that Manteo had begun dressing and acting like the English."

The main street of town was bustling with tourists. David pointed to the New Moon when we turned the corner. A giant

"Closed" sign hung in the window, and the place was conspicuously devoid of activity. "Isn't that where you work? Why is it closed?"

I swallowed the lump in my throat. "Two of the employees died."

"Died?" He sounded alarmed. "How?"

I sludged through my exhausted brain, trying to remember what the official police statement said.

"Don't do that," he said, his voice thick with disappointment.

"Do what?"

"Whittle down your answer to some bite-sized nugget you think will appease me. Either tell me the truth or don't answer."

I stopped and looked up at him in amazement. "Where the hell were you three weeks ago?" Perhaps if I'd had his intelligence at my disposal, I wouldn't have gotten myself into this mess.

"I was biding my time in Chapel Hill, waiting to meet you, even if I didn't know it yet." The way he looked at me as if I were some kind of treasured prize made me wonder if he meant that I was more than just a giant puzzle for him.

We stood on the street corner, staring at each other longer than was appropriate while the tourists walked around us. I had an entirely new thought: Where was he *four* weeks ago when I was dating boring Dwight? Before Collin stole my soul?

Someone bumped into my back, and I stumbled into David's chest. He grabbed my elbow with one hand and then wrapped his other arm around my back.

"Are you okay?" he asked, still holding me against him.

"Yes." But I still didn't break free, my heart aching. This man was just another reminder of everything I'd lost, everything I could never have.

"Why do you suddenly look so sad?"

I forced a smile. "Let's file that under information you *might* learn down the road."

His hands dropped slowly and he took a small step backward. "Okay. I can live with that. For now."

It was easy to see that David Preston didn't back down from a challenge, and it was also easy to see he was used to getting his way. It was no wonder. He was a force to be reckoned with. If he didn't get his way the first time, he could probably wear the opposition down with his endless questions.

"How did the employees die?" he asked again.

I turned away from him and walked across the street, waiting until he was next to me. "They were frozen."

He stopped in the middle of the street. "What do you mean *frozen*?"

I grabbed the crook of his arm and pulled him onto the curb and out of the way of an oncoming vehicle. "Frozen. Solid."

"How could that happen?"

"The police are still trying to figure that out."

"That's bollocks, Ellie." He sounded irritated.

I stopped and put a hand on my hip, giving him a glare. "I'm guessing 'bollocks' is similar to 'bullshit,' and I can promise you that it's not, Dr. Preston. The police *are* still looking into it." I glanced back at the entrance to the restaurant, where their bodies had been found. "I pay attention to what they know."

"What do *you* know?" His voice softened. "And call me David, please."

"Well, *David*, I know more than they do, but I don't quite feel comfortable telling you yet, especially not out in the open like this."

"Okay."

I glanced up at him in surprise.

"I pick and choose my battles," he said. "I'll get this answer soon enough."

I shook my head and walked toward the entrance of Poor Richard's Pub.

"*When* did they die?"

I took a breath. "A little over two weeks ago."

"After the colony reappeared."

There was no use denying it. "Yes."

"And your father died too."

I swallowed the lump in my throat. "Yes."

"Was he frozen?"

After Ahone accepted Daddy as my sacrifice, I had been terrified that he would be frozen like the others, but it didn't happen.

"Ellie." David sounded concerned. "I'm sorry. It was insensitive of me to ask."

"I don't have time to be sentimental." I squared my shoulders. "The answer is no, he wasn't."

"Did anyone else die?"

I stopped in front of the menu board and pointed. "Their pulled pork sandwiches are really good here."

His mouth pressed together in a thin line as he looked from me to the board. After we ordered—David insisted on paying—we sat at an empty table while we waited for our food. The dining area was nearly full of tourists, discouraging him from asking me more questions.

"When did you move to the States?" I asked.

"When I started graduate school."

"I'm guessing you like it here since you specialized in Native American studies. There can't be much demand for that specialty in the United Kingdom."

"You're correct on both counts. It's a good thing I prefer the sunshine and the heat to the cold, rainy weather in England."

"What part of England are you from?"

"London."

"You must have had a fascinating childhood."

"I'm sure it wasn't any more fascinating than growing up in Manteo."

The cashier called our number and David grabbed our bag. I led him out the back and we walked along the boardwalk back to my apartment.

"Did anyone else die?" he asked when we were out of earshot of the tourists.

I was hoping he'd leave that one alone. I should have known better. "Yes. One other person."

He waited.

"A man. He was the first. He was found underneath the statue of Queen Elizabeth in the Elizabethan Botanical Gardens. He was frozen too."

"And what was his connection to you?"

My head jerked up. "Why do you assume there's a connection?"

"Because there was with the other three."

Crap. Telling him might be enough to scare him away. But then again, if he was getting involved, he had a right to know. "I went out with him a few times."

David stopped on the boardwalk, tilting his head to the side. "Why was he killed?"

"Why were any of them killed?"

"I'm asking you."

"Why do you think I know?"

His eyes narrowed. "I'm not a fool, Ellie. Please don't treat me like one."

"You are the last person on earth I would ever suspect of being a fool." I meant it.

"So why were they killed?"

"As punishment. For me." As soon as the words were out of my mouth, I wished I could retract them. I started walking again.

David sensed my reluctance and thankfully didn't press the issue, not that I presumed he'd let it drop. He was just biding his time. I was learning that it was something he did a lot.

I led him between the New Moon and the retail shops that faced the sound. My apartment was in the back, the last unit on the third floor. We climbed the exterior wooden steps to my porch. When we reached the landing, I wasn't sure whether to curse or be thankful.

Collin had redone the marks.

David stared at the door, his mouth open in wonder. "You have to tell me what this means."

"I don't have to tell you anything." I said, snippier than I'd intended. I rubbed my forehead with the back of my hand. "I'm sorry. That was uncalled for. I'm tired. I haven't had a decent night's sleep in weeks."

"Why not?"

"My sleep has been riddled with nightmares."

I could see he wanted to ask me about my dreams, but instead he turned his attention back to the door. "You've already told me the symbols are there for protection, and I know you don't want to tell me what you're protecting yourself from. But if you were to indulge me with an explanation of their meaning, it might jar a memory about Ahone."

I shook my head with a smirk. "Well played, David. Fine." I pointed to the corners and started with the explanation Collin had given me. "The stars and the moon in the corners represent nighttime, which is when I need the most protection. The sun is on either side. This asks the sun to provide its far-reaching power to the night." I pointed to the symbols on either side of the sun. "Next are lightning and rain, representing the air. They are placed on either side of the sun. This asks the sun and the night to provide me protection from the wind—" I stopped short of adding *gods*. I stared at the center of the design. Collin had added his sign of the land. The only symbol needed for the protection code to be complete was mine for the sea. I bent down and grabbed the piece of charcoal I kept hidden in a flowerpot. "The symbol in the center represents what's being protected. What's there now is the symbol for land, but it's incomplete." I added my wave symbol to all four sides. "I am the sea."

When I stood back and looked at the door, the charcoal still in my hand, I waited for him to respond in some way.

He was silent for so long I wondered if he'd been enchanted. Finally, he licked his upper lip. "I have so many questions that I don't know where to start. And I'm far from sure you'll answer any of them."

"Go ahead and try."

"Where did you learn all of this?"

"The other Keeper."

His head pivoted toward me. "The other what?"

"Keeper. His name is Collin Dailey, and he's a descendant of Manteo. These symbols have been passed down from generation to generation. He's the one who first put them on my door. His symbol is the land."

"The land and the sea?"

"When his symbol joins with mine, it provides additional protection." I paused. "But I'm not ready to tell you that part yet." I was surprised I'd told him the Keeper part.

138

"How can you be sure he's a real descendent of Manteo? There are no recorded relatives. He could be duping you."

I put the charcoal back into the pot and pulled my keys out of my purse. "Wondering whether Collin is a real Manteo descendant is the least of my worries. But trust me that he is. I have all the proof I need." I put the key in the lock and pushed open the door.

"And what's that?"

I held my palm open. "Collin has an identical mark on his hand."

"So what?" David scoffed, showing his first sign of cynicism. "He could have had it tattooed."

"This isn't a tattoo, David."

"Then what is it?"

"When I met Collin at the New Moon, he didn't have this mark on his palm. But when he left a few minutes later, we both had one."

"Do you realize what you're saying?" he asked.

I stepped inside my apartment and turned to face him. He was one step away from entering my world. "David, this is your chance to get the hell away from all of this. You suggested that the appearance of the colony was a supernatural occurrence, and I'm here to tell you that you're right. The mark on my palm is too. It just showed up on my hand the day before the colony appeared."

He remained expressionless.

"If you walk through this door, I will tell you everything." I wasn't sure when I'd decided that, but he needed to make an informed decision about whether to plunge into this madness or turn back. And if he decided to be a participant, the only way he could help me was if he knew everything.

He looked at the door, then back at me.

"I know it sounds crazy. I didn't believe it either, and I wasted a full day pretending it wasn't real. But the god's honest truth is that I really need the information you have. I didn't intend to tell you what was really happening, I only wanted to find out what you knew. But tonight I realized you're too curious to let it go at that."

He took a step forward, but I blocked his path.

"You asked about how I was connected to the deaths, and I told you that they were a punishment. I had to make a choice and each day I didn't choose, someone I knew was killed. Right now, they're leaving the people I care about alone, but I can't be sure that will last. At some point, the people who are close to me may be in danger again, and if you become part of this, I suspect you will be included in that. *Especially* you. You have information that can help me understand them, and that might make them feel threatened."

"I'm afraid to ask who is doing the threatening," he finally said.

"Good." I moved closer to him. "You *should* be afraid. If you do this, you might be afraid every day for the rest of your life. Because I'm fairly certain that once you become involved, you're in it until the end, whatever that might be."

He looked shell-shocked.

"Turn around while you can, David. Just answer my questions, study Manteo's hut, and go back to Chapel Hill. Keep yourself safe."

He took a step backward. Disappointment threatened to suffocate me, but I told myself it was for the best. I was asking him to commit to something serious without knowing all the facts. Any sane person would walk away after what I'd said.

I turned around and headed for the kitchen, in desperate need of a glass of wine. Opening the refrigerator, I pulled out my last bottle and closed the door. When I did, David was standing on the other side, a determined look on his face. "I told you I don't back down from a challenge."

And just like that, I was no longer alone.

∿ CHAPTER TWELVE ∿

I put the wine bottle on the counter and reached for a couple of wine glasses. "Would you like some? It's a fine vintage stock. I'm pretty sure it was on the shelf of the Piggly Wiggly for at least two weeks."

The corners of his mouth lifted, and he chuckled. "Yeah. I think I might need it."

Smart man.

He set the bag of food on my counter and sat on one of the bar stools. Collin had been sitting in that exact chair when I told him that I'd pawned my relic, a pewter cup. He'd stormed out, which was understandable. If our roles had been reversed, I probably would have stormed out too. Would David leave after I told him my story?

I uncorked the bottle, poured two glasses of white wine, and sat next to him. "I'm not sure where to start. How much can you handle? Should I tell you everything at once or ease you into it?"

He pulled our food out of the take-out bag and placed my sandwich in front of me. "You said you were running out of time. Tell me all of it at once."

"Do you mind if I eat first? Once I get into this conversation, I'm liable to lose my appetite, and I haven't eaten since this morning."

142

"Sure."

We ate in awkward silence, which twisted my stomach into a knot. Maybe this hadn't been such a good idea after all.

"Do you have any siblings?" David asked, trying to take away the strain of silence.

Some of the tension eased from my shoulders. "No. I'm an only child."

"Stepsiblings?"

"What? Oh, no. Daddy was Myra's first husband. And they were both in their forties, so they skipped the whole second family thing." I lifted my wine glass to my lips. I needed liquid courage to go through with this. "Do you have siblings?"

"An older brother. He's still in England with my parents."

"Do you see them very often?"

"Usually once a year. Around Christmas."

I pushed the rest of my food away and then wiped my hands on my napkin and stood.

His brow wrinkled. "Is what you have to tell me really as bad as you're making it out to be?"

"Worse." I took another gulp of wine and moved to the sofa. *Here goes nothing.* "Once I start this, I need you to listen, and then you can ask questions when I'm done. Okay? Because it's going to sound insane."

He got up and sat in the chair next to the sofa, his expression solemn. "Okay."

I took a deep breath. "It all started over four hundred years ago, when the colony disappeared due to . . . supernatural reasons. The colonists faced hardships, partially because of the Indian tribes around them. The governor of Virginia left his daughter and son-in-law and their newborn daughter behind when he returned to England for supplies and help."

"Anyone who studied the Croatan knows that, Ellie." Irritation crept into his voice. "But what most people ignore is that they had good reason to be hostile, especially after Sir Ralph Lane's heavy-handedness the year before."

I couldn't hide my tentative smile. For all his good looks and charm, he really was a history geek at heart. And the fact that he'd chosen his profession because of his outrage over the treatment of the Cherokee only warmed my heart to him more.

A sheepish grin spread across his face. "Sorry, I couldn't help myself. The assertion that the English were helpless victims infuriates me."

"That's okay." I shifted on the sofa, tucking my feet underneath me. "Deserved or not, Ananias was terrified for his family. Manteo came up with a plan that would not only help the colonists, but also his own people. As I'm sure you know, they believed they got their strength for battles from the gods. So Manteo and Ananias performed a ceremony to lock the gods and spirits in Popogusso."

His eyes widened. "*Hell?*"

I nodded. "Yes, but it went horribly wrong. Manteo's gods were bound instead."

"They're roughly the same deities, Ellie."

I narrowed my eyes. "I know. I'm telling you what I've been told. And you're interrupting."

He sank back into his chair. "Sorry."

"That's okay." I paused. "Their ceremony was successful, but the colony also disappeared because of the curse. Manteo knew the gods couldn't be contained forever, and one day they would escape. Manteo and Ananias were each charged with the job of Curse Keeper. The curse could only be maintained if the two Keepers were kept away from each other. They were forced to stay close to the island but away from each other. Once the curse broke, the Curse Keepers had until the morning of the seventh day to reseal the gate to Popogusso. Their oldest child would take the position when he or she turned eighteen. Obviously, it's been passed down for generations. Like I said, Collin is a descendant of Manteo, and I'm a descendant of Ananias Dare. We also have titles. Collin is son of the land and I am daughter of the sea."

"Do you realize how impossible that is?"

"You mean the logistics of Ananias finding a new wife?"

He shook his head as he set his wine glass on the coffee table and began to pace. "You realize this is all completely preposterous?"

My heart sank. "Yes, why do you think I didn't want to tell you?"

He stopped behind the sofa, looking down at me. "And you actually believe all of this?"

"Not at first. My father taught me about the curse before Momma's death, but after she died, I forgot everything. Daddy tried to reteach me everything, but I wouldn't listen." A new thought occurred to me. This was supposed to be a secret. The Keepers were charged with keeping the information to themselves at the risk of great punishment. For years, I'd been convinced that I was responsible for my mother's death because I had told Claire about the curse a few days earlier. Eventually, I'd come to regard it as a horrible coincidence, but now I had to wonder. What if I *had* been responsible for her death, as absurd as it seemed? I shoved down the avalanche of guilt that accompanied the thought and moved to another: Would there be repercussions for telling Drew and now David? Even though the curse had already been broken?

But I couldn't ignore that this man had been placed in my path exactly when I needed him, and he had the resources to help me save humanity. Did I really have a choice?

David sat down in the chair again, leaning back and looking at the wall. "Sorry. Go on."

"Collin showed up at the New Moon one day. I'd never seen him before, but I felt like I was suffocating when I was near him, which was also part of the curse. Probably designed to help keep us apart. He grabbed my hand before he left, and the marks showed up. Even before I finally acknowledged that the curse was broken, I knew it. I *felt* it happen. And when the colony reappeared the next day, I started to wish I'd paid more attention to Daddy's stories. I thought Collin was some nutcase when he insisted I needed to help him close the gate." I shook my head in disgust. "But he was using me all along. He wanted to permanently *open* the gate to Popogusso."

His face paled. "He wanted to *open* the gate?" I nodded and finished my glass, watching him as I drank. But he just stared at me, not even blinking.

"I thought we were closing and sealing the gate. And we did . . . after the gate opened and all the spirits and gods that had been locked away escaped. The spirits have been responsible for all the dead birds and animals that have stumped scientists around here. They're weak after being locked away for hundreds of years, and they're feeding off the animals' Manitou to regain their strength." I paused. "Do you know what the Manitou is?" I presumed he did with his knowledge of the Algonquian.

He waved in dismissal. "Yes. Go on."

"They especially want mine because I have a pure soul, which has earned me a title Collin doesn't have: witness to creation. Manitou are recycled, but mine wasn't, which means I was present at creation. I'm rare, and it makes my Manitou stronger. I had no way of knowing, and Collin claims he didn't know either until Wapi, the wind god of the north, tried to steal mine. Once Collin realized I was at risk, he painted the henna tattoo on my back, using Okeus's symbol. My tattoo matches the symbol the Manteo line gets inked on their chest on their eighteenth birthday."

David shifted in his seat, and I could tell he was dying to ask me questions, but he pressed his lips together and waited.

"Collin painted an identical mark on my back. But Okeus wanted me to fully pledge myself to him. When I refused, he killed someone I knew as a sacrifice each day for three days." I looked away, my voice breaking. "I never would have accepted Okeus, not that I even could . . . The curse is based on duality, and Ahone claimed me. After Daddy sacrificed himself to reseal the gate, Ahone said I had permission to put his mark on my body as protection, only he neglected to show me what it is. Which is why I'm so desperate to find it. Once my henna tattoo is gone, I'm completely vulnerable." I gave him a hesitant smile. "Okay, you can ask questions now."

"Collin gave you the henna tattoo, but the mark on your hand just appeared?"

"Yes, it was our sign that the curse was broken, and the marks are also the source of our power to close the gate. Or open it, as the case may be."

"And how did you get the diagonal slash mark on your palm."

"Collin."

David tensed, and when he spoke again, it was in a lower voice. "He attacked you?"

I shook my head, sadness washing over me. "No. He needed our blood for the ceremony. I had no idea how the ceremony was performed, and he didn't warn me. I suspect he was a little over-zealous." I paused. "We pressed our symbols together to open and close the gate. We have more power when we are joined than we do separately." I tried not to think about the *other* ways we had joined together.

David was silent for a moment. "The wind gods have no recorded names."

I released a soft laugh. He would pick up on that. "Then you'll be the first to record them. The wind god of the north is Wapi."

I took a gulp of my wine and then poured myself more. I sank back into the cushions of the sofa and closed my eyes. "Other than Collin, Myra, and my best friend Claire and her fiancé Drew, you're probably the only other living person who knows about this. And Myra doesn't know everything. I don't like to worry her."

He studied his hands for several seconds, then looked up at me. "That animal that eats dog hearts? What is it?"

"He's a spirit of some kind. He hasn't told me his name."

"He talks to you?"

"He comes to me in my dreams. Just like Big Nasty."

"Big Nasty?"

"The giant snake with horns. Mishiginebig. But that's too big a mouthful."

His eyes narrowed with distrust. "So there really is a giant horned snake loose on Roanoke Island?"

"Why are you looking at me like that?" I angrily swung my feet to the floor. "You were the one who was intrigued that there were three reports about a giant snake. *You* were the one who was convinced it was *something*."

"I know." His voice rose with frustration. "But suspecting something and hearing it confirmed are two entirely different things." He tried to sound neutral, but a hint of cynicism laced his words. Not that I blamed him. He was an educated man. He had a doctorate degree in this subject. Of course he was skeptical.

But I was toast unless he agreed to tell me what he knew anyway. "Well, thank you for your truthfulness, I guess."

"We promised to be truthful with one another." His tone was accusatory.

"I've been more truthful with you than I have been with anyone about the curse."

"You have to admit that this is a lot to take in."

How could I make him believe me? "I can prove it to you."

His eyebrows lowered over his eyes. "You can prove that the gods were locked up in Popogusso, and you're a Curse Keeper?"

I lifted a shoulder in a half shrug. "I don't know about that, but I can introduce you to a god or spirit."

"How?"

"Spend the night here and you'll see a deity before morning."

A strange expression spread across his face. "Is that some kind of euphemism? Has this all been a ploy to get me into bed?"

I stood up, shuddering. "*What?* Good God, no!"

His eyes widened. "Are you suggesting that the thought of sleeping with me is repugnant?"

Putting my hand on my hip, I shook my head in disbelief. "Which is it, David? Do you want me to *want* to sleep with you or not?"

"Neither!"

"That doesn't make sense!"

"I know." He slumped into the chair, covering his eyes with his hand. It seemed like all the fight had bled out of him.

I wasn't being fair. My father had raised me with the story of the curse, and I still hadn't believed it until the reappearance of the colony. Wouldn't I think less of Dr. David Preston if he took my words at face value without a hint of cynicism?

I sat back down on the sofa, closer to him. "Look, I don't blame you for being dubious. I didn't believe it myself at first. But almost every night at around three or four in the morning, I get a visit from some type of spirit or god. Sleep on my sofa tonight and you can see it for yourself."

His hand dropped, and he lowered his gaze to mine. "You're kidding, right?"

"I wish I was."

A war of emotions played across his face before resignation set in. "Okay." He stood and stared down at me with equal parts fear and irritation. "But first, I'm going to the inn to get a few things for the night." He headed to the door and stopped to examine the markings when he opened it.

I glanced past him and saw that the sun had set. The henna tattoo was still working, albeit barely. The spirits wouldn't attack me while we were waiting for Okeus to spring his special surprise, but what if they saw David as a threat? What if they tried to kill him? "I think I'd better go with you."

He grimaced. "Uh . . . that's not necessary."

He probably wanted to get as far away from me as possible. I was sure he wouldn't be pleased by the explanation if I told him I was coming along to offer what little protection I could. "I have to go back anyway to get my laundry."

"Okay . . ."

Both of us remained silent as we walked to the bed and breakfast. When we met at the side entrance five minutes later, he seemed distant, slinging his bag over his shoulder and opening the door so I could get through with my laundry basket on my hip. He followed me to my car and opened the back door as I put the basket in the back. He stared out the window on the short drive to my parking lot, doing his best to ignore me.

But when we got to my front porch, I shrieked and dropped my basket, some of my clothes flying out of it and onto the landing.

A mauled cat lay at my front door, its guts spilling out of its body. Blood was smeared all over the floor and splattered on my door.

My heart racing, I stepped backward and bumped into David's chest. His hands grabbed my arms to steady me, his fingers digging deeper than necessary as he too caught sight of the giant badger's calling card.

Turning away, I swallowed my rising bile.

David kept his hands on my arms. "*What did that?*" he asked.

"You and I both know." I forced myself to glance back at it. The animal didn't look familiar, not that I was a cat person. I supposed the badger hadn't had much time to find its next victim. But this also meant it knew something about my comings and goings.

It was watching me.

⌁ CHAPTER THIRTEEN ⌁

"Bloody hell." David still gripped my arms.

Trying to catch my breath and control my panic, I broke his hold and bent to pick up my fallen laundry. Some of it had landed in the blood, and I tossed it to the side.

"What *did* this, Ellie?" he repeated.

"You *know.*" Everything was suddenly too overwhelming. "I don't know how to make it stop." I shoved the basket to the side and sat down on the steps, turning my back to the mess in front of my door. I couldn't face this.

He took another look at the cat and then sat down beside me. "Why do you think you're responsible for the behavior of a wild animal?"

"Because I set it loose." I leaned my head against the post. "Not on purpose, but I was part of it all the same. It's like I told you, I thought we were closing the gate."

"You see these monsters in your dreams?"

"Yeah," I took a deep breath. "That badger. Mishiginebig. A couple of others. I used to just see blobs, which is how the messengers of Okeus and Ahone looked right after the curse was broken. But as they got stronger, they began to look like things. I'm guessing their previous images."

"Why does it eat the hearts?"

I squeezed my eyes shut. "The badger told me that their Manitou is purest in their heart."

David rested his forearms on his thighs. "*Bloody* hell."

I sighed. "It's taunting me. My neighbor's dog . . . my daddy loved that dog. And now this cat."

"Why would it taunt you?"

"I don't know." I sighed. "The animals come to my dreams every night too, begging me to save them from the spirits. And when I'm in the ocean, I can feel the creatures of the water crying out to me."

"What do you mean you *feel* them?"

I rested my elbow on my leg and my cheek in my palm. "It's hard to describe . . . I can sense them."

"Who?"

"The living things. Fish. Insects." I turned to look at him. "Plants, amoeba." I paused. "I can *feel* their Manitou."

"As a collective?"

I shook my head. "No. Individually."

"*Omniscience?* How can that be?"

I hadn't considered it that way. "I don't know, but it's the only good part of the curse. Collin told me that Manitou are recycled from being to being. But when the spirits and gods consume a creature's Manitou, it's not recycled and the being is doomed to Popogusso." I leaned over my knees. "I told you that Okeus's mark protects my Manitou from the supernatural beings that have been released, but they also tell me they've been forbidden to take it. Okeus says he's waiting for me to be 'ready.' I suspect that means he's waiting for me to be unmarked." I decided to keep to myself for the moment the fact that Okeus had vowed to make me suffer for four centuries.

"And then what?"

"I think he plans to take me."

He clasped his hands and whispered, "Then you really are running out of time."

"But I'm not entirely defenseless." I extended my hand, showing him the mark. "I can send the creatures away to protect myself, but I can't lock them away. I need Collin's help to do that."

"So where is this mysterious Collin?"

I shook my head with a grimace. "Doing what Collin does best." I stood and took a deep breath before I turned around to face the mess in front of my door.

David stood. "And that is?"

"Looking out for Collin."

That cat was lying on the mat. I stood in front of it, my stomach reeling as I leaned over and unlocked the door.

"Should we call Animal Control to clean this up?"

"In a normal world, yes. But one in which the Manteo police officers are watching every move I make? If I call, this will only make them more suspicious of me."

"Don't tell me that you want to clean this up yourself . . ."

I stepped over the cat and kicked off my shoes at the entrance so I wouldn't track blood. "The Native Americans you've spent years studying dealt with worse than this."

"Well . . . true . . ." but he didn't sound convinced.

I grabbed several plastic trash bags and a kitchen spatula, along with a pair of cleaning gloves Myra had left under my kitchen sink one time as a "subtle" hint. I handed the bags to David, who was still standing on the porch, staring at the cat with a gaping mouth.

"You're really going to touch it?"

I offered him a sweet smile. "Only if you won't." His eyes widened. "Okay, then hold the bag open."

He obeyed, watching me as I tossed the spatula to the floor and pulled on the kitchen gloves. I was suddenly thankful I hadn't eaten much for dinner.

Gagging, I squatted and folded the mat, turning my head in revulsion. David was jolted out of his shock, and he lowered the bag close to the floor so I wouldn't have to lift the mat very high to get it inside.

He quickly cinched the top closed and held it out from his body. "What in the bloody hell do we do with this now?"

"There's a Dumpster downstairs. That's where I tossed all the dead birds the spirits left on my porch." I glanced up at his pale face. "Don't ask."

David tromped down the wooden staircase, and I would have worried that he wasn't going to come back if he hadn't dumped his messenger bag on the steps first.

I went back inside and grabbed a pitcher of water, using it to wash as much blood off the wood slats as possible.

When David came back, he stood at the top of the stairs, looking apologetic. "I'm sorry I didn't help more."

"It's hard to take it in the first time you see it. I'll cut you some slack."

"How many times have you seen something like this?"

"Twice in person. Twice in my dreams." I grabbed the charcoal out of the planter. I'd inadvertently washed some of the marks off the bottom of the door, so I needed to replace them before we went inside. I'd never replaced only one section before, and for all I knew, it couldn't be done that way. I'd just have to do all of it over again to make sure.

I started on the bottom corners, placing the symbols for night, and then moved back up to the top, scratching over the still fresh symbols Collin had placed only hours earlier.

David stood behind me, watching in silence, and I was reminded of the night Collin and I had marked this door together. The night before his betrayal. Tears burned behind my eyes, but I blinked them away. It always swung back to Collin.

I moved on to the sun and the other signs, forcing myself to concentrate and mentally ask the forces to protect me. When I reached Collin's symbol, I placed my own beside it, hoping it would be enough.

"They're just markings," David murmured behind me. "But there's a certain amount of reverence in the way you place them."

"I felt that way when I watched Collin place them for the first time," I said. "But then again, he was placing them to protect me." I groaned. How could I be so stupid? "What are your initials?"

"What?"

"You don't have a symbol, so what are your initials?"

"Oh . . . DMP."

I scratched his initials below mine, concentrating on including David in the protection spell.

"And this will work?"

I released a heavy breath. "It will protect us when we're on the inside. Outside we're fair game."

"Maybe we should head inside then."

I opened the door and David glanced down at the spatula lying by the front door.

For the first time since I'd started my tale, a smile cracked his lips. "Were you planning on flipping it over?"

I laughed. "Shut up. At least I cleaned it up. You just watched."

He shook his head with a derisive grin. "Why do I have a feeling you'll never let me live that down?"

"Probably because I won't." I picked up the spatula and tossed it into the sink after we walked back into the apartment. "I'm going to go clean up. I feel disgusting."

He set his bag on the coffee table. "Don't worry about me. I have some unfinished work to tend to from before I left Chapel Hill."

I held onto the doorknob of my bedroom door. "You're welcome to help yourself to anything in the kitchen, although I have to warn you that there isn't much there."

"Thanks." He sat on the sofa and pulled out his laptop.

I struggled with the strong desire for a shower versus the need to make my tattoo last as long as possible. In the end, I decided I couldn't wait any longer to shower because I needed to wash my hair. I put on a pair of shorts and a tank top and wandered out to the living room to find David focused on his laptop.

"You're still here," I said.

He looked up at me and lowered his reading glasses.

It struck me again: David Preston was a very good-looking man. I wondered how all those college girls ever took notes in his class during his lectures.

"You think I would miss the chance to meet an Algonquian god?" There was a teasing lilt to his voice, but his eyes were serious.

I picked up the wine glasses and took them into the kitchen. Thank God I'd cleaned the apartment up a few days ago during one of my bouts of insomnia.

"I e-mailed my friend, and he's agreed to FedEx the books to your mother's bed and breakfast."

"Oh." I stopped wiping the counter. "You remembered."

"Honestly, I almost forgot with all the excitement. He's also promised to thumb through some passages to see if he can find the symbol before he sends them off."

"Thank you."

He shrugged. "I figured you were pressed for time. One day could make all the difference."

"So you believe me now?"

His eyes locked with mine. "I'm getting there."

I offered him a tight smile.

"I've been searching for anything about a badger in the Algonquian legends."

I shook my head. "I've searched every which way on the Internet, and there was nothing."

He grinned. "I'm a professor. I have access to papers online that you wouldn't have been able to find."

My eyes widened. "Really?"

He put his glasses back on his nose. "Do you have any coffee? I'd like to stay up awhile and spend more time on this."

I finished cleaning the kitchen as the coffee brewed. I poured us both a mug and took them out to the living room, setting David's on the coffee table.

"Is that it?" he asked, looking at my shoulder blade.

My hair had tumbled over my shoulder, exposing my back. "My henna tattoo? What's left of it."

"Can I get a closer look?"

"Sure." I sat on the sofa next to him. I had stripped down to my bra when Collin applied the tattoo, but I couldn't bring myself to do that with David. Instead, I turned away from him and pulled down my tank top strap, exposing my back.

"Have you checked this recently? Okeus's mark is barely visible."

My shoulders stiffened. "What about the rest?"

"It's just as faded." He studied my back in silence. "Do you know why it was designed the way it was?"

"No. It's identical to Collin's as best as I can tell, except mine is henna. Like I told you, Collin said all the Keepers in his line get this tattoo on their eighteenth birthday, so I think it's been handed down for years. Maybe centuries."

"Why is yours henna?"

"Collin knew I'd never agree to a permanent one. After Wapi attacked me, he was worried the other spirits would realize I was a pure soul, and I'd be on their most-wanted list. He marked me that night after I got off work."

"So you need to duplicate this?"

"I think so . . . except for Okeus's mark, of course."

He pulled the strap back onto my shoulder. "Would you e-mail me the photo you showed me? I'd like to send it to one of my friends and see if he can give me an opinion."

"Sure." I sank back into the cushions next to him. "Do you want to take a shower or change clothes? You're welcome to use my bathroom."

He picked up his coffee mug and took a sip. "You don't mind?"

"Of course not. I hope the shampoo isn't too girly for you."

He laughed. "I have some in my bag. I'll just finish this up first."

I propped my feet on the coffee table and listened to the clicking of laptop keys—an oddly relaxing sound. My eyelids grew heavy, and before I knew it, I fell asleep.

The animals were back, like always, calling out to me for help, but tonight was different. The air was full of static, making the hair on my arms stand up. In the distance I heard the faint sound of my name, "daughter of the sea, witness to creation," but instead of the usual pleading, it was slurred and threatening.

My heart sped up as I walked through a marshy field. The faint odor of salt stung my nose and the water came up to my thighs, making the folds of the dress I was wearing cling to my legs.

"Daughter of the sea and witness to creation," a different voice called out. "You have abandoned us."

I pushed through the last section of reeds—to find the gate to Popogusso.

I tried to take a step back and hit a wall that hadn't been there before.

Chip was standing behind the black metal gate, his guts spilling out of his abdomen. The cat I'd found on my porch was next to him, along with half a dozen other animals in varying states of decay.

The stench of rot and dank blood filled the air, and my stomach roiled in protest.

Chip lowered his face. "I was sacrificed for you, witness to creation. Will you save the others?"

My tongue felt thick. "I'm trying."

His eyes narrowed and glowed yellow. "You must find a way. Tonight he is moving on to bigger prey."

The horrified screams of a woman filtered through the darkness.

My chest burned with fear. "*No!*"

"You must save them . . ." Chip's voice trailed off as the light behind the gate faded.

The screams still echoed in my ears.

⌁ Chapter Fourteen ⌁

Something touched my shoulder and I jumped, shrieking in fright. David's anxious face was bent over mine when my eyes flew open.

"Ellie, are you all right?"

I sucked in deep breaths to control my panic. "We have to stop it." I tried to get up, but he grabbed my arm and held me down.

"You're okay. It was only a dream."

The woman's screams still haunted me, and I shook my head as a new fear was added to the long-standing ones. "No. No, it wasn't. I need my phone."

David released me as I jumped up and grabbed my cell phone from my purse on the kitchen counter. I fumbled for Claire's number with shaky fingers.

David moved next to me. "Ellie, who are you calling? It's two o'clock in the morning."

I ignored him.

Claire answered on the fourth ring, sounding panicked. *"Ellie? What's wrong?"*

I collapsed onto the bar stool. "Thank God. You're okay."

"What happened?"

"Do *not* go outside. Promise me you won't go outside for any reason at all tonight. *Do you understand?*" I knew I was coming across as angry, but I had to get through to her.

"Okay, I won't. But what's going on? You're scaring me."

"That thing that's ripping out animals' hearts is going to have a human victim tonight." My voice shook. "I had to check on you."

David gasped beside me, his eyes widening.

"Oh, God," Claire whispered. "What can I do?"

"Just stay inside. *Please.* I have to go. I need to check on Myra. I called you first because I figured you were more likely to be out at this hour."

"I'm okay, Ellie. I promise I won't go outside until daybreak."

"Not until you see the entire sun."

"Okay, I promise."

I hung up and pulled up Myra's number next.

David leaned in toward me. "How do you know for sure that it's going to kill someone tonight?"

"My neighbor's dog told me." I knew it sounded absurd, but worrying about whether Dr. David Preston believed me had gone down a few notches on my priority list.

"Ellie, are you okay?" Myra's anxious voice filled my ear. "Oh, thank God you're okay."

"Ellie. What's going on?"

"Promise me you won't leave until the sun comes up . . . and you can't let anyone else leave either."

"What's going on, Ellie?"

I explained the situation, trying to keep the panic out of my voice.

"Oh, dear God." Myra's voice was faint. "I don't want you to be alone. Either come over here, or I'll come over there."

"No, Myra. Don't leave the inn. *Promise me you won't go outside!*"

"Okay, I won't. I'm just scared for you."

I looked up at David, wondering if I should tell her that he was with me. "I'm not alone," I finally said. I bit my lip, searching his face for permission.

He nodded, his eyes wide.

"I'm with Dr. Preston."

She hesitated. "Where are you?"

"I'm in my apartment. I walked with Dr. Preston to Poor Richard's for dinner, and then we came to my apartment so he could help me with some research on the curse."

"He knows about it?"

"I told him."

"And he *believes* you?"

I sighed. "He's getting there."

"Why didn't he come back here for the night?" I was a grown woman, and Myra was still trying to keep track of the guys I took home.

"We were doing research, and I fell asleep on the sofa. I'm going to make him stay the night because I don't want him to go out in the dark with that thing on the loose."

"Okay," she relented. "I just worry about you, Ellie."

"I know, Myra. And I worry about you. I'll see you in the morning."

I hung up the phone and rested my head on the counter, overcome with exhaustion.

"What happened?" David said.

Lifting my head, I searched his face. "I told you that I have dreams every night. The animals beg me to save them. Then I usually get a visit from a monster. Tonight I got Chip and the cat."

David slowly sat on the stool beside me. "I'm going to ask you a question that's not meant as an insult. It's just . . . a fact-gathering type of thing." He paused. "What type of medication are you currently taking?"

I shook my head with a snort. "I wish it were that simple."

He still looked unconvinced, not that I blamed him. I wasn't surprised he'd fallen back into disbelief. For a while, I'd wobbled back and forth looking for a logical explanation too. If he was like me, it was going to take a visit from a god or spirit to settle him firmly in the believer category.

"Did you find out anything about the badger?"

"No, not really."

"Which is it? No or not really?"

His face scrunched in irritation. "Bloody Christ, Ellie. I'm sleeping on your sofa with you snoring next to me, waiting for some unseen boogeyman to show up. Then I'm awoken by you moaning and crying in your sleep. Why don't you give me a chance to come to my senses? You scared me half to death!"

"I don't snore!"

He tilted his head to the left and lifted his eyebrows. "Out of everything I just said, *that's* what you chose to fixate on?"

I scowled. "Well, I don't." I got off the stool and began to pace. "I'm sorry. But I have to stop that thing before it does any more damage."

David leaned his elbow on the counter and shook his head. "You keep saying that, but I'm still not convinced it's up to you."

I stopped and swung around to face him. "I helped set it loose. *I'm* a Curse Keeper, and it's my job to make this thing go away. Ideally, I'd do it with Collin, but Collin won't help. He thinks we should let these things run amok until they settle down. But it's hard enough to watch animals die. How can I stand back and watch it kill people?"

"You're not getting my point, Ellie. There are *professionals* who deal with this sort of thing."

"You saw that cat on my porch. Do you really think that was done by a normal animal?" I pointed to the front door. "It was left for me."

"Maybe it wasn't for you. Maybe it just happened to be on your porch."

"And the neighbor's dog just *happened* to be next to my house. What a coincidence." Leaning my head back, I groaned. "This is not an animal. This is a spirit. And it won't stop until I stop it."

"For argument's sake, let's say you're right. How do you stop it?"

I lifted my chin. "That's where *you* come in."

He sighed and moved to the sofa. "If you're hinging everything on my knowledge, then you're going to be sorely disappointed." He grabbed his laptop off the coffee table. "When I did a search for an animal that eats hearts, I only found a short reference—just a couple of lines."

"And?"

"It's a sort of mythical creature." He pulled up the document. "It's said to resemble a badger more than anything else. It has claws like a predatory cat, teeth like a wolf, and night vision like a bat."

I sat down next to him, lifting my feet onto the sofa and crossing my legs. "Bats use sonar to see, not their actual sight."

"Don't be so literal. This was written well over three hundred years ago. You get the point."

"So it's like some hybrid mix."

"It's not uncommon for these mythical creatures."

"Does it say how to kill it or what it's called?"

"Unfortunately, there's nothing about how to kill it, but it does give it a name. Ukinim."

"A name is something. It's better than nothing."

The wind picked up outside, the gusts rattling the door and windows.

David cast a hesitant look toward the door. "I didn't think there was a storm in the forecast for tonight."

My shoulders tensed and I uncrossed my legs, my feet touching the floor. "I'm sure there wasn't."

Despite the fact that I had almost nightly visits, I was rarely awake when they showed up. They usually woke me up by pounding on the door. And despite the fact that they visited so often, I still dreaded every encounter. Especially this one. What if the redrawn symbols on the door weren't strong enough to protect us?

"Are you suggesting what I think you are?"

I didn't look at him, trying to psych myself up for the encounter. "We'll know soon enough."

He closed his laptop and set it back on the table. "What happens when they show up?"

"They usually wake me up by banging on my door and shouting 'Curse Keeper.' I open the door to see what they want—"

"Wait. Why in bloody hell would you open the door?"

"The symbols protect the threshold. They can't get in. If I didn't open the door, they would keep yelling. I worry that they'd wake up my neighbors and kill them."

His lips pressed together in a tight line.

Several seconds later, the door shook with pounding and my palm burned. "Curse Keeper!"

I stood and took a deep breath, then looked down at David. "Showtime."

His pale face turned toward the door, his knuckles white from gripping the arm of the sofa.

Grabbing hold of the doorknob, I pulled the door open and prepared for the usual blast of wind.

It was frigidly cold. Wapi.

This was good. David was sure to believe me now.

Wapi was perched on the porch railing. I still wasn't used to seeing him in his physical form. His white hair blew around his bird body in the wind. I stood aside so that David could get a good look.

He gasped behind me. "Bloody fucking hell."

"What do you want this time, Wapi?"

"Who are you to speak to a god in such a disrespectful way?"

"I am Curse Keeper, daughter of the sea, and witness to creation. Enjoy your time on the earthly plane because I'm sending your ass back to Popogusso as soon as I can."

"I am here with a warning from Okeus." Wapi's beady eyes narrowed, and he looked over my shoulder at David. "You are not alone."

"So what's new? You always bring a warning." I prayed that the door protections would work, but it would be best to try and distract him from David. If that were even possible.

"You have a threat that is greater than Okeus at the moment."

I had no idea how that could even be possible.

"Okeus has made it clear that you are his and his alone, but Ukinim refuses to listen."

I swallowed my panic. That was the name David had found. "Who's Ukinim?"

"He left a present on your doorstep this evening."

"He's the spirit that's been killing the dogs?"

"Yes." A wicked smile lit up Wapi's eyes. "I have something you want. Information."

"There's no way you'd just give me information. Everything you and Okeus offer comes at a price. I don't have anything you could want besides my Manitou, and I know how scared you all are of Okeus."

167

Wapi's wings fluttered, then settled close to his body. "Don't be so sure about that."

A sliver of fear ran down my back. "Which part?"

"That all of us are frightened of Okeus. I was created eons before him."

"And yet he's still got you running scared."

Wapi jumped backward off the railing, flapping his wings so that he hovered in front of the porch. "You go too far, Curse Keeper. I answer to no one."

"Do I? I'm not so sure. Why are you taking orders from him when you are clearly smarter and more powerful?"

He laughed again, and it sounded like a screeching sound. "Are you suggesting I defy Okeus and take your Manitou?"

Perhaps baiting him hadn't been a good idea after all. "No, I'm suggesting you and your other wind god friends join forces and overthrow him. You did it with Ahone."

"Ahone was different."

"Are you so sure about that? He tricked you into creating Okeus. Then Ahone lent his power to Manteo to create the curse that locked you away for hundreds of years."

Wapi landed on the porch, mere feet in front of me. His head came up to my mid-thigh.

"Ellie . . ." David warned, standing next to the sofa.

I flexed my right hand, ready to blast the wind god away if necessary.

Wapi shook his head. "What do you know of the curse? You call yourself Curse Keeper, but you are ignorant. Just like the *toshshonte* who helped the *nuppin*."

Mishiginebig had used those same words. What did they mean?

"I'm here to warn you as a favor to Okeus, but I will leave if you mock me."

I crossed my arms. "I'm listening."

Wapi cocked his head and turned one eye toward me. "Ukinim does as he pleases. He cannot be restrained. Do not presume the threat of Okeus's wrath will protect you from him. Being locked up has changed him into something none of us recognize."

"How can I defeat him?"

Wapi laughed. "Why would I tell you that?"

"To protect me."

"I don't care if you are protected. I only relay Okeus's warning." He bobbed his head toward my door. "Stay behind your fortress, but the day is coming when it will no longer be enough."

That got my attention. "What does that mean?"

Wapi grinned and then flew away.

I stood gaping in the doorway as terror trickled through my body. Soon my door wouldn't be enough. What would I do then?

"What in bloody hell was that?"

I turned back to face David. He was standing and holding onto the back of the chair, his face a ghastly white.

"Wapi, the wind god of the north. He was particularly chatty tonight."

"He was . . . a large bird with a man's head."

"And white hair. Don't forget the white hair. That's the most significant way to tell him apart from his brothers."

His eyes widened. "His brothers?"

"The other wind gods, but I haven't had the pleasure of getting to know them like I have Wapi."

He stared at the still open door. "I have so many questions."

I surveyed the marks on the front of the door and then shut it once I was satisfied. "It's always hard to go back to sleep after one of them visits, so I've got nothing but time." I sank onto the sofa and David sat next to me.

"You mentioned several things I've never heard of before. You said that Wapi and his brothers overthrew Ahone. How did that happen?"

"Ahone created humanity and put them into a bag."

He shivered and tensed. "I've heard that, but in the story I'm familiar with, the creator was the Great Hare."

"From the little information I can find, I suspect Ahone and the Great Hare are one and the same. The four wind gods were jealous of everything that the creator god made, but they were most jealous of humanity. They told Ahone he had until the morning of the seventh day to hand humanity over to them or lose his power. Ahone couldn't bring himself to hand either over, so he tricked them. He split himself in two, creating his twin Okeus. Okeus got all the negative traits of Ahone, but he also got the majority of their power. So Ahone still kept his power, although in a much lower concentration, *and* he saved humanity."

"How do you know this? This isn't recorded anywhere that I'm aware of."

"I saw it happen. Like I told you, I was a witness to creation." I twisted my neck to glance at him. "I saw the birth of the universe and the world." The look of disbelief on his face wasn't surprising. "I was clueless to any of this until Collin and I pressed our hands together while we were in the ocean. I saw it all then. The birth of the gods, and the wind gods' threat to Ahone and humanity. The birth of Okeus and his children. I saw them all while they were locked behind the gate to Popogusso. And heard their threats. They vowed to make me suffer for what Ananias Dare and Manteo did."

"But not Collin?"

"He's pledged himself to Okeus. He's protected."

David shook his head. "You saw them imprisoned?"

"Ahone sought revenge for what the wind gods had done, and he wanted to shut Okeus and all his offspring down too. The Great Horned Serpent and that thing eating hearts? They're some of Okeus's offspring. When Ahone learned of Manteo's plan, he lent him the power to lock the gods away. Now they're all pissed at the creator god, and he's hiding in the heavens."

"How is Okeus's power greater than the wind gods' if they could collectively threaten Ahone." He rubbed his temple with his fingertips. "That doesn't make sense." His eyes, wild and desperate, locked with mine. "None of this makes sense."

"I know," I whispered. "I'm sorry I dragged you into this. I'm no better than Collin." I realized the truth of it as I said it. But without David, I was doomed . . . we all might be.

"Why do you say that?"

He was on the edge of what he could handle right now. I stood and headed for the kitchen. "I think we need a drink."

David didn't answer, his eyes locked on the wall.

Wine didn't seem strong enough so I searched for a bottle of whiskey an old boyfriend had left when we broke up. I grabbed it out of the cabinet and carried it to the living room with two juice glasses, pouring a generous amount into each glass.

"I'm not whiskey drinker," David said.

I pressed a glass into his hand. "Neither am I, but tonight both of us are."

I took a sip, surprised the liquid didn't burn as much as I'd expected. I rarely drank the stuff and never straight. But desperate times called for desperate measures.

David took a big gulp. "I've studied these things, but they're

Native American gods. They're like the Easter Bunny or Father Christmas. They certainly aren't supposed to be *real*."

"I know." I sat back and took another sip, letting him get it out of his system.

"But here they are—in the flesh. This is my opportunity to learn so much about the Algonquians, but no matter how much information I glean, no one will ever believe me."

"I know."

"The *tosh-shonte* and the *nuppin*. I've heard of those words. Do you know what they mean?"

"No, but Big Nasty used those words with me before."

"Big Nasty, the snake who talks to you?"

"Yep."

He took another big gulp.

"Big Nasty told me that the *nuppin* feared him and soon the *tosh-shonte* would too."

David closed his eyes. "I'm sure the *nuppin* were the Indians. Like I said, the story of the Great Serpent crossed multiple tribes. He lived in lakes and ponds and killed unsuspecting people. They were terrified of him."

"So if *nuppin* are the Indians—"

"The *tosh-shonte* must be the English, or in this case, all non-Native Americans."

"That doesn't sound good."

He lifted up his glass in salute. "No, it bloody well doesn't." He took another drink.

"But right now our biggest threat is Ukinim. I have to figure out how to kill it."

"It's a spirit, Ellie. Or, based on what I read and what Wapi said, a demon. Technically, I don't think you can kill a spirit or demon."

I shuddered. Though we were still talking about the same thing, the word "demon" brought an added level of terror. "I only know how to get rid of these things with Collin, which isn't an option. We have to figure out another way."

He turned to look at me. "That tosser opened the gate and left you to deal with the consequences?"

"I guess he figured I was protected by my henna tattoo and the marks on my door. And to be fair—although I have no idea why I feel the need to be fair—he keeps trying to convince me to pledge myself to Okeus."

David shook his head. "Okeus is supposed to be evil. That would be a very bad idea." His words were beginning to slur.

"I know, but if I don't find Ahone's mark, I'm doomed. And the more my mark fades, the worse my dreams get."

He poured himself more whiskey and then topped up my glass. "I know what you need."

"What?"

"A dream catcher. It's supposed to protect you from evil. More specifically, it catches the bad dreams and lets in the good."

I tried not to get excited. "Do you really think that will work?"

"It sure couldn't hurt to try it, right?"

"I thought dream catchers were from Southwestern Indians."

He shook his head and took another drink. "Nope. They're traced to the Ojibwa."

I lifted my eyebrows. "Is that supposed to mean something to me?"

"They belong to the Algonquian." He waved his glass. "Although this tribe lived up north. And in Canada."

I tried not to laugh. "Canada *is* up north." David was getting thoroughly sauced.

"We'll get you a dream catcher tomorrow and see if it works." His eyes pierced mine. "I'll help you fight these creatures, Ellie."

"This isn't your fight, David. You didn't ask to be part of it. All I need from you is information, and then you can walk away."

"Did you ask to be a part of this?"

"No."

"Then how is it *your* fight? Sure you were born to it, but you could walk away from it just like Collin has."

"I guess. But I won't."

"Do you believe in fate, Ellie? Destiny?"

I took another sip to stall. "I don't know. Maybe. I dismissed it, but then I think about the fact that I'm a pure soul and Collin says those occur once every several hundred years. It can't be a coincidence that I'm a pure soul and the Curse Keeper to witness the breaking of the curse."

"Is there any way Collin knew you were a pure soul when he broke the curse?"

"No, he said he discovered it by accident when we joined hands."

"You actually believe him?"

"Well, the first time we touched marks—accidently—he said he could sense that I was a pure spirit, but he didn't tell me until . . . later." I paused, the familiar sense of loss filling every part of me. "After I'd seen creation and Wapi had terrorized me in the ocean, Collin must have realized the full significance of what he'd done. He begged me to make the mark permanent. He claims he never would have put me at risk by opening the gate if he'd known, and oddly enough, I believe him. He cares about me in his own way."

David turned sideways, watching me with a strange look in his eyes. "You slept with him."

My face burned. "That's a personal question."

"I can see it in your face when you talk about him."

"That I slept with him?"

"That you care about him."

I shook my head, gritting my teeth. "He had his chance. I can never forgive him for what he did."

"That prat really left you in a lurch, didn't he?"

I had to laugh at his word choice. "Yeah."

"What a wanker."

"Among other things."

David set his glass on the table and turned back to me. "I asked you if you believe in destiny." He swallowed and looked down at my open palm, then into my face. "Well, I do. I almost didn't get my doctorate in Native American studies. My father kept trying to convince me to be a barrister. He said I'd never make much money living in the States and teaching history. Even my American mother didn't want to lose me to the States, as she put it. But something told me it was the right decision. And then this archaeological site." He waved toward the front door. "I wasn't supposed to be here, Ellie. I couldn't get my schedule cleared to make it happen and then suddenly it worked out." A burning intensity filled his eyes.

"You think this is destiny? They could all be coincidences that brought you to a *very bad place*." I sighed. "Look, David. You're drunk, and you can't make this decision lightly. I have a guilty enough conscience as it is."

"Fair enough," he drained the last of his glass and then set it on the table. "You're right. I need to give this serious thought." He startled me by grabbing my chin and swinging my face around to his. "But I promise you this: if I decide to help you, I'm totally in. I won't leave you to face this alone."

I swallowed the lump in my throat, trying to find the words to respond. I didn't trust his promise. I'd lost too many significant people in my life to believe such promises could be made.

Finally I smiled and said the only thing I could bring myself to say.

"We'll see about that."

⚝ CHAPTER FIFTEEN ⚝

David had a headache when he woke up. After he took a shower and dressed, I asked him how he felt and he said, "I'm surprised I'm not still wankered."

If "wankered" meant drunk, I was impressed. He'd sucked down the equivalent of four shots of whiskey in about ten minutes, less than four hours ago.

I dug through my salvageable laundry for something to wear for my lunch shift at Darrell's and then bagged up the clothes that had landed in the blood for relaundering.

David was drinking a cup of coffee when I entered the living room.

"Ready?" he asked.

"Yeah."

We had barely seen each other while we were getting ready, but on the walk to the inn, everything we weren't saying hung like a heavy cloud over both of us.

"Ellie—"

"Look, David—"

We spoke at the same time and I smiled. "Let me say this first." I turned to look up at him. "I don't know what you're thinking right now, but I really want you to give this serious thought today, okay? This isn't a game and it's not a challenge. If you decide you want to walk away, I'll understand. Honestly, I think you're crazy if you decide not to."

He stopped in front of a Mexican restaurant and turned to face me. "What happened last night seems like a bad dream, and getting pissed on whiskey didn't help matters much, but I know that all of this is real. And I promise to give it serious thought and consideration. I'll give you an answer tonight after I get back from the colony site."

"You can take longer than that."

He shook his head. "That's all I'll need."

We didn't speak the rest of the way until we went through the side door. He leaned close, lowering his voice. "I'll keep my eye out for anything I think will help you, whether I decide I'm in this or not."

"Thank you." I watched him walk away, feeling guilty about what I hoped he chose.

David headed for the living room with his laptop, and I snuck into the laundry room to pretreat my bloody clothes on the table by the washing machine.

"Oh, dear God," Myra gasped from behind me. "What happened?"

I dropped the heavily bloodstained shirt and spun around. "It's not how it looks."

Tears filled her eyes. "It looks like the night you came home after your father died."

That night, I'd been covered in my blood and Collin's from the slashes on our palms. Unsure of where to go, I'd come straight to Myra's house. I'd scared her half to death, still in too much shock to give her a rational account of what had happened. When I kept crying for Daddy, she rushed upstairs to check on him and was terrified to discover he was missing from his bed. Looking me in the eye, she asked if I knew what happened to him. When I nodded yes, she asked if he was alive and I refused to answer. It was no wonder the blood upset her.

"No, Myra." I shook my head, picking the shirt back up. "It's not my blood. I promise."

"Whose . . . ?" I know she hated to ask, but she needed to know.

"A cat. That *monster* left it on my front porch. It scared me when I saw the mess, and I dropped the laundry basket. The clothes fell in the splattered blood."

Some of the color returned to her face. "I think we should move."

"*What?*"

"It's too dangerous for you here, Ellie. We should go somewhere else."

I turned back to my laundry. "You know that won't help, Myra. These things will find me wherever I am."

Her arms wrapped around me and she trembled.

"I need to stay here, but you should leave."

Her eyes bulged. "Leave *you?*"

"You think it's bad now? This is only the beginning. And they're going to target you and Claire to get to me."

Myra's face paled.

Why had I been so blunt? I needed to protect her from this, not scare her to death. "It's going to be okay. David thinks he has some information that can help me."

"He's offered to help you?"

"I'm making him think about it before he commits."

"It makes me feel better that you won't be alone."

The thought made me feel better too, selfish though it was. "Do you need help with breakfast?"

"No, I've got it covered for now, but you can take the cinnamon rolls out when they're done." She started to leave the room but stopped in the doorway. "Ellie, one more thing. If you come across an old ring, hold onto it. Your father showed it to me a few days before he died and told me that you needed it." She looked down at her feet. "I didn't think much of it at the time. Even though he seemed fairly lucid, he was acting paranoid. He was quite upset that you didn't have it."

My heart lurched. "Where is the ring now?"

She shook her head. "I don't know. I tried to take it for safe-keeping, but he refused to let go of it. He insisted he'd give it to you himself. He'd been scribbling drawings of those symbols and scratching down notes, so I just chalked it up to his dementia. Now I'm worried you might actually need it."

"He was scribbling notes?"

"Yeah, on little scraps of paper."

What if those notes had the information I needed? "What did the ring look like? Do you know where he usually kept it?"

"No, I'm sorry. I'd never seen it before, but it looked very old and worn. He had it on a chain around his neck. There was another object you needed too, he said, but he couldn't remember what it was. He started muttering something about you needing time." Her mouth twisted into a grimace. "Maybe he was worried you were running out of time?"

"And you have no idea where the ring might be?"

"No. I'm sorry. He was on the front porch when I saw it."

I tried to hide my disappointment and focus on the positive. There was a ring that could help me somehow, along with the notes my father had written down. The ring and the notes had to be here somewhere. I just had to find them, and hopefully, the notes would tell me about the other object he'd mentioned.

When I finished in the laundry room, I headed to the kitchen and took the cinnamon rolls and fruit over to the sideboard.

Several of the researchers had already gathered in the dining room. David walked in just as I was finishing up, and his friend called out to him, "David! We missed you last night."

"I decided to call it an early night."

"I knocked on your door when we got back around dark and you didn't answer."

"I walked downtown to get dinner. Poor Richard's has great sandwiches."

"Are you feeling all right? You look tired."

David gave a halfhearted laugh. "You know how it is when you sleep in a bed that's not your own."

Or in this case sitting up on a sofa. We'd slept there together. After drinking copiously.

Feeling reassured that they had everything they needed, I went into the kitchen to clean up. I was halfway done with the dishes when David appeared in the doorway of the butler's pantry. "Can I come in?"

"Of course."

He moved toward me, concern in his eyes. "This morning has been . . . awkward, and I feel rude for ignoring you in there."

I put the pot I was scrubbing under the water to rinse. "It's probably better that you do. You'll make them all suspicious if they know you spent the night with me."

"In more ways than one," he conceded. "Steven would consider it greatly out of character."

My eyes widened as I realized what he was hinting. "Oh, you're gay." I shook my head, feeling like fool. "With all those girls after you at your college, I just thought—"

"What? No!" Horror filled his eyes. "No, I'm not gay." He frowned. "Not that there's anything wrong with being gay, but I can assure you that I'm not."

My faced flushed. "Oh."

"Me sleeping with a woman I just met would be completely out of character. I know we didn't *sleep* together." His face turned bright red. "But they don't know that. It's probably best to keep it quiet."

"Okay."

He rubbed his temple, closing his eyes. "Bollocks. Now it sounds like I'd be ashamed if they thought I'd slept with you." His eyes flew open. "Which I wouldn't be. You are a very attractive woman, Ellie, and I would love nothing more than to . . ." His voice trailed off and he took a step backward, pointing over his shoulder toward the door. "I think I should stop talking now. Perhaps I should just go."

I grinned, my hands deep in the soapy water. David blushed furiously, which made him look more attractive than ever. I found it hard to believe someone as good-looking as he was could feel anything less than confident.

He put a folded piece of paper on the counter. "This is my cell phone number, in case you need me for anything today."

"Thanks."

"Can I have yours? In case I need you?"

I laughed. "Is this a bad pickup line? It's pretty obvious you don't need them, so I can see that you've gotten a bit rusty."

"No. God, no." The red on his cheeks deepened. "I just figured if I found anything at the site . . ."

I grabbed a towel and dried off my hands. "I'm teasing. You just look so cute blushing like that, it was hard to resist."

He grimaced. "So does that mean you're giving me your number?"

I rattled off the number, and he plugged it into his phone.

When he had it entered, he slipped the phone into his pocket. "I mean it. Call me if you need me, Ellie."

"You haven't made a decision yet."

"Call me anyway."

I stared in awe at the man who was standing six feet away from me. He was so utterly different from Collin. Even though we hadn't known each other long, I could tell he was a man of character—a man who stood by his word. "I'm more worried about you, but you should be okay during the day. For now. Eventually they'll be strong enough to go out in the daylight, but today you should be safe."

"I'll promise to call you if you'll promise to call me."

"Deal."

He turned to leave, but then stopped as if he'd forgotten something and spun around. "Will you have dinner with me tonight?"

It was my turn to be shocked. "Um . . ."

"So we can discuss my decision. I think it warrants more than a phone call."

"Oh . . . yeah."

He playfully cocked an eyebrow. "See you tonight. Seven?"

"Okay."

"I'll pick you up at your flat if that's okay. Think of someplace that serves good seafood."

He smiled and his face lit up, making him look even more gorgeous than usual. If I were the swooning type of girl, I would have been in a heap on the floor. As it was, my stomach fluttered with anticipation.

"Have a good day, Ellie."

"You too." I watched him leave, wondering how he'd gotten the upper hand.

After working on the main rooms at the inn, I left for my shift at Darrell's.

When I got there, I reviewed the daily specials and headed to the dining room to check on the flatware, hoping for an uneventful second day.

Carly was standing behind the cash register counting money in the drawer, but she glanced up when I walked by. "Oh, Ellie. I forgot. I came in to work part of the dinner shift last night and a couple of guys were in here asking about you."

I froze in my tracks and tried to act nonchalant. "Really? What did they say?"

She thumbed through a stack of bills, then put it in the drawer. "They asked if I knew a redheaded woman named Ellie."

"And what did you tell them?"

"I asked if they knew you from the New Moon. I figured they were regulars of yours there."

"And . . . ?"

Carly scrunched her nose and shrugged. "I told them you were working the lunch shift today."

Carly was right. They could have been regulars from the New Moon. I was probably overreacting. "What did they look like?"

"A couple of beefy guys."

So much for my cockeyed optimism.

Carly unlocked the doors and the sight of a police car pulling into the parking lot actually gave me comfort. Talk about a 180-degree change.

A few customers trickled in and I kept a close watch on the door. Tom and his deputy friend weren't there, and though Collin showed up, he was seated in a different section. I caught him watching me, but I did my best to ignore him. I considered telling him about Wapi's visit and his information about Ukinim but decided to keep that to myself for now. Collin knew that animals were being killed. Did it really matter to him whether or not these particular deaths were sanctioned by Okeus?

The usual swarm of worries and fears was still swirling through my head, with the added worry that Marino's men had found me, so I was thankful I could concentrate on the lunch crowd and forget them for a while. I was starting to feel okay again when Tom came into the dining room wearing his police uniform. He looked like he was a man looking for something other than the seafood platter. Sure enough, his eyes searched the room and landed on me.

Oh, shit.

Collin, who had kept tabs on me throughout his lunch, watched as Tom strode toward me.

"Ellie, I'd like to ask you a few questions."

I glanced down at the table I was serving. "Can this wait, Tom? I'm in the middle of something right now. *My job.*"

"No." His voice was firm. "We can either go outside to talk or we can go down to the station. Which would you prefer?"

My face flushed with anger, but I stuffed it down. "I'm sorry," I said to the customers at my table, who seemed touchingly concerned about me. What with their Outer Banks and "The Lost Colony Lives!" T-shirts, they were almost certainly tourists.

Collin sat several tables away, in full eye- and earshot of our conversation. His complete attention was focused on me.

"This is my *ex*-boyfriend Tom, and he seems to have lost his mind." I tilted my head to the side and cast a glance at him. "We had a wild and crazy two weeks, but now he thinks he can dictate everything I do." I turned to Tom, whose mouth had dropped open in shock. "I don't care that you had my name tattooed on your ass, you don't own me, Tom Helmsworth. Using your uniform to make me do whatever you want is abusing your power." I winked at Collin. "Even if we had a wild night with those handcuffs."

Tom's face turned crimson.

Collin smirked, enjoying the show. Bastard.

184

I leaned closer to the table. "If y'all will wait just a few minutes longer, I'll get rid of him, and your drinks or dessert will be on me."

That seemed to appease them, even though I knew the comp was coming out of my tips. I shoved Tom's arm. "We need to get this settled once and for all."

Tom looked like I'd whacked him upside the head as he stumbled toward the back door. Carly stood staring at me bug-eyed from behind the cash register as I followed Tom outside.

"I'll be right back." I offered her a sweet smile, but I had serious doubts I'd be invited back to Darrell's Restaurant, either as a waitress *or* a customer, if the police kept questioning me while I was working.

The hot, humid air seemed to finally restore Tom to his senses after I shoved him through the back door. As he regained his footing, Collin's parked truck caught my eye.

"You can't do that, Ellie!"

I put my hands on my hips. "Seems like I just did."

"You know what I mean! You made me look like a fool!"

"And how do you think you made me look? All those people think I'm a criminal! My tips will suck."

"There are bigger things at stake here than your tips." Tom gave his head a hard shake and leaned against the Dumpster.

"What's so important it can't wait the two hours until my shift ends?"

"We found a dead body!"

Why would Tom specifically search me out and tell me about finding a dead body? Then it hit me. "Myra." I stumbled backward and clutched my chest. My head felt light and my knees began to buckle.

Tom's eyes flew open and his anger faded. "No. God, Ellie I'm sorry. It wasn't Myra." He saw my face and added. "Or Claire."

"I need to sit down."

To my surprise, Tom grabbed my upper arm and led me to the curb. I crouched down and put my head between my upright knees, taking several deep breaths until my head cleared.

"You're right. I should have handled this better, but I know you're hiding things, and I'm frustrated that you won't tell me what you know. If I knew what in the hell was going on, I might have a chance to stop it."

More like what had been loosed from hell. "You can't stop it," I mumbled and then closed my eyes. Now what on earth had possessed me to say that?

"Why not, Ellie?"

I sat up. "What made the colony reappear?"

He shuddered in surprise as he searched for a ready answer. "It was uncovered by a storm."

"That's bullshit and you know it. That storm was nothing compared to the storms we usually have. Hell, Hurricane Irene caused more damage than that pathetic storm."

His shoulders tensed. "That's the official answer."

"And what's the unofficial answer?" I was genuinely curious.

He looked out into the parking lot. "We don't know." Tom's face tensed, and he turned to me with a determined look in his eyes. "But I think you do."

I rolled my eyes with a groan. "I'm not rehashing this conversation. Ask me what you came to ask."

He turned serious. "Someone found the body of a young woman this morning, close to the marshes by the condos a little south of here."

A metallic taste coated my tongue and the screams from my nightmare echoed in my head. I fought a wave of nausea as I waited for what he was going to say, preparing myself not to react. "And?"

"Her abdomen was ripped open and her heart was removed, just like with those dogs."

"Wow. Have you called Animal Control yet?"

"Goddamn it, Ellie!"

I stood and looked up at him, balling my fists. "What do you want me to say? How did I become the resident expert in all things peculiar?"

"You are putting people's lives at risk by not telling me what you know!"

A dark sedan pulled into a parking space at the back corner of the restaurant. Two guys got out and I immediately recognized one of them. They were Marino's men. He and his now-dead partner had tried to abduct me before. They were pretty gutsy to pursue me in a restaurant with several police cars parked out front. Or desperate, which was always a bad sign.

It was time to play my temporary solution to two problems card.

I stood and turned to Tom. "You're right. I got mixed up in some kind of trouble. I'm scared and don't know what to do."

His eyes widened in surprise at my sudden change in attitude. "Okay . . ." He gave his head a slight shake. "I can protect you, Ellie. Tell me what's going on."

"I'd love to give you a full statement, but while we were standing here talking, your two suspects just parked over there." I pointed to their car.

Tom's jaw tightened. "If this is some kind of joke—"

"It's not! I swear!" I grabbed his arm. "The inn was hit pretty hard by the hurricane a few months ago and we lost business. I was desperate for money, so I took a pair of silver candlesticks to Buxton. I hocked them there."

"What does that have to do with—"

"Listen to me! The guy I hocked them to mistook me for someone else and he thinks I'm involved with some crime deal. Those guys in that car"—I jabbed my finger in its direction—"They're after me. They tried to kidnap me down in Morehead City and I barely got away. Somehow they tracked me here. I think they're inside looking for me right now."

"Why didn't you tell me this sooner?"

"I was embarrassed. I thought I could handle it on my own."

"Could they somehow be responsible for the dog mutilations and the murder this morning?"

I hated to lie, so I came up with a half-truth. "I think they like to intimidate, and you have to admit it's intimidating. They've been searching for me for weeks. I bet they were trying to flush me out."

Tom pressed the radio attached to his shoulder and called for backup. Given that there were other officers in the restaurant, it seemed unnecessary. All he needed to do to get help was holler through the back door. He turned his attention on me. "What do they look like?"

I saw movement at the side of the building. The guys were opening their car doors. I nodded in their direction. "You can see for yourself."

Tom's head jerked up. After taking a moment to study them, he pushed me toward the door. "Go inside, Ellie."

"Tom, be careful." I said, hoping he took me seriously. "These guys don't mess around."

"Go inside," he barked, moving toward the car.

I opened the back door like I was about to go inside, then dashed behind the Dumpster while Tom had his back to me.

The guys were climbing into the car, their gazes fixed on Tom. His hand rested on his gun. "I'd like to ask you a few questions."

The passenger's gaze shifted to me and his eyes lit up with recognition. I could tell he wanted to come after me, and I was terrified he'd gun Tom down to do it. But after giving Tom another quick glance, he got inside the vehicle, slamming his door shut as the car jerked backward.

Tom pulled his gun from its holster and pointed it at the moving car. "Stop!"

The sedan tore out of the parking lot, tires squealing.

Tom ran around the corner as several sirens filled the air, coming from the front parking lot.

"You sure know how to stir up trouble," Collin said from behind me.

Startled, I spun around to face him. "What are you doing back here?"

"Checking on you. I wasn't sure if Officer Fife was going to arrest you or not." He gazed across the parking lot. "I'm not sure whether telling him about your suitors was a good idea. There's a good chance you've just exponentially increased the danger you're in."

"Not if Tom and the other officers catch them."

"There's always more on their heels, Ellie." He sounded tired, like he knew from experience.

I closed my eyes. I suspected he was right.

Collin grabbed my arm. "Come on."

I jerked out of his hold. "Why would I go anywhere with you?"

"Ellie, you're in real danger. Don't you get that?"

"The police can protect me."

He snorted. "And can they protect you from the thing that killed that woman last night?"

He had a point.

Collin's hand slipped into mine so easily and naturally that I actually let him pull me halfway across the parking lot to his truck. "Wait. Where are we going?"

"I'm going to hide you. We're going to my boat." He opened the passenger door.

I dug my feet into the ground. "For how long?"

"Indefinitely."

"What? No!"

Collin pushed me against the side of the truck, pressing his body into mine. My legs barely held me up. "Ellie, how many times do I have to apologize? I'm sorry, okay? Do you know how many times I've apologized in my life? I could count them on one hand, and most of them have been to you." His hand slid up my neck, digging into my hair, and my traitorous body leaned into him. His mouth hovered over mine, and I could tell he was trying to resist me as much as I was trying to resist him. We were supposed to be fleeing, not making out.

"I can't."

"*Why?* I can't stand here and watch you get hurt. Or worse."

"I have a date." I didn't mean to say it like that, but it was the first thing that came to mind.

Collin's hand stiffened in my hair. "You *what?*"

His reaction was enough for me to push on with my deception. He deserved it and more. "A professor of Native American studies is here working at the colony site. He's offered to help me."

His expressionless face barely registered my words, but a slight tic in the corner of his eye gave him away. "Help you how?"

"Help me send this thing away."

"*What thing?*"

"Ukinim."

He leaned back, moving his hands onto the truck, one on either side of my body. "What the hell is a Ukinim?"

"Are you serious? You really don't know?"

His blank face answered my question.

"It's the badger spirit that's mutilating animals and eating their hearts. And apparently, now humans."

"Is this something *he's* told you?"

"No, it's something Wapi told me."

His head jerked up and his eyes narrowed. "Why would Wapi tell you any of this? Why would he care?"

"Because Ukinim doesn't think Okeus's rules apply to him, which makes me fair game. Okeus isn't happy that I might not be around for his big surprise. Wapi was delivering a message warning me to be careful."

The color drained from his face. "Why didn't you come to me?" He had the nerve to sound accusatory.

"Because it happened last night. What would you have done, anyway?"

"Protect you!"

My anger flared white hot. "You gave up that duty when you betrayed me."

"Bullshit, Ellie. I told you the night before the ceremony that you would be my responsibility no matter what happened." Collin grabbed my wrist and shoved me toward the open door. "You're coming with me."

I jerked out of his grasp. "The hell I am!"

"For Christ's sake! Grow up, Ellie! How much of your tattoo is left?"

I didn't answer him.

"Have you found Ahone's mark yet?"

"No." And it burned a hole in my gut to admit that I hadn't.

"Your professor *boyfriend* doesn't know it? Then what good is he?"

"He's trying to find it for me. Which is more than you're doing."

His eyes narrowed. "*Trying* to find it. And what if he doesn't?"

"You know what."

Rage filled his eyes. "If you think I'm going to stand back and watch you get killed, then you're delusional. You need a new mark, and I'll tie you down if I have to and put a new one on your back myself."

"Like hell you will!"

His mouth found mine and I lost myself in him, which is undoubtedly what he had planned. He pushed me through the open door, lifting me up onto the seat, my legs straddling his waist.

"God, Ellie," he groaned. "How can you fight this?"

His mouth claimed mine before I could answer, and I found myself wondering the same thing.

His hand skimmed up my back, underneath my shirt. "We have to go," he said, but he didn't pull away.

"Collin." No one had ever felt as right as he did.

He was right. Our connection was more remarkable than anything I'd ever experienced. I was sure I would never find it with anyone else.

But I couldn't trust him.

I started to cry, my heart breaking all over again.

Collin pulled back, worry in his eyes. "What's wrong?"

I pushed him away from me. "I have to go."

He slid his hands down my back and up my arms, gripping my biceps gently. "Don't go, Ellie. I need you." There was a wistfulness in his voice I'd never heard before.

"I need you too." I looked into his eyes, my tears making his face blurry. "But it's not enough."

I expected him to get angry, but he leaned his forehead against mine. "I know," he whispered. He wiped a tear that had fallen down my cheek and pulled me to his chest, burying his face into my neck. "I just don't know how to live without you."

My throat clogged with tears. I couldn't stay here with him another moment. I pushed his shoulders again, and he released me this time, helping me down from the seat.

He grabbed my left hand, putting it on his chest, and I looked up into his face, searching for proof that I should stay. That this time I could trust him. But all I saw was hopelessness.

I gently pulled my hand from his and walked toward the back door of the restaurant.

Collin's truck started and pulled out of the parking lot.

My heart left with him.

CHAPTER SIXTEEN

Tom showed up a couple of hours later as I was finishing my shift. The look of defeat on his face told me everything I needed to know.

"You didn't get them."

He shook his head. "No. They got away. I'm sorry."

I took a deep breath. Collin was right. I was in deep trouble.

Tom's back stiffened. He was in full Manteo Police Officer mode. "I need to get a statement of everything that has happened to you up until now. And you might need to go to Buxton and Morehead City to give statements there too."

My eyes flew open. "Why?"

"You said they tried to abduct you in Morehead City. We don't have jurisdiction there."

I shook my head vigorously. "No. I'm not going to press charges." I didn't have time to travel hours away, and undoubtedly it would get messy with everything else I was dealing with.

"Ellie," Tom groaned in exasperation.

"I'll tell *you* what happened, but no one else. And I don't want to go down to the station. I want to give you my statement at the inn."

"That's a lot of conditions, Ellie."

"Do you want me to cooperate or not?"

194

His eyes narrowed. "If you don't cooperate, I can have you detained overnight for obstruction of justice. Or filing a false police report."

"I didn't even file a police report!"

"You made an accusation that involved a high-speed car chase. Don't think I won't lock you up to prove my point."

If Tom locked me up, I'd be safe from Marino's men, but I'd be totally at the mercy of the spirits without the protections on my door and the salt around my windows. I sighed. "Will you meet me at the inn or not?"

"Yes. Fine." He released a heavy breath and glanced out at the parking lot. "I'll meet you there in an hour."

On the short drive to the bed and breakfast, I sorted through the story I planned to tell Tom. I'd been mulling it over for the last hour of my shift, but I still hadn't worked out all the details. I couldn't tell him everything, of course, and I needed to decide whether to include Collin. Instinct told me to keep him out of it, if nothing else than because of his criminal record. But I wasn't sure how my story would make sense without him.

When he arrived, we sat down in the living room of the residential house. I hoped the researchers didn't come back early. The last thing I needed was for them to see me delivering a statement to a uniformed policeman. And I sure didn't want to worry Myra. "Tom, whatever I tell you, you can't tell Myra. She's upset enough over Daddy. There's no need to involve her."

"I can't guarantee anything," he said with a nod. "But I'll do my best."

It was all I could ask. "I'm not sure where to start."

"Why don't you start by telling me how you ended up in Buxton."

"I'd heard about a loan shark there. We were behind on the mortgage, so I sold him a pair of silver candlesticks."

"How did you hear about the loan shark? Why not somewhere closer? There's a couple of pawnshops in Kill Devil Hills and Kitty Hawk."

I shrugged. "A customer at the New Moon told me about him."

"And who was this customer?"

"I don't know," I said in exasperation. "Just some guy. I heard him tell his friend about hocking something to a guy in Buxton. He said he bought stuff for top dollar. So I got the guy's information and took the candlesticks to him."

"Can Myra corroborate this?"

My eyebrows rose. "Am I under suspicion for anything?"

His face hardened. "I just want to make sure I have all the facts."

My gaze shifted to the doorway. I resisted the urge to cringe when I noticed that David was standing in the foyer. Our eyes locked and his eyebrows rose slightly. I gave him a slight nod. I wanted him to hear this. "She knows I sold the candlesticks to get money, but she has no idea who I sold them to and I don't want her to know."

Tom shifted in his seat. "Who did you take them to?"

"A guy named Marino. He works in the back of a nasty thrift store."

"Why are his men after you?"

"I told you, Marino thought I was part of something he called the Ricardo deal."

Tom's eyes lit up. "Are you?"

I shuddered in surprise. Tom obviously had some idea what it was. Now I was even more curious. "No. The first time I heard of the Ricardo deal was when I showed up at his warehouse. I got away, but his men have been asking around about me ever since. He knew I'd pawned stuff in Kill Devil Hills, which is how he tracked me here."

"What were you doing in Morehead City?"

Damn it. Why had I told him that part? I paused, trying to come up with a story, knowing I was starting to look more suspicious with each second. "I was there with a guy."

"Why the hesitation?"

"Because I'm worried this is all going to get back to Myra. I had just broken up with Dwight and . . ." I sighed and clasped my hands together. "Myra already thinks I date too many guys, but I don't usually run off and shack up with one the day after I met him."

He tilted his head. "Is that what you did? Shack up with a guy the day after you met?"

My eyes were drawn to David's expressionless face. He was standing several feet outside the doorway and to the side.

Too late now.

I lifted my chin. Guys slept around all the time. Why should I be ashamed? "Yeah, I did. I met him in Buxton at a bar and he took me to a motel in Morehead City for a few days. Marino's guys showed up and tried to kidnap me. I got away and came home."

Tom shook his head in disbelief. "You just *got away*?"

"Don't make it sound so inconceivable. I can take care of myself."

His eyes found mine. "Before I came here, I did some digging about odd occurrences in Morehead City."

"Did you now?" I asked, crossing my legs and casting a glance toward David. Lord knew what he thought of me now. "You move quickly."

"People are dying. I'm trying to prevent more deaths." He cleared his throat. "Guess what I found?"

I rubbed my forehead, "I'm too tired for guessing games."

"Then I'll cut to the chase." He leaned forward. "A man was found dead in the parking lot of the North Carolina Outer Banks Museum the night before your father died."

"People die all the time. Just because I was in Morehead City doesn't mean I brought the Grim Reaper with me."

"This guy was frozen solid, Ellie. And his fingers on one hand were broken off."

My stomach rolled and I swallowed, looking away.

"I can see you know something about it."

I jerked my gaze back to him. "Why? Because I had the decency to look upset that some guy's fingers were broken off?"

"He was known to associate with a man named Joseph Marino."

My mouth gaped. "You already knew about Marino?" My anger flared. "And you let me think you didn't?"

"I never insinuated that I did or didn't know about him. I wanted to find out what you knew. Or at least what you'd share with me. Do you know how Mr. Denton died?"

"You just told me. He was frozen."

"No, Ellie." His voice hardened. "You told me Marino's men tried to abduct you. One of Marino's men was found dead and frozen. Notice a pattern?"

My stomach clenched. Telling Tom about Marino's men was supposed to get him off my back about the supernatural occurrences. Instead, it had only made things worse.

"I think you saw Mr. Denton die in that parking lot. The look on your face tells me that maybe you even saw his fingers snapped off."

I tried to stop my cringe. I failed.

"The coroner said it looked like his fingers were wrapped around something. Maybe your wrist?"

"You think *I* froze that man? How would I do that?"

For the first time since his interrogation began, Tom's face softened. "No, Ellie. I don't think you froze him. But you're obviously caught up in something bigger than what you're telling me.

Marino and the Ricardo Estate are just the tip of the proverbial iceberg."

"I didn't kill that man and I don't know how he died. One of the guys I saw at the back of Darrell's and his associate tried to take me from the parking lot of the hotel where I was staying. The guy I was with freaked out and took off. I got away from Marino's men and came home."

"What's the name of the guy you picked up in Buxton?"

He made it sound so crass, but then again, that's how I'd painted it. "Roy."

"Roy what?"

I shrugged and glanced over to where David was standing in the shadows near the doorway. What would he think of me? It didn't matter; I had to play this out. "I don't know. I didn't ask."

Tom sat back in his chair. "You're telling me you picked up a guy in Buxton, whose last name you didn't know, drove with him to Morehead City, and hooked up with him for a couple of days in a hotel until Marino's men showed up."

"That sounds about right."

"No wonder you don't want Myra to know."

I squirmed in my seat. "Do you have any more questions? Because I need to start my second job here at the inn."

"That's all for now. But I'm sure I'll have more later."

"You know where to find me," I sighed as I stood, not surprised by his words. I headed for the doorway, hoping I could repair any character damage I'd incurred through this interview, but I stopped short and swung around to face Tom. "What the hell *is* the Ricardo deal, anyway? If I'm in trouble because Marino thinks I'm a part of it, at least tell me what it is." Collin had refused to enlighten me, telling me the less I knew the better, but that wasn't good enough.

Tom stood and took a few steps toward me. "The Ricardo Estate is an antique collection that was set to be shipped to Sotheby's in New York for auction. Only it turned up missing."

I shook my head. "You mean someone stole it?"

"Presumably. It was locked up in Charlotte in a secured, guarded warehouse, but when the time came for it to be transported, the room was completely empty."

Had Collin been mixed up in the theft? "What were the antiques?"

"Late sixteenth-century English pieces."

My breath caught. Could this be a coincidence? "Furniture?"

"No. Some knives and swords, clocks, jewelry, candlesticks. Mostly pieces forged in metal. A few Indian artifacts."

"Indian artifacts? Like what?"

Tom tilted his head. "Why the interest?"

I scrambled for an answer. "I'm trying to piece together why Marino thinks I'm a part of it. And we've already established that I'm fascinated with Algonquian culture."

"You said you just sold him candlesticks."

"I did. But I also mentioned to Marino that I had other old antiques," I lied. "Maybe he thought it was too much of a coincidence."

Tom glanced around the room. "Well, most of your things are off by a couple of centuries to fit the Ricardo auction profile, so I'm not sure that's it. In the meantime, I can have a police cruiser swing by the inn and your apartment to keep an eye on things."

I wasn't sure it was a good idea, but while I could defend myself against the supernatural, I was pretty sure I wasn't immune to bullets. "Thanks."

I walked Tom to the side door and he paused as he opened it. "I know you're not telling me everything, but I'm going to let it drop for now. I hope you'll see that I have your best interest and your safety in mind and you'll come to me with the rest on your own."

I nodded, releasing a sigh. "I know you do, Tom. Thanks."

As soon as I shut the door, David's voice broke the silence behind me. "How much of that was fabricated?"

I spun around to face him. "I'm not sure about London, but here in the States eavesdropping is considered rude."

His eyebrows rose. "What really happened in Morehead City?"

I shook my head with a grudging smile. "That's an interesting tale that needs tea to accompany it."

"Fair enough."

He followed me into the kitchen and scoffed when I pulled out tea bags. "It never ceases to amaze me that you uncivilized Americans call that tea."

I put my hand on my hip as I held the dangling tea bags in my other hand. "It *is* tea."

He shook his head as he sat on a bar stool. "Someday I'll show you what *real* tea is. In the meantime, this will suffice."

I boiled some water in the microwave, and I could see it was killing David that I wasn't making tea the "right" way, whatever that was. But I also caught his use of "someday." I was dying to ask him if he'd reached a decision, but I imagined he might have reservations after listening in on my little chat with Tom.

I put the tea bags into a couple of mugs and set them on the counter. "The ceremony to close the gate required the use of the original relics that had been used to seal it the first time. Mine was a pewter cup belonging to Ananias, but Collin's was a wooden bowl that was in the North Carolina Outer Banks Museum in Morehead City. We went there to get the bowl."

He shook his head in confusion. "It was on display? But I

didn't hear about any break-ins involving the theft of ancient Native American artifacts. I'm certain I would have heard."

"Let's just say we got it safe and sound and leave it at that."

David started to speak but stopped himself.

"We were leaving the museum and Marino's men were looking for me. Okeus's messenger killed the guy who was trying to shove me into their car. His hand was curled around my wrist and Collin had to break his fingers off since he was frozen solid."

His face paled. "So Marino's men really *are* after you?"

"Yeah, unfortunately. Like I was telling Tom, Marino's got in his head that I know something about the Ricardo Estate."

"So not only do you have ancient spirits and gods out to get you, but you also have the goons of a crime boss on your tail. You're a popular girl."

I pulled the measuring cup with water out of the microwave and poured it into the mugs. "Apparently, I'm a freaking lightning rod for trouble." I stopped pouring and looked into his face. "I'm glad you were listening to the statement I gave Tom. You need to know *everything* you're getting into."

"You didn't pick up some guy in Buxton and shack up for several days. That was a story you cooked up to cover Collin's sorry arse, wasn't it?"

I grimaced. "Guilty as charged. If he's locked up, he can't change his mind and help me."

"You think he will?"

I shrugged. "Collin tried to kidnap me today and hide me so Marino's men couldn't find me. He also threatened to tie me down and rehenna my back to protect my Manitou. At least he's still trying to protect me."

"Perhaps he still cares about you."

"In his own Collin Dailey way, he does. But he always puts his own best interests before anyone else's." I pulled my tea bag out of my mug and added some sugar. "The fact that I have a backbone must be a novelty to him, but he would have lost interest in me sooner rather than later. He just can't stand the fact I rejected him first. Don't you men all love the thrill of the chase?" I looked up at him and winked.

A devilish grin lit up his face. "I can't speak for *all* men."

"I don't want to talk about Collin anymore." I dragged a bar stool from the kitchen side of the counter to face him and sat down. "What are you doing back so early? I didn't expect to see you for another couple of hours."

"I was eager to get back and speak to you."

"Oh." I looked down at my mug, flustered. Was that a good sign? "Tell me about your day. Did you get inside Manteo's hut?"

"I did, but we're still cataloging, so I couldn't really touch anything. I did take a more careful look than I had the day before, though."

"Did you see anything interesting?"

He grinned. "Yeah, I did. I thought maybe I'd bring you tomorrow so you can see for yourself."

I set my mug on the counter, not believing what I'd heard. "Are you serious?"

His smile widened. "Yeah."

I jumped off my stool and ran around the counter and hugged his neck. "Thank you! You have no idea how much this means to me."

One of his arms pressed against my back in an awkward hold. "I had to pull some strings to make it happen, and I owe Steven a round of golf, but I got you a pass to the archaeological site."

He smelled good, a mix of his herbal shampoo and laundry detergent. I dropped my arms and stood up straight, suddenly embarrassed. We needed to maintain our boundaries. I wasn't going to screw this up by having anything other than a working relationship with him. "That wasn't very professional. I'm sorry."

His eyebrows arched. "Is that what this is? A professional partnership?"

My chest constricted, and I took a step back and sat down on my stool, wrapping my shaking fingers around the mug to hide my nervousness. "Do you want to have this discussion now?"

"I have a few questions."

I nodded, forcing myself to breathe. "That's good. You need to make an informed decision."

"You said many spirits were released from Popogusso. Do you have to send all of them back?"

I shrugged. "I don't know. This didn't exactly come with an instruction manual."

He was silent for several moments. "Will you need me here in Manteo very often after my two weeks here are up?"

I leaned back on the stool. "I don't know. If you're asking if I think this will all be resolved in two weeks, then the answer is no. I don't see how it could be. I guess we can correspond remotely once you're back in Chapel Hill."

"And what if I wanted to be more hands on?"

My heart beat faster. "What do you mean?"

He kept his voice neutral. "What if I accept and I want to spend more time in Manteo? How would you feel about that?"

"Oh." I set my tea on the counter, worried I'd drop it. How *did* I feel about it? If he were here, he'd be more readily available when I needed him. And it would be easier to make sure he was okay. But that would mean he'd have to upheave his entire life. I was already asking so much from him. It didn't seem fair to ask this too. "I don't want to inconvenience you."

His eyes lit up. "I assure you that this is something that interests me. I could see more of these things for myself."

I tried to hide my own excitement. If David was here more often, that meant I wouldn't be doing this completely alone. "But what about your job?"

"I spoke with someone at the foundation this afternoon about setting up a sabbatical at the archaeological site for the fall semester."

The blood drained from my face and I felt light-headed.

Worry flooded his face. "Does that upset you?"

I shook my head.

"Talk to me, Ellie. Did I overstep my bounds?"

"No. The opposite. I can't believe you might actually be *here* to help me."

"It's not official. I still have to get permission from the foundation and the university, but I suspect it will all go through."

"I don't know what to say." I looked up at him. "Does this mean you've made a decision?"

"I promise, I've given the proposition extensive consideration, but I knew this morning that I would accept."

"I don't want you to do this because you think I don't have anyone else to help me."

"I'd be lying if I said that wasn't part of the reason, but the biggest reason is that this is a once-in-a-lifetime opportunity. I've read and studied the texts, but this is my chance to see everything firsthand. It's a historian's dream."

"But it's dangerous. I might not always be able to protect you."

"Did it ever occur to you that I'm worried I might fail *you*? My first task—a huge one—has been unsuccessful so far. I haven't found Ahone's symbol yet. My friend didn't find anything before he overnighted the books to me. At this moment, you're no safer than you were before you met me."

"You might find it yourself when the books arrive tomorrow."

"I hope so. And like I said, I've sent out word to a few colleagues. But we should also step up the search for your father's notes."

I leaned on the counter. "Myra remembered something this morning. She said that Daddy had started scribbling notes the week after the curse broke. And at one point he showed her this old ring he said I needed. She thought he was being delusional at the time, but she realized that it might be important. She said he told her I needed time."

"Time for what?"

"I don't know and neither did she." I closed my eyes. "I wish I'd been around more that week to ask him questions instead of putting all my trust in Collin."

"Ellie, you had no idea he'd betray you, and your father had full-blown Alzheimer's. Of course you were counting on Collin to help you."

"Well, look where it got me."

He reached over and covered my hand with his. "You did what you thought was right. You can't go back and change anything, so stop beating yourself up about it. All you can do is move forward, and I'll help you anyway that I can."

I looked up into his warm hazel eyes. "Thank you." I'd always wondered if I could trust Collin, right up until the end. But David didn't seem to have any ulterior motives. Still, I didn't trust my own judgment. I pulled my hand from his. "I need to start cleaning the rooms upstairs. I'm behind after talking to Tom."

"But we have dinner plans."

"Oh," I said, flustered again. "I thought that was to talk about you helping me."

"We still have to eat. And after hearing you tell what I suspect were a bunch of half-truths and lies, I'd like to get to know the Ellie Lancaster who existed before hell broke loose."

"Well . . ." I wasn't sure getting close to David was a good idea.

He sensed my hesitation. "And I'll tell you all about growing up as the son of a famous barrister."

My eyebrows lifted. "Your father's famous?"

"I guess you'll find out tonight." He winked. "Why don't you get your work done while I see what I can dig up about the Ricardo Estate."

I locked eyes with him. "You caught the coincidence there too?"

"I did. It could turn out to be nothing, but a collection of sixteenth-century English and Native American objects disappearing around the time the curse broke is highly suspicious."

"Especially since Collin is somehow tied to it."

He turned serious. "Agreed."

I went upstairs to start working, feeling guilty about not telling David the entire truth about my connection to Collin. Since he was putting his safety on the line to help me, he had a right to know that I had bound my soul to Collin's. Still, I wasn't ready to tell him. I could barely admit the truth to myself.

I cleaned all the rooms, leaving my old room for last. I told myself that I'd grown up in there, so there was absolutely no reason to be afraid of it now. But the moment I stepped over the threshold, the hair on my arms stood on end. I made the bed and dusted off the dresser, shifting a stack of books to the side. The title of one of them caught my eye: *The Head in Edward Nugent's Hand.*

It was David's. David was staying in my old room.

I froze with my hand on the book, telling myself it didn't mean anything. There were four available rooms up here, so it wasn't that odd that David was staying in this one.

When I finished an hour later, I found David at the dining room table in front of a legal pad and his laptop, lost in concentration, a pair of reading glasses perched on his nose. He looked up when I paused in the doorway.

"All finished?"

"Yeah. Did you find anything?"

"Not much more than we already know, but I'll keep digging. The collection was set to go to auction three weeks ago. The police appear to be baffled by how it was stolen. There was video surveillance, but it doesn't show anything untoward. It's rather odd that I hadn't heard of it, given that the collection contained Native American antiquities. I'll ask some colleagues to see if they've heard mention of it."

"Okay." I hesitated. "I wonder if we should skip dinner and just look for Daddy's notes and the ring."

He pulled off his glasses and set them on the table. "I'd agree with you if I didn't know that they were closing the site early tonight, and Myra offered to cook the team dinner."

My mouth dropped open. "Myra's cooking?" Before Daddy got sick, they used to host dinner parties all the time. Myra was a fantastic cook; she just hadn't done any entertaining in years.

"Forgive me if I'm overstepping my bounds, but I think there might be a connection between her and Steven."

"*What?*"

He held up a hand. "It's nothing really. Not yet. But I can see that there's something there."

"But isn't Steven married?"

He shook his head. "No, widowed."

I sagged into the door frame. "Oh." I could understand his appeal for Myra. He was an attractive man, and for several years

Daddy hadn't been the man she'd married. I was the last person to judge her. It just felt strange to think of her with someone else.

"I think Myra's invited a few other people too, so it will be a full house. We'd have no hope of finding anything with so many people around."

I bit my lower lip, jumpy with anxiety. Now that I had confirmation that Daddy really had hidden information around the house, I was eager to find it. But David was right. It would be better to wait. "Okay. But I want to start tomorrow. After we visit the colony site." I swept a few stray strands of hair that had fallen out of my ponytail from my face.

"Why don't you go get ready, and I'll take you to dinner. When do you want to go?"

I didn't want to take a shower, and it was too humid to do anything with my hair. Besides, it wasn't like we were going on a real date. "Forty-five minutes?"

"Okay." He grinned. "I'll pick you up then."

I drove my car home, mulling over everything I'd learned in the past twenty-four hours. I was sure I was missing something, but I couldn't put my finger on it. I washed my body off with a washrag, checking out the mark on my back in the mirror. It had faded quite a bit in the last day. I figured I had a couple of days at most. The thought filled me with terror, but I had to believe that David would find something.

No. It was time for me to depend on myself. I would find a solution and David would hopefully contribute. I'd start searching the house for the notes tomorrow. Daddy would have wanted me protected, so Ahone's mark had to be in his notes somewhere. I tried to ignore the fact that he hadn't recognized the mark that had been passed down in Manteo's line from Keeper to Keeper.

David showed up exactly on time, wearing khakis and a short-sleeve button-down shirt, open at the collar. He looked more handsome than ever. My stomach did a little flip, and the look of appreciation in his eyes made me suck in my breath. I suddenly worried that he might be interested in me for something other than our professional relationship.

I had to put a stop to that.

His eyes scanned the pale green sundress I'd pulled on and then landed on my face. "You look lovely, Ellie."

"Thank you," I murmured as I let him in. "I just need to grab a pair of shoes."

David followed me inside while I went into my room. When I emerged, bending over to slip my feet into my sandals, he smiled. "Have you figured out where we should go?"

"Yeah." I gave him directions to a restaurant on the highway to Nags Head. When we arrived, we were told there was a ten-minute wait, so we sat at the outdoor bar in the back of the restaurant, overlooking the sound. We ordered drinks and watched the water in silence as I tried to figure out how to handle David's possible interest in me. I couldn't afford to offend him.

Other than Drew—Claire's fiancé and my own friend since we were all kids together—Collin was the first man I'd spent time with without pursuing a romantic relationship. That intention had lasted all of a few days. Now here I was committing to a long-term working relationship with a very attractive man, and I wanted to keep it platonic. I snuck a glance at him. Could this really work, or was I just fooling myself?

David kept his gaze fixed on the sound. "How did things suddenly get so awkward?" he said after a while. "I can tell you're anxious. You described what's between us as a professional relationship, so why don't you just think of this as a business dinner."

He'd caught me watching him. "Sorry. This is all new for me."

"I didn't mean to make you uncomfortable. I just thought it might make working together easier if we were better acquainted personally."

I released a long breath. "Yes, you're right. I'm sorry I'm so edgy."

"You're dealing with a lot right now. No one can blame you for feeling anxious." He studied me for a moment. "If you don't mind me asking, how old are you?"

"Twenty-three."

He stiffened slightly. "You're not much older than my students."

My brow wrinkled in confusion. "You make yourself sound ancient. You said you were in your early thirties, right?"

"Thirty-one."

I snorted. "I have a dress older than that."

He laughed. "Isn't that supposed to be my line?"

I glanced over at him and grinned. "You have dresses tucked into your closet?"

His face flushed.

"I never took you for the blushing type, Dr. Preston," I teased.

"I never used to be until I met you."

Our banter eased the underlying tension, and after we were seated at our table, we spent dinner finding out about each other's lives, avoiding anything to do with the curse by unspoken agreement. We couldn't discuss it much in public anyway, and although I instinctively knew I could trust David, hearing more about him made me feel better about our alliance. Our lives up until now had been nothing alike. While my father was regionally known for his Lost Colony expertise, David's attorney father had gained national attention before David's birth, representing a victim of the South

London race riots. Consequently, his upbringing was more *Downton Abbey*, while mine resembled *Hart of Dixie*. Still, I felt a connection with him that I couldn't explain. Maybe David was right about fate. Maybe we *were* supposed to work together. And dinner made me feel better about his possible attraction to me. He'd been a perfect gentleman all night, completely professional. I assured myself I'd imagined his interest.

By the time we left the restaurant several hours later, I was sure that contacting him had been the right decision. But I also realized the risk we'd taken. The sun had set while we were at the restaurant.

As we drove home, I told David to park at the inn and I'd walk home.

"I'm not sure that's such good idea."

I scowled. "It's far more dangerous for you to be outside after dark than it is for me."

His face tightened and he gripped the steering wheel. "I want to suggest something, but I'm worried you'll take it the wrong way."

"Okay . . ."

"Until you get your new tattoo, I don't think you should be alone after the sun sets."

"Myra wants me to move back in with her, but I just can't make myself do it."

"I understand. I can't begin to fathom moving back in with my parents." He laughed, but it was hesitant.

"Besides, my room is currently taken." I wasn't about to tell him that I'd discovered that he was staying in it.

"That's not what I'm suggesting." He glanced at me. "I'd really like to stay at your apartment with you."

I froze. "Oh."

"I'd sleep on the sofa. You would be in your bed."

It was tempting. But it would be so easy for me to begin to rely on him. I needed to learn to rely on myself. "David, that's really sweet, but I don't think so."

"Ellie, I assure you I have honorable intentions."

"If anyone else said that to me, I'd laugh. But I know you mean it." I put my hand on his. "I think we need to take this slow. Even if it is a professional relationship." As I said "professional," I realized that touching him was contradictory. I removed my hand and put it in my lap.

"You've called it that twice now. Is that how you see it?"

I shrugged. "I'm not sure how to classify it. How would you?"

"A professional relationship sounds so cold and calculated. I have a feeling we're going to get to know each other fairly well. We're going to need to trust each other. I'd like to call it a partnership."

It all sounded like semantics to me, but he was right. We needed to define exactly what we had here. "Okay, you're right. I like partnership. But we need to make rules too."

"Okay." He seemed hesitant.

"I'm in charge since I'm the Curse Keeper and have the power to actually do something to these things. You'll have to trust my judgment."

"Is that an absolute rule, or can we have a healthy debate if I disagree?"

I bristled. "Is that how I'm coming across? Dictatorial?"

"No, Ellie. You're right. We need to lay the ground rules. But I need to know if I can present a contradictory opinion if I disagree."

"Of course. I value your opinion, David. If I didn't, you wouldn't be here."

He nodded.

"But if we're in a dangerous situation, I need to know that you'll listen to me first and argue later. If we come face-to-face with Ukinim—and I'm sure we will—I can't worry about you going rogue and putting yourself in danger."

David didn't answer for several seconds, staring out the windshield. "Okay."

I released the breath I'd been holding.

His eyebrows rose. "You were worried I wouldn't agree?"

"Let's just say I know someone else who wouldn't."

"Okay," he said softly. "What else?"

I leaned my elbow on the window. "That's the only one I have."

He kept his eyes on the road, but I saw the cords in his neck tighten. "I have a few."

Surprised, I dropped my arm and sat up straighter. "Okay."

"This will only work if we're completely honest with each other." He turned to me for a second, his eyes burning bright. "In all things."

"What does that mean?"

"It means you can't hide anything from me to protect me, even if it's just my feelings."

"You think I'm going to hurt you?"

"Not intentionally, Ellie, but we're both coming into this with past experiences, and it's easy to see that you're still hurting over that wanker."

Collin.

His hand tightened on the steering wheel. "He's the other Curse Keeper. We're bound to cross paths. If he wants to let the release of the spirits run its course as you say, he's not going to appreciate my involvement."

I turned my face to the window. "Well, the two of us are history."

"It may be over between you two, but he's still going to be around. He's still marking your door and threatened to kidnap you to protect you, for Christ's sake. It's safe to assume that his involvement is far from history."

My anger ignited. "Do you want him to stop?"

"God, no! Not with your mark almost faded. You need the protections on your door to be as strong as possible."

I rubbed my forehead, suddenly exhausted. I didn't want to talk about Collin, let alone think about him. "I don't understand what you're getting at."

"I'm telling you that if a situation arises where you're faced with telling me the truth or sparing my feelings, I need you to tell me the truth."

What did David foresee that I didn't? We weren't emotionally involved. I couldn't imagine a situation where my actions would hurt him unless he really did have an interest in me other than our agreement. But I was lying to Myra and Claire to protect them, so perhaps he had a point. "Okay. I promise."

His shoulders relaxed.

"What else?"

"You need to agree to listen to me if I make a suggestion or request about something other than the curse."

"Why?" I asked. "What are you planning on telling me?"

"Nothing. Yet. I just want to know that you'll consider my advice if I feel the need to give it."

I couldn't see any harm in that. I wasn't promising to obey him, just to listen. "Okay. Anything else?"

"No." He pulled up next to the inn and parked at the curb. The car idled as he took my hand in his. "But I want to thank you."

My stomach fluttered. "You're thanking me? Why?"

A sad smile covered his face and he looked out the windshield toward the side door, its protective markings visible from where we sat. "I've been at a crossroads this past year. I haven't been happy with how things were going in my life . . . It felt like my life was on hold, and I was waiting for *something* to occur." He looked at me, his smile fading. "Now you think I'm barmy."

"No. I felt exactly the same way. I couldn't figure out what I was supposed to do with myself, but it seemed like everything I tried didn't fit." I squeezed his hand. "Until the curse broke. Then I realized this was it."

"Yes," he said softly. "When you came to Chapel Hill, I knew you had to be a loon, and yet . . ." His voice trailed off. "And then I came down here and saw those markings on the doors and heard about the snake. *You* were here. After I saw Wapi, I just knew this was it. My whole life has been one long journey to *this*."

His thoughts were so similar to my own that he was scaring me. "Ahone's messenger told me he couldn't give me Ahone's symbol because searching for it is part of my journey." My heart exploded in my chest, and I looked up wide-eyed. "Meeting you, having you help me, is part of my journey."

David looked just as startled.

"I'm sorry," I whispered. Once again, the fucking deities were messing with me.

"*Why?* This is exactly where I want to be."

I couldn't imagine why. I was certain this situation wouldn't end well. "I have to go." I let go of David's hand and reached for the door.

"Ellie, wait. Why are you upset?"

"Because I'm not sure I'm strong enough to protect you, and it scares me."

"We can do this together. And thank you for being honest."

"That's part of the deal, right?" I sighed. "But I really do need to get home. When should I come to the site tomorrow?"

"Are you coming over to the inn tomorrow morning?"

"Yeah, and thankfully, I already have a day off from Darrell's. If I still even have a job after my first two days."

"What happened during your first two days?"

I shook my head with a half laugh. "We'll leave that sordid tale for tomorrow."

"I can only imagine what's in store for me. Do you want to just come with me to the site for the whole day?"

"Sure."

He opened his car door and came around to open mine. I was already climbing out.

"You don't have to open car doors for me, David."

"Some habits die hard. I don't think I'll ever break myself of that one." He glanced down the street, in the direction of my apartment. "I'm worried about you getting home okay. This doesn't feel right."

"Shelve your chivalry. In this particular instance, I can take care of myself much better than you ever could."

He placed his hand over his heart. "You really know how to wound a bloke."

His face broke out into a mischievous grin that made my insides flutter, but I ignored it and gave his arm a playful shove. "Get inside already."

His grin faded. "Text me when you're inside your flat so I know you're safe."

"Now you sound like Myra."

He winked, and I couldn't help but notice his gorgeous, long eyelashes. "I just got an awesome new job. I need to make sure my boss is still around so I can keep it."

I shook my head with a laugh. "I'll text you. Now go."

I watched the door close before I started down the street, trying to stay alert to any possible danger around me. My hand flexed instinctively at my side. I hadn't used the symbol on my palm since the night the curse broke, but the few times I had needed to use it, instinct had taken over for me. I had to trust that it would again.

My ears strained for any hint of danger, but the bugs were singing their nightly chorus. They'd be gone if any of the nasties were around.

When I got to the top of the stairs, the marks on my door were fresh, but there was a new symbol in the middle. A diamond shape with an X. What did that mean?

I grabbed the charcoal out of the flowerpot and added my own mark, worried about the new symbol. Could Collin be setting me up? But even as the thought occurred to me, I knew there was no way he would intentionally hurt me. If I was sure of anything where he was concerned, it was that he wanted to keep me safe.

Damn him.

I shut the door and placed my back to it. My cell phone started to ring and I dug it out of my purse, not surprised to see David's number on the screen.

"I just got in. I was about to text you."

"I forgot to tell you that I left something for you on your kitchen counter."

"What is it?"

"Go find out."

I found a small brown bag on the counter against the wall. How had I missed it earlier? I picked it up and shook it, surprised it didn't weigh very much. Reaching inside, I felt a wooden hoop and strings. My heart constricted as I pulled it out. "It's a dream catcher."

"Hang it over your head. On your bed frame if you can manage it. The legend about them might just be a story, but lots of things we thought were stories are turning out to be real. I figured it was worth a try."

"I don't know what to say, David," I said in amazement. How had I been lucky enough to find him? "Thank you."

"You're welcome, Ellie. Sweet dreams."

I'd be happier if I had no dreams at all.

⊰ CHAPTER SEVENTEEN ⊱

My sleep was blissfully dreamless and more restful than anything I'd experienced in weeks.

Until a woman's screams made my eyes fly open.

My heart raced as I bolted upright in bed, my heavy breathing the only sound as I tried to orient myself. For a moment I thought I'd imagined everything, but then the screams came again, just as anguished. Someone was in trouble.

I scrambled out of bed and looked for my cell phone, intent on calling the police, when my palm began to itch. I nearly dropped to my knees in fright.

The threat was supernatural.

I lifted my phone from the kitchen counter with a shaking hand, wanting desperately to call someone, but who? Collin? I had no idea where he even was, let alone whether he could make it here in time. David? He was two blocks away, but I didn't want to put him in danger. Tom and the police were out.

It was up to me.

Oh, God.

I dropped onto a bar stool, trying to control the panic bursting in my chest. I had no idea what to do.

The woman screamed again.

I sucked in several deep breaths and set the phone down, forcing myself off the stool. If I didn't go out there, someone would be killed. Could I live with that?

I hesitated when I reached the threshold. I'd saved *myself* before, but could I save someone else?

Throwing open my front door, I stood in the doorway, my ears straining to try and place the sounds. Halfway down the stairs, I heard the scream again. It was coming from behind my building. From the sound.

I ran around the side of the building toward the water, cursing that I'd forgotten to put on shoes. I ignored the fact that I was wearing short pajama pants and a tank top with no bra. My hair was down and loose.

When I reached the street, the night was eerily silent. Not a single person was investigating the cries. While I was thankful there weren't any potential witnesses or additional victims, I was also highly suspicious.

The woman screamed loud and long. A cry of pain.

My stomach roiled. What if I was too late?

The cries echoed off the water, coming from the direction of the marsh lighthouse.

Had Big Nasty cornered someone out there? I found myself hoping so . . . Anything would be better than Ukinim.

A low layer of clouds was rolling in toward land. It was particularly dense around the short, one-story replica of an original marsh lighthouse, built on a deck at the end of a narrow pier. The structure's lights were noticeably dark.

My feet were bare, but my footsteps thudded on the wooden planks, the only sound in the still night. Even the insects were silent. It was yet another sign that something supernatural was out there waiting.

I had no hope of sneaking up on whatever awaited me, so I decided to go in big and bold. I had two choices once I reached the deck of the lighthouse. I could stay on the lower, wider walkway, or I could head up to the raised walkway that hugged the perimeter of the building. I chose the lower deck and circled the back, the blood rushing in my head. When I rounded the corner to the back section, I found nothing but swirling, transparent clouds.

My breath coming fast and shallow, I took tentative steps across the surface. I had made it halfway across the deck when I heard a sound behind me. Terrified, I slowly turned around, my heart squeezing with fear.

A large, grey, furry animal with glowing yellow eyes and sharp, pointy claws stood ten feet away. I would have laughed if I wasn't so terrified. It looked fluffier than I'd expected, kind of like a giant demented teddy bear.

Ukinim.

I forced myself to stay silent as I started to slowly back away from him.

His squatty legs looked ridiculously inadequate to support his three-foot-tall and four-foot-long body. I moved to the side of the building, and his glowing eyes tracked my every movement.

I took several steps backward.

"I knew you would come," he said with an evil smile, his voice a garbled growl.

I glanced around the area, still trying to keep an eye on Ukinim. "Where's the woman who was screaming?"

The creature laughed, and when he opened his mouth again, a woman's cries came out.

I had walked into a trap.

"You stupid human. I knew you couldn't stay away," Ukinim said, pacing back and forth across the deck, blocking any possibility of an escape except through the water. "I don't see what's so special about you."

Fighting hysteria, I flexed my hand by my side as I continued to walk backward toward the opposite end of the lighthouse. But the badger switched directions, pushing me toward the upper deck surrounding the building. "You should compare notes with Mishiginebig. He said the same thing."

The badger growled at the mention of the snake.

I knew that I should use my mark to send the stupid thing away, but I hoped this excursion wouldn't be for nothing. Maybe I could at least get some information out of it. If it didn't manage to kill me first. "Why do you want me?" I asked. "Other than the obvious."

His eyes narrowed and he snarled, "Because Okeus does."

"Why? What did Okeus do to you?"

He stopped and lifted his chin. "I was a great warrior, but Okeus was jealous of my glory."

"You were a *person*?" Could Okeus turn people into demonic animals?

The badger snapped and I jumped backward, jamming my shoulder into the railing behind me.

His head lowered. "I was until Okeus tricked me with the promise of untold riches and power. He betrayed me and forced me to live underground. I was only allowed to come out once a year to see the sun. But the tables have turned. In Popogusso, we were all on equal ground, and I vowed to seek my revenge. Okeus no longer has control over me. I want to take the thing he wants above all else. You."

"Why does Okeus want me so much?"

"I don't care. It only matters that it will cause him great pain to lose you." He was three feet away, and the stench of blood, dirt, and decay clogged my nose.

Great pain? How could that be?

My palm burned. Ukinim was close enough that he could easily slash my belly with his claws. "I want to get even with Okeus too. Maybe we could work together."

The creature laughed. "I'd rather eat your heart."

"But I still have Okeus's mark. My Manitou is safe."

"That's what you think."

Oh, shit. I lifted my palm. My mark glowed white, the light filling the dark night, and I began to recite the words of protection.

"I am the daughter of the sea . . ."

The wind picked up, blowing my hair into my face. A low growl rumbled in the badger's throat as a faint white vortex appeared behind him.

"Born of the essence present at the beginning of time and the end of the world . . ."

The badger snarled and lunged for me. I jumped sideways as he swung out a paw, his claws slamming through the wood with a loud crash, creating a two-foot hole.

Oh. Shit.

My hand still raised, I continued my chant in a shaky voice as I walked backward along the back of the building. *"I am black water and crystal streams . . ."*

The vortex wind grew stronger, and I struggled to stay upright. The badger fought against the gusts as he tried to follow me.

"The ocean waves and the raindrops in the sky." I had almost reached the opposite end and was preparing to turn and run when I heard another low growl. I looked over my shoulder and shrieked.

A second badger was inching toward me, its nose low to the wood deck.

There were two of them.

My hand dropped in my shock and the vortex disappeared.

I was screwed.

The second badger swung his paw, his claws gleaming in the moonlight that shone through the misty fog. I jumped close to the railing abutting the water as he crashed through the decking, creating another hole. They had me cornered.

The water bubbled violently in the sound, and Mishiginebig burst to the surface, his mouth open and hissing.

"Who dares defy Okeus?" his voice boomed through the darkness.

The badgers hesitated, and I took advantage of the moment to run toward the raised walkway, leaping onto the edge of the two-foot-high deck and then scrambling over the railing. I pressed my back against the siding of the lighthouse as both badgers charged. They crashed through the wood railing on either side of me, leaving gaping holes in the deck. I was trapped on a three-foot-wide section of sidewalk with three-foot holes to my left and right.

One of the badgers tumbled into the water, squealing as it tried—and failed—to gain purchase. The other ignored his friend and charged the section of the deck where I was standing.

Mishiginebig lunged toward the badger, grabbing its neck and dragging it away from me. The badger wounded the snake with a vicious slash, and its thick black blood leaked into a puddle on the deck.

I took advantage of the distraction and climbed onto the railing. Balancing on the balls of my feet, I stood and jumped, grabbing an extended support beam from the low-slung roof. I pulled my body up so that my chest was leaning over the beam, then swung my legs up, my knee hitting the edge of the metal roof. I ignored the pain that shot through my leg and dug my knee onto the slick roof, releasing the beam with one hand and gripping the raised metal seam to pull myself the rest of the way up.

The building shook violently and I began to slide back down, my lower legs hanging over the edge.

The second badger had climbed out of the water and slammed back into the building. Extending his claws, he dug into my left calf.

I cried out in pain and tried to climb higher, tamping down my bubbling terror. I had to get to the widow's walk at the top of the lighthouse.

Blood dripped down my leg, the slash throbbing with every heartbeat, but I climbed higher on the roof, grabbing hold of the lower edge of the widow's walk and pulling myself up. I climbed over the short railing and stood, grunting when I put a small amount of weight on the foot of my injured leg.

The other badger had broken free of Mishiginebig's grasp and was now climbing onto the deck's railing with its identical friend.

I lifted my palm, my chest heaving from exertion and fright as I began to chant again.

"*I am the daughter of the sea, born of the essence present at the beginning of time and the end of the world. I am black water and crystal streams.*"

The wind gusted as the vortex reappeared.

My hair blew in all directions, partially obstructing my vision, and all three spirits fought against the suction.

Mishiginebig took advantage of the badgers' distraction and grabbed one of them, dragging it toward the water. It clung to the railing, its back half hanging over the sound. The other one ran across the deck and leaped for the roof, its claws sinking into the metal of the lower section.

"*The ocean waves and the raindrops in the sky. I am life and death and everything in between.*"

The badger slunk up the gently sloped roof until he was almost level with me. A smile lifted his mouth, his sharp teeth glistening

226

in the moonlight, just before he swung his claws toward my stomach. I cringed, waiting for the pain as I forced myself to finish the last line.

"I compel you to leave my sight."

The badger was lifted into the air, his claws just inches from my face, and sucked into the vortex. Mishiginebig and the other badger shrieked as they suffered the same fate. Mishiginebig's head was sucked inside and his long, serpentine body continued to lift from the water into the twister for what felt like forever. The swirling circle grew tighter and tighter until the tip of his tail disappeared, then the vortex with it.

I collapsed against the railing, fighting sobs of fright and relief. Sirens filled the air and I whipped around to see red flashing lights bouncing off the fog clouds that shrouded the streets. Several police cars screeched to a halt.

I was on top of the one-story lighthouse with no easy way down, destruction all around me.

Now I was really screwed.

∙⌣ Chapter Eighteen ⌣∙

I sat against the railing for a moment, waiting for Tom to appear. A crowd had gathered at the end of the pier. The cloud layer and lack of lighting still hid me from the people on the street. I could either wait to get caught and be forced to come up with a logical explanation. Or I could try to get away.

Climbing over the railing, I glanced back toward the street again. Several police officers were heading down the pier.

I hunched down, trying to stay hidden in the darkness as I lowered myself to the metal roof. I slid on my backside to the bracket I'd used to climb up. Leaning over, I grabbed hold of it and lowered myself to what was left of the upper deck. A bolt of pain shot through my leg when I landed.

The clump of footsteps on the pier sped up my heart. There was only one way to escape.

I stepped through one of the holes the badgers had created and plunged into the water.

Vegetation brushed my legs while my head was still submerged, causing me to panic. I pushed up to the surface, telling myself I was in salt water, my new natural habitat. But the usual energy surge I felt in the ocean was missing, replaced by a dull thrum.

I swam backward, under the lighthouse, as approaching footsteps clattered on the deck over my head.

"What in God's name destroyed the deck like this?" Tom's voice was unmistakable.

"I thought I saw something on the roof," someone else said.

I needed to find a way out of here quickly. It would be a matter of minutes before they started searching the water for a suspect.

Moving slowly so I didn't splash, I started swimming around the lighthouse support beams, heading toward the pier. I had to duck under the horizontal supports of the pier, but thankfully a crowd of curious onlookers appeared to have gathered near the lighthouse, and their loud voices covered the small splashes I made. If I could continue under the boardwalk and around the edge of downtown to the swimming ladder behind the Tranquil Inn, I'd be able to climb out with my injured leg, and I'd hopefully be far enough away that no one would notice me.

My plan worked perfectly, but it took me several minutes of slow swimming to reach the ladder, and I needed to dodge a few docked sailboats to get there. By the time I pulled myself up the metal ladder, my leg was throbbing.

I skirted the side of the hotel, looking at the crowd that had gathered down at the end of the street. I had no idea how I'd get to my apartment in my sopping wet clothes without attracting attention.

I hobbled a couple of blocks west, then south. Thankfully, most of the people who were still out were gathered by the pier.

The insides of the Dare Inn and the residential house were both lit up. I ducked in the side door of the house and headed to the laundry room to grab a towel from the dryer. Wrapping it around my shoulders, I slipped into the butler's pantry to get the first-aid kit that Myra kept hidden there. I had just pulled it out when David appeared in the doorway, his face drawn.

"Ellie. Where in bloody hell were you? Myra is frantic. We rang your mobile and went to your apartment. She's waiting over by the lighthouse; she was sure you had something to do with the disturbance there." His gaze dropped to my leg. "I'm guessing she was right."

"Call her and tell her that I'm fine. I don't want her to worry."

He pulled his phone from his pocket and called Myra, speaking in hushed tones. After he hung up, he frowned.

I flinched as I dabbed the five-inch-long claw marks on my leg with an alcohol swab.

"I hate that I just lied to your mother. You're obviously not fine."

"I will be."

"What happened?"

"Ukinim."

He paused. "What do you want to do?"

"I want to go home, but I can't go looking like a drowned rat. If Tom sees me, he'll know straight off I was on that pier."

"I'll run upstairs and get you some of my clothes, but you really need to take care of that gash. Is it from Ukinim?"

"That or his buddy."

"There are two of them?"

I sighed. "I'm full of all kinds of good news tonight."

David went upstairs while I taped large gauze squares over the wound.

He returned with a T-shirt and I pulled it over my head, my damp tank top still underneath.

"Can you walk home?"

"It's not like I have a choice."

We hobbled down the street, my leg throbbing with every step. David helped me up the stairs, following in silence. There were still a number of people milling about behind the apartment building,

230

and a cacophony of sounds bounced around in the night. I was so eager for the safety of my apartment that I didn't notice the person sitting in one of the plastic chairs on my porch until I almost stumbled upon him.

Collin leaned back in the chair, narrowing his eyes. "Well, aren't you the cute couple?"

David's arm stiffened around my waist.

I groaned. "Not now, Collin. I'm too tired for more drama."

"What happened out there, Ellie?"

"Ukinim showed up, that's what." I pushed David's hand away and started to look for my key when I realized I hadn't locked the door. In fact, I hadn't even closed it. Collin must have.

"Why in God's name would you go out there alone?" Collin asked. He shot David a condescending look. "Or did you take your new friend with you?"

"I went alone." I lifted my eyebrows. "Satisfied?" I leaned into the railing, white-hot pain shooting up my calf. "I woke up when I heard a woman screaming. Since my palm was itching, I knew it was supernatural. Which meant calling the police was not an option. I considered calling you, but I wasn't sure you could—or *would*—help. So I went alone."

"Why would you even go at all?"

"Because we let those things loose, Collin." I stepped forward and jabbed his chest with my finger. "You and me. If you think I'm going to let some woman get her insides shredded while I lay in bed listening, you don't know me at all."

"You could have been killed, Ellie! It was stupid and reckless."

"Maybe so." I lifted my chin in defiance. "But I'd do it again."

Collin's face contorted in rage, and he turned his attention to David. "So you're the college professor who's supposed to be helping her? Where the hell were *you*?"

Fury blazing inside me, I shoved Collin's chest, and he stumbled backward.

"*Excuse me?* Do you think he *owns* me, Collin Dailey? Do you think I'm some witless girl who needs a man to boss her around? *No one* tells me what to do. I thought you would have figured that out by now."

His face darkened. "He's going to get you killed, Ellie. He doesn't know a goddamned thing."

"Well, at least he's trying, which is a hell of a lot more than you're doing."

Collin's gaze dropped. "What happened to your leg?"

"A gift from Ukinim or his friend."

He stiffened. "You're bleeding."

Blood was seeping through the gauze. "Gashes from claws will do that," I said with a snotty tone.

Before I knew what he was doing, he grasped my right hand with his, pressing our marks together.

The sensation of every living creature in the vicinity filled me. I felt the heartbeats of the seventy-two humans by the sound. The flutter of mosquito wings in the parking lot below. Grass in the park, stretching upward.

Collin stared into my eyes and I felt the yearning in his heart. The ache that soaked every cell of his body.

A burning sensation engulfed my calf, and the gashes on my leg closed, the cells repairing and knitting together.

Collin pulled his hand from mine and dizziness swamped my head.

"What did you just do?" I gasped.

He looked down at my leg. "Testing a theory. It looks like it worked." His jaw clenched. "But I might not be around to help you next time." He pointed to David, getting angrier by the second. "And that fool sure as hell can't do anything."

Collin stormed down the stairs, and my mouth gaped open as I watched him go.

"What just happened?" David asked.

"He healed my leg."

I opened the apartment door and went inside, David following behind me. I bent down and ripped the gauze off my leg, still amazed. There was no sign of the injury. Not even a scar.

"He's right, you know."

My anger rekindled and I spun around. "About what?"

"I might get you killed."

I shook my head and sat down. "I don't expect you to know everything, David. Any information is better than none."

"I have something new on Ukinim."

I froze. "*You do?*"

David sat on the sofa beside me. "I found a text that lists him by name. It says he was a warrior turned into a badger."

"Yes! That's what he told me." I stood up and went into the kitchen.

He turned to watch me. "You had a *conversation* with a demon?"

"Once I realized it was a trap, I figured I might as well get something out of it." I grabbed two bottles of water from the fridge, handing one to David as I sunk back into the sofa cushions.

He twisted the cap off his bottle. "What else did you find out?"

I looked up. "Well, there are two of them. That caught me by surprise."

"The text said the second one's his wife. They were cursed together."

"His wife? How did that happen?"

"I copied the text into an e-mail. Hold on a second." David grabbed his phone out of his pocket, pulled up the e-mail, and scowled, enlarging the text. "The story says that Ukinim was the greatest warrior in all the tribes. He was boastful and claimed he could beat Okeus in a wrestling match. One evening at twilight, Okeus walked into the camp and accepted Ukinim's challenge, but Okeus insisted on setting the rules. If Ukinim won, he could have everything he wanted—power and wealth. But if Okeus won, Ukinim would be banished; he would spend the rest of his life ostracized from his people. Ukinim accepted. If neither of them won, they would walk away with nothing. Their match would be the next night.

"Word spread far and wide, and many people arrived to see the great Okeus take on the warrior Ukinim. They brought offerings to the god of war, piling them so high they rose into the heavens, attracting the attention of Ahone himself.

"At twilight, Okeus walked into camp. Ukinim's wife, Ilena, heard the cheers of the *nuppin* and became furious that her people wanted the god to beat her husband. The contest lasted for hours. The people grew weary, but Ukinim's strength never wavered and neither did Okeus's. The sun had begun to rise, and yet the warrior and the god still fought.

"Ilena believed her husband deserved to win. What other *nuppin* had dared to challenge Okeus? What other *nuppin* could stand against him for so long? So she approached the edge of the circle where the warrior and the god were fighting and tossed a handful of dirt into the face of the god, temporarily blinding him. Ukinim took his chance and pinned the god, winning the challenge. Ukinim strutted around the circle, boasting that he was better than the gods.

"Okeus was furious that Ukinim had dared to claim he was his better and that the man had won by cheating. The ground shook and the *nuppin* screamed in terror. Ukinim swore he didn't know his wife had cheated, but Okeus didn't care. He banned them both from the *nuppin* and changed them into badgers, forced to live underground except for one day out of the year."

I rested my head against the cushions of the couch, completely exhausted. "Does it say how we can defeat them?"

"From what I've read, a god can kill them."

"Oh, good. I'll just ask my good friend Okeus to get rid of them for me. When he springs his surprise."

He grimaced. "Don't be so cheeky."

"Is there anything else?"

"Yes." He hesitated. "But it's vague."

"What is it?"

"It says that a conjurer with strong power can defeat them and send them to Popogusso."

I sat up. "A conjurer?"

"Conjurers were real members of the Algonquian tribes and were said to have magical powers. They had a connection to the spiritual world that the *nuppin* and the priests, the other spiritual leaders, lacked."

My chest tingled with excitement. "So where do we find a conjurer?"

A hint of a smile appeared as he leaned closer, his face inches from mine. "Ellie, *you're* the conjurer," he whispered.

"What?" I leaned back. "Does it say how I can defeat them?"

"No."

"So we're no closer than we were."

"Not true. Collin told you it took both of you to banish them. This is singular. I think you can do it on your own."

A huge weight fell off my shoulders. "David . . . this changes everything. How?"

"I don't know. But if it's out there, we'll find it. I promise you that."

I reached around his neck and pulled him in for a hug. "Thank you."

David pulled back and stared into my eyes, his smile fading. "But next time, don't run out there on your own. If something happens to you, we'll all be lost. We're partners now, remember?"

That was still going to take some getting used to.

⌁ CHAPTER NINETEEN ⌁

When David and I showed up at the inn the next morning, Myra gave me a long hug and told me not to scare her like that again. While I hoped I wouldn't, I also didn't offer any promises.

After I helped with breakfast, I told Becky I wouldn't be able to work with her today.

"Don't worry about it." A wicked smile lit up her face as she leaned to the side to watch David talk to his colleagues. "Myra already made arrangements for someone else to help me today."

"She did?"

The side door opened and Becky laughed. "Talk about perfect timing."

I turned to see who was walking through the door. "*Claire?*"

She laughed. "Don't sound so happy to see me."

"Why aren't you working at the Tranquil Inn today?"

"It's my day off. Isn't that weird? I never get Thursdays off, but my boss called me last night and told me I could take the day off to get ready for my wedding. With pay, even. How weird that Myra asked for my help on the same day."

Another eerie coincidence. "If you got the day off to work on your wedding, what are you doing here?"

She shrugged, looking over my shoulder. "That's really him."

"Him, who?"

Her eyes widened in exasperation. "Hot British Professor him. Who else?"

"I already told you he was here."

"I wanted to meet him up close and personal for myself." She pushed past me and walked up to David, extending her hand. "Hello, I'm Claire, Ellie's best friend. I saw you in Chapel Hill, but we weren't introduced, Dr. Preston."

He looked down at her, amusement dancing in his eyes, and shook her hand. "David, please. And we weren't introduced because I was about to call campus security on Ellie."

Steven was sitting at the dining room table eating his breakfast, but he glanced up at us. "Ellie came to see you in Chapel Hill?"

"Yes," David said. "It's a long story that I'll share with you later."

Claire couldn't stop grinning. "So you're taking her to see the Lost Colony."

He winked. "It's not lost anymore."

Claire turned toward me. "I like him. You can keep him."

I groaned and grabbed her arm, dragging her toward the kitchen. "Thank you. I feel so much better to have your blessing."

"It was nice to officially meet you, Claire, Ellie's best friend," David called after us.

"I'm serious," Claire said when we reached the butler's pantry. "I like this guy."

"You like his accent and his build."

"Well . . . that too."

I laughed and put a dirty plate into the dishwasher. "This is a working relationship. No flirting. No fooling around."

"But fooling around is the best part of a relationship."

My eyes widened in frustration. "There is no relationship. There is no us. This is a professional partnership."

"Uh-huh."

I shook my head and stared out the window over the sink. "I don't want to royally screw this up. If we keep it professional, it will be easier for us to work together."

"Uh-huh." She sounded far from convinced.

"Stop trying to force something that isn't there."

"Hello, Ellie! He's hot! And that accent!"

"Collin was hot too."

"Collin doesn't count."

"He most certainly does. I don't trust my judgment when it comes to men."

"Then trust mine. Do not let Dr. David Preston get away. This man is perfect for you."

I scowled. "You don't even know him."

"I see the way he lights up when he talks about you. And the way you get flustered when I bring up the idea of him getting in your panties."

"Umm . . ." David was standing in the doorway, his face flushing. "Ellie, I'm ready to go when you are."

I squeezed my eyes shut. "'I'll be ready in a minute." I waited a moment. "Is he gone?" I asked in a whisper.

Claire laughed. "Yep."

I opened my eyes and smacked her arm. "Thanks a lot! You knew he was there, didn't you."

A wicked smile lit up her eyes. "It should be an interesting day now."

I dried off my hands. "Just for that, you can clean up the kitchen on your own."

David was waiting in the dining room, and he didn't say a word as we got into his car. The silence was awkward, so I tried to break the tension. "I meant to tell you that the dream catcher worked."

His eyes widened. "Really?"

"Not a single dream. I didn't even see the animals this time. I woke up when I heard the woman's screams."

"That's fantastic news. You'll have to sleep with it every night. And tonight, I insist on sleeping on your sofa."

"David—"

He parked his car in the Fort Raleigh National Historic Site lot and held up his hand. "Nope. You agreed to listen to my suggestions and concerns. I'm not trying to hover over you, although I have to admit that I'm protective of the people I care about. But if we're going to be partners, we need to watch out for each other. I want to keep an eye on you . . . and at the risk of emasculating myself, I'd feel better if you were there to protect me if I need it too."

There was no way I could refuse him if he truly felt safer with me. And besides, his argument made sense. If Collin had a problem with us working together, it stood to reason that the spirits and gods wouldn't like it either. I couldn't count on the marks protecting David at the inn. I suspected he was a lot like me. If he heard someone screaming for help in the middle of the night, he would be the first person out the door. "Okay."

"Now that wasn't so hard, was it?" he teased, opening his car door. "Now let's go check out Manteo's hut."

Manteo's hut. My stomach churned with anxiety.

David got me checked in at the foundation office, and they gave me a guest pass marking me as a visitor. When we left the building and started down the sidewalk, David snuck a glance at me. "You look nervous."

"I am. There's a lot riding on this."

"We know it's not our only potential source of information. But I do think the hut is going to give us some guidance."

The village came into view as we rounded a bend and I froze, my feet sticking to the sidewalk.

"Have you seen it since it reappeared?" he asked quietly.

"Only what they showed on TV the day they found it." I took a deep breath. "Both my parents worked in this park, and I've been here more times than I can count. But this . . ." I hesitated. "I wish Daddy could have seen it."

David rested his hand on my arm. "If you don't feel up to this . . ."

"No." I turned to him, pleading. "I do. It's just that Daddy lived his entire life to see this. There were over four hundred years of Keepers in our family, and it all boils down to me. I don't feel worthy."

"Ellie, I'm sure your father would be proud of you. And for what it's worth, from what I know of you, you *are* worthy."

I nodded. I wasn't sure I believed him, but I was the one who was here. It was up to me. "Let's go."

After we passed the visitors' center and walked through a patch of trees, the entire village was spread out before us. My mouth hung open.

"It's overwhelming when you first see it. Give it a minute."

I could see why. A six-foot-tall chain-link fence surrounded the buildings. The village had disappeared hundreds of years ago and reappeared exactly where it had once stood. Daddy had told me that the landscape of the island had changed over time. The shore itself had crept inland and the ground was higher. Most of the trees in the clearing next to the original fort mounds were less than a hundred years old. But the village didn't seem to care about the landscape when it reappeared. It had blended in with what was already there.

Close to thirty buildings covered the ground; trees shot through some, and others were partially underground. Strings that had been set up by the researchers had created a checkerboard pattern. I was no stranger to archaeological sites, but they were usually all dirt and holes. This was truly something different.

"Ready?" David asked after several seconds.

"Yeah."

We went through the gate and checked in with the guard, showing him our credentials. David pointed out several structures as we walked the perimeter—a blacksmith shop, lodging quarters for the single men in the colony, family homes. He pointed to a slightly larger house close to the edge. "I know you want to see Manteo's hut, but I thought you might also be interested in this one." He grinned. "We think it belonged to Ananias Dare."

My stomach fluttered. Instinctively, I had known it would be there, but I had been so focused on what information might be found in Manteo's hut that I hadn't stopped to think about it.

I shook my head in awe. "They were just stories. I never believed them. Not really. Especially after Momma died. But now it's all here." I waved my hand toward Ananias's house. "And I'm standing here thinking about what Ananias went through . . . what drove him and Manteo to even consider doing such a thing."

David was silent for several moments. "Ananias had a wife and newborn child to protect. Manteo was trying to save his people. They were desperate, Ellie. They would have done anything to save the people they loved and cared about." He paused, lowering his voice. "We're not totally unlike them. You're trying to protect the people you love. We're trying to save our people. Humanity."

"What if we screw up like they did?"

He looked down at me with a tender smile. "We'll just have to make sure that we don't."

"You sound so certain."

His smile faded. "We don't have a choice. It's our only option."

I nodded, not trusting myself to speak. I was surprised by how much I already needed him. Not only for information, but for support. He believed in me even when I didn't believe in myself.

"Do you want to look inside?"

"Ananias's house?"

He grinned. "Yeah."

"Okay."

We carefully stepped over strings as we headed toward the structure. Several people were writing things down while a couple of others were taking photos. Steven stood to the side, holding a clipboard and talking to a woman.

As we walked over, he glanced up and smiled. "Good morning, Ellie. Welcome to 1587."

"Thank you." My voice croaked and I tried again. "Thank you for giving me the chance to be here."

"Of course. I know how much your father and your mother would have loved to see this."

A man walked over and turned to David. "Excuse me, Dr. Preston. We found something that might be of interest to you."

My attention perked up.

"Of course," David said. He turned to me, searching my face. "Are you okay with staying here for a little bit?"

"Don't worry about her." Steven waved David away. "If she shares the interest her parents and stepmother have in early American history, she'll want to stay all day."

David hesitated, waiting for permission from me. My original goal had been to examine Manteo's hut, not Ananias's. But if David was leaving me here, I knew there had to be a reason. Collin had spent our entire time together hiding information from me.

The frustrating part was that I'd known it without being able to do a thing about it. David, on the other hand, had never given me any reason *not* to trust him. He shared everything he knew and freely admitted when he didn't know something. I knew without a doubt that David would tell me about any discoveries he made without me. I smiled. "I'm going to hang out here with Steven for a while."

David gave me a relieved smile and then took off across the eerie village. Steven watched him go and chuckled, shaking his head. "He's got it bad."

"What?"

He just laughed and ignored my question. "Ellie, I'm not sure if you realize this, but your father was very highly regarded. His expertise on the Lost Colony was world renowned."

I knew he'd been important as the head park ranger here, but I hadn't realized that he'd had a reputation off the site. "Really?"

He nodded and wrote on some paperwork, silent for several seconds. "Not just your father. Your mother too, before her death." Steven handed a young woman his clipboard and took several steps toward a small timber-post house. "Your father was brilliant. We were sorry to see him go."

I stepped over an exposed tree root as I followed. "It was hard on Daddy when he began losing his memories. For a man who valued intelligence and education so highly, it was difficult for him to accept."

Steven stopped and swung his gaze to my face. "We'd lost him several years before that, Ellie. We lost him when your mother died."

I blinked, confused. "What are you talking about?"

"Your father traveled and delivered lectures about the first English colonies, particularly the ones in North Carolina. He was greatly sought after."

I vaguely remembered him traveling, but I'd never thought about the fact that he'd stopped doing so after Momma's death. "He must not have wanted to leave me."

"I thought so too at first, but about a year after she died, I invited him to a conference that was being held in Chapel Hill. I understood his fear of leaving you, but the conference was close enough that he could attend for just the day and even bring you along. My wife was going to be there, and she offered to watch you. John knew Margaret well, but he still stubbornly refused." Steven paused and looked out into the trees. "I drove up to Manteo and took your father out to dinner. We all knew how much he loved your mother, so I suspected that he was still grieving. I thought perhaps I could convince him that he still had a purpose in life. That your mother would want him to continue doing what he loved and that we still needed his expertise.

"He drank too much that night, and I encouraged it in the hopes that it might help me change his mind, but it only made him melancholy. He told me that your mother's death was his fault. That the colony had killed her, and he would never lecture about it again. His answer made no sense to me, but when I asked him what he meant the next day, he refused to elaborate."

"But Myra told me the police suspected that Momma was killed by a man who was mad at Daddy over some zoning issue that was brought to the council."

"I'm sorry to dredge up bad memories, Ellie. I only know what your father told me."

"Thank you. Daddy kept so much hidden from me and now that he's gone, I'm trying to piece together anything and everything I can. Especially about the Lost Colony."

He took a step toward Ananias's hut, then stopped and turned to face me. "There is something else, but it never came to anything."

My eyes widened in anticipation.

His mouth pursed, and I could tell he was struggling with whether to continue.

"Please, Steven. If you know anything, I'm eager to hear it. No matter how inconsequential it may seem."

"That's what worries me about telling you. You just lost your father, and I don't want to reopen old wounds from your mother's death."

I grabbed his arm before I realized what I was doing. "Anything you can tell me would be helpful. Please. I've been having dreams about her death, and the events play out differently than I remember them. I need to know what happened."

He sighed and put his hand over mine. "Of course, Ellie. If it involves your parents, you have a right to know." He stared into my eyes. "Your mother called me a week before her death, which was unusual. She was an archaeologist, although the only digs she had worked on in quite some time were the rare excavations on the Raleigh grounds. She spent most of her time at the foundation doing paperwork and publicity on site, which aggravated her to no end at times. I usually only talked to her when she was with your father."

"Why did she call you?"

He took a deep breath. "She told me that she'd stumbled upon something, a private collection that she suspected had been stolen. She'd been invited to view it but had to sign a nondisclosure agreement before she was given access. She wasn't supposed to tell anyone, of course, but she wanted to discuss the situation with someone who was knowledgeable in the field without worrying your father. She said the collection contained English and Native American antiquities. When I pressed her, she admitted that she suspected there were objects from both Roanoke colonies."

"*Both* colonies?"

"Yes, Sir Ralph Lane's fort from 1586 as well as the infamous Lost Colony."

I leaned against a tree. "Wow."

"We ended the call with her planning to come to Chapel Hill and Duke the next week to search the libraries at both campuses. But days before I was supposed to meet her at Duke, I heard about her death. I immediately contacted the Manteo police."

My breath caught. "You think the collection had something to do with her death?"

"I thought it was suspicious, but when the police investigated, they couldn't find any information about any such meeting or collection, and no one at the foundation knew anything about it."

I bristled. "Do you think she made it up?"

His brow furrowed at my accusation. "No. If your mother was correct, and I have no reason to believe otherwise, I suspect the collection was so secret there wasn't a paper trail for the police to follow."

I took several breaths, letting his information sink in. "Did Daddy know about this?"

"Yes, but he insisted the culprit was the man the police suspected."

"And what do you think?"

His face softened and he gave me a sad smile. "Honestly, Ellie, I don't know. Your father said that whoever broke in wanted you. If your mother was killed because of the collection, why would they be looking for you? Your father's explanation seemed more plausible."

I nodded, my throat tightening. I wasn't sure what to believe anymore. Was her death related to the curse as I'd always thought, just in a way I hadn't suspected? Could the collection she'd examined have been the Ricardo Estate?

"This was a lot to throw at you and not the best place to do it. I apologize. But with the appearance of the Lost Colony and hearing about your father's death, it's been heavy on my mind. I felt compelled to tell you."

I shook my head. "No. I appreciate you sharing this information with me. Thank you."

"Just don't let the past consume you, Ellie. It's the curse of the historian, I'm afraid. It makes losing people that much more difficult." His voice sounded scratchy, and he cleared his throat, patting my arm. "Why don't you take a moment, and then I'll show you the inside of Ananias and Elinor Dare's home."

I nodded again, my shoulder pressed into a tree as I took several deep breaths. Steven had given me more information about my parents than I'd ever hoped to get. But it was overwhelming after finding nothing at all for weeks. Or years. How much had my father kept from me?

He'd done what he'd thought necessary to protect me, and I would never fault him for that. Perhaps if I hadn't shut him down so effectively about the curse, he would have shared this information with me. The blame belonged squarely at my own feet.

But wallowing in guilt wouldn't help me find out who'd killed my mother, nor would it help me lock away the evil that roamed the earth. There was a reason I was at this site—to find any helpful information that Manteo or Ananias might have left behind. Standing here feeling sorry for myself was a waste of time and resources. I squared my shoulders and joined Steven at the opening of the hut.

"Ready to step back in time?" he asked with a smile. When I nodded, he ducked through the doorway. "All I ask is that you don't touch anything."

"Of course."

"This home is actually larger than most of the others because of the Dares' status, but it's still quite small by today's standards."

I stood in the center of the dirt-floored structure as my eyes adjusted to the dim light, amazed that a family of three had lived comfortably in here. A bed, slightly larger than full-size, sat in one corner, a skeleton tucked beneath the quilt.

I gasped as I realized I was staring at my namesake, Elinor Dare.

Steven turned back to me. "I'm sorry. I should have warned you that the bodies haven't been removed yet. Do you need to get some air?"

I shook my head. "No, I'm fine. It just caught me by surprise."

"As a father, the cradle is much more difficult for me," he murmured.

The cradle. My eyes sought it out, next to the head of the bed and in Steven's shadow. I took a step closer. A tiny skull was visible at the top of the infant's bed, a cap covering its head.

"We're fairly certain this is Elinor and Virginia Dare, but there's no sign of Ananias."

"You're sure this is their house?"

"Not one hundred percent, of course, but as certain as possible. We've found a Bible with Ananias's name inscribed inside, as well as other papers leading us to believe he lived here." He pointed to the table on the opposite wall from the bed. A stack of papers sat in one corner, a candle in the middle.

I took a deep breath, the full impact of the situation hitting me. Ananias had sat at the table. He had slept in that bed next to his wife. Held the tiny baby that now lay in the cradle. How had he gone on after realizing he'd lost everything and everyone? "What was in the papers you found?"

"We've only begun to scratch the surface, so I can't really answer that question yet. The two weeks we've been granted isn't nearly enough time for us to examine everything. After David requested an extension, I've decided to file one as well. I'd like to be the lead researcher." His mouth twisted, and he shrugged. "We'll see if that happens or not. Only the fates decide."

"Do you believe in fate, Steven?"

"I never used to, but I'm becoming more and more of a believer."

I was too.

David returned about thirty minutes later. We were standing outside when Steven saw him coming. He leaned close to me and lowered his voice. "I'm not a meddler, Ellie, but David is like a son to me." He rubbed his chin. "He doesn't get close to people very easily. I can see there's something going on between you two."

"Oh." We'd tried to be discreet with our partnership, and I felt bad that Steven had misunderstood, thinking our mutual interest was romantic.

"What you two do is your own business, but it's obvious he's taken with you. I wanted you to know how rare that is for him."

I considered setting him straight, but what was I going to say? I'd have to let David take point on this one. "Thank you for showing me the house, but more importantly, for telling me about my parents."

David approached us with a leery expression. "What are you two talking about?"

I laughed. "You, of course."

Steven laughed with me and placed an arm around my shoulders. "You've met your match with this one, David. I suspect her father would approve."

I offered him a smile. "I'm sure Daddy would." Steven was talking about romance, but I knew Daddy would approve of David's eagerness to help me.

David's face flushed. "I think I've heard enough." He shook his head and reached for my forearm, dragging me away. "There's something I know you'll want to see."

Several feet away, he slowed down and stopped pulling, but his hand didn't drop; it just shifted so that he was lightly gripping my wrist.

"I meant what I said about Daddy."

He looked amused. "Oh, really?"

"Daddy would have loved you. If he could have handpicked someone to help me, I'm certain it would have been you."

David gave me a strange look, and his eyes flickered with something I didn't recognize. Then he shook his head, his excitement returning. "Come on. I really do have something to show you."

"What?"

"It's a surprise." He led me to a hut that was smaller than the others and located at the edge of the clearing. Several primitive symbols were painted by the door, a few of which I recognized.

"Manteo's hut," I murmured.

"Yes, but that's not the surprise." He led me around the side of the structure, to a table that had been set up under a canopy. "Ellie, look at this."

There was a slat of wood, covered in symbols.

"We just found it inside. Look at this." He picked up a pen and pointed to a few of the symbols, keeping the tip several inches above the wood. "Recognize these? The night, the sun, the land, the sea."

"They're almost identical to the ones on my door."

"I know. The symbols for things often changed from tribe to tribe. Collin's family must have carefully preserved these for the ones he's using to be almost identical."

At least thirty symbols covered the slat, and I didn't recognize about half of them. One symbol in particular filled me with excitement. "Okeus." I pointed to it. "That must mean that one of these stands for Ahone."

"Yeah, but the question is *which*."

Some of my excitement faded. "How do we find out?"

"The books my friend borrowed should arrive at the inn today. Even if Ahone's symbol isn't in the text, we might be able to narrow the options down through the process of elimination."

"How long do you think that will take?"

"That's what I'm worried about. It might take days or even weeks. How much time do you think you have left?"

I twisted my lips as I thought about what Ukinim had said. "I might already be out of time. Ukinim suggested he wouldn't have trouble taking my Manitou."

David's eyes widened. "Why didn't you tell me?"

"What good would it have done? Knowing won't help us find Ahone's mark any faster."

"You can't go out after dark anymore."

I grimaced, finding it hard to agree. My Manitou was now fair game. Okeus could spring his surprise on me at any time.

I only hoped I would survive it.

⸲ Chapter Twenty ⸲

Over the next few days, David worked at the colony during the day, and I worked at the lunch shift at Darrell's. Collin hadn't shown his face at the restaurant—he was probably still angry with me about involving David. Still, he had continued to visit my door night after night, putting his mark and the new symbol in the center. David hadn't found any reference to the symbol in the texts that had arrived from New York, and he hadn't found Ahone's symbol either.

I considered finding Collin and asking him what he knew about the Ricardo Estate and to define his involvement, but I knew it would be a wasted effort. Collin wouldn't tell me anything he didn't want me to know. And I was certain this fell under that category.

David moved out of Myra's and started staying in my apartment full time. I expected to feel resentful about having my space invaded, but now that the mark on my back was completely gone, I found his presence reassuring, even if he couldn't really do anything to help me if Okeus came calling. He insisted on sleeping on the sofa every night, even though I suggested that we take turns rotating on my bed.

When we weren't working, we spent all of our time together. We walked to the inn every morning before he left for the colony site.

Then he'd come straight to my apartment at around seven. We'd eat dinner and do research. His progress had been slow but steady.

Neither the badgers nor Big Nasty had made a reappearance.

"Maybe you sent them back to Popogusso on your own, Ellie," David suggested. "Maybe your words of protection are enough, and it just didn't work before because the gate hadn't been resealed. It makes sense if my theory that you're a conjuror is correct."

I hoped so, but I wasn't about to count on it. I suspected they were lying low, waiting. For what, I wasn't sure. I was scared to find out.

The researchers staying at Myra's were planning to go home for the weekend. When I arrived at the inn on Friday morning, Myra stood in the kitchen, her forehead knit with worry.

"Something's bothering you," I said. "What is it?"

A guilty look crossed over her face. "How comfortable would you be if I left for the weekend?"

"Oh." I could see why she would be hesitant to leave me after the lighthouse incident. "Please go. I'll be fine. Nothing has happened in days."

"Steven has invited me to go home with him for the weekend. He thought it might be a good idea for me to get away from everything for a couple of days. But I'm not sure I should leave you."

I tried to hide my surprise. Myra and Steven had become nearly as inseparable as David and I were, although I suspected that David was right and their interest wasn't strictly professional. "That's wonderful. Of course you should go."

"I was worried how you'd feel if I ever met someone other than your father."

"Myra, I've seen how you two look at each other and I think it's wonderful. Steven is a great man, and you deserve to be happy."

"I don't want to leave you." She wrung her hands. "Maybe I should tell him no."

I grabbed her shoulders. "Don't you dare. David will be with me. You go have fun."

She sucked in her lower lip, giving me a pensive look.

I recognized it well. She often got that look in my teen years when she thought I was about to do something she thought I'd regret. "Spill it, Myra."

"I'm just worried about you."

"I know. What in particular?"

"Ellie, I love David, and I know how much your father would love him too. I just worry about you jumping into a relationship so soon after your father's death. And what happened with Collin."

I looked up in surprise. "Why do you think there was something between me and Collin?"

She touched my cheek with her fingertips. "You wear your heart on your face." Her hand dropped to cover mine. "I didn't see you much when you were with him, but I saw you after. I know you were upset about your father's death, but I could tell there was more."

I took a deep breath. "What Collin and I had wasn't real, or at least it couldn't be in the long term. Collin is too selfish to be in a long-term relationship."

"I know he's the other Curse Keeper. Don't you still need him?"

I was surprised she was discussing this with me. She had ignored everything Curse Keeper–related before my dad's death, but even now she rarely mentioned it. "Collin refuses to help me. He thinks the spirits and gods should be loose. I disagree." I shook my head. "Besides, there's nothing between me and David. He's helping me research. I know he's sleeping at my apartment, but he's staying on the sofa."

Her worry faded and she studied me with a knowing look. "Okay," she smiled. "I'll stop meddling."

"Go have fun this weekend. I'll stay here at the house while you're gone and take care of the guests." Since the researchers would be gone too, all the rooms in the residential house would be vacant. David and I would have almost forty-eight hours to perform a more thorough search for Daddy's papers and the ring Myra had mentioned. Our searches so far had been done in snatches of time between our shifts and the other guests' arrivals and departures.

"If you're okay with this, I'll leave straight after work today and come back on Sunday night with Steven. He still hasn't gotten his extension granted, so next week might be his last one here."

I kissed her on the cheek. "Go and relax. You work seven days a week. And after everything . . . You need a break, Myra. You deserve one."

She started to leave, but I blurted out a question. "Did Daddy ever mention anything about something called the Ricardo Estate?"

Recognition flickered in her eyes. "I believe I remember him mentioning something about it years ago, but he was on a phone call. I only remember because he stopped talking when I entered his office. I worried that he might have found someone else and Ricardo was her last name." She shook her head, guilt flooding her face. "Later, I was ashamed for thinking such a thing. Your father was loyal to a fault. After I found out about the curse, I realized that it must have been related to that."

My body stiffened. "Wait. Daddy was talking to someone else about the curse?"

"I don't know for sure, Ellie. I'm only guessing." She grimaced. "I'm sorry I can't be more helpful."

"You've been more helpful than you know."

Myra went upstairs to pack, and I found David on the front screened-in porch with his laptop, sitting in the chair that had been Daddy's favorite.

I stood in the doorway watching him, and my breath stuck in my chest. The morning sunlight bathed him in a warm glow. The wind blew his hair against his forehead, but his gaze was focused on his computer screen. He had on a short-sleeve button-down shirt with a pair of jeans that I recognized. They fit his backside remarkably well.

Myra has assumed there was something between us—along with everyone else—and I kept dismissing the suggestion, but as I watched him now, I found myself wondering: *What if?*

He looked up at me and smiled. His eyes lit up and my heart fluttered, catching me by surprise. But how could I be with someone else if my soul belonged to Collin? Still, my stomach somersaulted as I started to consider what it would be like if David and I had more than a professional partnership.

His smile faded into something more serious, more meaningful, and a quiver of fear vibrated my insides. Could we really be together? Things had gone so badly with Collin. I had no problem admitting that I both wanted David around and needed him. What if we tried to have a relationship and it failed? Then I'd be completely alone. I wasn't sure I could survive that.

"Myra—" My voice stuck in the back of my throat, so I looked away and tried again. "Myra is going home with Steven this weekend and the other researchers are going home Sunday night. I thought we"—I shook my head—"or I, if you don't want to, can spend the weekend at the inn, looking for Daddy's papers." I dared to cast a glance at him.

He'd turned in his seat, setting his laptop down on the table next to him. "Of course I want to help you."

I sat in the chair next to him, twisting my hands in my lap. "I just told Myra she works too hard, and so do you. You need to take a break." I offered him a soft smile. "Maybe you want to go home for the weekend too." I hesitated. "I never even asked if you had a girlfriend."

"First of all, it's the pot calling the kettle black for you to say I work too hard." He picked up my hand and held it between his. "And how can I take a break when you're completely defenseless?"

"I'm not your responsibility, David. You had a life—friends—before you showed up on Roanoke Island. I have no right to expect you to drop everything for me when I can't even offer you anything in return."

His smile was bittersweet. "Ellie, I told you the night I accepted this arrangement that I'd been searching for something, and I was sure this was it. Well, I'm even more certain of that now. You *have* given me something." His hand squeezed mine. "You've given me a purpose. Don't underestimate that."

I looked down at my lap, overwhelmed.

He reached over and lifted my chin so that my eyes met his. "This is exactly where I want to be. With you."

His touch sent shivers down my back, and my gaze lowered to his mouth.

"And for the record"—his lips twitched slightly—"I don't have a girlfriend."

I heard footsteps on the stairs, and someone called David's name.

He grimaced and slowly lowered his hand from my face. "Duty calls."

"I hope you have a good day."

"I'm more looking forward to the evening."

Butterflies danced in my insides.

"Oh, and I just found two more symbols. The plank has thirty-six symbols and I've now figured out twenty-two of them."

"That's great, David."

"But not good enough." He stood and pulled me to my feet. We were less than a foot apart and I shivered again. I couldn't believe how ridiculous I was being. I'd been close to David several times over the last week without feeling anything like this.

He studied my face, looking like he wanted to say something, and then the hint of a smile appeared. "Call me if you need me."

My gaze locked with his. "You too."

He picked up his computer and eased past me into the house. I stood next to the chair, looking out toward the sound as I took slow, steady breaths to keep from hyperventilating.

I was in trouble.

A couple of hours later my cell phone rang while I was cleaning a bathroom. The number surprised me. It was the New Moon.

"Ellie, how are you getting along?" It was Floyd, the owner, but he'd handed all responsibility to Marlena. He rarely stepped foot in the place.

"Hey, Floyd. I'm getting by. I've been picking up some shifts at Darrell's."

"I've hired a new manager for the restaurant, and I'd like to reopen next week."

I kept myself from gasping in surprise. I couldn't imagine someone else managing the restaurant, but of course someone else would. Time moved on. "That's great."

"I'd already heard that you've been working at Darrell's. Are you interested in coming back?"

"I've only been filling in there. But I do have a request."

"Okay," he said, his voice hesitant.

"I can't work the night shift anymore. Only day shifts."

"You know I can't guarantee that, Ellie. From what I've seen, you used to work both."

"Then I guess I'll just keep working at Darrell's."

He groaned. "Oh, all right. You can have days only. But it's going to piss the other waitresses off."

I shrugged, even if he couldn't see it. "Oh well." After all the angry spirits I'd gone up against, pissed-off waitresses were nothing.

"I'll see you for the lunch shift next Wednesday."

I might have gotten my job back at the New Moon, but I still had a shift at Darrell's to fill. The customers were all strangely subdued. I was trying to figure out what was wrong when Tom came in with the sheriff deputy he'd been dining with on my first day. I froze, hiding around the corner in case they were there to question me. The hostess seated them in my section and the muscles in my shoulders tensed. There was no evading them now.

I forced a smile and took menus over to them. "Good afternoon, Tom. Deputy Moran. Can I get you hardworking officers a drink?"

The deputy obviously liked to hold a grudge based on the scowl he shot in my direction.

Tom didn't look much happier.

I was waiting on a table opposite theirs after I took their drink orders, and I caught snatches of their conversation.

"... location isn't similar to the previous one," Deputy Moran said.

"But we haven't found any pattern whatsoever other than Ellie. The dogs were found to the north and west of the island. Another one was found next to Ellie's family home."

They were talking about Ukinim.

"The first victim was found south of Manteo," Tom continued.

First victim. Had there been more? I hadn't had a single dream since David gave me the dream catcher, so no spirits had been tormenting me in my sleep. And I sure hadn't heard about another death.

Deputy Moran lowered his voice, and I struggled to hear. "I heard the two from last night were found in bizarre locations."

Two? I grabbed the edge of the table.

"The locations themselves aren't bizarre, it's how they're spaced. One was placed exactly a quarter of a mile north of Ellie's apartment, and the other was a quarter mile to the west of it."

"So somebody's baiting her?" Deputy Moran asked.

"Not if she doesn't know."

I took an order back to the kitchen, sucking in big gulps of air. So I *hadn't* sent Ukinim and Ilena back to hell. While I wasn't surprised, it was disappointing. David still hadn't found out what the conjurer had to do to destroy the badgers. I had no idea how to get rid of them for good.

But more importantly, the badgers were killing more people. We had to find a way to stop them.

On the way back to the dining room, I stopped in the hallway and grabbed my phone out of my pocket, texting David about what I'd heard.

He replied within seconds. *Are you okay?*

Yeah.

Call me when you get off.

"Who are you texting, Ellie?" Tom asked from several feet behind me.

I shoved my phone into my pocket and whirled around to face him. "Are you my boss now? Was I supposed to get permission first?"

"Ellie." He sounded exhausted.

I couldn't begrudge him for pestering me after hearing how strongly all the recent strange incidents were connected to me. Why hide it? "I was texting David."

"You're spending a lot of time with him." Tom leaned his shoulder into the wall. "He came to town about the time the bodies started piling up, didn't he?"

"Are you seriously accusing David of murder? I suspect he doesn't even kill spiders."

"The timing is pretty coincidental, Ellie."

I narrowed my eyes, tilting my head. "Check that time line again, Tom. David came to town after the dog was killed in my yard."

Tom scowled.

"You must be desperate if you're randomly accusing a renowned professor of grisly murders."

His voice lowered. "You know I'm desperate. And you also know there have been more murders."

My anger faded. "Two more?"

"Three."

My eyes widened as my stomach churned. "But I heard you say—"

"That was just last night, Ellie. The third one was two nights ago."

I leaned my back against the wall. "I heard you say the last two were a quarter mile north and west of my apartment. Where was the other body found?"

"At the lighthouse. We've done our damnedest to keep these under wraps."

I closed my eyes. "Their hearts were eaten?"

Tom leaned closer. "Yeah. Whoever is doing this is baiting you, Ellie. And I don't think it's Marino's men. Have you seen them since that day of the high-speed chase?"

I shook my head, feeling sick to my stomach. "No. I was hoping that you permanently scared them off."

"There's not much likelihood of that. Maybe they figure they don't need you anymore."

My back straightened. "Why do you say that?"

He ignored my question. "Tell me about the guy who showed up behind the restaurant the day of the chase. The guy with the red pickup."

"How do you know about him?" I shook my head and frowned. "It wasn't him. He would never do this."

"How can you be sure?"

"I know him. He just wouldn't."

Tom grinned like he'd woken up on Christmas morning to a room full of presents. "What's his name, Ellie?"

I took a deep breath. *Damn it.* He'd set me up.

Tom leaned his face close to mine, raising his eyebrows. "What's his name?"

I gritted my teeth. Damn my mouth. "Collin."

"Collin what?"

"Collin Dailey."

"And how do you know Collin Dailey?"

What could I tell him? "I met him at the New Moon. We hung out a lot the week the colony reappeared."

"What a coincidence."

"Are you basing your entire case on coincidences?"

"It's all I fucking have at the moment, Ellie."

I leaned the back of my head against the wall and looked up at the ceiling. What a mess.

"Where does Collin Dailey live?"

"Buxton." That seemed far enough away to draw them away from Collin, and it helped that it was true.

"Buxton." He looked over his shoulder and then back at me. "I've seen him here every day until our encounter a few days ago. That's quite a drive to Manteo each day."

I scowled.

"What were you doing in Wanchese last week?"

I fidgeted.

"Collin Dailey is in Wanchese, isn't he? And if I find out you lied to me, I'll throw your ass in jail for twenty-four hours just to prove I'm done playing around."

I didn't answer.

"Does Collin Dailey live in Wanchese?"

Oh, God. Collin had admitted that he had some kind of criminal record. And although he hadn't told me what it involved, the fact that he carried tools around in his truck to break into places was a good clue. "I don't know."

"*Ellie.*"

I glanced at Tom. "His boat is in Wanchese, but I don't know where he's living right now."

"He has a boat?"

I nodded. The less I admitted the better.

"Were you visiting his boat the night they found the guy floating in the cove?"

"No."

"Ellie."

"I went to see Collin. I never saw his boat."

"Why?"

My heart raced and I felt light-headed. "Do I need an attorney?"

Tom pressed his back into the wall next to me and leaned close to my ear. "I don't know, Ellie. Do you?"

My head flooded with panic. I knew Tom didn't have any evidence to press charges against either of us, but I knew I couldn't afford to spend even one night unprotected, especially with my mark gone. But could Collin? His mark seemed to protect him more than mine did. Could I risk it?

I squeezed my eyes shut. "We had a . . . thing."

"A relationship?"

"Well as close as Collin will probably ever have to a relationship."

"You sure do plow through men, don't you, Ellie?"

I cringed.

"So you went to see him because you were . . . *seeing* him?"

The closer I stuck to the truth, the better. "No. We were done. But he had something of mine I wanted."

"And did you see him?"

"Yes, but we got into an argument and he drove off."

"Where did you see him if you never saw his boat?"

"His truck was there. I figured he had to be out in his boat, so I waited until he came back. We had an argument, and he left." I flushed, remembering the part I was leaving out.

"*He* left. *You* didn't?"

Tom was perceptive. "I left afterward."

"How did that guy end up dead in the cove?"

I was already spilling my guts, so I might as well share what I could of this to make it look like I was being cooperative. "After Collin took off, two guys showed up." I grimaced. "There was a misunderstanding about who I was."

"What does that mean?"

I looked up at him. "Don't play stupid with me, Tom Helmsworth. You already think the guy who was killed tried to rape me."

Tom's body stiffened and his voice deepened. "Did he?"

I studied the crack in the floor. "It didn't get that far."

"What happened?"

"When he dragged me over to the boats, I hit him in the head with a wrench I found on the boat and it dazed him. I was getting away when a giant snake appeared out of the water. Then it ate him. His friend took off and so did I."

Tom's shoulders sagged. "Why in God's name didn't you tell me all of this in the beginning?"

"It was a giant snake, Tom. Seriously, who was going to believe that?"

"Ellie, I already told you that the other guy said it was a snake."

I shrugged. "I don't know. It just seemed better to try and forget it."

"And the destruction at the lighthouse?"

"Why do you think I know about the lighthouse?" Tom had never questioned me about the incident that night, and I'd incorrectly assumed he hadn't made the connection.

Tom studied the opposite wall. "Don't you play stupid with *me*, Ellie. I know you're wrapped up in it somehow."

I pressed my lips together.

"I don't think a snake is killing these dogs and people. Their abdomens were all ripped open with large claws."

"And you think I know what it is? You think I know who it's going after next?"

A cocky smirk lifted his cheeks. "I'm more worried about you. If I weren't so sure this was an animal, I'd say it's after you. Have you pissed off anyone other than Marino lately? Is Collin upset that you broke up with him?"

I cracked a grin. "And how do you know *I* broke up with *him*?"

He laughed. "Because any guy who broke up with you would be an idiot. And that guy doesn't look like an idiot."

Carly rounded the corner and frowned when she saw me

talking to Tom. "Ellie, you have orders ready and customers waiting for their checks."

I cringed. *Damn it.* "Coming."

I stepped away from the wall. "I *did* break up with Collin, and although he wasn't happy about it, he wouldn't resort to terrorizing me. We've reached an amicable truce."

"But he still cares about you? Enough to stalk you and try to intimidate you?"

My eyes flew open and my heart slammed against my chest. "No! Collin would never do anything like that."

"Is he capable of violence?"

I shook my head, getting frustrated. "Listen to me, Tom. I know you really want to find out who is doing this, but it's not Collin. You're looking in the wrong place."

"Then where should I be looking?"

I sighed. "I wish I knew. And that's the truth."

I took the orders and checks out to the tables and kept an eye on Tom, desperate for the chance to call Collin. About fifteen minutes later there was a slight lull, so I headed into the women's restroom and hid in a stall.

Collin answered on the second ring and sounded worried. "Ellie? Are you okay?"

"I'm fine, but you need to hide."

"What are you talking about?"

"That police officer who was questioning me last week behind Darrell's? He tricked me into admitting I know you. He told me if I didn't answer his questions he would lock me up for twenty-four hours just to prove his point." My voice broke. "I'm sorry, Collin."

"What did you tell him?"

I filled Collin in on everything I remembered.

"He's grasping at straws if he's making those leaps," Collin finally said.

"He's desperate."

"Obviously."

"I'm sorry."

"No, Ellie. You did the right thing. We can't risk you getting locked up." He paused. "How much of your mark is left?"

"None."

I expected him to blow up, but instead he asked, "You haven't found Ahone's symbol yet?"

"No."

"I'm giving you three days, Ellie." He sounded like the Collin I'd first met. Dictatorial and condescending.

"We have bigger issues, Collin. Tom thinks Ukinim is baiting me."

"Then that's exactly why the disappearance of your mark is our biggest issue."

"They'll still kill me, Collin. Ukinim doesn't care about my Manitou. He just wants to get me before Okeus does."

"*Fuck*, Ellie. Stop being so stubborn. You have to let me protect you."

"Let you protect me?" I spit into the phone. "You're the reason I'm in this situation. The marks on my door are still working."

"Ellie, be reasonable."

"Tell me what you know about the Ricardo deal."

"No."

"You owe me something for dragging me into that mess, along with everything else."

"Forget Marino and focus on the bigger issue. This thing is getting stronger, Ellie. The daylight is protecting you for now, but I suspect it will soon be able to make short excursions into the sunlight."

The blood rushed from my head. While I knew that day was coming, I'd hoped it would be further off. I'd become a prisoner in my apartment. "Then help me get rid of it."

He hesitated. "I can't."

"Why not? You'd seriously let this thing kill me rather than help?" Hurt and resentment filled my chest. "If you really wanted to protect me, you'd help me send this thing and his mate back to Popogusso. To hell with your principles."

"*His mate?* What are you talking about?"

"You really don't know anything about Ukinim or his wife?"

He paused. "No." A low grumble filled my ear.

"And you were so certain that David would be pointless and get me killed. Well, he's the one who's actually giving me information instead of trying to keep me in the dark. Unlike you."

"Ellie," he pleaded.

The bathroom door opened, and I flushed the toilet. "I have to go. But watch out for Tom." I hung up before he could respond and washed my hands, ignoring the strange look from a young mother trying to corral her two small children into the other stall.

As soon as I got off work, I started ripping the house apart. Whatever I needed to protect myself had to be in Daddy's notes.

Because I couldn't consider the alternative.

~ Chapter Twenty-One ~

David found me in the living room, on my hands and knees under a small writing desk in the corner.

"If you'd told me we were playing hide-and-seek, I would have counted first." He looked around the trashed room and whistled. "I see you started without me."

I looked up. "I have to find those notes."

"I know, love." He reached his hand out to me. "But come up here and let's figure out a plan, because you've searched this house countless times and come up with nothing."

I took his hand, my heart stuttering at his term of endearment. Had he meant anything by it, or was it just one of those things people said? I stood and he pushed me back toward the chair, guiding me into a sitting position on the arm. Then he took a step back and surveyed the room.

"I've spent the better part of the day trying to get into your father's head." He shot me a frustrated look. "Not an easy task since I didn't know him." He ran his fingertips across a pile of guidebooks on the desk. "But Myra told you that he was anxious and paranoid when he started compiling his notes, right? And he would have hidden them somewhere he thought you'd be able to find them."

"Yes, but I've already looked in those places."

"So let's consider this logically." David sat on the arm of the chair next to me, our legs pressed together. I was hyperaware of his presence. "Have the Keepers before you ever written the information down?"

"I'm not sure, but I suspect not. It's an oral tradition, and it was a secret. To tell someone who wasn't family about the curse would bring dire consequences."

His brow furrowed. "Do you believe that? Is there evidence this actually happened?"

"I remember my father impressing the importance of keeping it a secret with horrible tales of death and injury, but I never really believed it." I looked up at him, guilt eating my insides. "Until I told Claire."

His eyes widened. "You told Claire?"

"When I was eight. She knew I had a secret, and she couldn't stand it. So I told her about the curse. Just the part about Manteo and Ananias and the gate." I sucked in my bottom lip and wrapped my fingers around the edge of the chair's arm.

His body stilled. "What happened?"

"My mother was murdered a few days later."

"Oh, Ellie. I'm sorry." His hand covered mine.

"I forgot every single thing I learned about the curse that night. When Daddy tried to reteach me, I refused to listen. I didn't want any part of it."

"I'm sure it was a coincidence . . ." His voice trailed off at the end, and the tone of his voice told me he wasn't sure he believed it.

I offered David a tired smile. "I used to tell myself that too. But now I'm not so sure. I'm not so sure about anything." I sighed and looked up at a tiny stain on the ceiling. "You knew that Steven knew my parents."

"Yes. He told me that he highly respected your father's work." David shifted on the seat, but he kept his hand on mine.

Tingles shot from my hand through my body. "He said Daddy was known worldwide for his expertise about the Lost Colony. But he stopped giving lectures after Momma's death. Daddy told Steven she died because of the colony, and he'd never lecture about it again. He blamed himself for her murder."

David slid his hand up my arm, resting it on the back of my neck, leaving goose bumps in its wake. His hand slipped under my hair and rubbed my tense muscles. "It sounds to me as if there was a lot of unnecessary guilt associated with her death. The person who killed her is the only one to blame." He gave me a gentle smile.

"You're right," I said, acutely aware of his hand on my neck. "But there's more I haven't told you."

"What?"

"Steven said Momma had been invited to see a private collection of sixteenth-century English and Native American pieces the week before her death. She called him about it because she was concerned they were stolen."

David stood and turned to face me. "Why didn't you tell me this sooner?"

I shrugged. "I don't know. It was stupid not to. It's just that it was the first big piece of information I'd heard about my mother's murder in years, and I needed a few days to absorb it. Besides, my mother died years ago. We had bigger and more pressing issues."

"Ellie. Any information about your mother's death is important, even if it doesn't help us with the curse. It's important to *you*."

"Finding Ahone's mark is our biggest concern," I sighed. The information seemed like a coincidence, but David was right. There were no coincidences. "Steven said he notified the police, but they couldn't find any evidence such a collection existed. No one Momma worked with knew anything about it either."

"So he thinks she made it up?"

"I asked him that and he said no." I looked up at him. "This morning, I asked Myra if she'd ever heard Daddy mention anything about the Ricardo Estate and she says she did once, years ago."

"You think the collection your mother surveyed was the Ricardo Estate? If so, it might be related to her death."

"I don't know. Steven didn't call it the Ricardo Estate, but Daddy did—if Myra remembers correctly, that is. She said Daddy was talking on the phone and was secretive."

"It does seem like there's a connection. We just need to find a reliable source."

"After my conversation with Myra this morning, I asked Collin about it on the phone this afternoon, but he refused to tell me anything."

He scowled. "Like I said, we'll find a *reliable* source."

"One more thing." I shifted my weight. "When the curse broke, the dreams about the animals and the spirits weren't the only ones I started to have." I told him about the dreams I'd had about my mother's death and the bloodstains on the floor of my bedroom.

"So I was really staying in your old room?"

I stood. The familiar anxious feeling I always experienced when I thought about her murder made me jittery. "Yeah."

"I'm so sorry." He stepped in front of me and his arm encircled my waist, pulling my head to his chest.

Holding my breath, I rested against him for several seconds, taking comfort in his embrace. Something in me yearned for more. I looked up into his face.

His gaze was on my mouth.

David wanted this too.

It would have been so easy to lean closer and press my lips to his. To see if I could actually feel something with another man after Collin.

But would that be fair to David? He had given up everything to help me, so how could I risk breaking his heart?

I took a step backward, my hands trailing down his shirt, knowing I needed to break contact, yet so desperate to stay in this moment.

If I was destined to live a life without love, what was I even fighting for?

His face searched mine, confusion and desire jostling for control of his features.

I reached my hand to his cheek, rubbing his stubble with my fingertips. I was fighting for David. So that he and the other seven billion people on this planet could live their lives without facing the terror lurking outside my door each night. The countless monsters hell-bent on destroying us all.

This was no time for me to explore my romantic life. My hand dropped and I turned away. "We need to keep looking."

David didn't answer for several seconds.

I spun around to face him, the desire on his face nearly my undoing.

"Ellie."

I shook my head. "David. I can't."

He ran his hand over his head, looking at the staircase. "That wanker did a number on you, Ellie, but I'm not him." He walked out of the room, leaving my heart and emotions in a tangled mess.

I grabbed my purse and keys and ran for my car, feeling a sudden, unstoppable need for the ocean. I hadn't been in days, not since my encounter with Ukinim and Ilena. When I reached the beach, I parked my car in the lot and, leaving my shoes in the car, ran for the water, needing that burst of power to recharge my body and weary spirit.

By the time I got back to my car, I realized over an hour had passed and the sun was nearing the horizon. I hadn't thought to bring a towel, although by now I should have been smart enough to pile a bunch in my trunk.

The evening was unusually cool, and I shivered when I parked the car at the curb of the inn.

David was in the doorway when I walked up to the building. "You scared the hell out of me, Ellie. I tried calling you and you didn't answer."

"I forgot my phone. And I would have told you, but you were angry—"

"I wasn't angry." Resignation covered his face. "Hurt is a better word." He shifted his weight. "I shouldn't have stormed out like that. And I shouldn't push you into something you're not ready for. I'm sorry." He grabbed my arms and held me back. "Why are you all wet? You smell like seawater."

"That's because I was in the ocean."

His eyes flew open in alarm. "What happened?"

I shook my head. "Nothing bad. It's a perk of the curse. Daughter of the sea and all that. I get these overwhelming urges to go to the ocean. Sometimes I'm in the water before I even realize I've left the house. The ocean recharges me." I rested my hand on his arm, immediately glad for the physical contact. "I like it because I'm one with the Manitou. Tonight reminded me what I'm doing all of this for."

His eyes softened. "And what's that?"

I simply smiled and broke loose of his hold, heading for the staircase. "I'm going to take a shower, and then I'll cook us dinner. It's dark enough that we shouldn't go outside."

He didn't say anything.

"Oh, I brought your bag from my apartment and left it upstairs in the hall. I cleaned all the rooms so you get your pick, except for Myra's, of course."

I bolted up the steps, not waiting for an answer, stalling in the shower for as long as possible. At least my faded mark had one benefit: I could take showers whenever I wanted now. When I went downstairs in a tank top and shorts, my hair in a wet braid, I found David in the kitchen cooking.

"I would have made something."

He looked up from his pot with a mischievous grin. "Since I'm staying at your flat and I don't seem to be paying for my lodging anymore, cooking dinner seems like a fair trade."

"What are you cooking?"

"Well that, Ms. Lancaster, is where the bloom falls off the rose. I'm making macaroni and cheese. And let's hope it turns out well."

I laughed, thankful that he was making an effort to ease the tension between us.

I dragged a bar stool over to the other side of the counter and perched on it. "Beggars can't be choosers, can they?"

"Just remember that when you eat this mess." He stirred a pot of boiling water. "How was your shower?"

"Good. I feel much better." And I did, especially since he seemed to have let our earlier awkwardness go.

"So, do you want to go on a scavenger hunt after we eat?"

"Sounds like fun." I hopped down from the stool and disappeared into the butler's pantry.

"It's not fair if you get a head start," he called from the kitchen.

I found a bottle of wine in the wine cooler Daddy had installed when he remodeled the back end of the house. I carried the bottle, a corkscrew, and two wine glasses into the kitchen and set them down on the counter. "I've heard that a rich Bordeaux pairs nicely with mac and cheese."

He laughed. "And where did you hear that?"

I waved my hand, the corkscrew in my grip. "Eleventh-grade home economics." I lowered my voice. "Mrs. March was a lush. But *shh*." I held my finger to my lips. "We were sworn to secrecy."

"Your secret is safe with me."

"Along with all the others." I opened the wine and poured us both a glass, handing one to David, careful to not touch him.

He took a sip and set it down so he could drain the noodles.

I looked around the kitchen. "I really want to help with something. What can I do?"

"You can get the salad out of the refrigerator."

"You do realize that a salad blows the whole bachelor mac and cheese image to bits."

The grin he graced me with was infectious. After he scooped mac and cheese onto plates, we sat on bar stools at the counter.

I took a bite and released a contented sigh. "I haven't had macaroni and cheese in ages. It was my favorite when I was a kid. My mother used to make it for me, so it's full of happy memories." It was nice to have a happy memory associated with my mother after thinking about her death so much. I took another bite. "What was your favorite?"

He laughed, his eyebrows arching. "There's not a bloody chance in hell that I'll tell you."

His protest made me even more intrigued. "Why the big secret?" I shoved his arm. "I told you, now you tell me."

He cringed, but he was grinning. "I thought that game was usually played with the removal of clothing."

"Ha! Come on, just tell me. How weird can it be? What, did you eat liver with catsup? Are you *ashamed*?"

He lifted his chin, trying to look serious. "It was spotted dick."

I started laughing, noodles shooting out of my mouth. "It was *what*?" I choked out.

"See? I knew this would be your reaction. You Americans wouldn't know good food if it bit you on the arse."

"Do I even want to know what spotted *dick*"—I broke into more giggles—"*is*?"

"It's a bread pudding with currants." He smirked. "Do you think I was raised by paedos?"

"Sorry, I'll try to be more *civilized*."

He poured more wine into our glasses and we shared stories of our childhoods. As I watched him tell me about all his antics with his older brother, I smiled, but my heart ached. Why couldn't I have met this man before all this curse nonsense began? He was so much better for me than Collin ever could be.

But there was no point in dwelling on what-ifs. There was only the here and now.

We cleaned up the kitchen together, and when we finished, David hung a dish towel on the stove handle.

"Okay, Ellie. Let's figure this out. What was your father's routine?"

"He spent a lot of time in the living room watching TV with his caregiver. And he loved the front porch. He liked to watch the neighbor's dog, Chip." The thought of Chip still gave me a pang.

"That's a bloody good place to start. We'll check out the lounge and see—"

"The lounge?" I could figure out most of his British lingo, but this one was unclear.

He made a face. "What you would refer to as the living room. Americans need to learn to be more civilized."

I stood on tiptoe so that we were face-to-face. "And look where you moved to."

278

"The land of the uncivilized. Who knew it was still the wild frontier?"

"Very funny. Besides, you're half American and you're fascinated with the Native Americans. I'd think you'd like it that way."

He grinned mischievously. "I like some things wilder than others."

I ignored the obvious subtext as he followed me into the living room. I pointed out the chair and ottoman where my father had liked to sit.

David sat down and looked around, lifting a lamp and looking underneath it. He stood and turned around, removing the cushions from the chair.

I got on my knees and looked under the coffee table, shocked to find a folded paper stuffed into the cracks of two seams on the underside. "I think I actually found something."

David knelt next to me as I pulled out the paper and opened it. Daddy's handwriting filled the page.

"What does it say?"

I quickly scanned the sheet. "He tells how the curse was created and the rules for the Curse Keepers. Nothing new to me." When I finished, I handed the page to David. "But this means he really did write things down and that there are probably more hidden around here somewhere."

We spent the next half an hour looking in every nook and cranny in the living room and dining room without finding anything else. We searched the rest of the first floor until about midnight, when I started yawning.

David leaned his shoulder into the door frame to the dining room. "We should call it a night and go to bed."

His words sent a flutter through my chest. *Not together, Ellie*, I reminded myself. "Yeah, it's been a hard day." I couldn't help wondering if Collin had managed to evade Tom.

"Are you ready to go upstairs?"

I nodded, suddenly feeling self-conscience. Why was I so nervous?

David followed close behind as we climbed the stairs, and my anxiety increased with each and every step. His bag was still at the top of the stairs, and he picked it up, noticing my own bag outside the bathroom door. "Why didn't you put your bag in your room?"

"I was waiting to see which one you picked." Why did I say it like that? Did he think I was waiting for an invitation to his room?

"Why didn't you just put it in your old room?"

"Because you slept in my old room before you moved into my apartment. I thought you might want it again."

A soft smile warmed his face, and he walked down the hall to my room, standing just inside the doorway. "I wish I'd known this was your room when I was staying in here."

"Would it have made a difference?"

He shot me a wicked grin.

My insides turned to liquid fire and I forced a laugh. "I'll take that as a no." I brushed past him as I entered the room, every nerve in my body alive and begging for more contact. I turned on the lamp on the nightstand and sat on the edge of the bed. "I haven't slept here in years."

David dropped his bag inside the doorway and watched me with a grin. "I'm trying to picture you as a little girl in here. Or you as a little girl, period."

"That seems so long ago." I looked around the room. All hints that it had belonged to me had been removed, and it looked like a generic guestroom. But the dresser, the bed, and the full-length mirror in the corner were all mine. My fingers brushed the comforter. "I couldn't wait to leave home."

"That surprises me given how close you were with your father and the good relationship you have with Myra."

"It wasn't them." I scooted farther back onto the bed and crossed my legs. "I don't think I ever felt comfortable here after Momma's murder. And after we broke the curse and I started having those dreams . . . well, I couldn't even come in here."

"You're in here now."

My lips parted, and I stared up at him in surprise. "You're right."

He moved to the bed and sat on the edge.

"Maybe it's because you're here to protect me," I teased.

His smile faded. "I only wish I could."

I leaned forward and grabbed his hand. "David, you *are* protecting me. Or trying to. If you weren't here, I'd be completely alone."

Sadness flickered in his eyes. "But you wish you were with Collin."

Did I? I had to admit that his comment wasn't without a grain of truth. But David had been the one to stand by my side and help me find answers. Even though Collin probably had some of the answers, he refused to give them.

I stared into the hazel eyes of this man who was offering me hope and support, and more importantly, absolute trust. In that moment, I knew that David would be there for me until the end, whatever that turned out to be.

"No, David." I reached for his cheek, my fingers trembling as I touched his skin. "I want *you*. There's no one else I'd rather be here with now." The truth of it hit me like a lightning bolt.

His hand covered mine as he searched my eyes, hope flickering in his gaze.

"But you and I could never work. He ruined me."

"Because you still love him?"

I shook my head. "What Collin and I had wasn't love. And it wasn't real, even if he thinks differently. What we had was based on lies and schemes, hormones and magic. He used me." I lowered my hand while still holding his and stared at our joined hands. "Even when we started a relationship, he never once confessed that he had broken the curse on purpose." I paused. "Still, I know his feelings for me were real, or as real as Collin is capable of having."

"How can you be so certain?"

I looked into David's eyes. "Because when we touch our marks together, we not only feel the Manitou, we feel each other." I sighed. "We feel every emotion."

"You can read each other's minds?"

"No, we can just tell how the other person feels without knowing why. I knew he wanted me before we slept together, but he also felt tremendous guilt." I took a quick breath. "I thought it was because he felt bad about dragging me into this curse mess accidentally. But it turned out not to be accidental at all, of course." My stomach tightened and I felt nauseated. "I . . . I was the one who pushed him to sleep with me." I felt so ashamed to admit to it.

"Hey," his free hand cupped my cheek, his thumb stroking my cheekbone. "Don't be embarrassed. I've slept with other women, some I regret. We're adults. We have a past."

"I wish that's all this was." My eyes filled with tears.

A soft smile lifted his lips. "It can't be that bad."

"It is." A tear fell down my cheek. "It's worse."

"What is it?" He didn't look worried, only patient.

"Once . . ." This was so embarrassing, but I had to be honest. After all the deceptions and lies with Collin, I needed David to know everything. "Our marks . . . the more we use them, the more they seem to attract each other." I took a deep breath. "One time when we were having sex, we touched marks."

"And what was the significance of that?"

My chin trembled. "Our souls were bound."

He was perfectly still for several seconds. "And what does that mean exactly?"

I blinked and more tears fell down my cheeks. "I'm not sure. I didn't know it would happen, but it was my fault. I . . . I'm sorry."

He tilted my face upward. "Why are you sorry?"

"I can't be . . . that person for you."

"What person? I'm still not sure what's happening here, Ellie. Unless I'm greatly mistaken, you're attracted to me and want something more. So do I. What's the problem?"

"I don't know if I can love you. I don't know if I can love anyone. The night before the ceremony, Collin told me that one day I'd hate him. Stupid me, I thought he meant because of his past and the mess with Marino. I told him he was wrong, of course. We touched marks again, and he told me that he had ruined me for any other man. That no other relationship would ever compare to what he and I had."

Anger darkened David's face. He climbed off the bed and grabbed the bedpost with one hand as he looked out the window. "What a goddamned egotistical motherfucking wanker."

My chest tightened at his outburst. I'd never seen him so angry.

He turned to face me. "Don't tell me you believe that bollocks."

"I . . ."

"We both know he still wants you back. That was his way of ensuring he could always get you back. And look, Ellie." He shook his head as his voice softened. "It's working."

I didn't know what to say.

He sat on the bed next to me, his anger fading. "If you were ruined for all other men, would you still feel something for me?"

"I don't know," I whispered.

His hand slowly slipped behind the nape of my neck, pulling my face closer to his. My insides tingled with anticipation. "You're breathing more rapidly, Ellie. Does that mean you feel something?"

I closed my eyes.

His free arm encircled my waist, his hand slowly sliding up my back. His breath was hot on my face, his lips hovering over mine. "Do you feel this?" His mouth pressed softly to mine, and he ran his tongue along my bottom lip.

My chest burned with desire that shot straight to my core.

He placed gentle kisses along my cheek and down my neck, finding the spot that made me squirm. "How about this?"

My hands gripped his back, holding him in place.

He returned to my lips, his tongue exploring my mouth. My tongue joined his and an explosion of need erupted inside me. My grip on him tightened.

David lifted my tank top over my head and pushed me backward on the bed, leaning over me on his elbow. His free hand cupped my breast, his thumb softly brushing my nipple through my bra. His mouth hovered over mine, making me desperate for him to kiss me again, while his eyes watched my face. "You feel this, Ellie. I can see it in your eyes and the way your body is reacting to me. You want this and so much more, but I'm not Collin. I won't coerce or cajole you into anything you don't want. I want this to be just as much your choice as it is mine."

He placed a soft kiss on my lips and then got off the bed.

I rose up on my elbows, confusion replacing lust. "Where are you going?"

He picked up his bag and smiled softly. "To bed. I'll see you in the morning."

I stared at him in disbelief as he left my room, my body crying out for more. Was David right? Was there a chance I could feel something with someone else? To my surprise, I realized how badly I wanted it to be with him.

↭ CHAPTER TWENTY-TWO ↭

I went into the bathroom to brush my teeth, glancing at the closed door on the other side of the hall. David's demonstration had left me wanting more. I considered going into his room to finish what he'd started, but I'd been the pursuer in my last several relationships, and I liked that I was the one being seduced this time. David was taking things slow, so I'd wait for him.

When I headed back to my room to get my bag, I looked down the long hallway, my gaze inexorably drawn to the place where my mother had died. I squeezed my eyes shut as the memories of her ragged dying breaths filled my head. I stepped back into the bathroom and flipped on the light, leaving the door cracked open. I knew it was babyish to need a night-light, but there were too many memories in this house.

I stood in the doorway to my old room, wrestling with whether I should get my bag and move into another room. But maybe it was time for me to face the demons of my past as well as the demons of my present. After I changed into a pair of pajamas, I left the door to my room open so I could see the bathroom light. I pulled the dream catcher from my bag and hung it on the bed over my pillow. I lay there for several minutes, listening to the wind blow tree limbs against my window as I began to get drowsy.

I thought about David in the other room, probably happy to be sleeping in a real bed for the first time in several nights. I wondered what it would be like to be curled up next to him, his mouth on mine, his hands roaming my body.

Fatigue had taken over and my mind hovered in the purgatory between wakefulness and sleep. A bird squawked repeatedly outside my window. My foggy mind struggled to identify the creature. I blinked and tried to focus, then gasped.

Wapi was sitting on a tree branch watching me through the window, a ghoulish smile on his face.

Had I put fresh markings on the doors? Was there still salt on the window ledges?

I tried to sit up, but the tentacles of sleep refused to let go, pulling me deeper. Panic exploded as I was pulled under. This was no normal sleepiness. Somehow, supernatural forces were controlling me. "David," I called out, but the sound was drowned out by Wapi's cries.

"Witness to creation, Okeus is ready for you," Wapi said, and then everything turned to darkness.

I came to in a dark earthen tunnel, the smell of dirt and mildew flooding my head. I lay on my side, and tiny rocks poked my legs and arms. I sat up, feeling groggy and unsure of where I was or what I was doing. A dim light shone at the end of the tunnel.

This was a dream.

I climbed to my feet and held onto the wall to right myself.

A scream echoed through the tunnel, and I pressed my back against the earth wall, my heart racing. This felt more real than any of my other dreams, even those with the spirits and the ones about my mother.

The scream echoed again and I had two choices: find a way to escape, or help whomever was screaming. I really wanted to leave, but I couldn't live with myself if I made the decision to walk away. Still, I wasn't sure I could purposely make myself go toward the screams either. Especially after the way Ukinim had tricked me at the lighthouse.

But I took one step forward and then another. The light grew closer and closer as I moved toward it. The end of the tunnel opened into a big room, and when I was only a few feet away, I stumbled on a pile of bones. I covered my mouth to hold back a cry of fright, while another scream came from ahead. The smell of decay and blood hung heavy in the air.

I was in the badgers' lair.

Trying to stay in the shadows, I pressed my back against the wall and edged closer to the entrance. A woman stood in a corner, her feet spread in a defensive stance, her face a mask of terror. The badgers paced in front of her. Each time she tried to slip by, one of them would slash at her with their claws.

I couldn't stand here and watch this. I held up my palm and began to recite the words of protection, keeping my voice low.

"*I am the daughter of the sea, born of the essence present at the—*"

Nothing happened.

The badgers heard me and slowly turned around, their eyes glittering in the moonlight that streamed through a hole overhead.

"Witness to creation," Ukinim growled, his eyes enlarging.

The woman saw me and became frantic. "*Help!*"

The badgers slowly advanced on me, and I caught sight of another opening on the other side of the room. I took several steps backward, and the woman began to sob.

"Don't leave me. Please!"

Squatting, I reached into the pile of bones and grabbed a long one with a jagged point, trying to ignore the muscles and slimy bits that were still attached. "Go!"

She headed for the opening, but the smaller badger blocked her path. Her sobs echoed off the walls.

"Let her go," I said, rising again, my voice shaking with fear. "I'm the one you want."

"Wrong," Ukinim said with a growl. "We want you both."

Ilena trapped the woman in the corner as Ukinim advanced on me.

I raised the bone in my hand, ready to strike.

Ukinim lunged and I jumped to the side, barely escaping his claws as I jabbed the bone into his eye with as much strength as I could muster. The badger shrieked and rushed toward me but veered sideways and bumped into the earthen wall, jamming the bone deeper and eliciting more shrieks. I scrambled backward and grabbed two more bones while keeping my eyes on my enemies, staying on Ukinim's blind side.

Hearing her mate's distress, Ilena turned and growled, hunkering low to the ground.

"You must die, witness to creation."

"Not if I can help it," I mumbled as I approached her and her intended victim.

Ukinim squealed behind me, violently shaking his head.

Ilena crouched lower and then pounced. I jumped out of the way, but her claws sank deeply into my upraised forearm.

I cried out in pain.

The woman continued to sob in the corner, even though the exit was clear. *Why was she still here?*

"Go!" I shouted.

Ilena lunged at me again, swinging high. I scrambled backward, trying to determine how to use the bone in my right hand as a weapon. It was shorter than the one still protruding from

Ukinim's eye, and I would be risking significant injury if I got close enough to strike.

Ukinim's cries had quieted and I noticed movement at my side. He was advancing toward me. "I will make you pay, witness to creation. I will take your own eye."

Blood ran down my arm, and my wound throbbed.

Now I was trapped between the two of them, and the woman was still in the corner.

"*Run!*" I shouted.

She finally ran for the exit, but Ilena spun around to chase her. Anxious to save the woman, I jammed one of the bones in the badger's ear. She squealed, but the bone fell to the floor. The wound wouldn't incapacitate her, but I had bought the woman enough time to escape.

The sound of Ilena's cries of pain caught Ukinim's attention, and a low, menacing growl filled the cavern.

Now I was alone with two very angry badgers. Fantastic.

But during the struggle, I noticed something: when Ilena cried out, Ukinim's good eye rested on his mate for a good second before returning to me, and Ilena had stopped tormenting the woman when I injured Ukinim.

I'd just discovered their weakness.

They paced and stalked until they had me in the corner where they'd set upon the woman. I had one bone left to defend myself.

Ukinim bared his teeth as he snarled and leapt. I cringed at the sight of his paw swinging toward me. I lifted the bone high, hoping it would offer some defense, but just as his claw was about to reach my face, I suddenly flashed to an entirely different location.

I stood next to a tall tree in a field of grass and white flowers. The full moon hung in the sky above me. I spun around, trying to figure out where I was, when an owl hooted above my head. I jumped backward, grabbing my bleeding forearm.

The owl flew down to a lower branch.

"You're Ahone's messenger." I tried to keep the bitterness from my voice.

"Your journey is almost complete."

"Does that mean you're going to kill me?"

The owl hooted, then said, "Neither I nor Ahone will kill you tonight."

"There are so many things wrong with that sentence," I mumbled, raising the bone I still held in my right hand. "Are you here to give me Ahone's symbol?"

"You have one more task on your journey."

"And then what?"

"And then you will be rewarded." The owl's eyes penetrated mine. "Some things are merely illusions. The beautiful becomes ugly when the scales of sleep fall from your eyes. The ugly becomes beautiful when you look for the truth."

I didn't like the sound of that.

"The dream world is shifting again. Ahone saved you from Ukinim, but he can't save you from where you are going now. That is up to you and how you use the resources you've been given."

I blinked and suddenly I was on an island. The moonlight glittered off the rippling waves. I was on the sound and not the ocean, I realized. My pajamas had been replaced with a flowing white skirt that blew around my legs and a gauzy white shirt that hung open, exposing a white bikini top. The wound on my arm was gone.

"I've been waiting for this moment with great anticipation."

I spun around to face Okeus. He stood on an embankment, watching me with a patient expression.

It was my day of reckoning.

I froze, my heart slamming into my rib cage.

He smiled, and his face lit up with a beauty I hadn't expected. The last time I saw him—the night of the ceremony—he was wearing a loincloth, but tonight he was dressed in jeans and a fitted T-shirt that covered a well-developed chest and muscular arms. His jet-black hair had been long on one side and short on the other, but tonight it was all trimmed closer to his head, the breeze tousling his dark waves. Okeus was the manifestation of masculine perfection.

He held his hands out and chuckled. "Not what you were expecting?"

"No." I had to force the word out, my fear stealing my breath away.

"There's no need to be afraid, Ellie."

He used my name. Every other spirit and god used one of my titles. Never my name.

"Why not?" I asked, walking backward, drawn instinctively to the water. "The last time I saw you, you threatened to torture me for hundreds of years."

He walked over and offered his hand as I entered the sound. "I spoke in haste, Ellie. Before I had a chance to think. You're perfectly safe." But the sentence sounded unfinished—the "*for now*" was unspoken but understood.

I refused his hand, crossing my arms under my breasts. I stayed in the water, taking another step into it. Now it reached my calves, and the edge of my skirt was brushing the top of the waves.

"I wish to start over."

"Why?"

"Because I think we each have something the other wants."

Was this how his messenger had approached Collin?

He tilted his head as he studied me, a pensive look on his face. "Come, dine with me. I have a meal prepared for you. As well as a surprise."

I took a step backward, moving still deeper into the water. "What is it?"

He winked. "If I told you, it wouldn't be a surprise."

"I'm not hungry."

"Come sit with me anyway." He reached for me again, but I stepped to the side. I couldn't get away from him by walking into the sound. I only had one option: to hear him out and look for a way to escape. I began to step out of the water, swinging wide of him.

He laughed and climbed the embankment, turning to wait for me.

I glanced down at my palm with dismay. The words of protection hadn't helped me with the badgers. I was trapped, especially since Ahone wouldn't intervene this time. Without the mark on my palm, what resources did I have to save me from Okeus?

So far, Okeus was nothing like the monster I'd seen the night of his escape. The god who'd carved his mark into my arm with a razor-sharp claw. The question was, why? What did I have that he wanted, other than the obvious? But if he wanted my Manitou, wouldn't he just take it? And if he planned to take me to Popogusso to torture me as he'd threatened in the past, why waste time trying to butter me up?

I followed him to a table covered in a white cloth that was fluttering in the breeze. Multiple candles crowded the table, their flames flickering. Several platters of fruit and cheese covered the rest of the space. There were two chairs at either end, and Okeus pulled one out for me.

I reluctantly sat, grabbing the sides of my seat with my hands.

He took the chair opposite me, an amused smile on his face. "You look nervous, Ellie. I only wish to talk."

"Why are you calling me Ellie?"

One of his dark eyebrows arched higher than the other. "Ellie is the name you prefer, correct? As opposed to Elinor?"

"Yes. But the others call me by my titles."

"They use them as a sign of respect."

I wanted to point out that I was sure it wasn't, but I was more interested in getting some other answers from him. "Why are you dressed like that?" I asked, waving my hand toward him. "The last time I saw you, you were dressed more . . ."

"Native?"

I nodded.

"I thought you'd be more comfortable if I looked more like you."

I hated to admit it, but he had a point. In fact, his clothes, the table, his manners were all setting me at ease in spite of myself. "Why do you care if I'm comfortable?"

He laughed and passed a plate of sliced peaches toward me. I loved peaches, and the smell wafting toward me made my stomach grumble.

"Have a slice, Ellie."

I knew enough about folk- and fairy tales to not to accept any food from him. Too many stories ended with people getting stuck places as a result of eating something they shouldn't. "No, thank you."

"Suit yourself." He set the plate down in front of me, sighing in disappointment. "I suppose you want to know why you're here."

"Yes."

He leaned back in his chair. "I've already told you that I realized I spoke in haste over a fortnight ago. And I would like to offer a proposition to you."

"What kind of proposition?"

"Ahone took something from you, something you love. I would like to give it back."

My breath stuck in my chest. "Daddy?"

His smile widened.

I was smart enough to know it wouldn't come without a price. "What do you want in return?"

"Are you always this cynical, Ellie?"

I forced a grin. "You said we both had something the other wanted. What is it that you want?"

Something was off. I knew this was a dream, but everything felt a bit too perfect. The food was too beautiful. The temperature too comfortable.

The owl had warned me. *Some things are merely illusions. The beautiful becomes ugly when the scales of sleep fall from your eyes. The ugly becomes beautiful when you look for the truth.*

I stood up. "I think I'm ready to go."

Okeus stayed seated, and I saw irritation flicker across his face before it was replaced by his jovial demeanor. "But Ellie, you just got here. Sit. Please. We'll discuss a business proposition."

Business. "I can hear it just fine standing."

His eyes narrowed. "I must insist, Ellie. I still haven't shown you your surprise."

I slowly sat down, keeping my eyes on him. I was ready to flee if necessary, even though there was nowhere for me to go.

"Would you like to have your father returned to you?"

"That's impossible." But was it? Hadn't I spent the first days after his death stalking the hidden gate to Popogusso, hoping I could somehow get him back?

"See for yourself."

A light glowed in the trees and a shadowy figure appeared in their midst.

My breath caught and my head was swamped with a cloud of confusion and disbelief. I stood and took a step toward the trees.

"Ahone was wrong to take him from you."

I spun to face Okeus, finally finding my anger. I latched onto it like a life preserver. "You wanted to take him from me first."

He stood and moved toward me, stopping several feet away.

I stiffened with fear, trying to catch my breath.

He lowered his voice until it sounded like a caress. "I was wrong, Ellie. I was wrong about so many things, and I'd like to make it up to you. Giving you back your father is the first step."

"Your spirits kept telling me you were waiting for me."

"I was, but not to do you harm. I had to wait until you were ready."

"Ready for what? What determined that?"

"The mark Collin drew on your back had to be completely gone for you to make your choice. Ahone or me. You must choose."

"Ahone has claimed me."

He waved his hand as though swatting a gnat. "That means nothing." He held his hand toward me with a soft smile. "I claim you. Now you have a choice."

"Why would I choose you?"

His eyes lit up in amusement. "Why would you not? I've protected you, Ellie. Where was Ahone when Ukinim and Ilena attacked you? Where was Ahone when you were attacked by that man at the dock?"

"Mishiginebig saved me. Not you."

"My children wish to please me. You know full well that he protected you on my behalf. Where was Ahone?"

I had to concede that Okeus had a point. Ahone had remained aloof, at least until a short bit ago. "Ahone saved me from the badgers tonight."

Okeus's smile quivered. "And that carries more weight than all the other times when he neglected to help you?"

I refused to admit the bitterness I felt about Ahone's lack of assistance. "You say you want to protect me, but who will protect humanity from your children? At least Ahone leaves them to live in peace."

"If you prefer Ahone, then why are you unprotected? Why don't you have Ahone's symbol?"

I didn't answer, my eyes drawn to the figure in the trees.

"You don't know what his mark is, do you? Ahone gave you permission to use it, but he neglected to give it to you. *Ellie.*" His voiced softened. "Does that sound like a god who wants to protect you?"

My pulse pounded in my head. He was right. Where had Ahone been? His messenger had told me I needed to complete my journey to receive it. But based on the way Ahone had been acting, he'd probably just disappear again and leave me to my fate after I got his mark tattooed on my body.

"Ellie, I've acquired a reputation of malevolence, but I assure you that it was acquired because I protect what is mine."

I turned to look at him, suddenly unsure about everything.

His face softened and his voice was hushed. "I would like to make you mine."

"What does that mean?"

"It means I'm offering you my protection. You've seen firsthand that not all of my creations follow my wishes. Some like Ukinim choose to go their own way. You're here with me now because I've chosen to help you. Otherwise you'd already be dead."

He made it all sound so reasonable. "What about Collin?"

"What about him?"

"He sold his soul to you. Isn't that what you're asking me to do? You want me to give you my soul for Daddy's life?"

"You make it sound so dramatic. '*Sell your soul.*' What does that even mean, Ellie? It simply means you would be committing yourself to me."

It had to be more than that.

"You're partially mine anyway, you know," he said in a conspiratorial whisper.

My eyes widened.

"Your soul is bound to Collin's." He shifted closer to me. "You've wondered what it means . . ." He paused. "It means you're bound to Collin in all things."

My heart sank. "So I have to spend eternity in Popogusso too."

"It's not so bad."

I shot him a glare. "Then why were you in such a hurry to get out?"

Okeus laughed. "Why are you resisting, Ellie?"

Why *was* I resisting? Okeus had protected me while Ahone had abandoned me. If I was going to Popogusso anyway, why not get his protection? "What do you get out of it?"

"Why can't I simply offer you my protection?"

"Collin said you offered him something and then you reneged. Who's to say you won't do the same with me? But more importantly, Collin agreed to open the gate to Popogusso and *free you*. You gave him quite the responsibility, and I suspect his reward was much less significant than what you're offering me. What could I possibly have that you want enough to bring someone back from the dead?"

His eyes glittered with excitement. "You're a smart girl. It only makes you more perfect." He reached a hand toward me. "Come sit with me, Ellie." He walked backward, his hand extended, beckoning me to follow.

I ignored his hand but moved toward him.

There was a light behind him, and I could see a canopy daybed with gauzy curtains blowing in the wind. Candle-filled lanterns hanging from poles as well as candles on the ground surrounded the bed, their flames flickering brightly.

"What is that?" My heartbeat sped up and fear crawled up my spine.

He ignored my question and sat down in the middle of the bed. "Do you realize how extraordinarily unique you are, Ellie?" He shrugged. "I'm not surprised if you don't. I didn't realize it until after I was released from Popogusso." He crossed his legs and gave me a half shrug. "But you *are* correct. I was planning to destroy you until I considered your potential and realized you were too important to waste. Too perfect. Not only are you a pure soul, but you also have the power of a Curse Keeper."

My stomach rolled into a tight ball as I stopped several feet from the bed. What could he possibly hope to gain from that? "I'm not sure how that helps you."

He leaned back on his elbows. "Mishiginebig and the others— do you know how they came into existence?"

I had seen it in my vision in the ocean with Collin when I'd reexperienced creation. "You created them."

"Yes. Some. There are spirits who were created by Ahone that are still loyal to him, but they are weak."

That was news to me. I hadn't realized there were benevolent spirits.

"But there are others, Ellie. Half man, half immortal."

"Like Ukinim and Ilena?"

"No, they were humans who were turned into animals." He leaned forward. "There are others who resemble humans—some more, some less. But none are perfect. Yet."

I shook my head, my nerves on edge. I was afraid to hear the rest.

"I made my creations to rival Ahone's precious human race, but when he split himself apart, he kept the essential piece that made men and women. I couldn't make them on my own, so I sought help."

"Where? Who?"

"How were you created, Ellie? How did *you* come into the world?"

The blood squeezed from my head, fear of what he might be suggesting making me light-headed. "My parents."

"Exactly. You had *parents*." He stood and moved next to me. I backed up until my shoulder bumped into a lantern post. "My later creations also had parents—a human mother and myself. But their mothers weren't strong enough and their humanity was overpowered by my own traits. I need someone stronger."

I shook my head, hysteria bubbling in my throat. "No."

"You are *perfect*. Your soul is pure and you have the power of the sea. Together we can make children to rival Ahone's."

"No!"

"I can offer you anything you desire if you cooperate, Ellie. Anything." His smile was warm and adoring.

"*Why?* Why would you do this? You have enough monstrosities running loose. Why would you want more?"

"Because you're exactly right. They are monstrosities. I tried over and over again to perfect them. Is it so wrong to want a perfect child? You can help me."

"No." I shook my head repeatedly. "I won't do it."

He stared into my eyes lovingly, his smile so genuine and understanding. So deceiving. "Ellie, you don't have a choice."

"The hell I don't." I shoved his shoulder hard and burst free, intending to run to the beach.

Daddy stood at the edge of the trees.

I froze, my feet digging into the sand. I almost fell forward. "*Daddy?*"

"Ellie." He held his hands out to me. "You can bring me back."

I wanted Daddy, but at what cost? I looked over my shoulder at the god behind me.

"Ellie, I was wrong about Okeus. He's really on our side."

I never remembered Daddy talking about Okeus other than being concerned about me having the god's symbol on my back. "What are you talking about?"

"Ellie, you need to listen to Okeus. He can bring me back."

Collin told me that no human could go to Popogusso and come back alive. So how was my father here? "Daddy, he wants me to do something terrible."

He stepped toward me and placed his right hand on my arm. His fingers were cool and clammy, not the warm hands I remembered. His face was my father's . . . but not my father's. It looked wrong, almost plastic. And Daddy always smelled like cinnamon with a soft hint of leather, even after he'd taken ill. Now he smelled like nothing. But that was to be expected, right? Okeus had brought Daddy back from the dead, so it made sense that he wouldn't be quite himself.

But I knew in my heart that this wasn't him, and having his likeness in front of me made the pain of losing him fresh all over again.

"It's okay, Ellie. Okeus is going to help us. We should help him too."

I shook my head and took a step back, tears burning my eyes. "No. You're not Daddy."

His face twisted in dismay. "Ellie, how can you say that?" He held his hands out from his sides. "It's me."

"No. My daddy would never let anything terrible happen to me."

Okeus approached from behind. "Can you be so sure about that? How well did you *really* know your father? You didn't even know that your father was world renowned in his field. Or the role he *really* played in your mother's death. Your father was supposed to be home the night she was killed, but he was somewhere else."

Fear tickled the back of my head, stealing my breath. "He went to a board meeting."

Okeus's eyebrows lifted in mock surprise. "Did he? You think you are beginning to know what happened the night your mother was killed, but it's only the tip of the iceberg."

"You're a liar." I pointed to the man who looked like Daddy. "That is *not* my father."

Okeus's eyes narrowed. "What do you want most, Ellie? What is your heart's desire? Is it your father? Maybe not . . . maybe it's the truth about your mother's death." He gave me a smug smile. "I know the truth and can share it with you."

"Liar," I spit.

"Or is it Collin? I know you think he betrayed you, but he only did what he thought was best for all concerned. I assured him you would eventually understand."

"I understand all right. I understand that you lie and manipulate and bend the truth to get what you want."

"Ellie." I heard impatience in his voice.

"I have proof that you're a liar. You promised Collin payment and you didn't follow through."

Okeus's eyes narrowed, his temper creeping in. "He disobeyed me."

"For protecting me? Isn't that what you said? But now *you* want to protect me too, so maybe you should pay him now."

Okeus's eyes flashed red before returning to their normal dark brown. "I do not tolerate disobedience."

"Then this thing between us"—I waved my hand from him to me—"It's not going to work out, because I have a real problem with obedience. Just ask Collin." I looked up at the thing pretending to be my daddy. "And too bad that's not my daddy—he would have told you the same thing."

I stomped toward the water, but Okeus grabbed my arm and pulled me back. "We aren't done here."

"Well I am." I jerked my arm out of his grasp, and blood soaked through my white shirt as my arm began to throb where the badger had clawed me. I stopped to stare at it in confusion, but Okeus took advantage of my distraction.

Wrapping an arm around my waist, he pulled my back to his chest and picked me up as if I weighed nothing. He stomped toward the canopied daybed.

I kicked his shins and clawed his arms, screaming, but he never so much as flinched.

He's a fucking god, Ellie. Could I physically hurt a god?

I swallowed a sob of panic.

"Ellie, you're a disappointment. I thought you were smarter than this." He threw me down on the bed and the skirt and shirt instantly disappeared, leaving me naked.

I scrambled backward on the bed, but Okeus grabbed my ankles and dragged me toward him.

This is just a dream.

That's right. It was just a dream. All I had to do was wake up.

"You bear my mark on your arm, but you refuse to take my mark of protection on your own." A claw extended from his finger as his other hand pressed down on my shoulder. "So now you shall bear another." He lowered the nail to my exposed abdomen, the tip sinking into the skin above my belly button, slicing his zigzag pattern there.

I screamed until I was hoarse, thrashing to get away, but it only made the pain worse.

I had to wake up. Why couldn't I wake up?

Okeus looked down at his completed mark with a smile. "I claim you as my own, Elinor Lancaster."

302

"Fuck you," I shouted through my tears. I *had* to wake up. Ahone's messenger had told me to use my resources, but what other resources did I have other than the mark on my palm?

David.

"David!" I screamed, hoping this would work. It was the only plan I had. *"David!"*

Okeus began to unbuckle his jeans.

"Ellie!" I could hear David's voice in my head.

"David. Help me!" I sobbed. I felt my physical body being shaken, and I scooted backward.

Anger spread across Okeus's face. "No!" He grabbed my legs and pulled me toward him.

I closed my eyes to concentrate. *"David!"*

A hard jerk shook me, and I opened my eyes to David's terrified face.

∽ CHAPTER TWENTY-THREE ∽

I was back in my dark room—the only illumination a glimmer of light from the open bathroom door. David sat on the bed next to me. His hands were on my shoulders, shaking me. I sat up, wincing as pain shot through my abdomen, and threw my arms around his neck, sobbing into his shoulder.

He held me tight against his chest with one arm, his other hand cradling the back of my head. "It's okay. You're okay."

I continued to cry, beginning to hyperventilate.

He gently pulled away enough to look in my eyes. "Ellie, you're safe. It was just a dream."

I shook my head, my shoulders shaking with my tears. I struggled to catch my breath. "It *wasn't* just a dream." I looked down at my arm.

"You're bleeding." His voice rose in alarm as he dropped his hold on me and grabbed my arm. "These are claw marks."

"Ukinim."

His eyes widened. "When did you leave the house?"

I shook my head. "I didn't."

"*This happened in your dreams?*"

The sheet covering my body had fallen to my lap, and his gaze lowered to the blood trickling from the carving on my stomach.

Oh, God. I was naked.

I grabbed the sheet and pulled it up to cover my chest.

"And your stomach? What did that?"

"Okeus." My voice hitched.

His body tensed, and he looked out the window before turning back to me. "I'm going to get something to clean you up." He got off the bed, and my chest exploded with panic at the thought of being alone.

"Don't leave me! *Please.*" I started crying again and grabbed his arm. "Please don't leave me." I knew I was irrational, but nothing about what had just happened was rational.

He pulled me into his arms. "I won't, Ellie. I promise I won't leave you."

I clung to his neck, terrified. I knew I was safe at the moment, but my hysteria still refused to believe it.

He tugged the top sheet off the bed and wrapped it around my back. "Let's go into the bathroom."

I hiccuped a breath, gaining control of my tears. "Okay." I slid off the bed with his help. My legs shook and began to buckle, but he slid an arm around my back, supporting my weight.

David guided me through the bathroom door, moving sideways, and helped me sit on the closed toilet lid. The brightness of the room helped soothe my frazzled nerves, and I looked up into his worried face. Blood covered his T-shirt where I'd grabbed him. He lifted my arm, his brow wrinkling with concern. "How the bloody hell did this happen?"

"I don't know. Wapi was outside my window when I fell asleep."

"What about your dream catcher?"

I took a deep breath. "I had it."

He dug a first-aid kit out from under the sink and opened up several alcohol pads. "Why didn't it work?" He sounded angry, but his touch was gentle as he dabbed at the wounds. "And even if you had dreams, they shouldn't have manifested themselves this way."

I flinched as the alcohol burned my gashes. "I don't know what happened." My voice broke.

He dropped to his knees in front of me. "Ellie, I'm sorry. I'm not mad at you. I'm just frustrated. I thought I had figured out a way to protect you while you were asleep and it failed." His mouth turned down. "I failed you."

"No. You saved me. If you hadn't called my name, I don't think I would have woken up and Okeus . . ." I started crying again, helplessness washing over me. I'd given myself the illusion of being in control, but I wasn't in control of anything.

David grabbed my shoulders. "You're here now."

I nodded, forcing myself to calm down. I took a deep breath and held it for several seconds.

"These wounds are deep. I think you should go to the hospital to get stitches."

"No. They'll ask questions and Tom will find out that I saw Ukinim. He already thinks they're stalking me. I can't deal with the questions."

He took my hand and squeezed it. "Okay. We'll get you some butterfly bandages in the morning."

"Thank you."

He kissed my forehead and then continued to clean the wounds. He found bandages in the first-aid kit and wrapped my arm with gauze. His gaze fell to the bloody sheet that I was clutching to my breasts. "I need to look at your stomach."

"Oh."

He pointed his thumb toward the door. "I'll step out and let you get things . . . situated, and then I'll be back."

"Where are my pajamas?"

"I don't know. You were naked when I found you. I figured that's why you locked your door, which seemed odd. You never even close the door all the way in your apartment."

"I went to bed in pajamas and I left the door open so I could see the bathroom light."

His face paled. "Ellie, your door wasn't just closed; it was locked."

"Oh, God." Those things had access inside the house somehow.

David's eyes widened with fear. "I'll go look for your pajamas."

"No." I shook my head, frantic. "Don't leave me."

"Okay. I'll just turn around." He stood in the doorway, facing the hallway.

I dropped the sheet to my waist and pulled a towel off the rack to cover my breasts. "Okay."

He turned around and took a step toward me, freezing when his gaze landed on my stomach. "God, Ellie. What did he do? That's his mark." His voice cracked, and his eyes glassed over.

My chin quivered. "He claimed me as his own."

David swallowed. "Does that mean—?"

"No. I still have to choose, but both sides have claimed me now, whatever that means."

He put his hands on my shoulders and pushed me backward so that my shoulder blades were pressed against the back of the toilet. His voice softened. "What happened?"

"My dream was real. First I saw the badgers, where I got this." I lifted my arm. "Then I saw Ahone's messenger, who promised to show me Ahone's mark after the next part of my dream, which was when Okeus cornered me."

"Did you see the mark?"

"No." I didn't hide my bitterness.

He dabbed my stomach with a wet washrag and I flinched.

"I'm sorry."

I gritted my teeth as he continued to clean it.

"This thing is a good twelve centimeters long. I think it's going to scar." He sounded devastated.

I closed my eyes and swallowed the lump in my throat. "I think that was his intent. He wanted it to match the one he gave me on my arm."

"I'm sorry."

I opened my eyes and offered him a small smile. "Quit saying you're sorry."

"I can't help it. This happened to you while I was across the bloody hall."

"Well, I don't want to think about what would have happened to me if you hadn't been here."

"What happened with Okeus, Ellie? I know he did this, but why?"

Total disclosure. "Okeus promised to give me back Daddy."

His mouth dropped open. "Can he do that?"

"No, I don't think so. Daddy was there, but it wasn't him. His look-alike tried to get me to accept Okeus's agreement."

"To get his mark?"

"That too."

"What else?"

I looked away. "He wants to use me as a breeding mare."

He sat back on his heels. "What the *bloody hell* does that mean?"

"The demons are Okeus's creations. But his ultimate goal is to create children who look like him. Like us. So he moved on to making babies the old-fashioned way. Only his babies were still monsters. He thinks my pure soul plus my Curse Keeper blood will make the babies he's always dreamed of."

"*He wants to impregnate you?*"

"So it would seem."

David sat on the side of the tub and took my hand. "You were naked."

"If you're asking me if he was successful in his attempt, the answer is no. But if I hadn't woken up when I did, I'm sure it would be a different story."

"Ellie, I'm sorry."

I put my finger on his lips. "You didn't do anything wrong. You saved me. Thank you."

His fingers wrapped around mine, and he placed a kiss against my fingertips.

"Are you done with my stomach?"

"I've cleaned it up. I'm not sure what else to do other than give you something for the pain." He stood and found a bottle of ibuprofen in the medicine cabinet. He handed me two with a cup of water.

I swallowed the pills and then pulled the sheet up to cover my breasts. "Okay," I said as I clutched the covering and stood. "I'm going to get dressed."

He reached for my arm, but I shrugged him off. I needed to feel like I was in control of something, like I wasn't completely helpless. "I'm better. I can walk now."

He followed me into my room. Standing at the foot of my bed, he combed the room with his eyes, coming to a stop at the window. He stepped forward for a closer look.

"It looks like the salt is missing."

"So that's how they got in my dreams?"

"I don't know." He moved to my bed, slightly lifting the dream catcher that hung from the headboard. "I wish to God I did."

"Well, one thing's for certain. I'm not going back to sleep until the sun comes up."

"I'll stay up with you." He bent over and picked up my pajama bottoms and camisole top off the floor, handing them to me. "If you want to get dressed, I'll turn around."

"Thanks." It seemed stupid. He had seen me naked earlier, after all. My eyes drifted to the busted door frame.

"I had to break the door in."

"Thanks."

He nodded and turned around as I slipped on my clothes. My arm and my stomach throbbed, but I managed to do it without causing myself too much pain.

"I'm done."

He spun around and watched as I moved toward him. The pain and guilt in his eyes was nearly my undoing.

I stopped in front of him. "David, don't do that. Don't feel sorry for me. I can't take it."

His eyes widened, incredulous. "Is that what you think this is? You think I *pity* you?" He lifted his hands and rested them on my upper arms. "You're the strongest person I know. I don't pity you. God, far from it." His hand rose, his grip tightening as he cupped the side of my face. "Ellie," his voice broke. "I can't stand the thought that I wasn't able to protect you from this . . ." His other hand rose to touch the other side of my face. "I'm supposed to be helping you, but I keep failing at every turn. You're better off without me."

My back stiffened. "Don't you *dare* say that, David Preston. You just saved me from . . . that monster. And you have found more information for me than I ever would have found on my own. But you've given me so much more than that." I grabbed his

310

cheeks and pulled his face closer. "I don't care if you ever find another piece of information. I still want you here. I can't do this alone. I *need* you."

His mouth lowered to mine, his kiss tender and hesitant.

I wrapped my arms around his neck, opening my mouth to his probing tongue.

He groaned and placed a hand on my lower back, pressing me to him as his mouth and tongue grew bolder.

I slid my hands from his neck, needing to feel more of him. I lifted his shirt up and he lifted his head to let me pull it the rest of the way off.

My hands landed on his chest and my fingertips glided across his skin.

David searched my eyes. "Are you sure you want to do this, Ellie?"

My only answer was to pull off the shirt I'd just put on.

His gaze landed on my breasts and then moved up to my face. "I don't want to do this in here."

I nodded and he took my hand and led me to his room, tugging me to the bed. He kissed me, one arm around my waist as his other hand explored my breast. I buried my hands into his hair, and he pressed his stomach to mine as our kisses deepened. I winced, releasing a cry of pain from the cut on my abdomen.

David released me and tried to step back, his eyes filled with worry. "I don't want to hurt you."

I wrapped my arms around his upper back, pulling him back to me. "I'll be fine. We can make this work."

He sat on the edge of the bed and pulled me between his legs, wrapping one arm around my waist. His mouth found my breast and I moaned, burying my hand in his hair to hold him in place. Still, I needed more.

As if reading my mind, his head lifted and he stared into my eyes as his thumb hooked the top of my pajama bottoms, pushing them over my hips and down to the floor.

Standing, he gently pushed me down to the bed. He began to tug his own pajama bottoms down, but then stopped.

I looked into his questioning eyes. "David, I want you."

His gaze lowered to my stomach. "I'm scared that I'll hurt you."

I smiled. "We'll figure it out."

He went to his bag and returned with a condom. Dropping his pants, he stood between my legs, which hung off the sides of the bed, and rolled on his condom. He leaned down, resting his elbow next to my head, his body hovering over mine as his tongue licked my bottom lip and then sucked it into his mouth, biting lightly.

White-hot lust spread through my veins and I instinctively lifted my hips up to his.

He groaned and lowered his mouth to my breast, while his other hand slipped between my legs. I pressed into his hand, needing more, needing this man.

"David, I want you," I repeated. "Now."

A growl rumbled from his chest as he rose, standing in front of me, the desire and devotion in his eyes making me even hungrier for him.

He grabbed my hips and leaned between my legs, filling me in a slow plunge.

I cried out and lifted my hips higher so he could get deeper. I wrapped my legs around his waist as he sank into me again. His head leaned back and a guttural sound erupted from him. His pace quickened as we climbed and I clung to him, desperate for more.

The pressure built, but I held back, my whimpers encouraging him to quicken his pace, moving deeper and faster. When I couldn't hold back any longer, I arched my back and pushed against him. Wave after wave washed over me as David gave one last grunt, staying deep inside as my orgasm finished.

He rested his knees on the bed, still inside me, and then leaned over, raining kisses on my face and neck. "You're so beautiful."

I lifted my mouth to his, reaching around his neck and holding him close as my tongue sought his.

He pulled back, giving me a reluctant smile. "I need to go clean up. Will you be okay if I leave you alone for just a moment?"

I stared into his eyes and nodded.

He left the room and I forced myself to get up and pull down the covers, crawling on my hands and knees. My butt was in the air, facing the door, when he returned. "Now there's a welcoming sight."

He helped me pull the sheet down and then slid in next to me, still naked. Wrapping an arm around my back, he pulled me to his side. I rested my cheek on his chest. He lifted my chin and stared down into my eyes, worry wrinkling his brow. "Are you okay?"

I smiled. "Yeah."

"No, I mean really okay?"

My smile faded. "As okay as can be expected." I kissed his chest. "If you're asking if I'm okay with what we just did, though, I'm more than okay. But the rest . . . I'll need a bit of time."

He bent down and gently kissed me. "Understandable." Worry and fear tightened his face. "But despite what just happened between us, I still wonder if you should be with me."

I rose on my elbow and started to protest, but he put his finger to my lips.

"Hear me out, love. I need to say this."

"Okay," I said softly, terrified of what he was going to tell me.

"I want you, Ellie. Not just for your body, but your mind, your wit, your stubbornness, and your courage. I look at you now—like this—and I can't believe you've let me into your life." He swallowed. "But I can also see that you're loyal, and I don't want that to be your downfall."

My lips parted to respond, but the pressure of his finger increased.

"The day may come when I'm no longer a help but a hindrance. If it does, I need you to promise me that you'll let me go."

Anger surged through my body. "No!" I sat up, wincing at the pain. "You don't get to tell me what to do!"

Sitting up, he rubbed the back of my neck, bringing my face closer to his. There was no anger in his face, only patience and devotion. "I know that, Ellie. I would never dream of telling you what to do, but back when we made the agreement for our partnership, you agreed to give all of my suggestions and concerns consideration."

"What are you doing, David? Is this your way of trying to leave me? Just like every—" I stopped.

Sadness filled his eyes. "Like everyone else? Your father and your mother? Hell, even Collin left you—he just forced you to be the one to walk away with his lies and deceptions." He sighed and closed his eyes. "God, how could I be so *stupid*?"

Tears filled my eyes. "Do you want me or not, David?"

"Christ, Ellie," he pleaded. "It's not about wanting you. I just want what's *best* for you."

My chest tightened, my words thick with emotion. "You don't get to decide. I do. It's my decision."

"Okay, okay." His hand caressed my cheeks, wiping away my tears. His eyes burned with intensity. "Elinor Lancaster, I pledge to never leave your side of my own free will. I will stand with you and always be at your service. The only way I will leave is if you send me away."

My mouth dropped open and I shook my head in disbelief. "You can't promise me that."

A teasing smile lifted his lips. "I just did."

"But—"

"Ellie, you need to know you can count on someone to be there for you, no matter what. No matter how hard it is or how dangerous. I am promising to be that someone."

"But why?"

His lips pressed against mine, his hand gliding across my bare back. His fingertips dug into my skin as he sucked my upper lip into his mouth.

I panted with need, clinging to him.

His head lifted and he looked into my eyes, all the teasing gone. "Do you remember when I asked if you believed in destiny? *You* are my destiny, Ellie Lancaster. You."

We made love again, slow and gentle, but with reverence as we explored each other's bodies.

Afterward, sunlight crept through the drapes, and I rested my cheek on his chest.

His arm tightened around me. "Do you still think you're broken?" he asked, sounding sleepy.

What David and I had shared was special, but if I were honest with myself, it wasn't close to what I'd experienced with Collin. He and I had shared body and soul with each other—a once-in-a-lifetime experience. But we'd also shared deception and betrayal. Collin and I were fire and ice, love and hate. When you climb to soaring heights, the fall is much more deadly.

What I had with David was deeper and more meaningful, and yet . . . it was not quite enough. Collin was right. I'd never experience anything like the pure completeness I had felt when we were connected, but those moments had been fleeting, and our passion had come at a steep price that wasn't worth it. The sad truth was that Collin couldn't give me what I needed, because he couldn't give *himself* what he needed.

I needed to make a choice and I needed to stand by it. David deserved the same commitment that he'd offered me. I knew that once I picked, I couldn't go back.

I stared into the face of the man sleeping beside me and brushed the hair off his forehead. I knew in my heart he was perfect for me.

I leaned down and brushed a kiss on his lips, whispering. "I choose you."

Then I laid my head on his chest and slept a dreamless sleep.

⌁ Chapter Twenty-Four ⌁

We only slept a few hours before I got up to make breakfast for the guests in the inn. With Myra gone, I couldn't forget the real reason I was staying in the house.

I hung around the office and small kitchen of the inn, greeting guests and giving them directions and suggestions for sightseeing. David got up with me and hovered nearby for most of the morning. Normally, it would have felt claustrophobic, but after my real-life nightmares of the previous night, I was freaked out enough to not want to be alone. And I knew David wasn't the hovering type. He was staying close to me because he knew I needed him.

I pushed him into the office and reached up to kiss him. "Thank you."

A wicked gleam filled his eyes. "And what exactly are you thanking me *for*?"

I kissed him again and stepped back. "Everything."

When the guests left for their day of sightseeing, David followed me upstairs to help me make the beds and clean the bathrooms.

"You don't have to do this," I said, tucking in a sheet. "You can go do something fun."

"No. I've always been fascinated about the role of an inn-keeper."

I laughed. "An innkeeper, huh? You make me feel like I'm sixty." I leaned over in the bathroom connected to the room and grabbed some damp towels off the floor, wincing as I stood.

"Ellie, you shouldn't be bending over like that."

"I'm fine. It doesn't hurt or anything. It just stings."

He took the towels from me. "Where do I put these?"

"The basket in the hall," I said, turning on the water I'd need for cleaning.

He dumped them where I'd told him. "Want me to get started in the next room?"

"David, you don't—"

"Ellie, let me help. The sooner we get done here, the faster we can get back to searching for your father's notes."

I nodded and then rushed out into the hall to give him a quick kiss. "Okay, as long as you don't mind."

He grinned against my lips. "Don't you have a bathroom to clean?"

I lifted my eyebrows in mock surprise. "Oh, yeah."

He disappeared into the other guest room and I returned to the bathroom I was cleaning, surprised to see that the mirror had already steamed up. I leaned over to crack open the window and gasped.

"*David.*"

He was through the doorway in seconds, worry on his face. "Are you okay?"

I pointed to the window. In the steam was the outline of a symbol. It was a four-pointed star. It looked weirdly familiar, but I couldn't place it.

"How did that get there?" David asked, moving closer.

"I don't know. When I came back, the window was steamed up and it was there."

"Ellie, this symbol is on the plank."

"Do you think it's Ahone's?"

He shook his head in amazement. "I don't know. It could be."

"Could be isn't good enough. I *need* to know. I can't just tattoo some random symbol on my back." I ran my uninjured hand through my hair and turned toward him. "I'm sorry. I'm not upset with you. I'm pissed at Ahone. Why does he have to be so damned illusive? Why can't he just say, 'Here's my symbol'?"

"I don't know. I keep wondering why Okeus's symbol is still known but not Ahone's. It could be because the people offered regular sacrifices to Okeus and pretty much ignored Ahone. They rarely gave him thought, so why record his name? Or perhaps Ahone's name is like the ancient Hebrew name for God, and only the priests knew how to pronounce it. God's name was considered too reverent to be spoken by just anyone."

"Hopefully Daddy will have recorded it somewhere. If we can find any of his other notes."

"We will."

He sounded more certain than I was.

"Tonight I think we should sleep in your apartment," he said. "Last night was the first time you dreamed since you started sleeping with the dream catcher. But I'm going to sleep with you so I can check on you and make sure you're okay."

I bumped his shoulder. "You just want a reason not to sleep on the sofa."

He laughed. "That's right. You caught me. I seduced you only so that I could have a mattress." He pushed me against the wall and leaned over to kiss me.

I wrapped my arm around his neck, closing my eyes as I let myself be sucked into the moment. It struck me—*this* was what I'd been looking for before Collin showed up and shattered my life. I wasn't in love David, but I was *falling* in love with him. Even this early, it was easy to see he was *the one*—the guy I'd been waiting to show up and fill my life, the guy who could give me the love and happiness my parents had shared. Sighing with momentary contentment, I pushed him away. "As romantic as making out in a guest's dirty bathroom is, I'm afraid I need to get back to work."

"You are a very cruel woman, Ellie Lancaster."

"And you are easily distracted, Dr. Preston. Now go make a bed." I gave his arm a playful push.

After he stole another kiss and headed into the other room, I found myself staring at the fading symbol again.

With the two of us working, we finished within an hour. David insisted on carrying the dirty linen to the laundry room and starting the wash. When I protested, he mock scowled. "I'm a bachelor, Ellie. I've lived alone since I was eighteen. I know how to do laundry."

"Okay . . ." Was I really going to fight him over him doing the laundry?

"Now that we have this symbol, I'm going to e-mail a few colleagues to find out if they've ever seen it. I doubt we'll get confirmation, but we might be able to eliminate it if they recognize it as something else."

"Okay, how about I order a pizza? The best place in town doesn't offer delivery, but I'll go pick it up while you're sending your e-mails."

Worry filled his eyes. "Do you want me to go with you?"

"No, I'll be fine. It's daylight." Although I wasn't sure how much longer that would give me security.

"Okay. Be careful."

He headed for the front porch with his laptop, and I called in the order, realizing as I did that my car was back at my apartment. I grabbed my purse and walked the two blocks home. My arm throbbed after using it all morning, reminding me that it still needed butterfly bandages. I had a box in my bathroom, so I figured I could run upstairs and grab them.

When I reached my front porch, I knew something was off. The symbols on my door were smudged, and that *never* happened. Fear squeezed my lungs. Had Tom arrested Collin?

But when I unlocked the door and pushed it open, I realized what was really going on. One of Marino's men—the one who'd tried to kidnap me in Morehead City—sat in my overstuffed chair with a handgun on his lap. The box that held Daddy's remaining watches was out on the coffee table.

"Ellie Lancaster, you're a hard woman to find."

Oh, shit. I froze in the doorway, my hand still on the doorknob.

"Come on in, Ellie. We need to have a little chat."

I hesitated. "I'm not feeling very chatty today." I started to take a step back.

He lifted the gun and pointed it at me. "Don't underestimate my willingness to shoot. You've been a pain in my ass for weeks, and I'd as soon shoot you and be done with it. Just give me a reason." The look on his face told me he meant it.

Forcing myself to take slow, steady breaths, I walked inside.

"Shut the door."

I cast a quick glance over my shoulder. The one time I wished Tom was hanging around and nagging me to talk, he was nowhere to be found. Figured.

"Have a seat."

I took my time sitting on the sofa, staying as far away from him as possible. Why did he have Daddy's watches? He must have been snooping in my closet.

"Tell me what you know about the Ricardo deal."

"I don't know anything."

He leaned forward, his face reddening. "I'm not a patient man. So let's try this again." His eyes narrowed. "What do you know about the Ricardo deal?"

Why was he questioning me here instead of taking me to Marino? I wasn't sure what that meant. "I don't know anything. The first time I ever heard of it was when I met Marino, and Collin refused to give me any details. Officer Helmsworth told me it was a collection of antiques that had been stolen. That's all I know. I swear."

"Then what are you doing with these watches?"

"They were my father's."

He shook his head with a disgusted look and banged his hand on the table next to the box. "Try again, Ellie."

I jumped, fighting the sob that was building in my chest. Where was Mishiginebig when I needed him?

He opened the lid and pointed to the older watch. "Where did you get this?"

"I told you, it was my father's." I forced myself to take a normal breath. I had to control my fear.

Reaching down to a bag next to his chair, he pulled out a folder and set it on the table before sliding it over to me. "Take a look at that."

I opened the folder with shaky fingers, trying to make sense of the photos inside. Then I realized I was staring at the contents of the Ricardo Estate. Maybe I would learn something I could use if I survived this encounter.

I flipped through the photos slowly, hoping I wasn't being too obvious with my cataloging. Swords and daggers made of gold and silver were displayed on tables. Some were intricately carved, others plain. The next photo held candlesticks and silverware, but the third photo was what had made him suspicious. Pocket watches were mixed in with buttons, brooches, hairpins, necklaces, and rings.

"Take a closer look at that one. Upper left corner."

I picked up the photo and tried to figure out what he wanted me to see. When I saw it, I gasped. The watch was identical to the one sitting on my coffee table, the one Oscar had told me would need its own insurance policy. But how could that be? These watches had been in Daddy's family for years, centuries even.

"Now you know that I have evidence of your involvement, so let's stop fooling around. Where did you get the watches?"

I obviously didn't have the answer he wanted, and he obviously had information I could use. I had two choices. I could keep insisting on the truth, or I could take a lesson from Collin's playbook. "Collin gave it to me," I said after a moment.

He eased back in his chair and gave me a condescending grin. "Now we're getting somewhere. Why did Collin give it to you? As payment?"

"Payment for what?"

"Come on, Ellie. Once I figured out who you were, it didn't take much digging to put two and two together. Your mother was known for her expertise on Elizabethan and Jacobean antiques. And your father"—he leaned forward—"he was an expert in all things about the colonies. *Of course* Dailey would find you. Most people see his looks and charm and dismiss his cunningness, and he definitely uses that to his advantage. The question is how long did he string you along before you realized what he *really* wanted?"

Was there any truth to his question? Had Collin given any thought to who I was besides the fact that I was the other Keeper? I was desperate to know more about the Ricardo deal, particularly now, which meant I had to give this guy something to keep him talking. I gave him a bitter smile. "It was a carrot. He gave it to me to get me intrigued."

A real smile lit up his face. "And did it?"

I lifted my eyebrows. "What do *you* think? You said it yourself—he has the looks and the charm." I lowered my chin. "Let's just say he used every trick he had to get me involved."

"Did he tell you where it was?"

I held my breath. Did Collin actually have it? "No. He just gave me the watches to appraise. He never mentioned where anything else was." Was I doing the right thing? I had no idea how Collin was really involved in the Ricardo deal. For all I knew, I was screwing him over. But I had to survive this encounter, and throwing Collin under the bus was the only way I saw that happening. I'd deal with the fallout later.

"Did he plan to take you to the collection?"

I hesitated, not sure of what the right answer would be. "We never got that far."

His eyes narrowed. "Marino was never certain whether Dailey had it or not. He claimed he didn't, but we all know that every other word out of his mouth is a lie, so we've been watching him and biding our time. Marino had begun to believe Dailey really didn't have any part in the theft." He grinned. "Until you showed up with those candlesticks. So many alarms went off in that one visit."

My heart sped up. "So you think Collin *does* have it?"

"That or he knows where it is. Doesn't this watch he gave you prove it?" He sat back a bit and I let out my breath. "Marino thinks that map he loves so much might have a clue about where the collection is hidden. Did you ever see anything on the map that might support that?"

"No." I shook my head. "I barely saw it. I've been trying to get the map myself."

He perked up. "You've been trying to get the map? Do you still have access to Collin?"

Oh, crap. "I see him around."

His jaw tightened as he gripped the arm of the chair with his left hand, his right still holding the gun steady. "Are you or are you not still working with Collin Dailey?" His eyebrows lifted ominously. "Think carefully about your answer."

Shit. What should I say? Both yes and no seemed fraught with danger. If I said no, then he'd probably take me to Marino, and I *really* didn't want to go there. If I said yes, he might kill me because of my association alone. Neither sounded like a good option. God, I hoped I was making the right choice. "Neither."

"What *the fuck* does that mean?"

"I'm a middle-of-the-road kind of girl and I'm not big on commitment. Collin comes to me every now and then to ask me a question about antiquities. Sometimes I answer, sometimes I don't." I gave him a wicked smile, trying to keep my chin from quivering with fear.

He stood. "I think we need to make a trip to Buxton."

Wrong answer. I stood and scooted around the arm of the sofa. "I'm sorry. I already have plans today."

He pointed the gun in my direction as he leaned over and closed the lid to the box. "Change them."

He was going to take Daddy's watches and I really needed them now. How could I get out of this situation alive and *with* the watches? "Wait. There's one more." My words came out shaky. I had to get myself together to make this work.

His head lifted. "One more what? Watch?"

"Yes."

"How do I know you're not lying?"

I pointed to the box. "If you look closely, there's an impression of the third watch in the case."

He lifted the lid and leaned closer. "I'll be damned." He looked up, his eyes hard. "Where is it?"

I forced myself to take slow, steady breaths. "I hid it. In case Collin ever tried to take them back. Insurance."

"Smart girl."

"If you give me some time, I can try to get Collin to tell me where the rest of the collection is."

He looked dubious. "You think you can really get him to cooperate?"

I put my hand on my hip. "I'm not like all of Collin's other sluts. Don't underestimate me. Give me until next week and I'll have more information for you."

"You have until tomorrow night. I'll be here at eight."

"My neighbors are extra nosy. Make it eleven."

"Deal."

I released my breath, trying not to make it obvious.

He picked up the box and tucked it under his arm.

"Wait! I still need those."

He paused, his eyebrows raised in anticipation.

Oh, crap. What rational explanation could I come up with? "Collin is expecting them back. He won't take me to see the entire collection if I don't have them."

"This better not be a trick."

"It's not. I swear." I was surely going to hell for all the lies pouring out of my mouth lately, but then again, Okeus had pretty much confirmed I was going there anyway.

326

He moved toward the front door. "See you tomorrow night, Ellie Lancaster."

"Yeah," I mumbled as he walked out the door. "I can't wait."

After giving myself a few moments to recover, I grabbed the watches and bandages from the bathroom and headed for my car. When I got back to the inn, David was on the front porch, his full attention focused on his laptop. I parked my car on the street and walked across the yard, the box tucked under my arm.

When I opened the screen door, he looked up in surprise. "You're back already? Where's the pizza?"

"Something happened."

His eyes widened in alarm. He closed his computer and set it to the side. "Are you okay?"

I nodded. "Just shaken up." I paused. "Marino's guy was in my apartment."

He jumped out of his seat and grabbed my hand. "*What?*"

"He found Daddy's pocket watches, and he thinks it's proof that I'm involved with the Ricardo Estate."

He shook his head, confused. "What watches?"

"Let's go inside and I'll show you."

David picked up his laptop and opened the front door, locking it behind us once we were inside.

"They won't be back until tomorrow night," I said when I caught him scanning the street.

"Tell me everything."

We went into the kitchen and I showed him the watches. I confessed to pawning the third one and told him everything that transpired in my apartment a few minutes earlier.

"Do you think Collin made the same deductions about your parents' background that Marino did?"

I shook my head with a sigh. "No. He refused to tell me anything about the deal, saying the less I knew the better. He never once tried to get information from me about any of it."

"Okay. So what do you want to do about tomorrow night?"

I opened the lid to the box. "I don't know yet. Maybe tell Tom. I want to think about it. But we're safe for the moment."

He nodded.

I looked inside and gasped, picking up my favorite watch. "It's the symbol." The four-pointed star had always blended into the background of smaller stars, but after seeing it in the window this morning, it was like a neon sign.

I'd had it all along.

David reached for the watch, and I reluctantly handed it to him.

"Daddy used to carry one of two pocket watches every day. When I was little, before Momma died, we'd play a game. Every morning at breakfast, I'd try to guess which one he had in his pocket."

"Surely he didn't wear the other watch in this box. It looks like it should be in a museum."

"No, it was this one and the one I sold. But this one was always my favorite. The other one was prettier, but for some reason I was always drawn to this one."

A soft smile lifted his mouth. "I guess we know why."

"I take it you haven't heard anything yet?"

"No. But I just sent the e-mails out. Let's give it a little time."

I nodded. We didn't *have* time, but pointing that out wouldn't help anything.

Then it hit me: Myra said Daddy said I'd needed *time*. The watches. He'd given me a clue but I was too stupid to put it together. What else had I missed?

I shook my head. "I forgot to pick up the pizza."

He leaned over and kissed me. "We'll figure something else out." He grabbed my hand and placed the watch in my palm. "But do me a favor: don't ever consider selling these two pieces unless you are so desperate you have no other option."

I glanced down at the timepiece, then put it back into the box. "I won't."

We made sandwiches for lunch before we searched my old room. After an hour of looking in every nook and cranny, we came up with nothing.

David pulled me into a hug. "Let's take a break. I'll check my e-mail, and then we can figure out which room to start on next."

I put in some more laundry, fighting my rising frustration. I was beginning to accept the fact that I might never find the rest of Daddy's notes or that mysterious ring Myra had mentioned. The most pressing issue was figuring out Ahone's mark. The four-pointed star had turned up twice in the course of a few hours. Could I trust that we'd found it? Enough to permanently put it on my back? When I finished, I found David in the kitchen, sitting at the counter with his computer.

I opened the lid to the box and picked up the starry-sky watch and opened the cover, examining the face. It hadn't been wound in ages, and the hands were frozen. Clutching it in my hand, I closed my eyes as warm memories of my childhood washed over me. I was a little girl again, sitting at the kitchen table with Daddy as Momma served us breakfast.

"Okay, Elliphant," Daddy said, running his hand over the pocket of his uniform pants. "Which one today?"

"Um . . ." I tapped my chin like Daddy sometimes did. "You wore the silver one yesterday. Maybe you wore it again to trick me."

"You'll never know until you guess."

"You picked my favorite. You wore the starry sky."

Grinning, he pulled it from his pocket, unhooked it from its chain, and put it in my hand.

"I was right!" I bounced in my seat.

"This is your *watch," Daddy said. "I'm just holding onto it until you need it."*

Momma scooped scrambled eggs onto my plate, then kissed the top of my head.

Daddy beamed at me, picking up his fork. "As soon as you finish breakfast, you can look for the quarter I hid."

My eyes flew open. "I know where to look."

David glanced up from his computer. "You do?"

"Daddy and I used to play a game when I was really little—preschool age. He would hide a quarter and I had to find it. We didn't do it for very long. Momma said I was too good at finding them and I was getting too much money. I had completely forgotten until a moment ago."

"So where do we look?"

"Outside." I jumped off the stool and ran out onto the front porch, David on my heels. "I was little, but Daddy used to say he couldn't make it too easy. He told me a good archaeologist had to know where to look. That was half the battle." I knelt in front of the two-foot brick wall that ran along the front of the house. Running my hand over the bricks, I stopped when I found a loose one and gave it a tug. "And the adventure."

The brick came free in my hand, and I stuck my hand inside. Something was there. My fingers snagged the folded paper and I slid it out, carefully unfolding it in my lap.

The sheet was written in neat handwriting that turned to barely legible chicken scratch at the end. I began to read:

"When Ananias discovered his village and family were gone, he headed south toward Florida to St. Augustine, where he took a French wife."

I looked up at David in surprise. "There were French in Florida in the late 1500s?"

He nodded. "Virginia Dare may have been the first English child born in the Americas, but a Spanish child was born in this country at least twenty years earlier. If Ananias needed a wife to continue the Dare line, Florida would have been the logical place to look."

"But this says he took a French wife."

"There was a colony of French as well. Your Anglican history books tend to neglect such facts."

"And how do you know this?"

"They had interactions with the Native Americans."

"Oh."

He leaned over the paper and continued where I left off:

"Ananias had three children with his second wife, Marie, and three generations of Dares lived in Florida, passing the legend and the curse down to the next Keeper. The history, the symbols and words of protection, how to close the gate, how to send back the gods and spirits if the gate remained open, the feud between the brother gods, and many other things.

"In 1620, Ananias LeBlanc, fourth-generation ancestor of Ananias Dare, felt a pull north. It was an inexplicable feeling, but it caused him great discomfort to ignore it. He took his wife and two children to Jamestown, Virginia. The Curse Keepers resided in Virginia until 1650, when John Williams took his pregnant wife with a group of Virginians to colonize Albemarle Sound in North Carolina. The Curse Keepers and their descendants have resided in North Carolina since, never being able to travel more than fifty to two hundred miles from Roanoke Island."

"Yes!" I squealed. "I always thought it was agoraphobia. Only mine was worse, depending on the day. I could usually go fifty miles before feeling anxious, but I always felt uneasy about leaving the island."

David looked up. "Do you still have it? You came to Chapel Hill."

"No, I didn't have it at all that day." I shifted my weight. "And I didn't have it when Collin and I went to Morehead City. He was the one who told me that the feeling was insurance for the curse, to make sure we never got too far away from this place."

"Maybe the feeling is like a barometer. You were meant to meet me. You and Collin were meant to get the bowl."

"But who gets to decide?"

"Who or whatever is controlling your fate. Ahone?"

I scowled. I didn't like the idea of any deity controlling my fate.

"You and Collin got his bowl for the ceremony. Where are the relics now?"

I paused. "Collin must have taken them. I wasn't thinking straight at the time." Could they have been in the locked glove compartment of his truck? Along with the map?

I kept reading:

"*The Keeper's duty passes to the oldest child, who assumes the responsibilities of Curse Keeper upon their eighteenth birthday. In the event that the oldest child cannot assume the duties, the role passes to the next child in line.*

"*The stories must be told and preserved. In the event that the line dies off, the gate will open and the spirits will escape.*"

My chest tightened. "No."

David looked up, his eyes wide.

"I can't do that, David. I can't have a child and force this upon them. What kind of parent would do that?"

"Your father had you and he wasn't horrible. He was a loving father whom you adored."

"He also didn't have me after the gate had been opened. He didn't have me knowing I'd have to face all these monsters."

"Let's think positive." He leaned forward. "We'll send all the demons back and figure out a way to make sure they stay locked up."

I nodded, but I didn't believe it. Ahone's messenger had told me that the curse was flawed from the beginning. If the spirits weren't mutilating animals and people, I might have been inclined to side with Collin about letting things even out. But I knew they'd only just begun their reign of terror. They wouldn't settle down until a lot more innocent animals and people were killed. "I found out there are good spirits too. But I didn't see them escape when the gate opened."

"There were far more kind and gentle spirits in the Native American belief system than evil ones. So it makes sense that both types still exist. The question is: Where are the good ones?"

"We get more and more questions, but we're not getting any closer to answers."

"Ellie, you have to be patient. The curse was over four hundred years old. It stands to reason that you can't learn everything about it in a few weeks."

"I learned all about creation in a matter of minutes. I didn't have to wait days and weeks for that."

And then it hit me. Why hadn't I thought of it before?

I got to my feet. "I have to go."

David grabbed my hand and pulled me back. "Wait. Where are you going?"

"I know how to find our answers, and I'm an idiot for not thinking of it sooner." I paused, worried about how David would react. "I have to go find Collin."

"Okay, why?"

"When I saw creation, so many of my questions were answered. But I was touching marks with Collin. He'd purposefully taken me out into the ocean to see what would happen. I need to do it again."

Fear flickered across David's face. I could tell he was trying to come up with a response. "That sounds like a good idea," he finally said. "I'll come with you."

I shook my head, feeling terrible for doing this to him. "I have to do this alone."

He studied my face, searching for reassurance.

"David. Trust me."

Finally, he swallowed and nodded. "Okay."

I grabbed his shirt in my fist and pulled him to my chest. I kissed him deeply, showing him how much I wanted *him*, not Collin.

His hand buried in my hair and he deepened the kiss, tilting my head back. His free hand rested on my neck and I clung to him, wanting as much of him as I could get before I went to see Collin. I needed a memory I could draw upon since I knew I'd be walking into certain temptation. I wasn't stupid enough to think my attraction to Collin would be gone when I saw him. But these memories of David would make me strong enough to resist it.

"Ellie," he said, lifting his head. "I don't want to lose you."

My heart skipped a beat. "I'm coming back to you. I promise."

His mouth lifted into a smile "I want to come to make sure you're safe, but I have no doubt he'll protect you." I could tell that it killed him to admit it.

"Maybe *I'll* protect *him*."

Amusement filled his eyes. "That wouldn't surprise me."

"I'll see him and come straight back."

His arms tightened around me. "I want you to call me when you find him. And then I want you to call me as soon as you get back to your car." He lifted my chin, his eyes boring into mine. "Promise me."

"I promise." Then I added, "If I'm not back in time, make sure to leave for the apartment before it gets dark."

"I will. Just go."

I stood on tiptoes and kissed him. "Thank you."

"Do you know where to find him?"

Unfortunately, I was pretty sure I did.

✦ CHAPTER TWENTY-FIVE ✦

The closer I got to Wanchese, the more my stomach clinched. The thought of going back to the first place Mishiginebig had protected me was bad enough. But the thought of facing Collin made me nauseous. I called David as soon as I got there.

Collin's truck was parked in the spot where it had been last time. He could be out on his boat, or he could be hiding from Tom. Either way, I probably should have called him to make sure he was around, but I thought the element of surprise could work to my advantage.

I parked next to Collin's truck and walked to the dock, the memories of my last visit clinging to my skin, making me feel dirty. I stiffened my back. I hadn't done anything wrong. That bastard who'd attacked me had gotten exactly what he deserved.

Maybe if I kept telling myself that, I'd stop feeling guilty.

The slap of my flip-flops was the only sound as I walked down the concrete sidewalk next to the boats. I figured that since Collin's truck was here, his boat would be out, but it couldn't hurt to check. So when I saw *Lucky Star* on the back of the second boat—the one the guy had tried to drag me onto—I stopped and reconsidered my plan.

Why did my life suddenly feel like a tapestry woven by fate? Should I just give in to whatever destiny had in store?

Collin popped up, a fishing net in his hand.

I sucked in a deep breath and walked to the edge of his boat. "So you really are a fisherman."

He stood, the net still hanging from his hand as he stared at me in shock.

I nodded toward the net. "There was lots of fishing talk when we were together, but I never saw any fishing action."

The hint of a smile lifted his lips. "Maybe you kept me so busy with other action that I didn't have any time to fish."

My face burned. I'd set myself up for that one.

His gaze landed on my bandaged arm before he returned to his task. "What are you doing here, Ellie?"

"Did Tom find you?"

"If you're asking if *Officer Helmsworth* came to see me, then the answer is yes."

"You talked to him?"

He looked up with his cocky grin in full force. "Sure. Why not? He would have been more anxious to find me if I'd tried to evade him. I didn't have anything to hide."

"He didn't think it was a coincidence that the guy was on your boat?"

Collin's smile fell. "What guy was on my boat?"

My stupid mouth. I didn't answer.

"The guy who was killed?" He waited a second.

"What does it matter, Collin. It's done." I paused. "Marino's guy came to see me today."

The color left his face. "Where?"

"I came home and found him waiting in my living room. He found a pair of antique watches that belonged to my father and presumed it was part of the Ricardo Estate."

His eyes sunk closed. "Fuck."

"He was going to either shoot me or take me to Marino. I had to lie. I told him you gave me the watches to appraise. I'm sorry." My voice cracked with my guilt.

"You did the right thing. That was quick thinking." Pride filled his eyes. "But then again, you're a natural."

"Do you know where the Ricardo Estate is?"

His face hardened. "Ellie."

My temper flared. He still wasn't going to tell me. "They know who I am, Collin! They think they have proof I'm involved. I have a right to know!"

"I don't have to tell you shit, just like you don't have to listen to my warning that your professor is going to get you killed." He grunted and threw the net into a pile. "You could have told me this in a phone call. Why are you really here?"

"I need you to take me out onto the ocean."

He put his hands on his hips. "Why don't you have your boyfriend take you?"

"Because I need *you*."

He stared at me for several seconds. "No."

"*No?* What do you mean *no?*"

"I mean no. I'm not your errand boy, Ellie. The last time I offered to help you, you blew me off."

"You wanted to hide me on your boat!"

"I wanted to protect you." His voice broke, and he turned to look out at the sound.

I took a deep breath. "I wouldn't be here if it wasn't important."

He started working on his net again. "There are lots of charter boat businesses around here. Go hire one of them."

My anger exploded, and I opened my purse, digging out my wallet. "You want money, Collin?" I grabbed what little cash I had and held it out to him. "Here." I shook my hand. "Here's some god-damned money."

His face softened, defeat in his eyes. "I don't want your money, Ellie."

"Collin, please."

He watched me again, and then he took a step to the edge of his boat and reached his left hand out to me. I took it and stepped over the edge. He didn't move backward, so my stomach bumped into his.

I flinched in pain, but Collin didn't seem to notice.

"Why do you want to go out onto the ocean?"

"I need some answers, and I'm hoping it will help to be in the ocean. Like when we went to the beach and pressed our marks together."

"You *want* to press our marks together?"

"Yes."

He watched me for several seconds. "Okay. But we do this my way."

I sucked in a breath. "What does that mean?"

"It means we do it *my* way."

"I'm not having sex with you."

A sneer crossed his face. "Because you're having sex with him."

I couldn't look into his eyes. "Don't do this, Collin."

He stiffened. "My way or not at all."

Did I have a choice? "You'd really force me to have sex with you?"

"I can assure you, I wouldn't have to force you, Ellie." His cockiness was back. "How badly do you want me to help you?"

That's what it boiled down to: What was my life worth? Could I live with myself if I had sex with Collin when I wasn't even sure I'd get my answers? Still, I couldn't sit back and wait to be killed, or worse, play mother to Okeus's monster babies. Collin held all the cards. "Do you really want me to hate you even more?"

His eyes narrowed. "You realize that's not helping your case, don't you?"

"Fine."

He stepped to the side and said in a snotty voice, "Well, welcome aboard the *Lucky Star*."

The deck of the boat was a mess full of rope and nets. I looked around for a place to sit.

"It's a fishing boat, Ellie. Not a yacht."

"Whatever. As long as this rust bucket can get us out there, that's all that matters."

"Well, that's the spirit," Collin muttered. "You can sit inside or outside. Which do you prefer?"

"Outside."

"Have a seat right here." He pointed to a raised metal box just outside the wheelhouse. "I'll start up the engine and we'll be off."

I nodded, still pissed.

"Any particular place you want to go?"

"Wherever you think this will work."

The engine started and Collin untied the boat from the dock before heading out onto the sound.

I underestimated the amount of time it was going to take for us to get to the ocean. The sun was already dipping into the horizon by the time Collin found a place to stop. He shut off the engine and came out of the cabin, looking toward shore. He moved to the end of the boat and unfolded a metal contraption over the side.

My stomach twisted with nerves. What if we didn't get back to shore before dark? But we were already here, and I wasn't turning back now. Besides, Collin and I could protect each other if anything happened.

Right now I needed to focus on why we were here. "Do I need to get completely in the water?"

"You can sit on the bottom of this ladder and put your feet in." His tone was gentler than I expected. "Your legs were all that were immersed the first time we did it."

"Okay." I nodded and looked over at the seat at the bottom of the ladder. I could manage that.

I maneuvered over the edge and managed to sit on the metal slats, dangling my lower legs in the water. I felt the rush of power as the waves rocked the boat, splashing onto my lap and chest. I was going to be soaking wet when I finished this thing. Collin reached out to me and I lifted my right hand, preparing my body for the surge.

I pulled my hand back slightly. "Don't let Mishiginebig eat me." Now that I'd pissed Okeus off, there was no guarantee that I was still protected.

He grimaced. "I'm more worried about you falling off and drowning. Last time we tried this, you were completely oblivious to what was going on around you." His gaze flicked to the shore, then back to me. "Besides, I doubt he'd come out this far. It's too deep. I'm more worried about other things."

My eyes widened. "How do you know it's too deep?" I ignored the implication that there might be other waterborne demons out there.

He shrugged. "He likes shallow water."

My voice rose. "And you didn't think I needed to know *this*?"

Exasperation covered his face. "Ellie, if you'd given me the fucking time of day, I might have told you."

"You mean if we were still fucking."

He shook his head in disgust. "You wanted to come out here, so I brought you. I'm helping you, Ellie. Quit giving me shit. I don't have to do this."

He was right. What was I doing? "Okay, let's do this."

Collin started to lean over again, then stopped and stood.

Oh, God. I'd pushed him too far.

He stripped his T-shirt over his head and tossed it down, then unfastened his jeans, dropping them to his feet.

"What the hell are you doing?" I hissed.

Collin stepped off the edge of the boat and into the water. He disappeared with a splash, and his head popped up in front of me a few seconds later. "I'm making sure you don't drown, although I'm not sure why. You are the biggest pain in the ass I've ever known." He spread my legs apart and grabbed the end of the metal ladder, pulling himself up so that he was almost level with my face.

I gaped, surprised by his sudden intrusion into my personal space.

He saw my shock and gave me his shit-eating grin. "I said we'd do this my way."

But I knew it had been a spur of the moment decision. I swallowed, my body already reacting to his nearness. "Okay."

His smile fell, and his gaze landed on my lips. "Loop your arms through the ladder."

I struggled to breathe. "What?"

He released his hold, dropping into the water again, and reached up and threaded my right arm and then the left around the ladder so that the crook of my elbows caught on the support. His grabbed the ladder and pulled himself up again, weaving his arms above mine. "Lift both your hands and hold on with your left."

I did as he asked and looked into his face, expecting to see his usual arrogance there. Instead, I saw desperation and longing.

He reached up and grabbed the bar with his left hand before reaching his right across his chest to mine.

"Don't let us drown," I whispered.

"I'm already drowning, Ellie."

His mouth lowered to mine, and my breath caught in my chest as fire shot through my body. I started to turn my head, but then his hand grabbed mine, and my senses were jolted by the Manitou. The life force of millions and millions of beings poured through me at once. The sensations flooded every part of my being. I leaned my head back and gasped, staring up into the now darkening sky. A star shone brightly overhead.

Collin's feelings washed through me in thick waves of desire and sadness, guilt and stubbornness. His pulse quickened. He wanted me more than he'd ever wanted anything in his life, but something was holding him back. Something that frightened him.

His breath became more rapid and the star overhead began to pulse, expanding and contracting over and over again until it swallowed me whole.

I found myself standing in a field that was flooded with bright white light. It should have been blinding but wasn't. The colors of the grass and flowers, the stream that gurgled nearby, the mountains in the distance, and the blue sky full of puffy clouds were vibrant, but they seemed washed out at the same time.

"Ellie?"

I spun around and gasped. Daddy was standing in front of me. I stumbled backward, splashing into the stream. "No. You're not Daddy."

His face softened, a warm smile lighting up his face. "Yes, Elliphant, it's me."

Tears stung my eyes, and my breath came in pants in my attempt to keep control. "No." I shook my head. "Okeus tricked me before."

"Ellie, it's me." He took my hand and smiled. His was warm and soft. "I can't come back to you in the earthly world, but Ahone has allowed me to see you."

I threw my arms around his neck and he held me tight. His familiar smell surrounded me. It was the right one this time.

"Ellie, I'm so proud of you. And so is your mother."

I pulled back to look into his loving face. "Momma?"

"She's with me. We're together."

My heart shattered, and my voice broke. "She's in Popogusso too?"

He shook his head, tenderness washing over his face. "No, baby. We're not in Popogusso. We're in heaven."

"But how?" My knees felt weak, but he grabbed my arms and steadied me.

"I sacrificed myself to Ahone, not Okeus."

I started to cry. "I thought you . . ."

"I know. I wanted you to know that I'm fine. You have so much to worry about, and I don't want you to worry about me anymore."

My chin trembled. "Daddy, I'm so scared. I can't do this."

He reached up a hand and gently stroked my hair. "You can, baby. You can and will do this and so much more."

"I'm so sorry. I should have listened to you."

He shook his head, grabbing my face with both hands, ferocity burning in his eyes. "Everything is as it should be. You're on a journey. Watching you face these challenges is the hardest thing I've ever done, but I have faith in you, Ellie. You will save the world."

I shook my head. "How can *I* do anything? Collin has all the answers, and he won't share them with me."

"Collin has his path to follow and you have yours. Eventually, they will merge, but your journeys are separate for now."

"I can't do this alone."

His smile was full of tenderness. "But you're not alone."

Was he referring to David? "The mark on my back is gone, and I'm unprotected. Both Ahone and Okeus have claimed me. And

Okeus says I'm bound to Collin in all things, but Collin is destined to go to Popogusso. I don't know what to do."

"There's always more than one answer. I taught you that."

I shook my head. "I know. But even if I decide to use Ahone's mark, I don't know what it is."

"Yes, you do." He smiled and pointed up. It had grown dusky, and a star burned in the sky, growing brighter and larger until it assumed the shape of the four-pointed star.

"You must do it soon, Ellie. It's almost too late." His face tightened. "But the mark can only protect your Manitou. It doesn't protect you from Okeus's plan."

Tears clogged my throat. "You know what he wants."

"I wish I could protect you. I'm sorry."

"Okeus tried to trick me into agreeing to cooperate. He said you should have been home the night Momma was killed. Was he lying to confuse me?"

Pain filled his eyes. "There's so much I regret."

"Was she killed because of the Ricardo Estate?"

The corners of his mouth lifted slightly. "There is much for you to learn. But the watches are important."

"The pocket watches?"

"They hold a key."

"What is it?"

"Finding the key is part of your journey."

I sucked in a breath, becoming frustrated. "Ukinim is coming to kill me and Collin isn't helping. David thinks I'm a conjurer and can banish spirits to hell on my own right. Is he correct?"

"You have more resources at your disposal, but finding them is part of your path. Remember that it's not a weakness to use them. You don't have to do this alone."

My eyes flooded with tears. "I miss you."

"I miss you, Elliphant." His eyes darkened. "You must find Ukinim and Ilena tomorrow night and send them back."

"But I still don't know how to do it on my own."

"You will find the way."

"I need more answers, Daddy. I came to you for answers."

"Remember the star."

I looked up into the star, watching it expand and contract until it swallowed me again. I felt myself being jerked backward, and then I was bobbing in the ocean. Collin had an arm around my back and was holding onto the ladder with his free hand.

He searched my face. "I'm sorry. I tried to keep contact with you for as long as I could. But you fell off and—"

"It's okay. I got what I needed."

"That's good." He continued to watch me and then nodded toward the ladder. "Then I guess we can climb out."

I grabbed the rungs and pulled myself up, Collin following behind me. I stood on the deck, lifting my T-shirt and trying to wring all the water out of it.

He looked down at my stomach, his mouth hanging open. "*What is that?*"

The gauze had fallen off my arm in the water and the gashes were healed, but the wound on my stomach was a well-defined scar. I pulled my shirt back down.

His eyes widened in anger. "Ellie, what the hell is *that*?"

I took a step backward. "It's none of your business."

His face reddened. "You talk about me keeping secrets, but you keep a shitload of them yourself."

I put my hands on my hips. "What am I keeping secrets about?"

He flung his hand toward my stomach. "That, for starters."

Collin didn't deserve to know anything about my life, but he was right—this concerned him too. "You want to know what this

346

is?" I grabbed the bottom of my shirt and tugged it over my head, the wet cotton sticking to my skin. I threw it down and stood in front of him in my denim shorts and black bra. "Here it is, Collin. You're the guy with all the answers. Why don't you tell me what it is?"

He stared at my stomach, and his eyes were glazed with horror when his gaze rose to my face. "Okeus."

"Yeah."

"When? How?"

"Last night. He came to me in my dreams."

"How the hell did he come to you in your dreams?" he shouted, the veins in his neck bulging. "I put that goddamned mark on your door to protect you."

"*What?* I don't understand."

"You told me that they were coming to you in your dreams, so I put the diamond symbol with the X on your door. The diamond represents your dreams." He ran his hand over his head and looked toward the shore. "*Goddamn it!* I redid it last night to make sure it worked."

My stomach fell to my feet. "So it wasn't the dream catcher?"

His face wrinkled in confusion. "What dream catcher?"

I shook my head. "I wasn't home last night."

"You were with *him*." A sneer covered his face. "Your professor who doesn't know shit and is going to get you killed. How can you not see that?"

"At least he tells me the truth, Collin. Something you are completely incapable of." I took a deep breath. "Besides, you don't know I'm sleeping with him."

"Look who's incapable of telling the truth now." His face turned ugly. "Our connection works both ways, Ellie. I know you slept with him. I know that you have feelings for him. Hell, I could smell him on you the minute you got on the damned boat."

Shame and indignation swept through me. "Who the hell are you to talk? You've probably slept with half a dozen women since me."

"I haven't slept with anyone since you." His voice broke. "How could I even consider it after what we shared?"

I stumbled backward and sat on the metal box. How was that possible? Oh, God. What a mess.

He watched the water for several seconds. "What happened in your dream?"

"Okeus said he'd give me Daddy back if I gave him what he wanted."

"And what does he want?"

"Me to choose him."

"What else?"

I looked up at him.

He met my gaze. "To give you something that big, I know he must have wanted something in return."

I swallowed. "He wants me to have his baby."

"He wants you to do *what*?"

"My pure soul, plus my Curse Keeper power . . . he thinks he can finally make a real human baby."

"*What the fuck, Ellie!*" He looked devastated.

I didn't answer. There was nothing to say.

"And if you don't?"

"He said it wasn't a choice."

The water began to rumble off the side of the boat, bubbling about ten feet out.

I looked over the edge. "I thought you said we were out too deep for Mishiginebig to bother us."

"We are." Collin moved next to me. "This has to be something else."

"What is it?"

"I don't know."

"What if it's Okeus? I don't have a mark on my back."

He turned to me, horror on his face. "You haven't found Ahone's?"

"Not until a few minutes ago."

"*Shit.*" The water bubbled higher. "There's no time to mark you."

"Collin." I grabbed his arm. "We can fight this thing together. We can send it back to hell."

He shook his head, watching the water. "We don't even know if it's after you, Ellie. It could be a good spirit. They're getting stronger too."

My eyes widened. "So they really are out there?"

"I told you they were weeks ago. It's just taking them longer because they don't take other creatures' Manitou."

"How come you know this and I don't?"

He gave me a smirk. "I can't divulge *all* of my secrets."

The water began to shoot into the air, churning with an angry current.

A friendly spirit might even be able to give me information. "Do you think it's one of the friendly ones?"

Collin scowled. "No."

∻ Chapter Twenty-Six ∻

A large mountain lion head shot out of the water and then dove back into it, revealing a furry mountain lion body with jagged plates on its back, like a stegosaurus, and a long, lizard-like tail.

Panic gripped my chest as I watched it disappear into the water. "What the hell is that?"

Collin ran to the other side of the boat. "A water panther."

That didn't sound good.

He ran into the cabin and started the engine. "We have to get out of here."

I followed him into the cabin. "Why? We can send it back to hell."

"I can't, Ellie!" The engine roared to life and the boat took off toward the shore.

I fell backward into the wall. "*Why not?*" And then I knew. Okeus.

He grabbed my arm and dragged me over to the wheel. "We're heading north. Just keep it straight."

I grabbed the wheel, looking back at him. "What are you going to do?"

"Take care of this."

"Are you sure Okeus will *allow* it?" My tone was snotty. I knew I should be grateful that he was trying to save me, but I was pissed. Why wouldn't he take care of it permanently?

He ignored me and stormed out the back.

I hoped we had left the water panther behind us, but a quick glance back assured me it was following us. It seemed insane to think we could outrun a demon.

Collin lifted his hand and a glow filled the air as I heard him shouting his words of protection. A vortex appeared and the water panther screamed.

I slowed the engine and then killed it. This was ridiculous. We could get rid of the demon together.

Collin shot me an angry look through the open door, but he'd have to stop reciting his words of protection if he wanted to stop me.

The boat slowed enough for me to release the wheel, and I moved next to him and shouted over the wind of the vortex he'd created. "Collin, listen to me!"

But Collin's eyes hardened and he finished the chant.

"*. . . everything in between. I compel you to leave my sight.*"

The water panther screamed as it was lifted into the air and disappeared into the closing vortex.

Collin turned toward me, livid. "Why can't you just fucking do what I tell you? *Just one goddamned time!*"

I shoved his shoulder, my temper raging. "That's what it all boils down to, doesn't it? You want me to be a stupid girl and do whatever you say without asking questions!"

"Ellie, you're being ridiculous!"

"Take me home, Collin."

"Now look who's doing the ordering!"

I hated that he was right. My temper vanished, leaving behind sorrow. "Why couldn't you just trust me, Collin?" My voice broke. "I wanted to be with you. Why couldn't you just tell me the truth?"

His face softened and he wrapped his arms around my back, pulling me to his chest. "It's not too late, Ellie. I can make it up to you."

I stepped back, and his eyes fell to my stomach. "You chose your side, and I have to choose mine. You say you care about me, but you refuse to stop those things from killing me."

"How can you say that? I always make sure your door has fresh marks!"

"If you want to protect me, then tell me what's out there, Collin! At least let me know what's after me so I can protect myself."

He didn't answer.

I suddenly realized the truth. "You think you'll never see me again if I have all the answers."

He looked away.

"Why couldn't you trust that what we had was enough?"

His chest heaved as he released a breath.

"You can't manipulate someone into being with you, Collin. You can't build a relationship on that."

"It's not like that, Ellie. I swear. *I love you.*"

I gasped.

He reached for my hand. "Ellie, I love you. Look, you're right . . . I've never given a shit about anyone but myself my entire life. Until you." He pulled me to his chest. "We can make this work. I promise. I'll tell you everything."

"What about Okeus, Collin? Are you going to let him impregnate me?"

Horror covered his face.

"Will you stop him?" When he didn't answer me, my shoulders started to shake with silent sobs. "You're so blind in your devotion to Okeus that you would sacrifice even me to him." I shook my head, tears streaming down my face. "How could I be with you?"

He took a breath, tears in his eyes.

"I wanted you. I'd never wanted anyone like I wanted you. And you're right." I leaned into his face, my anger turning to hate. "You did *ruin* me. Sex with David is nothing compared to what we had."

Pain covered his face.

"But I can't trust you. I'm scared *to death*, Collin. I needed you to be there for me. I needed to know we were partners in everything, that we shared everything. But you can't even trust yourself."

"Ellie."

I put my hands on his chest. "If this was just you and me, and we hadn't opened that gate, I would have waited for you to figure things out, Collin. I would have waited." My voice broke at the realization. "But it's not just you and me. And I can't stand back and wait for these things to settle down, because a lot of people are going to end up dead. Including me."

"Ellie, please. You don't understand."

I shook my head. "No. I *don't* understand, because I would never pick Okeus over you. *Never.*"

His eyes narrowed and I could see he was closing himself off from me again. Not that he'd ever been completely open to me to begin with.

"I can trust David. I know that he's there for me despite all of this. And not because he's stuck with me because of some curse. He's with me because of *me*." I turned my back to him. "I want to go home. To David."

He stood behind me for several seconds and then turned around and started the boat.

I had myself under control by the time Collin pulled up to the dock in Wanchese. I was already climbing out of the boat when he emerged from the cabin.

"Ellie."

I stopped on the sidewalk, waiting. I needed to ask him a few more questions, but the more distance between us, the better. "Tell me about the Ricardo Estate. How are you tied to it?"

He shook his head, a determined look in his eyes. "Like I said: the less you know, the better."

"Marino thinks you're involved with me because of my parents' expertise in the field. Is that true?"

His face scrunched as he shook his head. "You know why I found you."

"Did my parents' professions make a difference to you?"

"I swear to you, Ellie. I never once took it into consideration."

"Where's my pewter cup?"

His body tensed. "In my truck."

"Locked in your glove compartment? With your bowl and the map?"

He didn't answer.

"I want my cup and the map."

His mouth tipped into an ugly grin. "Possession is nine-tenths of the law."

"And you declared that rule to be bullshit. *I want them now.*"

"No."

"I *need the map.*"

"You're going after Ukinim, aren't you?"

"He made it pretty clear last night that it was him or me. What would you do in my shoes? I need every resource at my disposal."

He swung his head away. "*Goddamn it.*"

"You *still* won't give it to me?"

"*No.*"

My temper rose and I considered finding a rock or something heavy to beat in his dashboard, but he'd stop me before I ever got the stupid thing open. I'd have to figure out another way.

As soon as I got in my car and headed back to Manteo, I picked up my phone and saw that I had five missed calls from David. Given that it was ten o'clock, I wasn't surprised.

He answered on the first ring. "Ellie, thank God. I've been worried half to death."

"I'm fine," I said, forcing my anger out of my voice. "It just took longer than expected."

"Did you find what you were looking for?" I knew what else he was asking.

"I did. I have a lot to tell you. I can't wait to see you."

I heard his sigh of relief. "I have something to tell you too. After I got back to the flat, I remembered something I read in one of the books I've got here. I think I've figured out how you can defeat Ukinim."

"How?"

"There's a chant that you can supposedly use. I think it's similar to the original curse."

Hope bloomed in my chest. "And do you know it?"

"Yes."

I released my held breath. "Oh, thank God. We have to do it tomorrow night."

"Why tomorrow?"

"I saw Daddy in my vision, and he told me that I have to defeat Ukinim and Ilena tomorrow night. He says I can do it on my own."

"That's the second best news I've heard all day."

"And what's the first?"

"That you're coming home to me."

I expected to be attacked by some demon or god before I got home, but I pulled into the parking lot without incident and ran up the stairs, stopping outside the door to stare at the symbol in the middle of the door.

But as I stared at it, the door flung open and David appeared in the doorway. I wondered what he thought. I was just in my shorts and bra, as my shirt had disappeared when we were fleeing from the water panther. But he gathered me in his arms, holding me tight.

"I was so scared, Ellie."

"I know. I'm sorry."

He dragged me across the threshold and closed the door, pushing me against it and kissing me thoroughly.

I laughed against his lips. "I've been gone a few hours, not days."

He lifted his head. "I swear to you, I'm not the clingy type, but I'm also not used to the woman I care about being in constant danger."

My smile fell. "I'm sorry."

He shook his head. "I knew what I was getting into when I agreed to this arrangement."

"But it's a different arrangement now. You couldn't anticipate that."

He didn't answer. "Do you want to go first or me?"

"You," I said. "But I need a cup of tea." I nudged his arm. "Rumor has it that Englishmen are experts at making tea."

"Is that so? Well, you might be right. I'm brilliant at making tea even with tea bags. Do you have any in the apartment?"

I laughed. "Yeah. In the kitchen." I went into my room and grabbed a T-shirt, pulling it over my head.

David had found the tea bags and was looking for the kettle. His gaze lingered on me, questions in his eyes.

"You're probably wondering where my shirt went."

He looked into my eyes. "I trust you, Ellie."

"I know, but I want to tell you anyway."

"Okay."

"After I got out of the ocean—after my vision—I was wringing the water out of my T-shirt when Collin saw Okeus's artwork." I sighed. "I'll admit that I was pissed that he was still defending Okeus, so I tore my shirt off to show him what Okeus has done to me."

His voice softened. "I trust you, Ellie," he repeated.

I threw my arms around his neck, clinging to him. "Thank you."

His mouth found mine as his hands held me tight. He lifted me up so that I was sitting on the kitchen counter and slid his hands under my shirt and up my back.

I wrapped my legs around his waist and pulled his shirt over his head.

"You probably think I'm some sex-crazed Brit who can only think about shagging."

I gave him a saucy look. "Lucky for me I want a sex-crazed Brit who only thinks of shagging."

He picked me up off the counter with my legs still around his waist and carried me to my bed.

"Hey," I said as he unfastened my shorts and pulled them off. "Where's my tea?"

David shed his jeans and straddled my waist, pinning my arms over my head and grinning. "You'll get it when I'm done with you."

My skin flushed and my hips instinctively rose. "I like the sound of that."

His mouth lowered to my breast and I arched up to him while he still had my arms.

"Ellie, how can I be so attached to you after so little time?" he murmured, trailing kisses over to my other breast.

"I don't know," I panted. "But I don't know what I'd do without you."

He slid up, his mouth hovering over mine. "Then let's not find out."

I lifted my head to kiss him. He released my arms and rolled me over to my side, facing him as his mouth lowered to my breast again. My leg straddled his waist and his erection pressed against my thigh.

He had me out of breath and begging him to enter me within minutes. When he started to roll away to get a condom, I held him in place. "I have an IUD and I'm careful. I don't want to use a condom if you don't."

He brushed a hair off my cheek. "You didn't ask about my sexual history."

I stared into his eyes. "I trust you. If it was unsafe for me, you wouldn't do it."

He shook his head in wonder. "How can you trust me so completely, Ellie? Not just in this, but in *everything*. I feel like you have offered yourself to me completely without even considering that I might abuse the privilege."

"Because I know you wouldn't. It's why I'm with you."

He picked up my right hand and placed a gentle kiss in my palm, in the center of the circle, and then looked up at me. "I don't know what I could have possibly done to earn such blind trust."

"It's not blind." My eyes penetrated his. "I swear to you, you are the one person on this earth I want to be with."

David's mouth lowered to mine as he rolled me onto my back. His hand lifted my hips as he entered me and I tilted up so he'd slide deeper. He lifted his head and stared into my eyes as he began to move.

I watched him through blurry eyes, overcome with emotion. How had I been so lucky to find such a gentle and trustworthy man?

His hand stroked my cheek, worry in his eyes. "Am I hurting you?"

"No." I shook my head, my voice tight. "I'm just so grateful that you're mine."

"Oh, Ellie," he murmured. His pace quickened, and he buried his face in the nape of my neck. I clung to him, wanting him to go even deeper.

When I came, it wasn't the earth-shattering experience Collin used to give me. Instead, it was something I needed more.

I felt like I'd come home.

CHAPTER TWENTY-SEVEN

We lay in bed for an hour, wrapped in each other's arms. David lazily stroked my body, and I felt a peace and contentment I'd never known.

I told him about Collin taking me out to the ocean and my vision, but I left out some of the details. I worried that I was being deceitful, but I didn't want to hurt him. He knew some parts were left out, but he didn't ask any questions. When I mentioned there was more, he gently kissed me and smiled softly. "I trust you," he said.

"But now that I know Ahone's mark, I can get my tattoo."

"And how do you feel about that? I know you've been resistant."

"I think it offers less protection than I originally expected. The demons will still be able to kill me; they just won't be able to steal my Manitou."

"Well, at least that's something, love."

"And Okeus can still try to be my baby daddy."

David stiffened. "I'll figure out a way to protect you."

"Short of a hysterectomy, I'm not sure there is one."

"No need to get that drastic just yet." He rolled me over and kissed me.

I sobered. "I found out about the mark on the door. It stands for dreams. I had told Collin that I was having nightmares, and

360

he put it on the door. It was the same night you gave me the dream catcher."

He was quiet for several seconds. "So, Collin, huh?"

I tilted his face down to mine. "I don't need Collin to put marks on my door. I can do that myself."

He nodded.

"Hey." My eyebrows rose. "You said the salt was missing from the window in my old room. Maybe that's why the dream catcher didn't work."

"The symbol is probably the reason why you're not having dreams, Ellie."

"Well, I'm sleeping with both. I'm not taking any chances. We'll find answers on our own. Collin keeps things from me as a way of controlling me. I'm done with it."

"Okay." His fingers traced Okeus's scar on my stomach. "Tomorrow we need to go to that tattoo place your friend recommended to get you your mark. I don't want you to face Ukinim without it."

"But I hear those things hurt. Do I really want to get it before I go head-to-head with a demon?"

"Ellie, you're running around with Okeus's mark carved into your skin like it's nothing. You can handle a tattoo."

"How would you know? I don't see any ink on your skin."

"Humor me." He kissed my palm. "If your father said you need the watches, we need to buy back the watch you sold to the pawnshop."

"I sold it. I didn't pawn it. I don't know if it's even there anymore."

"We'll just hope for the best."

As embarrassing as it was, I had to tell David the truth. "Even if Oscar still has it, I don't have enough money to buy it back."

He shifted so he was lying on his side. "Ellie, we're in this together. *I'll* buy it back."

I cringed, my humiliation deepening. "That's not what I'm asking."

"I know. But I'm part of this too now, and if we need the watch, it's in my own best interest to get it back."

I buried my head into the nape of his neck. "I don't know what to say."

"Don't say anything. Trust me, Ellie. It will help me feel an ownership in this endeavor."

"Okay."

He lifted my chin and gave me a slow, lingering kiss, then pulled back grinning. "Now that wasn't so hard, was it?"

I snorted.

David smoothed my hair back from my face. "We have to figure out how to get more information about the Ricardo Estate. Inquiries with my own sources have turned up nothing."

"Collin is out, so maybe I should give Marino's guy something tomorrow night, even if it's a false lead. If I string him along, he might give me some helpful information."

His eyes widened. "Do you hear what you're suggesting? Stringing along a thug to use him? I think you'd be better served turning him over to Officer Helmsworth."

"Other than Collin, Marino's our best lead on the collection."

"You do know how wrong that is on *so* many levels?"

"It's all we have at the moment. Until I figure out a way to break into Collin's truck."

"Let's not resort to theft just yet."

"We've moved way past theft, and you know it." I yawned, exhaustion overwhelming me.

"Ellie Lancaster, Curse Keeper and petty thief."

I closed my eyes and murmured. "That's me, never a dull moment."

Before I knew it, I started to doze off.

Several hours later, David woke me with a kiss. "How are your dreams?"

I cracked my eyes, still groggy. "Dreamless."

"Good." He kissed me again. "Go back to sleep, and I'll wake you in a few more hours."

The next morning we got up early and headed to the inn. David called the tattoo shop and made an appointment for early afternoon. When we showed up several minutes early, my nerves were a jumbled mess. "It seems like committing my soul to a deity should come with a bit more pomp and circumstance."

"You want a ceremony?" David teased. "I can give you one."

I shook my head with a grin. "Just hold my hand. I really have no idea what will happen when this thing is on my back. When Collin did it with henna, I didn't feel anything until he put his mark on it. But this is real. I'm worried I'll do something stupid when the needle hits."

He bent down to kiss me. "I'll be with you the entire time."

"Thanks."

True to his word, David held my hand the entire time, and I struggled not to compare the two experiences—the solemnness and seductiveness of the ceremony with Collin and the sterility of the tattoo application. I only hoped it would work.

We spent the rest of the afternoon and early evening at the inn, coming up with a plan to lure in Ukinim and Ilena and practicing the chant that David had found.

"Daddy said there were many resources I could use."

David didn't look so sure. "If I had the choice, we'd hold off and practice this on something less threatening." His mouth pressed into a tight line. "Are you positive your father said you had to do it tonight?"

"Yes, I told him I didn't know how to send them back, and he said I'd find a way." The pocket watch box sat on the kitchen counter, and I opened the lid. "He also said the pocket watches were important, but I'm not sure how." I picked up the one with the starry-sky background. "I can bring them, but I have no idea how I'd use them."

He took a deep breath. "I think I'll bring some holy water for backup."

My jaw dropped. "You're kidding, right?"

"No. I'm deadly serious." He stood. "I can't believe we're doing this. Maybe you should call Collin for backup."

I jumped to my feet. "I'm not calling Collin."

"Don't be stubborn, Ellie."

"You said I was the conjurer and that I could send them away on my own."

"I *do* think you're the conjurer." His breath came in short bursts. "I'm just frightened for you. I can honestly say I've never been more frightened in my life."

"Why? Because you think I can't do it?"

"No, because I've never risked losing something so precious to me."

I grabbed his hands and held them between my own. "Why would my own father tell me to do this if I wasn't going to be successful?"

"Does he know the future, Ellie? Can you be certain?"

I hesitated.

"No. You can't. You could die tonight."

My shoulders stiffened, and I dropped his hands. "You knew the danger coming into this, David. Do you want to back out now?"

"Is that what you want?" he asked. "You want me to leave? Like everyone else?"

"That's not fair!"

"It's perfectly fair, but guess what? I'm not leaving you, Ellie. I'm not going anywhere. You're stuck with me."

"Why?" I pleaded, trying to understand. "Why would you do this to yourself?"

"Because I love you."

I grabbed the edge of the counter. "What?"

His eyes widened. He was obviously as surprised by his announcement as I was. His face softened. "I love you."

"David."

He took a step toward me. "I don't expect you to say it back. I didn't mean to say it at all."

"I . . ." I tried to catch my breath. "How long have you known?"

"Longer than you would believe." He leaned down and kissed me. "It doesn't matter whether I said it or not. We need to focus on what needs to be done."

I shook my head. "Don't do that. Don't minimize your feelings."

"Ellie, I'm sorry. It slipped out. Now isn't the time to discuss it."

"No." I looked up at him in shock. "Now is the perfect time to discuss it."

"I know your soul is bound to Collin. I know I'll always be second to him." He took my hand. "I'm okay with that."

My heart ached. "How could you be okay with that?" I knew that I would never be.

"Because I told you: I know beyond a shadow of a doubt that *you* are my destiny."

I closed my eyes, feeling nauseated. I was so unworthy of his love and devotion.

"I'm thirty-one years old, Ellie, and I've never been in love before. Don't go and die on me tonight and leave me broken-hearted."

I wrapped my arms around his neck and kissed him. "Then I shall try my very best not to die tonight. Just for you."

He murmured against my lips with a grin. "Thank you." Then he released me and grabbed his car keys off the counter.

"Where are you going?"

"To get some holy water," he said as he walked out the door.

I stared at the empty room. I had time to kill, and I wanted to look for more of Daddy's notes and the ring, but I wasn't sure where to look next. David and I had searched the other guest rooms, turning up nothing. I knew I needed to relax and try to remember specific incidents of when Daddy and I had played the hiding game. But I was four or five years old at the time. I was surprised by how many of the memories from my early childhood I had lost. How ironic that Momma had made Daddy stop the game because I was too good at finding the quarters, and now all I could find was a single hidden note.

I went upstairs to Myra's room and was searching there when my phone rang. Claire was miffed. "I didn't think you were ever going to call me again," she pouted. "It's been *days*."

"I'm sorry. I've just been busy."

She heard the smile in my voice. "You totally hooked up with that hot British professor. Am I right?"

"Well . . ."

"*You did!* I was joking! Is he as hot naked as he looks in his clothes?"

"Claire!"

"Well? Is he?"

"Let's just say I'm fairly certain I have a date to your wedding next weekend."

"That doesn't tell me anything about how hot he is sans clothes. And my cousin will be extremely disappointed."

"He'll get over it." I paused. "Say, I hope you don't mind but I'm going to have a tattoo on my back in that halter dress you got me."

"You found Ahone's mark?"

"Yeah, finally."

"Where?"

"It's a long story, but I got the tattoo this afternoon."

"It had to hurt like a son of a bitch to get it on your shoulder blade."

"People say that about pretty much every body part." I shook my head. "And it didn't hurt too bad. David held my hand."

"Is it okay if I gag now?"

"Stop!" I laughed.

"I'm happy for you, Ellie. He seems like a really great guy. He's much better for you than Collin."

"Yeah." So why was I so sad for Collin? "Say, Claire. Something dangerous is going to happen tonight, so be sure to stay inside, okay? Do I need to come remark your door?"

"No, my door is fine. And why do I think you're about to take part in this dangerous thing?"

"Because you're smart *and* perceptive. Just stay inside."

"Be careful, Ellie. Do you know how hard it will be for my sister to fit into your dress if you get yourself killed?"

"Ha! I'd like to see that. But sorry, I'm not planning on getting myself killed." I heard noises downstairs. It sounded like the researchers had arrived. I needed to go down and make sure they got resettled. "I'll call you tomorrow, okay?"

I hung up and went downstairs, happy to see Myra setting her bag down by the back door.

"Did you have a good weekend?"

She looked up and smiled. "I did. How about you? Everything go okay?"

"Yeah, great." I smiled.

She studied my face and her eyes glittered. "You look happy."

"I am."

"David?"

I nodded, blushing.

"That's wonderful, Ellie. David's a wonderful man. Your father would have loved him."

"I think so too." But I could tell that she looked happy too. Her face had a soft glow to it, and she seemed more relaxed than I'd seen her in ages. "Steven's a good man too."

She blushed.

"And he and Daddy were friends, so we *know* he'd approve."

"How do you feel about it?"

"Honestly?" My eyebrows rose. "It's a bit weird. You're my *mom*. But I love you, and if anyone deserves love and happiness, it's you."

"Thank you, Ellie." She threw her arms around my neck and squeezed, then stepped back. "I heard David had applied to get a longer position at the colony site. It sounds like it's going to go through."

"Yeah, he's excited about it and I have to confess that I am too."

"That's great." She looked down.

"What's wrong?"

Her brow wrinkled and she forced a smile. "What are you talking about?"

"Myra, I know you. You're sad about something."

"Steven only has a week left here on site before he has to go back to Durham. His university won't let him stay longer." She swallowed, refusing to meet my gaze. "There's a position that's opened out of the blue, one I'm a good fit for. Steven had mentioned it, but I didn't think much of it until we had dinner with the department head on Saturday night. He's asked me to formally apply. It's nothing prestigious and although it's highly unusual, Steven thinks I have good chance at being hired if I want the position."

"*Oh.*"

"I'm not considering it. Steven just wants me closer to him, and he knew that at one point in my life I wanted to teach at a university." She paused and her face softened with affection. "But he doesn't know anything about the curse. He doesn't know the danger you're facing and how much I worry about you. I could never leave you, Ellie."

"I never knew you wanted to teach."

She waved her hand. "That was long ago."

Funny how I'd never given any thought to my parents' lives before me. But David was right. There were no coincidences. A position opening up out of the blue? The farther Myra was from all of this, hopefully, the safer she would be. I had known this time was coming, I just hadn't known goddamn fate had decided it for me. "I think you should apply."

Her mouth dropped open in surprise. "What?"

I smiled, refusing to cry. "If you want to do it, you should. I'll come visit you or you can visit me. We'll be fine."

"*Ellie.*"

"Promise me you'll really think it over, okay?" I hugged her again. "You deserve to be happy. *And safe.*"

She jerked back and searched my eyes.

I could tell there were a thousand questions she could ask me. I shook my head. "Don't ask, Myra. I love you, and nothing is going to change that. I have to get home." Before she could say anything, I grabbed the box of watches and went out the side door, my gaze landing on the rope swing hanging from the tree in the front yard.

"Swing me higher, Daddy!" I squealed. "Higher."

"If you go any higher you'll touch the stars, Elliphant."

"Can I really touch the stars, Daddy?"

He laughed. "A child of opposites. You want to touch the stars while you dig into the earth."

I used to bury things under that tree.

I ran underneath it, finding a patch that looked like it had been recently disturbed. Using my hands, I dug up the loose dirt until my fingertips hit a flat metal surface. Excited, I crammed my fingers around the edge of the object and pried a mint tin free. Something metal clanged inside. My fingers trembled as I opened the lid.

A dull gold ring on a chain lay inside.

I'd found the ring. Now what did I do with it?

Pulling out my phone, I texted David that I'd found something important, asking him to meet me at the apartment.

He arrived only minutes after I did, bursting through the door. "What is it?" he asked, breathless.

"I found Daddy's ring."

We examined it together, and had I not known that he'd told Myra it was important, I never would have suspected. The band resembled a wedding band, but it was engraved with symbols. Some we recognized, some we didn't.

"Symbols for nature," David murmured, turning it in his fingers yet again. "But no signs for gods—that we know of. There are about half a dozen I don't recognize, and most of them aren't on the plank from the colony site." He looked inside the band. "But the most noticeable thing about it is the fact that the entire inside of the ring is engraved with alternating signs for the land and the sea."

"The question is how do I use it?"

David's jaw hardened. "I wish I had more time to figure that out."

"So I show up to fight these monsters carting my assortment of good luck charms like I'm going to play bingo? Because without knowing how to use them, that's all they are at the moment."

His mouth quirked. "I'm sure that might be more amusing if I knew what it meant."

"Don't worry your pretty little head about it." I gave him a kiss. "We need to figure out where to find Ukinim."

David pulled a map of Roanoke Island from a bag he'd brought in and laid it out on my table. "You said Tom told you that the victims were found at the lighthouse, and a quarter mile west and north of the apartment. That leaves east."

I looked up. "That's Festival Park."

He nodded.

"Well, that's good, right? It will be closed and deserted after dark. Less of a chance that someone else will get hurt."

"But we'll have to break in."

I shot him a grin. "All we need is a pair of bolt cutters." When he looked surprised, I winked. "I learned a thing or two from Collin."

"Ah, the education of the American youth."

"So what time do you want to do this? We need to be here at eleven when Marino's guy shows up."

"Ellie, I cannot express my disapproval of that idea strongly enough."

"And your disapproval is noted, David, but he might know something important."

"So we wait for you to have tea with a thug before we go off to fight demonic badgers? Just another Sunday night in sleepy Manteo. What do you plan on telling him?"

"That Collin is taking me to see the collection this week."

"You know this is absolute madness, don't you?"

"Yeah."

David sighed. "Well, if anyone can pull it off, it's you." He took my hand and pride filled his eyes. "And you can send Ukinim and his mate back to hell. I believe in you, Ellie."

I nodded. I was glad someone did.

The wait was agonizing. We came up with a skimpy plan for dealing with Marino's guy and one that wasn't much better for fighting the badgers, but at ten minutes after eleven, I was beside myself, pacing the living room floor frantically.

"Marino's guy doesn't seem like the fashionably late type. Where is he?"

David leaned his back against the kitchen counter. "I don't know. Maybe they changed their mind about you."

Dread cramped my stomach. "No. Marino doesn't change his mind."

My cell phone rang in my purse. I dug it out and anxiety stole my breath when I saw the unfamiliar number. "Hello?"

"Ellie, this is Tom."

"Hey, Tom. What can I do for you?" My gaze searched out David, and he moved across the room toward me.

"Just thought I'd let you know that we picked up two known associates of Joseph Marino crossing the bridge to the island about thirty minutes ago."

I sat on the sofa, my body tense. "You're kidding."

"It was a routine traffic stop, but when we ran their licenses we turned up some outstanding warrants. They're currently in the Manteo jail."

Would Marino blame me for this one? "That's great, Tom, but why are you telling me?"

"I thought you'd like to know that this mess might be over now."

I closed my eyes, resisting the urge to sigh. Little did he know, it had only just begun.

◦ CHAPTER TWENTY-EIGHT ◦

It was much easier to get into the park than I expected.

When we mapped out a quarter mile east of my apartment, it put us squarely in the English camp of the re-created settlement of the first Roanoke colony of 1586 that had consisted entirely of men. The section featured a guardhouse, a blacksmith shop, a woodworking lathe, and an officer's tent.

"So cliché," I muttered for the fifth or twentieth time.

"Yes, Ellie, I know," David murmured softly, keeping his flashlight beam low so we wouldn't be seen by anyone across the cove in Manteo.

I clutched the strap of my backpack, which carried the watches. The ring was around my neck on the chain. I still didn't know how to use them, but I hadn't known the words of protection and how to use the symbol on my hand until I needed them. I hoped the same would prove true tonight. "How are we supposed to lure them here?"

"You're the bait, love."

"That's reassuring." But true. "If things get too intense, maybe we can lure them to the water and Big Nasty will come save me." I snorted. "It's a sad day when you hope a giant evil snake will save you."

"Indeed."

When I got nervous, I got chatty. Obviously, David got quiet.

When we reached the middle of the English camp, I looked around. "I haven't been here in years."

He spun around, taking in the buildings. "I've never been here."

I pointed to the south. "The sound is just on the other side of that brush."

"So that's our escape plan. Pathetic as it is." He spun in a circle. "There doesn't seem to be a high place around here like the lighthouse."

"Well, there is," I corrected. "The tents are worthless but the roof of the blacksmith's building is a good two stories tall. It just isn't easily accessible."

He disappeared into a tent and dragged out a round table into the middle of the clearing. "This isn't much, but it's better than nothing. Climb on top of it after you finish marking your symbols."

"What are you talking about? We aren't going to try to get up on the blacksmith's building?"

"Ellie, look at it. Even if you get up there, you're liable to break your neck if you fall off. Besides, you need to be more tempting to them. So lower it is." He walked over to the woods and grabbed a long stick, then handed it to me. "You work on the markings, and I'll get started with the candles."

I nodded and reached for the stick. Our hands brushed, and I looked into his eyes.

He smiled softly and leaned down to give me a gentle kiss. "You can do this, Ellie. Just stick to the plan, as arse about tits as it seems."

I started giggling, relieved that he'd broken some of the tension. "Arse about tits?"

He grinned. "I have so much to teach you."

I began marking symbols in a big circle in the dirt, using the same ones I used on the doors, while David set up candles around the perimeter and lit them. When I finished the outer circle, I started on an inner circle of markings while David pulled a container of salt from his bag and poured a thin line around the candles.

When I finished the second circle, I stood up.

"According to Cherokee and Algonquian tradition, we either need seven circles or four," he said. "Nothing in between. We have four now, counting the salt and the candles. How's your palm?"

I lifted my hand. "It's fine. It doesn't itch or burn."

"Then make another circle and I'll make two more salt circles."

"Okay." My job was easier since I had a smaller circle to mark and I finished just as he ran out of salt, halfway through his next to last line.

"Remember to stay up there on the table unless they break through. If they do, run for the water." He pulled another salt carton from his bag and began to pour. "When both of them are in view, start the chant. Read it. I know you probably have it memorized, but in the Cherokee belief system, the wording has to be exact to make a spell work. We're not sure what we're dealing with here, so it's safer to hedge our bets. Read it slowly and *don't stop*. If you do, start over again." He looked up at the sky, then back at me. "Use your torch even if you can read the text by moonlight. It may be cloudless now, but you know how quickly the wind gods can summon a storm."

I dug the book out of my bag along with a flashlight and set them on the table, leaving the bag on the ground. "I'm scared."

He looked up, his determination written across his face. "I'm past scared, love. I moved into scared shitless about an hour ago while we were waiting for Marino's guy to show up. But just stick to the plan. You can do this."

I nodded. "Yeah, you're right." Why else would Daddy have told me it had to be tonight? I had to trust my instincts, but I had to admit that something about this didn't feel right.

I climbed on the table as he continued with the line.

"I'm going to be up in the tree right here." He pointed to a large oak tree next to my planned escape route.

"I'd feel better if you were in here with me."

"Ellie, we've discussed this already. The temples were considered sacred and only priests and conjurers were allowed inside. We just made you a temple. If I went in there with you, I'll dull or negate your power. Then all of this would be for naught."

I climbed on top of the table and picked up the book and flashlight. "Make sure that you're high enough in that tree so that they can't jump up and claw you. One of them got to the top of the lighthouse roof."

When he was halfway finished pouring the salt circle, my palm started to burn. A low growl rumbled in the woods, and my heart took off like a racehorse. "David, get in the tree."

He turned to look into the trees behind me and then continued to pour salt. "I'm almost done."

"David, get your ass into that tree now, or I'll come over there and push you into it."

"I'm not done—"

"If you think I'm lying, you don't know me very well." I moved to the edge of the table, ready to leap off.

"Ellie, don't you dare! It has to be seven full circles or it won't work."

He was right, but I didn't like admitting it.

He finished the circle and ran for the tree, tossing the salt container to the ground. He'd made it to the first branch when red eyes became visible in the woods. The badgers were on opposite sides of the clearing, hunching down amidst the trees.

Ukinim stepped out first. "Witness to creation, you brought me a snack." His right eye glowed bright red, but the left one was noticeably paler. Was physical harm permanent to them? Did that mean they could die?

The wind picked up and clouds began to form on the horizon. "An eye for an eye." Ukinim sniffed the ground. "Or in this case, an eye for something of worth."

Fear gripped my chest. "No!"

David was on the second branch when Ukinim bashed his head into the trunk, shaking the tree.

David lost his foothold and hung from a branch, his legs hanging over the badger. Ukinim's claw made a large swing, digging into David's thigh.

David cried out and pulled himself up onto the branch.

"David!" I moved to the edge of the table.

"Ellie, no!" David shouted. "Stay where you are!"

I tried to catch my breath. I had to keep my wits about me, but this wasn't going according to plan. *I* was supposed to be the bait, not David. I needed both badgers to be close for this to work. *If* it worked.

Ilena appeared from the opposite side and bolted for the tree. She threw her body into the trunk, shaking the branches so hard that David began to slip.

I fumbled to turn on the flashlight and started reading the text, my voice faltering as the pages fluttered in the gusts.

"Louder, Ellie!" David shouted over the wind. "Start over."

Ukinim leapt for the first tree branch, pulling himself up by his claws.

I started over, reading the ancient words in a booming voice.

The clouds billowed overhead and lightning shot from cloud to cloud, casting an eerie glow on the re-created village.

"That's good, Ellie! Keep going." David scrambled to the next branch, barely out of Ukinim's reach, but the badger was on the move again even as his wife smashed the tree trunk.

I held the book vertically so I could keep an eye on David over the top of the pages.

A splitting sound filled the air. I forced myself to keep chanting. David had climbed up to the smaller branches at the top of the tree. Soon they wouldn't support his weight.

I was more than halfway through the chant and nothing was happening. The vortex always started to manifest as soon as I started to recite the words of protection. The weather had changed, but it seemed to be the work of the wind gods rather than my own power. Were the wind gods here to protect me for Okeus? If so, that didn't mean they'd protect David. In fact, it was in their best interest if he wasn't around to help me.

Ukinim laughed as Ilena continued to ram the tree trunk. The splitting sound rent the air again, and the tree bent a few inches to the side.

All I had to go on were my instincts, and my instincts told me this wasn't working. Even if I finished the chant, David would be dead—either by the claws of the badgers or the power of the wind gods. I threw the book down and jumped off the table, stepping over the first two circles of symbols. I needed to protect David from the most immediate threat first. "Hey, Ilena. Don't you want *me*?" I walked over the third circle. "Come and get me."

"*Ellie!*" David shouted, fumbling to get his backpack open. "Get back in the bloody circle."

I had managed to attract Ilena's attention. She sniffed the ground, eyeing me with wary suspicion and greed.

Ukinim's nose lifted into the air.

"That's right." I held my hands out higher. "I'm out in the open. Don't you want me? Won't it piss Okeus off when he finds out you've killed his precious treasure? He cares way more about me than he does about that guy." I stepped over the fourth circle of candles.

Ukinim jumped to the ground.

David was climbing down the tree when I heard a loud cracking sound. The tree fell the rest of the way to the ground, David deep within its foliage.

"*David!*"

The badgers bent their heads low to the ground, pacing around the outer salt line.

David groaned, pulling himself up through the branches. "Ellie, get back to the inner circle!"

"It didn't work!"

"I know. Now you need to protect yourself."

But even if I listened to him, I wasn't sure how long it would help. The badgers were kicking dirt over the salt, breaking the outermost circles.

The clouds overhead rolled furiously and thunder rumbled long and loud as if in protest.

"Hey, you wankers!" David shouted, holding the bottle of holy water in his hand. "Look at me!" He stood on the fallen tree trunk, waving his arms in the air.

"David! No!"

But the badgers had turned to face David, who was seemingly easier prey. His leg was dripping with blood, which had to only increase their interest in him.

He held out the bottle of holy water and shook it toward the nearest badger. Ilena squealed in pain and bolted backward, crashing into a tree as the scent of singed skin and hair filled the clearing.

Ukinim stopped charging David and turned toward his mate, sniffing her back and licking her face.

I knew David's intention was to distract Ukinim and Ilena so that I could get back to the table, but I needed another plan, since the first one had failed. Right now I needed to get the badgers away from David, or I needed to use the words of protection to send them away temporarily. Which meant we would be back at square one.

Daddy had told me I had the resources to send them away. Why hadn't my instincts kicked in yet?

Ilena was still howling but Ukinim turned toward David, his menacing growl filling the air. "I will make you pay, *tosh-shonte.*"

I headed over to the path that led to the replica of the *Elizabeth II*, which was docked several hundred feet away. "Hey, Ukinim!" My voice was barely audible over the blustering wind.

"Ellie!" David shouted in irritation. "Stop!"

But Ukinim's attention turned to me.

Rain began to pour from the sky and lightning struck the ground on the other side of the park, filling the air with the stench of burnt wood.

"Come and get me!" I walked backward. I was leading the badgers away from David, but what would protect him from the wind gods? He couldn't run on his injured leg.

The circle. It had protected me from all the gods and spirits except Okeus at the gate ceremony.

"David, get into the circle!" I turned around, making sure the badgers were following, and sprinted for the ship that was anchored in the cove, hoping he would listen.

I had no idea how fast giant badgers could run, but I had a feeling it was faster than me. The wind shifted direction, pushing me forward instead of impeding my progress. I scrambled toward the ship as they chased behind me, smashing the wooden floor as they went.

I only realized what they were doing when it was too late to change course—they were destroying my escape path.

I made it to the dock and ran over the gangplank onto the boat. Now I was really trapped unless I jumped into the sound. I knew they could swim, but all the information I'd found indicated that they preferred not to. Of course, they might decide I was worth the effort.

Where was Mishiginebig when I needed him?

Ilena walked along the edge of the dock and growled. A large bald spot covered her back where the holy water had doused her. "We have you now, Curse Keeper."

I flexed my hand, ready to use my power. I knew that I should. My instincts had yet to kick in. But stubbornness won out. If I sent them away, they'd only come back again . . . and the next time they'd be even angrier. Daddy had said to do this tonight. I had to trust him.

Ilena leaped over the gap between the dock and the ship, landing on the deck, while Ukinim blocked any attempt I might have made to jump back onto the dock.

Crap.

I started climbing the rope ladder up one of the masts.

"You've got nowhere to hide, Curse Keeper," Ukinim slurred.

Movement at the side of the dock caught my attention, and the torrential downpour slowed to a sprinkle. "You are the *biggest* pain in the ass," Collin shouted, climbing over the edge of the dock.

"*Collin?*"

Ukinim turned toward him. "Son of the land."

Collin stood on the wooden platform, cocking his head to the side. "You and Ellie have more in common than you think."

He took a step closer to the ship. "You both hate Okeus. Just let her go."

"*Let her go?*" Ukinim lowered his head and turned his good eye toward Collin. "Okeus stole what was most precious to me. My humanity," he growled. "And now I will take what's most precious to him."

"Goddamn it, Ukinim. Okeus will never let you get away with this," Collin spit. "It's not worth it. Just let her go."

"Never."

Ilena rammed her body into the mast and the rope ladder shook. My foot slipped from its rung, and I clung to the ladder as the mast shook again and began to tilt over the dock.

"Ellie!" Collin shouted.

Ukinim laughed, swinging his claws, but I jerked out of the way and skittered back down the pole, reaching for a rope ladder attached to another mast. Grabbing hold of it, I crouched on the wood beam and leaped for the nearby pole, sliding and fighting for purchase as my legs became tangled in the ropes. At least I was back over the ship.

My relief was short-lived. Ilena hit the new mast and I screamed as my hands slipped, my legs still entwined in the ropes. I now dangled upside down over the deck, just barely out of Ilena's grasp.

"*Ukinim.*" Collin sounded desperate. "Let her go or I'll be forced to destroy you."

The badger swung his head around, his red eye glowing even brighter. "All the spirits know you aren't a threat. That's why they leave you alone. For now. If you do this, you will be as much of a target as she is."

"Listen to me!" Collin shouted in frustration. "Don't you see that if you kill her, Okeus will hunt you to the ends of the earth to make you pay?"

Ilena laughed. "Don't you think he knows that? He doesn't care."

Collin shot me a worried glance as I pulled myself up and fumbled to free my legs from the lines.

Ukinim slinked over the bridge onto the boat and laughed. "I'm going to send you straight to Popogusso, Curse Keeper."

"Don't waste your time," I said, finally freeing myself. "My Manitou belongs to Ahone now."

Ilena rammed the mast and the wood cracked, the pole leaning over the front end of the ship. I struggled to keep my hold.

The clouds rolled and lightning struck the lighthouse on the other side of the bay, the building erupting into flames.

"Ellie!" Collin shouted. "Start your words of protection."

"No! If I send them away, they'll just come back."

"*Trust me.*"

Two words, so simple but so elusive. I would have given anything to trust Collin, but he'd proven himself untrustworthy time and again. Still, he'd always gone out of his way to protect me. I knew he'd do it this time too. Wasn't that why he was here?

Collin took a running leap onto the ship.

Ukinim's feet gripped the pole, and he started inching up toward me.

I lifted my hand, but it was too late. Even if I started my words of protection, Ukinim would get me before I could stop him.

A bright, warm light appeared toward the shore, and I gasped. A golden deer appeared on the dock. Every part of him glowed, including the massive antlers on his head.

The badgers stopped their pursuit and turned toward the creature.

"A *wutapantam*," Collin said beneath me, his voice a combination of awe and grief.

"What is it?" I struggled to catch my breath. The animal was the most beautiful creature I'd ever seen.

"A sacrificial deer."

Tears welled in my eyes.

The badgers crawled to the edge of the ship while the deer watched, its head lifted high.

"Ellie." Collin stood about six feet below me. He lifted his hands up. "Jump while it distracts them. They won't be able to resist its lure."

The badgers were mesmerized, and they moved as if in slow motion across the gangplank toward the dock.

Collin reached for me as I dropped, his arm wrapping around my waist to keep me from falling to my knees.

My palm felt like it was on fire as the badgers advanced on the deer. "Collin! We can't let them kill it!"

"It's too late. It doesn't want to be saved." His words were filled with agony.

Ilena circled the deer, but Ukinim stopped and shook his head, releasing a low growl. "I won't fall for Ahone's trickery." He spun around to face us, lowering his nose to the wooden slats. His red eye burned bright.

Collin wrapped his left arm around the small of my back, his fingers digging into my waist as he pulled me against his chest.

Ilena pounced on the deer, throwing it to the dock and ripping its abdomen apart.

I felt the loss as a crushing pain in my chest, and my knees buckled.

Ukinim arched his back as he prepared to leap back onto the ship.

Collin's body tensed and his hand tightened on my side. "Put your arm around my back." He was already reaching his right hand toward mine.

"I don't know what to do, Collin."

"Yes, you do. You're the witness to creation. You've known all along." He pressed our marks together, and power greater than anything I'd yet experienced jolted through my body and Collin's. The presence of the Manitou was stronger than ever, and they were all grieving the death of the *wutapantam.*

Collin pulled me closer to his chest, guiding our pressed hands over our heads.

Fear stole my breath as Ukinim pounced at us. I cringed, releasing a shriek as Collin held me in place, but the badger hit an invisible shield—just like on the night of the ceremony. My gaze jerked up to Collin. He was right. I did know what to do.

"*I am the daughter of the sea . . .*"

Collin's eyes bore into mine.

"*Born of the essence present at the beginning of time and the end of the world.*"

My vortex appeared.

"*I am the son of the earth, born of space and heaven.*" His face grave, he nodded to me.

"*I am black water and crystal streams. The ocean waves and the raindrops in the sky.*" I stopped and looked up into his eyes.

Lightning shot through the air and the wind gusted. I struggled to stand, but Collin helped me remain upright.

"*I am black earth and sandy loams. The mountain ranges and the rolling hills.*"

My voice grew louder. "*I am life and death and everything in between.*"

"*I am the foundation of life and the receiver of death and everything in between.*"

Our blended voices echoed off the water. "*I compel you to leave my sight.*"

A crack appeared in the sky, ripping the seam between our realm and the spiritual one. The badgers screamed and cursed. The ground shook and the boat swayed violently, but Collin spread his feet apart and stayed upright, our hands still joined.

Rays of bright white light shot from the badgers' bodies, filling the boat and nearly blinding me. The creatures shrieked with agony and fear until their bodies exploded in a ball of white light. Then a million pieces that looked like fireflies were sucked up into the crack overhead. When all the pieces were gone, Collin looked down into my face, fear and devastation in his eyes.

He slowly pulled his hand from mine but kept his arm around my back. "Do you even realize what just happened?"

I swallowed the lump in throat, my chin trembling. "I'm not sure about the *wutapantam*, but we sent the badgers away."

"Yes," he whispered. "We sent them away. But at what cost? A *wutapantam* sacrificed himself *for you*. Do you even understand the significance of *that*?"

I didn't know for sure, but the loss I'd felt at its death had left me dazed.

"There are *four*, Ellie. Four in all of existence, and one is now gone because of what you started tonight."

Tears burned my eyes. "I didn't know, Collin," I choked out. "I saw Daddy when we were in the ocean and he insisted that I had to do this tonight."

He shook his head, disgust pinching his mouth. "He told you what Ahone wanted you to hear, Ellie! He tricked you into doing what he wanted. Just like he tricked Manteo."

My mouth opened, but I didn't know what to say. I didn't know what to believe anymore.

"We've both learned something tonight," Collin said. "*None* of the gods are to be trusted. We're all pawns in an eons-old power struggle, and both sides will sacrifice *everything* and *everyone* at their disposal to get what they want, including their own creations. The Croatan and the colonists. Manteo and Ananias."

My chin trembled. "You and me."

He swallowed, lifting his hand to my cheek, longing in his eyes. "Especially you and me."

"I'm sorry."

"We are responsible for destroying three creations tonight. For eternity."

I shook my head and jerked out of his grasp. "I'm devastated about the deer, but I'm not sorry about the badgers. That's what we're supposed to *do*, Collin. We're supposed to send those things back where they belong. That's our job! We're *Curse Keepers*."

Sadness filled his eyes. "We earned new titles tonight. *Destroyers of life*."

"They thought nothing of condemning innocent lives to Popogusso, so why should we feel sorry for them? They were going to kill *us*, Collin."

"No, Ellie. They were going to kill *you*." He paused. "And they wouldn't have stopped until they succeeded." He looked toward the town, sirens blaring in the distance. "I'm not sorry we destroyed them. I couldn't let them kill you. But we crossed a line we can never uncross. There's a good chance that we just declared war on Okeus's demons. My only hope is that they see the badgers as enemies of Okeus and think we did them a favor." He turned back to me. "But even so, they'll no longer trust me."

"Your allegiance to Okeus protects you."

He shook his head. "Not necessarily anymore. Not after this."

"So what happens next?"

"We stay on guard and wait to see if they attack us. They won't kill *you*, not unless they've gone rogue like the badgers. Okeus still wants you."

Like that was supposed to make me feel better. I clenched my fists. "If the others start killing people too, I'll send them back, Collin."

"Not if I don't help you." His face hardened.

"There's a way for me to do it without you, and I'll find out how." I instinctively reached for the ring hanging around my neck.

His gaze fell to my chest and he reached for the band, lifting it up to study the symbols. His face grew stern as his eyes lifted to mine. "Where did you get this?"

"It was my father's."

"No, it wasn't, Ellie." His voice was harsh. "Where did you get it?"

And then I knew. "It's part of the Ricardo Estate," I whispered.

His fist tightened around the ring. "Did you get it from Marino?"

I shook my head.

The sirens grew louder.

"Ellie!" David shouted from the shore. He leaned against one of the still standing poles.

"We have to get out of here, Collin."

Collin dropped his hold on my chain and nodded, looking dazed as he examined the dock.

We picked our way across the splintered wood and circled around the damage and holes until we reached David on the shore.

He was sitting on a rock, both of our backpacks slung over his bare shoulders. He'd tied his shirt around his leg and his face was pale. "You did it."

We had, but Collin's words worried me. At what price?

Collin had healed my wounds from the badgers with our marks. I considered trying the same on David but instantly knew

389

it wouldn't work. The ability to heal was one more resource for us as Curse Keepers.

David and I had already planned an escape route at the back of the park. We hurried toward it in silence, David hobbling to keep up.

Collin stayed with us until we slipped through the fence, and then he got into his truck and drove away.

～ CHAPTER TWENTY-NINE ～

The following Saturday night, the summer evening had cooled off and a breeze tickled the hair hanging down my back. Drew and Claire were dancing their first dance in the middle of the Grand Ballroom at 108 Budleigh, and Claire was gorgeous. She had gotten her dream wedding.

David leaned down toward my ear. "You do know that the maid of honor isn't supposed to be more beautiful than the bride, don't you?"

I looked up into his loving face and smiled. "I'm pretty sure you're the only one who thinks that."

He pursed his mouth into a mischievous grin. "Nope. That bloke over at two o'clock hasn't stopped watching you since you walked down the aisle."

"That's Claire's cousin and he's had a crush on me for years. He doesn't count."

After all the recent craziness, I couldn't believe we were doing something normal. It felt good.

For the last week I'd replayed the events in my mind, and I couldn't see how we could have done things differently. Especially when I took into account that Daddy had told me to do it. But was Collin right? Had Ahone tricked me by using Daddy? Did Ahone have his own secret agenda? Whatever the original agenda, the new one was clear. There was a good chance that Collin and I had giant bull's-eyes on our backs. Everyone in our lives was fair game too.

Claire and Drew's dance ended, and they invited the rest of the wedding party onto the dance floor.

David hobbled out with me. "Your dress is too beautiful to waste, Ellie." He'd needed to get multiple stitches for his leg wound, and he had trouble getting around, but he still insisted on dancing with me. Tom had questioned him endlessly, but ultimately he let it rest after the attacks stopped.

I had to admit, Claire was right. The emerald-green gown clung to my curves and the color perfectly complemented my auburn hair and hazel eyes. I really did feel beautiful, even if just for a night.

David wrapped me in his arms, and I looked up into his face, feeling both blessed and guilty. When the song ended, I helped him back to our seats.

My mouth dropped open when I saw Collin standing in the back of the room, dressed in a suit. He walked toward me, then looked down at David. "Would you mind if I steal a dance with Ellie?"

David stiffened slightly, then covered my hand with his own. "It's not my decision. It's Ellie's."

I nodded, my breath catching. I hadn't seen him since we'd earned our new titles.

Collin took my hand and pulled me to the center of the crowd, placing his hand on my hip and keeping a respectable distance between us. "I've never seen you look more beautiful, Ellie."

I flushed. "Thank you, but then again, I never really dressed up or wore much makeup when we were together."

"You don't need those things to be beautiful." His voice was husky.

I flushed.

"Are you happy with him?"

"David?" I glanced up at him through my eyelashes, hesitant to answer. He watched me with an expression I'd never seen him wear before. I nodded.

"When you came to me and asked me to take you out onto the ocean, I told you that I knew from our connection that you had slept with him."

I looked away, pain shooting through my chest. "Collin, don't."

"But I felt something else. I felt the contentment and peace he gives you. I never felt that from you when you were with me. And I was jealous."

I closed my eyes.

"I told you that I love you, Ellie, and I do. But I want you to be as happy as you can possibly be given our circumstances." He lifted my chin and forced me to look into his face. "He makes you happier than I ever could. He can give you what I can't. You deserve someone who's good to you. You should be with David."

Tears stung my eyes. "But what about our souls being connected?"

"There's no changing that, and I confess, it will kill me to see you with him, but he's what you need. Not me. Perhaps you and I aren't meant to be together in this lifetime. Maybe we're supposed to wait for eternity."

"Do you really believe that?"

He stopped dancing and his eyes clouded. "I have to, Ellie. It's the only way I can bear to live without you."

"Collin." My voice broke as my heart shattered.

"I want you to know that I'll always be here when you need me. I told you that you became my responsibility when I broke the curse, and I stand by that. You may be with David now, but you and I are far from done. We'll be seeing a lot of each other once the rest of the demons gain their strength." He leaned down and kissed my cheek. "I hope you find happiness while you can, Ellie."

"I need you to tell me about the Ricardo deal."

He stopped dancing, his shoulders tensing as his gaze landed on the ring, which I now wore on the middle finger of my right hand. "Ellie, let it go. You may have gotten lucky that Marino's guys got picked up on a routine traffic stop, but they are only a couple of many. Marino is far from done with you. The less you know the better."

"I don't care about Marino. I want to know the connection to my mother's death."

His eyes widened. "Why do you think there's a connection?"

"I just do. Will you help me?"

"You have to let this go, Ellie." He dropped his hold and turned to leave.

Maybe he wouldn't tell me now, but I'd wear him down. "Collin."

He stopped and looked over his shoulder.

"How did you know I'd be there last Sunday night?"

His eyebrows lifted in surprise. "You really don't know?" A soft smile lifted the corners of his mouth but pain filled his eyes. "David called me earlier that evening and asked me to come help you." He took a couple of steps and then stopped again. "There's a surprise for you in your apartment. Something you've been wanting."

"The map?"

He grinned.

I watched the man who had changed my destiny walk out the door, then turned to face the man who would shape my future.

However short that would be.

ACKNOWLEDGMENTS

They say writing is a lonely profession, but somehow I always seem to be surrounded by people. Perhaps it's all the kids running around with all my dogs. But I'm blessed with friends and associates that not only make my job much easier but also more fun.

This book wouldn't be what it is today without the invaluable assistance of my editor Angela Polidoro. Her patience has been put to the test since she became my editor with this book. I love that she gets what I'm trying to say even when it's not quite there yet, and her suggestions are always spot on. Her email inbox had to have been on fire with the final edits of this book. I'm sure I owe her a bottle of wine. Or maybe a case.

I'd like to thank my copy editor, Jon Ford, who added his own very valuable insight to both *The Curse Breakers* and *The Curse Keepers*. I'd also like to thank the 47North team—especially my editor, David Pomerico, who was crazy enough to take a chance on an urban fantasy based on the Lost Colony of Roanoke after what had to be the worst pitch of all time in the history of pitches.

My beta readers not only give me valuable feedback in the revision process, but keep me sane pre-release when I begin to doubt myself and my books. I can count on Rhonda Cowsert, Stormy Udell, Christie Timpson, Emily Pearson, and Anne Childon to tell me the truth. Rule number one of beta reading: friends don't let friends look stupid in print.

I wouldn't be able to spend as much time writing as I do if it weren't for the patience of my children. We're striving to find a "normal" that works for all of us. I think we're almost there. Well as normal as the Grover Swank household will ever be . . .

And finally, I'd like to thank you—my dear reader. You take a chance on me and read my books, then recommend them to your friends. If it weren't for you, I wouldn't be doing what I love: living the life of a full-time writer. I've never worked so hard in my life, and I've never been so happy. Thank you.

ABOUT THE AUTHOR

© 2013 Cathryn Farley Photography

Denise Grover Swank was born in Kansas City, Missouri, and lived in the area until she was nineteen. She then became a nomad, living in five cities, four states, and ten houses over the next decade before moving back to her roots. She speaks English and a smattering of Spanish and Chinese. Her hobbies include making witty Facebook comments and dancing in the kitchen. She has six children and hasn't lost her sanity. Or so she leads everyone to believe.